PENGUIN BOOKS

WHITE CARGO

'A remarkable first book about acting, travelling, exile, loving and losing; a book about families and, above all, a book about fathers and daughters. It contrives to be both a tribute to her father and a frank portrayal of him' Angela Lambert, *Good Housekeeping*

'A very honest and remarkable book . . . Felicity Kendal moves between past and present, skilfully interweaving stories of her extraordinary early life with poignant observations of her comatose father, whom she visits in hospital daily . . .' Veronica Groocock, *The Times Literary Supplement*

'Kendal's early years are told with such a fine, detached accuracy that the book transcends the autobiographical genre and becomes, quite simply, like a remarkable novel' Laura Thompson, *Independent*

'A touching glimpse of stardom' Judy Cooke, *Mail on Sunday*

'*White Cargo* is as much memoir as autobiography, since it is father rather than daughter who lies at its heart and whose rude, funny, high-toned letters provide its backbone . . . India was a magical place for a child and Kendal writes of it with real charm and affection' Kate Hubbard, *Spectator*

'A good and original book' Anne Chisholm, *Evening Standard*

Felicity Kendal is one of Britain's most successful actresses. She has played almost every leading Shakespearian role and has worked with a whole range of contemporary playwrights, including Peter Shaffer, Tom Stoppard, Michael Frayn, Simon Gray and Alan Ayckbourn. Her films include *Shakespeare Wallah*, directed by James Ivory, and Ken Russell's *Valentino*. She has appeared frequently on television and starred in *Edward VII*, *The Good Life* and *The Mistress*. She was awarded the CBE in 1995. She lives in London and this is her first book.

WHITE CARGO

FELICITY KENDAL

PENGUIN BOOKS

PENGUIN BOOKS

Published by the Penguin Group
Penguin Books Ltd, 27 Wrights Lane, London w8 5tz, England
Penguin Putnam Inc., 375 Hudson Street, New York, New York 10014, USA
Penguin Books Australia Ltd, Ringwood, Victoria, Australia
Penguin Books Canada Ltd, 10 Alcorn Avenue, Toronto, Ontario, Canada m4v 3b2
Penguin Books (NZ) Ltd, Private Bag 102902, NSMC, Auckland, New Zealand

Penguin Books Ltd, Registered Offices: Harmondsworth, Middlesex, England

First published by Michael Joseph 1998
Published in Penguin Books 1999
8

Set in Monotype Bembo
Printed in England by Clays Ltd, St Ives plc

For Ros

ACKNOWLEDGEMENTS

I would like to thank my dear friend, Brian Kellett, for nudging my memory where appropriate, and Tom Weldon, Mark Lucas and Sarah Hemming, without whom this book could not have been written.

The distinction between past, present and future
is only an illusion, however persistent.
— ALBERT EINSTEIN

CONTENTS

CONTENTS

LIST OF ILLUSTRATIONS

Sketch Map
showing places visited by

Shakespeareana

June 1953 ~ December 1956

✛ = 2, 3 and 4 visits

RISALPUR
⦿ ABBOTABAD
⦿ NAUSHERA ✛
PESHWAR ⦿ MURRAE
⦿ RAWALPINDI
SARGODA ⦿ JHELUM
⦿ SIALKOT
LAHORE⦿ AMRITSAR
JULLUNDA SIMLA
LHUDIANA SUSSOW ⦿ MUSSOURI ✛
⦿ AMBALA ⦿ DEHRA DUN
⦿ QUETTA ROORKEE
⦿ PATIALA
SAMRANTPUR
✛ DELHI
GURGOOR ⦿ NAINI TAL ✛
⦿ PILANI ⦿ ALIGARH
⦿ JAIPUR AGRA ⦿ DARJEELING
⦿ LUCKNOW ✛
⦿ NAWABSHA ⦿ AJMER ✛ CAWNPORE ⦿ GORAKPUR
⦿ TANDOADAM
⦿ HYDERABAD JHANSI
✛ KARACHI ⦿ PATNA
⦿ UDAIPUR ALLAHABAD
RAMGARGH
JUBBULPUR DHANBAD
⦿ BURNPUR
⦿ AHMEDABAD ASANSOL SANTINIKETAN
⦿ BARODA ⦿ INDORE RANCHI ⦿ ⦿ CALCUTTA
TATA NAGA
⦿ SURAT ✛ NAGPUR
⦿ NAUSARI
⦿ DEOLALI CUTTACK ⦿
⦿ BOMBAY ⦿ PANCHGANI
⦿ POONA ✛ HYDERABAD

⦿ MYSORE ⦿ MADRAS
OOTACAMUND
⦿ COIMBATORE

879 Performances of ~

OTHELLO
THE MERCHANT OF VENICE
HAMLET
THE TAMING OF THE SHREW
MACBETH
ROMEO AND JULIET
TWELFTH NIGHT
ARMS AND THE MAN
PYGMALION
SHE STOOPS TO CONQUER
THE SCHOOL FOR SCANDAL
THE IMPORTANCE of BEING EARNEST
GASLIGHT
CHARLIES AUNT
THE TEMPEST
DIRECTOR OF PRODUCTION ~ GEOFFREY KENDAL.

Patrons
THE RT. HON. COUNTESS
MOUNTBATTEN OF BURMA,
C.I. G.B.E., D.C.V.O.

HIS HIGHNESS THE MAHARAJA
SAHIB BAHADUR OF JAIPUR,
RAJPRAMUKH OF RAJASTHAN
JAIPUR

HIS EXCELLENCY
DR. K.M. MUNSHI, B.A., L.L.B.,
D. LITT., L. I.D. GOVERNOR OF
UTTAR PRADESH

CHAPTER ONE

NIL BY MOUTH

He is lying on his right side, staring at the wall. Paralysed by three mighty strokes that have left him immobile and speechless. Above his head is a sign, 'Nil by Mouth'. It's been up there for three years. The radio was blaring when I arrived and made my way up to the fourth floor of the nursing home to his tiny comfortable room with its lace curtains and candlewick bedspread. Radio London, and all that goes with it. He hated the radio, when he was still able to hate anything. 'Bloody stupid contraption making silly sounds for silly people.' What he really meant was that he was deaf and couldn't hear a thing, unless it was playing at a torturous level.

I turned it off before going over to him, kissing his forehead and saying in a louder than normal voice, 'Hello, Daddy. It's Foo. How are you?' What a stupid question. 'Anyhow,' I continued, taking off my coat and sitting beside his bed, 'I've decided to write a book — about my beginnings. I'm going to write about India, and you, and . . . about . . . about . . . about . . .'

I started again, trying to sound cheerful. 'I've decided to write most of it here in your room. It will be a way of spending time with you, without feeling so useless.' But what it really is, I thought, what it really is, is a way to make these endless days and hours seem sensible, a way of being with you while you're dying, ever so slowly, unable to speak. You, the great talker of the family, the man for whom the spoken word was a lifelong passion.

'Fill your belly full of air!' 'You'll never be any bloody good as an actor if you squeak!' 'Always remember, Foo, that your voice is your most precious instrument: the SOUND you make can move an audience to laugh or cry.' 'So, put your shoulders back and FILL YOUR BELLY FULL OF AIR!' I must have been seven years old when I first heard these often to be repeated words of wisdom – advice to me, your second daughter, the one who was supposed to be a boy.

I look at you now, your white hair in a long pony-tail spread out on the pillow, your silver chain round your neck with the medal of Saint Christopher, the patron saint of travellers (who, I believe, has been sacked), your false teeth firmly in place and, as far as possible under the circumstances, your dignity in place too. I gave instructions to the nurses when we moved here from the stroke ward at the hospital: 'No pyjamas to be put on him – he loathed them; his teeth in during the daytime, stuck in with very strong false-teeth glue, his hair left long and tied back; his beard trimmed, not cut.'

These are the few things I have been able to insist on. The nappies have had to be allowed, and, try as I might, I cannot persuade anyone to give you the whisky on a spoon that I do when you are sitting up, the 'Nil by Mouth' glaring down at me as you choke on your chota peg. 'Six thirty, time to open the bar,' you used to say. Wherever you were, and whatever the bar, six thirty was time for a peg. In a train on the way to Rawalpindi, at sea in a cargo ship, at home in a dak bungalow, sunset was the end of your day and, unless there was a show to perform, it was drinks time. Out would come your travelling silver peg measure with the Johnny Walker's or the Gordon's gin.

I can hardly believe, looking at your crippled, paralysed hands with the fingers locked into an ugly claw, that you were once my 'Daddy', your eyes once so piercing and bright, able, I thought, to see right through me and pluck out the very core of my being.

I used to think you were indestructible. 'Come along, Foo, I'll show you something glorious.' I'd hold on to your hand, smooth and strong, firm, beautiful hands with nails always finely manicured. 'Come along.' And off we'd go, down the dusty, hot platform, somewhere in the very heart of India, past the char wallahs and vendors selling sweet julabies, the beggars and the dogs, the coolies and the bearers in their dirty white uniforms taking orders for meals to be served at the next station down the line, till we got to the 'something glorious' at the front of the train, puffing and snorting, steam belching out, the driver and the assistant in their blue overalls working the levers and shovelling coal.

For the umpteenth time you would explain to me in detail how a steam engine worked. There was a lot about pistons, I seem to remember, and I don't think I ever quite got the hang of it, but I pretended to, faking my interest so well you never tired of our journeys to the front. And in later years they were to include boiler rooms in ships with even more about pistons. My childhood adoration of you made me pretend an understanding and interest far greater than I felt.

We were always on the move, travelling by train, bus, tonga or ship, in the luxury of first class one week and then the following week, when our luck ran out and the debts caught up, confined to a ghastly third-class compartment with wooden benches, complete with chickens, children, and the accompanying odour of garlic and stale sweat.

Images from my childhood crowd in on top of one another, the marbled palaces we slept in jostling for attention with the bedbug-infested guest-houses or the seedy small hotels with rooms for hire by the hour that were used by ladies of the night. I remember the blasting heat of the plains of India, the crispy, cold freshness of the hill stations, the thunderous monsoons and the balmy evening breezes on the Malabar coast, the hot chilli-spiced curries, the morbidly dull cutlets and rice and the ornately painted houseboats, nestling in the waterlilies on Kashmir's Dal Lake.

All this I remember, cheek by jowl. And, at the centre of it all — my father, Geoffrey.

*

'You stupid little bugger!' Geoffrey shouted at me. We were on the veranda of his bedroom, my mother sitting inside, pretending to read. I had tried to explain, for the umpteenth time, that I could not give up this chance to go and work in England.

'Daddy, my fare is paid for, I've been invited to the Berlin Film Festival, then on to the London Festival. It's a wonderful film. I'm bound to get *some* work out of it. How can I refuse?'

'You're a stupid little bugger,' he repeated. 'They won't appreciate you in England. You'll end up marrying the first clot you meet, who will want you to settle down with a bunch of screaming kids. You'll end up in hell with mortgages and misery! AND the climate's bloody awful. God, you're a fool.'

We had already spent days arguing, both of us stubborn and determined to win the other round. Neither was about to give in now.

'I've already got bookings for the next three months, you silly cow,' Geoffrey raged on. 'The tea gardens are coming up, then a short trip to Japan. Do you want me to cancel the lot for the sake of a bloody film?'

'I'm eighteen years old and I've been touring with you and the company all my life. I want to see what England is like, I want to try and get work in the theatre. Please try and understand,' I pleaded.

'After this wonderful life I've given you!' he roared. 'And you'll break your mother's heart.'

'Look, Daddy, if I come on this tour you've booked, I'll never be able to afford the fare, we'll end up penniless as usual, and I can't stay with you for ever.'

'I have nothing to say to such stupidity!' he bellowed, and walked out.

'And I'm damned if I'm giving up this chance for another round of the TEA GARDENS OF ASSAM!' I screamed at his retreating back. I turned to my mother and sought her complicity. 'You understand that I have to go?'

'You must do what you think right, Foo,' she replied. She had withdrawn into herself the last few days, conveying a mixture of hurt and quiet understanding. She would never go against Geoffrey in public, however foolish she may have thought him to be at times. Her loyalty to him was total. She only ever questioned him about matters to do with acting and then she could become fiercely argumentative. But now she was removing herself from the field of battle.

'You must try and understand Daddy, Foo. He thinks you're betraying everything he's been trying to give you. Try to understand – you're going back to a life we left years ago, a life your father scorned, of tatty reps and cheap cold digs, of critics and agents, of large profits and small horizons. But you must do what you think best.'

I knew she was desperately unhappy, and her trying to be so cool confused me. All my life she had been approachable, and now the curtains had been drawn. 'I love you, Mummy,' I whispered and went back to my room.

After the heat of the day's arguments, dinner that night was a sorry affair. In the dining room of this beloved hotel, which we had visited every year since I was a baby, the last supper was silent and sulky. We sat, not speaking – something unheard of in our family of chatterboxes. Somehow we got through the brown soup, the lamb chops and vegetable rissoles, the fruit salad and custard, but by the coffee I could stand it no longer, and, making 'packing' excuses, left the table. I had travelled all my life and packing held no mysteries for me, but I could not have got through the usually genial chota pegs after dinner with the company and hotel guests. I took my dog Chook for his evening piddle round the compound and went to bed.

I slept hardly at all, and now, here it was, the morning of my departure had arrived.

A white mist hovered over the sprawling Maidan. In the early hours of the morning the dry grass looked lush with the dew . . . the sickly sweet smell of the city had not yet taken hold of the day, and, in the cool air, the sounds of barking pye-dogs were still faint. Across the Maidan large black crows cawed and swooped at one another from the tall trees, and in the distance people walked and bicycled their way to work along the footpaths, municipal peons in their khaki shorts and bush shirts, pressed into starched creases that would not last till lunchtime, vendors in dhotis, their baskets of ware balanced perfectly on their heads, arms swinging freely in easy confidence.

It was not yet quite day and, as I stood on the edge of the vast parkland, I felt a sudden jolt of fear. I was leaving Calcutta this morning, flying first to Bombay, then on to Berlin, and, after a week . . . HOME. I was going home. But home was a strange land I remembered only vaguely. I had come to India as a tiny child. I could eat hot chillies, I spoke fluent Hindi, but, at eighteen, I had never been near a pair of stockings, owned a coat or worn gloves. My history lessons were of Nur Jahan and the great Mogul Empire; I hardly knew the difference between the Houses of Parliament and Buckingham Palace; but, nevertheless, I was 'going home' – going home to England, leaving my parents, the company and all I knew.

I had woken before it was light, had a shower, closed my well-worn suitcases and, slipping on my travelling dress and sandals, I had grabbed Chook's lead and crept with the dog out of the sleeping Fairlawn Hotel.

I made my way down Sudder Street, past the crumbling Georgian villas that once stood proudly in the centre of the British quarter during the days of the Raj, then picked my way round the sleeping bodies on the pavement of Russell Street, and came out on to the Chowringhee Road. Crossing the old tramlines that used to run alongside the great park, I let Chook off his lead to run free on the grass.

Behind me, overlooking the Maidan, stood the avenue of white columned houses that were built when Calcutta was a colonial port. They stretched into the distance – 'an entire village of palaces' was how one visitor described this spot in the nineteenth century.

I walked across to the giant tree under which, years before, my ayah Mary used to park me in the Victorian pram that travelled with us. She would adjust my tiny sola topi and sit fanning herself in the shade, eating peanuts. Later, when I grew older and the pram had long since gone, we would stroll in the early evening, while she told me fantastical stories in her pidgin English.

I breathed in the Indian morning. I was weak from a recent bout of paratyphoid, and shivered in my cotton dress. I was not excited. A calm had descended in the wake of the previous night's emotional outbursts about my departure.

I looked once more along Chowringhee, looking at the grand classical mansions with their ornate porticoes, stretching for miles. 'Come on, Chook. We've got to go back.' My little mongrel dog came running up to me, I put on his lead, and we started back across the old tramlines to the hotel.

The staff were busy, sweeping and polishing, and watering the lawn. 'Taxi here, Missy Baba,' the chowkidar informed me at the gate. I thanked him and asked him in Hindi to fetch the luggage from my room. There was no time for breakfast. I must have stayed at the Maidan longer than I thought. I ran to Mother's room to say goodbye. She was in her hair-curling rags and cotton nightie and, without make-up, looked young and delicate. She was still silent but tearful now. The lump in my throat was a hot pain. I bent over and kissed her sweet soft face. 'Goodbye, Foo,' she said. 'Keep safe.' She didn't cry aloud, but tears poured down her cheeks.

'I'll be back soon, you'll see.'

I went quickly down to the hotel lobby. Geoffrey was standing by the taxi, parked under the portico of the Fairlawn Hotel, with my luggage – a small pile of worn-out suitcases. 'Have you counted the pieces?' he barked.

'Yes, Daddy, there are three.'

'Chullow, driver, load up juldi juldi, or she'll miss the bloody plane!'

His dark brown eyes were steely, his expression set, and his mouth a thin line of disapproval. I recognized this look: it was the one he reserved for when things got really bad. He was very angry with me and unable at this moment of departure to communicate his hurt or feelings of loss. Thrusting something into my hand, he said roughly, 'That's a few bob sterling. It's all I could get my hands on. Hope it's useful.' I looked at the crumpled offering in my palm . . . it was thirty-five pounds!

'Right! Off you go, then,' he said fiercely – but his bony knees peeping out from under his khaki shorts looked vulnerable and pathetic. We didn't hug, we didn't know how to do this, we were not used to partings – I had hardly spent a night away from him in all my eighteen years. But nothing was going to make either of us give in to a sentimental leave-taking. He would not come to the airport to see me off: 'Waste of time!' And nothing on God's earth was going to make me repeat the weeping hysteria of my sister Jennifer's departure four years earlier, when she had left to get married.

No, I wasn't like Jennifer. I was the strong one. I could stand up to him. I wanted a career in the theatre of my own making, and I would not be bullied out of it. I would not cry and fling my arms about his neck, begging him to forgive my going, when going was a perfectly reasonable thing to do. I mumbled 'thank you', patted my little dog goodbye and got into the taxi. Sliding across the cracked plastic seat, I rolled down the window and waved until we turned the corner and the image of him was lost from view, standing straight and still, his palms together raised in namaste.

I booked on to the flight to Bombay in a daze. I felt no emotion, not even for the faithful little dog that I had loved for so long. It was only halfway to Bombay that I started sobbing. Tears flowed down my face, dripping and staining the front of my cream dress. I missed my mother, and the pain that she tried to hide hurt me more than my own.

I sobbed hot tears, but they were also tears of relief. I had done it; I was free. I had cut the cord – or so I thought. My life until that moment had been entirely controlled by my father and by the needs of 'the company'. No plans could be made, in case we left town or booked a show; no friendships could survive the constant travelling. My whole world had been a suitcase, packed and shipped to order, cargo or accompanied. But now my case was packed on my own terms, on its way to a destination of my own choosing. My life as a child was over.

CHAPTER TWO

THE LOTUS-EATER

The winter sun is shining through the window on to your candlewick bedspread . . . no smiles for me today when I came in, just turning away, you old bugger!

Your nails need cutting, and you are looking wild and cross.

I'll cut your nails later. I'm not having a good day. The play I'm in at the Haymarket is a flop, and we come off after only three weeks. You were very good at failure, having had so much of it! You just carried on regardless, a couple of whiskies, a few shouts at Mother, and you'd pack up and move on.

I wish you could say something. Here I am, banging away at my Olivetti, desperate for a word, a sign, anything to tell me I'm doing the right thing. Or the wrong one. But, what the hell, maybe you're just having a nice long think. Are you thinking about the tea plantations in the hills of India, sitting out at dusk with your whisky, watching the sun set over the plains beyond the valley? Or are you remembering tea and toast on the Punjab Express? Or the 'Kwality' vanilla ice-cream that you loved so much after a few laps of the pool in Bombay's Breach Candy Club? The club that was colourbar till only a short while ago in the early sixties. Only whites allowed; what a shocker. Or the dhows on the Hooghly River, the breeze filling their sails as they glide up and down the brown water past Calcutta, unchanged for hundreds of years?

It was from Calcutta, after I had left you to try my luck in England,
that you wrote to me about your autobiography:

My dear Foo,
   I hope you're well and gainfully employed. I'm still
on my Masterpiece and one thing is certain: that when I
do eventually join my Fathers, there will be a hell of a
lot of balls you can use for a fictional biography . . .
I'm living a lotus-eating existence – without the
lotus.

No lotus-eating today, that's for sure. Your 'supper' is being administered
– something like a banana milkshake piped through a blue tube into
your 'mouth' in your tummy. The magic blue feeding machine that
pumps it has become quite a little friend; the gentle squeak, squeak of
the revolving wheel as it administers the drip of life is soporific, and I
need regular doses of the nursing home's strong coffee to keep me from
joining most of the inmates in their twilight zone.

Reflecting on your bizarre existence, being drip-fed in a home for old
and bewildered gentlefolk, I think, what a way to end a life. But then
what a life. Swashbuckling your way through adventures and traumas
alike, and, despite all the ups and downs, managing to achieve at least
one of your ambitions: never, ever, to have owned a house.

Born in a small semi-detached in the town of Kendal, in the
Lake District, Geoffrey was the eldest of three sons and christened
Richard Geoffrey Bragg by his parents, a schoolmistress and a
travelling salesman (albeit a very smart one). After school, he
worked as an office boy and then as an engineering apprentice,
and was, in his words, 'hopeless at everything', until he joined
the amateur theatre and found his true vocation.

He started as the lowest of the low: assistant stage manager in a provincial touring company. But he had found his life's work, and engineering was forgotten. He played small parts with a number of reps around the country, then, at twenty-one, joined the Edward Dunstan Company. Cast as Romeo to Laura Liddell's Juliet, he fell in love – both with Shakespeare and with his leading lady. She clearly bowled him over, if his description of meeting her is anything to go by.

She was dressed in a brown-and-white checked costume, a suit it would be called now, with a swinging skirt and the highest heels imaginable. She wore a small brown hat over chestnut curly hair, gloves, and a coffee-coloured blouse. She had a pointed chin and a round face, deep brown slanting eyes and a *retroussée* nose that made her look almost oriental, and an air of enormous vitality. She was clearly a favourite, as the whole atmosphere changed. She came into the theatre with great glee, as though she had come home, and almost sighed with relief to be back . . .

Never had I seen a more lovely woman, or a more interesting actress . . . She pleased the public wherever she played. I thought of her as a person absolutely delicious, and I did two foolhardy things that were in defiance of the old actors' warnings. I carried her bag; and I allowed her to sew a button on my jacket without taking it off. I was terribly superstitious. I knew nothing could break her spell, and it never did . . . We stayed with the company for three years, then we married, at Gretna Green, on a lovely, sunny day in the spring of 1933. We had met at the age of twenty-one, and have stayed together ever since. For better or worse – a funny sort of better – no other would have worked.

The photograph of their wedding shows a sweet, young, round-faced girl, with brown curls and a shy smile, holding on to a thin young man in a tweed jacket, with slicked-back hair, standing proudly beside his new bride.

With marriage began the working partnership that was to last for the rest of their lives. As soon as they married, they started their own company, with Geoffrey as the actor-manager and Laura as leading lady. They registered as managers of the Bragg-Liddell Company and advertised for a cast. They had the princely sum of two hundred pounds. They bought some old scenery for fifteen pounds and put together a season of plays, although as yet they had not a single booking. They chose for their repertoire *Romeo and Juliet*, *Othello*, *The Merchant of Venice*, *Macbeth*, *She Stoops to Conquer*, *Saint Joan* and *Michael and Mary* (by A. A. Milne).

They were both in their early twenties, very much in love with their work and each other. Geoffrey was already showing signs of his eccentricity, coming up with ideas about cutting out all the scenery and relying on the spoken word. He was a rough-cut diamond next to Laura and her 'refined' finishing-school manners. He was abrupt and sometimes rude; she was soft-spoken and sensitive to other people. He liked to drink and be gregarious; she loved her solitude. Together they made a lifelong partnership that was indestructible.

These early days were tough, however. They toured all over England, but made very little money. Then, still on tour, Jennifer was born, in digs, with the landlady cast as midwife. Though my mother stopped work on stage during the last few weeks of her pregnancy, she continued to look after the costumes, and was in the theatre until late the night that Jennifer was born. It was a cold February night, and they were living in digs in Southport.

The landlady did not turn a hair when she was asked if the baby could be born in her house. She gave Mother a large supper before she went to bed and sent Geoffrey off to find the midwife. He wandered about the city for hours, unable to locate her. When he finally found her, on the outskirts practising her art,

Jennifer was on the verge of being born. She promised to come as soon as she had finished delivering the baby she was already attending, and so she did. She was tiny and old, and walked through the night carrying her bag of tricks, to arrive with Mother just in time.

Jennifer was born in the early hours of the morning and bedded down in a drawer, as Geoffrey fell asleep, more exhausted than Mother and still half covered in make-up from the previous night's performance of *Trilby*.

A few days later Mother returned to work, with Jennifer in a basket by her side. Apart from rejigging rehearsals slightly to incorporate feeding times, the company's schedule was scarcely disrupted.

Despite the Depression and the meagre bookings for shows, Geoffrey was determined that he would always run a theatre company and always be his own boss. He changed his name, taking 'Kendal' from his home town – thinking it more glamorous than Bragg and better suited to the profile of a romantic young actor.

When the war came my parents' lives were to change for ever. They were offered the chance of touring together with ENSA, travelling and playing to the troops in the Far East. This was a splendid job, with Geoffrey in charge of the company, and it was to be, for him, the beginning of a lifetime's passion for India. For my mother it presented an agonizing choice: she could either go with her husband and leave her child, or stay in England, not knowing whether she would ever see Geoffrey again. She chose to go. It was a decision she never regretted, but I think it affected my sister for the rest of her life. Jennifer (or Jane, as she was sometimes called by her father) was to grow up with a certain coolness towards her mother and an exaggerated need to be approved of by Geoffrey.

Leaving Jennifer to be cared for lovingly by her aunt, they sailed off on a troop ship to an unknown destination, not knowing when, if ever, they would see their child again.

ENSA Drama Division
Drury Lane

Jane Darling,

Having already written about five letters to you, I find I shall have to scrap them. The ship's security officer has just told us what we mustn't mention, and I'm afraid I've mentioned all of them. However, there's a chance of posting this very soon, so here goes.

I have done very little so far except eat and sleep. And I enjoy being on deck, it's grand! We have one compulsory duty every day and that is to appear at ten o'clock at a certain spot, attired in life-belts. We remain there until the ship has been inspected, which usually takes about an hour, and then the day is ours. Tomorrow I'm going to start my Russian studies.

After dinner we have coffee in the lounge and a soldier plays the piano. And we sit at the Captain's table for meals. But as yet, we haven't seen the Captain. We can buy sugared almonds at the shop, I will send you some, if they don't melt away in the meantime — the weather is getting hotter. Daddy has sat down and is writing reams to you.

All our love, darling. Mummy. X

Jennifer was about eight years old when these letters were written. There are dozens, still in perfect condition, filed away carefully by Laura, who must have retrieved them after the war. I found them among a lifetime of letters she had stuffed into worn and battered suitcases, hat boxes and old zip bags. There were ration cards from the war, school reports dated 1918, Mother's first elocution exam, a lock of hair, a pressed rose, Jennifer's navel button and endless letters, some bound up in ribbon, some thrust into old envelopes, letters to and from her friends, lovers and priests, all preserved, all yellow and faded.

Looking through them, I tried to piece together some of the past. I found Mother's letter of employment before she met Geoffrey, detailing the astonishing volume of work she was to take on:

Edward Dunstan and his Shakespearean Company

2nd Jan. 1930

Dear Miss Liddell

Will you please note that I have cast you in the following parts. Bianca (Shrew), Celia (As You), Ariel (Tempest), Olivia (Twelfth Night), Hermia (Dream), Lucy (Rivals), Constance (She Stoops), Constance (Three Musketeers), Dorothy (Nell Gwyn), Rosamuna (Becket), Cynthia (Pygmalion).

Learn the first three and Lucy (Rivals) to begin with, then the others are later on. I am not sure about The Merchant. You will be either Jessica or Nerissa – will let you know later on. You will find the cuts are the same as Mr Baynton's.

Yours sincerely

E. Dunstan

P.S. Tour commences Feb 3rd or 10th. We rehearse week previously, as the case may be.

There were passports full of exotic stamps and good luck cards to an actress of nineteen . . . all kept lovingly by Mother. The woman who had never owned anything much, apart from her books, had kept this record of her life and had travelled all over India with it tucked away in her cases. In later years, as the boxes mounted up, she parked some of them with Jennifer and some with me. I never bothered to look inside the cases and had no idea of the family treasure they contained. Sitting in my small study, up to my neck in musty old papers, I learned a lot about her life with Geoffrey and glimpsed something of their bravery and madness. Some were old airmails that she must have stolen back at some point, letters sent by her to her mother and sister, photographs and cards all kept, perhaps to give her some sense of security in her ever changing world.

The letters to Jennifer are strangely unemotional taken one at a time, but collectively they give the impression that Jennifer was painfully missed, and both her parents wrote to her almost every day.

Jennifer Darling,

We passed the famous Rock today! Tell grandad that this ship . . . can't give her name . . . was built in Barrow in 1926! Tomorrow we get our chocolate rations, I wish I could get mine to you . . . I write to you each day, Jane, but you won't know as dates are not to be mentioned, nor ports of call. It's pretty late, you'll be fast asleep.

Goodnight Darling.
Love you, Mummy. X

This last part of my mother's letter is heartbreaking, now. Jennifer was to die of cancer thirty-eight years later, and she would ask for my mother to sing lullabies to her to soothe her off to sleep. Sitting in the darkened hospital room, I would listen to 'Rock-a-bye Baby' and 'Golden Slumbers' being sung to my grown-up sister. And when she eventually fell asleep, before we crept out, Mother would kiss her face and say, 'You're fast asleep. Goodnight, darling . . . Love you.'

The tour played to the troops of the India Command and was a total success. The letters back to Jennifer spill over with enthusiasm and excitement. It was summer in India, and Geoffrey was clearly falling in love with this glorious land.

My dear Jennifer

There are some lovely things in this country, you know, it's so difficult to describe. Everywhere is so full of lovely colours – the dresses, the things they sell, it's all so grand. In the small towns you can watch people carving wood, making jewellery, making lace and leather work, all done by hand. You can buy a piece of leather and have it made into shoes while you wait for about 30 rs, and much nicer shoes than you see at home. I am sending you some pretty white ones. I have got a Sikh teacher for my Hindustani, very handsome – six feet and bearded.

How are you? I have written 17 letters to your 4! Do you know that all the men wear their shirts outside their trousers in India? And they always piddle sitting down. I must change into my 'Malaria Precautions' i.e. boots, long trousers, long sleeves. Damn silly isn't it? We put them on at sundown. We are off to the northwest frontier.

Rawalpindi
India Command

After a week in the train we arrived at the above. It's
different from Bengal and Tibet, though we can still
see the Himalayas. The people are taller and more
Arabian, veiled women, donkeys, lots of monkeys, etc.
You can get beer here WHOOPEE! A grand place. The
theatre we play at is next to a mosque and every two
hours the Muezzin calls the people to prayer – they call
in quite a high, falsetto note, and they always do it
during a quiet bit!

   You are a fool to pay £6 for a watch. When I was a boy I
wanted a watch and I pinched TWO . . . Now I don't expect
you to do that, but do be CAREFUL with your money, or
you'll turn into a half-wit. The world is full of
half-wits who waste their money. The people in our
company have bought all sorts of junk, all expensive
and useless, so I will be able to send you the £6 that
you have spent on the watch in my next envelope. My word
but it is hot here.

My love, you little gold digger.
Popeye

Mother's reaction to India was more muted. She describes
with some dismay and distaste 'the pavements covered with
sleeping people' and the native quarters with 'soothsayers, phren-
ologists, men sitting on the pavement taking a bath with their
clothes on, beggars, maimed and otherwise, dead cats and rats
just lying about and garbage littered around'. Her fastidiousness
made her recoil from the chaotic nature of the place.

But Geoffrey wanted his daughter to feel and share his passion.

His letters burst with the enthusiasm that he wanted to communicate:

My Dear Jennifer

  We are in Darjeeling, nearly in Tibet. A lovely place where I should like to live. The climate is like the best of English summer, there are no cars in the town, only rickshaws and riding ponies. Everyone rides, it is 2 rs an hour. And you can get a pony anywhere – children ride to school on them – there are lovely schools. The hills are covered in tea plants.

  We went to a Buddhist Monastery today – you can see Everest and Kanchunjun when it is clear – they are only 50 miles away! Did you get the parcel I sent off to you from Bombay? I'll get you some more sandals and a ghurka dagger and some boots. We are halfway through our time in India now, we should be home in January – with a bit of luck. I hope you're having a good time Jane. I wish I could bring you here. It's a wonderful country, you know, full of strange and charming people – all sorts – and everything is so different from the photographs.

                    Cheerio Jane Darling. Keep your bowels open.
                                        Love Popeye

He was not to know of course that Jennifer would spend nearly all her life in India. Nor did he realize that he would adopt India as his home, returning with his own company not once but twice: the first time with Jennifer and me as a baby, to tour for a few months; the second time when I was six, to stay for the next twenty years.

To begin with, however, my arrival scotched their immediate

plans. When the ENSA tour came to an end, they were sent back to rehearse another play at Drury Lane and take it back to India. The war was over, so security was lifted. Mother, however, was pregnant. She kept this to herself, knowing that she would not be allowed to travel, but, once back in India, a welfare officer who was in the same position 'spilled the beans', as Mother put it. When news got back to HQ, they were sent back to London – I should imagine in some disgrace.

Undaunted, Geoffrey set up yet another company, and opened with an old favourite, *White Cargo*, by Ida Simonton. He described the circumstances in his book:

For the first time since we had married in Gretna Green, Laura was not there, for even in the final days of her confinement with Jennifer, she had never left the theatre – continuing to look after the wardrobe until the fall of the curtain the night of Jennifer's birth. This time it was different. Laura's parents, who had moved to Olton in Warwickshire, insisted on her staying quietly at home. It was not for long, though. I came home one night after a performance of *White Cargo* to find it was all over without my help. On 25th September we had another daughter. We called her Felicity.

Nine months later we returned to India.

Mother refused to leave her children behind ever again, so this time, with Jennifer a beautiful, pubescent thirteen-year-old schoolgirl and me a plump baby, Geoffrey packed his family and the small company he had got together on to a ship and sailed towards the sun, leaving behind post-war England, food ration- ing, tatty dates and the coldest winter ever recorded. A nanny was to be found on arrival to look after me while Mother was working. Jennifer was to be put to work, as I would be years later.

There were no shows booked, but, undaunted and happy to be travelling as a family at last, my parents set off to fulfill their dreams of a life free from the mundane. They steamed towards the exotic land of princes and palaces, a place of warmth, welcoming them for the work they did and offering them a life of freedom and adventure.

CHAPTER THREE
MISSY BABA

FAIRLAWN HOTEL
Sudder Street, Calcutta

Hello Beula

We passed terrible floods on our way here, people living on roofs of houses.

Felicity rises with the lark. She simply gets up and murmurs 'Mama' through her cot bars. Honestly, she is so good. The order of her day is 6 a.m. up . . . then out with Mary after milk and banana. 9 a.m. back for breakfast, and if no rehearsal we have her until lunch time whilst Mary does her ironing and washing and usually takes a rickshaw or taxi to do a little shopping. 12 noon Mary gives her a bath and lunch and puts her to bed till about three, then I have her for an hour, we have tea, then when it's cool Mary takes her to the park or Maidan till 6 p.m., then another cool bath and bed.

XX

Mother's letter home to her sister

My earliest and most comforting memories are of the sounds of dawn in India. First would come the pigeons cooing, then the pye-dogs barking and the large black crows cawing. They would be joined by the local dhobi slapping his washing on the stone slabs, with a splat, bang, splat, as every button was broken in the effort of rendering the clothes spotless, if a little frayed. Days begin early in India, and soon these familiar sounds would swell to include the voices of vendors selling their wares, Muslim prayers being chanted from the mosque calling the faithful in to worship, and finally the continuous honking of cars and the ringing of rickshaw bells. Even in the remotest towns there would somehow manage to be a cacophony of sound to wake up to in the morning.

Mother's letter home, New Year's Eve, 1956

Dear Beula,

We had chota hazri at dawn. Felicity woke early. We are playing Othello tonight. Can you send some more sticks of no. 5 and 11. We use so much more in the heat and I am running out. Happy New Year, Darling.

Chota hazri would arrive: an early-morning snack of strong Indian tea, buttered bread and, sometimes, Madeira cake. Usually it was placed on a wooden tray covered in a simple white cloth and brought in by a bearer, who would silently pad into the bedroom in his bare feet, the obligatory old grey cloth on his shoulder, with which he would wipe the bedside table before putting down the tray and swishing away the flies that buzzed around the sugar basin and the jug of ice-cold, creamy buffalo milk. 'Chai liayer, memsahib, namaste, memsahib. I am bringing your morning tea, memsahib.' And, with another swish at the flies, he would be gone, making no sound as he shut the door and the flies settled happily on the bowl of coarse grey sugar.

My day would start with a sleepy visit to my parents' room. Wherever we were staying I would pad next-door or along the corridor of the hotel or guest-house, where I would find them already up and enjoying their early-morning tea. I would have a sip of my mother's, hot and sweet, then lie on the bed with my head in her lap while she talked and argued with my father, who was by now prowling up and down the room in his lungi, already wide awake and planning the day ahead.

They would start to talk to each other the moment they woke up and continue through the day and until last thing at night. They never exhausted their interest in each other's point of view, despite living in close proximity all their lives. There was nothing too important or too trivial to 'chew the cud over', and with this came laughter, sometimes anger and, on occasions, violence. At this age I had seen the shabby side of my father's character only once, and this was at night when he was drunk.

But in the mornings it was sweet tea and cuddles with Mother, sitting on her bed, she in her nightie and the hair rags that she slept in to curl her ramrod-straight hair, her sweet face devoid of make-up, and pretty. I would lie against her in the cool breeze of the fan, until Mary came to fetch me. 'Chullow, Missy Baba, time for your bath. Chullow now.' And she would lead me off to shower, then on to breakfast with the company.

Next to my mother and Jennifer, big, black African Mary was the person I loved best. On my first visit to India, when I was a few months old, Mary was picked to be my ayah from groups of servants lined up on the quayside in Bombay Harbour, waiting to be chosen by the burrah sahibs and memsahibs as they disembarked from the S.S. *Strathmore*. There were lines of drivers, bearers, ayahs and maids, all hopeful of employment.

Mary was spotted by Mother as the only one who was smiling. She was plump and commanding in a spotless white sari. Being the only black nanny on the dock may have contributed to the choice, my parents being drawn to the eccentric and unusual, but her great stature and glorious looks certainly played a part. She was large and beautiful, in an Amazonian way. She was, to my knowledge, the only black ayah in India.

C/O Thomas Cook and Sons

Hornby Road

Bombay

Dear Mother

  I must just tell you in haste that all is well. The AYAH IS MARVELLOUS! She is called Mary. They are fond of each other already, and she is so kind and looks so sweet. I must send you some snaps . . . Jennifer is enjoying herself immensely and the dress rehearsal today was surprisingly good. I must get some sleep now before the show tonight. It's beautifully cool in the evenings and not too hot during the daytime. Very different from the last time we arrived here during the war.

All love, Bye Bye Darling, Laura. X

Mary was to join the tour and look after me. My parents also hired a small south Indian bearer called Afonzo, who was to be the driver and 'go' boy. These two were to travel with us the length and breadth of India. For the next nine months Mary was on duty twenty-four hours a day, seven days a week. She looked after my every need and slept in my bedroom. I was still being breastfed for some of that time, so a large part of Mary's job was working out where my mother was and then taking me, if Mother was working, to the theatre or to the rehearsal, then back to the hotel, by taxi, rickshaw or whatever other transport was most convenient.

As long as she could go to early-morning mass on Sundays, Mary seemed not to want a life apart from me. She became a close and much loved member of the family. Mother adored her, and they would joke and cry together like mother and daughter. Mary had a great belly laugh and, apart from her moods, was a calming and soothing influence on everyone.

Mary could neither read nor write, and was given to embellishing her stories. So she may well have invented her past life, although the story she told never altered. She was born in Goa to an African father and Portuguese-Goan mother. Her mother may have been the town tart, as there was never any mention of her side of the family or of her friends – something unheard of in the East, where extended families reached, either through bloodline or wishful thinking, on into infinity. To have no family ties usually signified that you were an orphan or illegitimate.

She was married at thirteen to a local landowner, who beat her on a regular basis. After a couple of years, when she failed to produce a child, this abuse escalated, and finally, following a particularly brutal attack, she stole the few rupees she needed to take the long bus journey to Bombay. There she got a job on the outskirts of the city with a Goanese family, because she spoke Konkani and they wanted the children to have a Goan nanny. She stayed a few years, then moved on to other families. By now she spoke English and Hindi and, having some considerable experience with babies, she landed a job with the director of Bata Shoes in Bombay, staying until the little girl she was looking after went to boarding school. Then, having enjoyed working for her white memsahib, she turned up on the dockside tarmac, hoping for a similar post.

She was to be all mine. Looking back, our proprietorial attitude towards her seems appalling, but I felt that she *did* belong to us. And although my mother was hardly comparable to a real memsahib, she did expect total loyalty and a certain degree of subservience. But even if Mary was half slave, she was loved and respected, and there was a balance of power: she had acquired for herself the weapon of being indispensable, and she could shake my mother's otherwise cool equilibrium with her rare but gothic sulks.

> Playing Macbeth tonight . . . African Mary doesn't speak. She brought Felicity to me at tea time in silence. Something is on her mind. This mute fury will continue for a few days yet, and I will have to get out of her WHAT THE PROBLEM IS. THESE SULKS CAN GO ON FOR DAYS. Something is looming. But she still does her work and it makes no odds to Felicity.
>
> Mother's diary

Mary's silent tantrums were rare, but if the problem, whatever it was, was not solved, she would start to cry and ask to leave. Then my mother would start to cry and say she couldn't and call in Jennifer and Geoffrey, then, after a lot of wailing, Mary would end up with more money, and life would return to normal.

Every morning of my first tour of India as a baby, we would go through a ritual instigated by my mother. Mary would bring me out to the early-morning company meeting, and the company would greet us. 'Good-morning, Felicity. Good-morning, Mary,' they said solemnly, and then I would be taken away and the day's work could begin. This took place regardless of travel arrangements or fatigue. And it had a bonding effect. Many times during the coming years, if the company was suffering a financial setback or a crisis that seemed to threaten disbanding, Mother would call a meeting and somehow smooth the matter over, making everyone feel indispensable.

Once the company was rehearsing, Mary and I would go out. Sitting proudly in my Victorian pram, I was wheeled through the gardens of the compounds. In the more remote parts of India, children would crowd round and stare, intrigued by my strange mode of transport and even more so by my colour. 'Why is your baby all white?' was the question they asked Mary most often. 'I dip her in flour,' she would reply. 'Every morning she gets a flour bath – and now she is white all by herself.'

This tour lasted nearly a year, from summer 1947 to the following spring. Jennifer was a thirteen-year-old actress, Mother was the leading lady, Geoffrey the actor-manager, and there were four other actors. Geoffrey was back in the land he had fallen in love with during the war, but this time he was to witness the country shake off the shackles of the Raj, see the last durbar, and experience the beginning of the end of British rule in India.

The company toured the princely states, giving private per-formances, but the political climate was becoming more and more unsettled. India was struggling to become independent, and the conflicts between Muslim and Hindu, between Pandit Nehru and Mohammed Ali Jinnah, were coming to a head.

In the August before I was born, violent clashes had erupted between the two factions, leading to an orgy of killings, arson, violence and brutal mob murder. Jinnah had called for an inde-pendent Pakistan, and 'Direct Action Day' was 16 August 1946.

No one could have predicted the horror that lay ahead. But, in the general state of euphoria that accompanied Independence in August 1947, a few of the wiser were already cautious. Most telling of all, the Great Mahatma from his ashram in Calcutta expressed his shattered hopes and dreams of a united land: 'I have no message to give Independence, because my heart has dried up.'

On the eve of the day of the Transfer of Power, when the Union Jacks came fluttering down all over what had once been the Indian Empire, including the one that was never ever lowered on the Residency in Lucknow, Geoffrey recalled seeing a flag being used as a duster on the veranda of the guest-house. He described that time:

It was a time of change that was felt by all. Thousands squatted on top of railway trains, hoping for a free ride to safety. There was a different feeling about everything, not at once, but slowly, over the next few months, up until the new year. There were rumours, awkwardness, rudeness, excitement, and slowly the refugee troubles and the great massacres became generally known.

All sorts of stories were in circulation and on our travels we saw more than most people. We saw the great columns in the Punjab, the millions of homeless camping on every railway station, with children and old people sleeping on the pathetic bundles of household goods they were taking with them, and some with nothing at all. All this has been described in novels and films, but we were there and got the feeling, and that feeling cannot possibly be put down on paper. It was more terrible than you can imagine, and it went on and on. I think Partition was a wicked thing . . . there was no need to split the land in two. It was 'The Devil's Wind' all right!

There was unrest in the schools and colleges, and bookings became difficult. A British company was not so welcome at this time of unease. Then, one day in Bombay, they heard that the Mahatma had been shot dead in Delhi. India came to a standstill.

There was a sigh of relief when it became known that he was not murdered by a Muslim – that would have doubled the blood bath. His ashes were carried out to sea at Chowpatty in Bombay, and my parents watched with thousands of others.

And then we left India. We sailed on the P & O liner *Strathaird*. As the Gateway of India sank below the horizon, it seemed that our life in India was over, almost like a dream. There were no rehearsals on board ship now that we were sailing the other way. It got colder and greyer, and we were just a few more of the Raj going home.

CHAPTER FOUR

LIZARDS ON THE CEILING

The voice on the answering machine was calm. 'This is Sister Margaret, Felicity.' The gentle Irish lilt made it sound affectionate. 'Just wanted you to know that Geoffrey has a fever and is quite poorly. We've called in Dr Patrick, and we're keeping an eye on him until the doctor gets here.' The message continued, 'I'm off duty in half an hour, but Sister Rose will be here, if you'd like to phone us when you get in.'

I sat down at my desk, feeling suddenly tired and useless, when a moment before I had had boundless energy. Not now, I thought. Oh, God, please not now. I can't do death just now . . . Not with twenty minutes to spare before I leave for the theatre tonight.

I went into the kitchen for a glass of water, collected what I needed for the theatre, got into the car and drove down to the Embankment, into the square where there was never anywhere to park. I left a note on the windscreen, 'FATHER DYING . . . GONE TO HELP', and hoped that would stop me from being towed away from the yellow line. I ran into the nursing home, racing up the stairs, past the fish tanks, past the vases of fresh flowers, breathing in the all too familiar smell of disinfectant and room spray.

On the third landing, blocking my path, was a distinguished-looking gentleman, an ex-colonial army type, smartly dressed. He looked as if he should be propping up the bar at the RAC Club, not sitting in a stair chair halfway up, feeble and helpless, trapped by his old age into submissiveness.

'Should I come up with you?' he asked politely, attempting to get out of the chair and failing. 'No, I don't think so,' I replied, trying to squeeze past. 'I'd stay there if I were you.' I carried on up past him, hoping he would let me go. I had no time for this. 'Stay where you are. Sister will be up soon to help you!'

I felt rude and angry with myself for being so careless, for treating him in a dismissive fashion that he would not have tolerated twenty years before. Oh, hell, I thought, life is a pig. I hope he didn't notice my behaviour. 'I DON'T NEED HELP!' His voice followed me up the stairs. 'I'm Major Cunningham and I am leaving here tomorrow!' Please, God, let me die before I get like this, I prayed, as I reached Geoffrey's door.

I hardly know what to feel, now that I am here with you, and you are not dead, and not dying, but most definitely getting better. The nurse has just come in to say that since this morning, when they left me the message, your temperature has gone down and you are stable.

Am I relieved or not? I am relieved. The crisis, well, this crisis, has passed, and, for the moment at least, we can continue as before. I have fifteen minutes now before I usually start to get ready for The Seagull, *so if I leave soon it will be a tight squeeze, but I should make it. I like to get there an hour before every show, a habit drummed into me from years of your indoctrination. 'Always give yourself the luxury of time before and after a show,' you would preach. 'Never ever turn up in a rush at the half!'*

You started training me early. I can't have been more than five years old when you put me on the stage. We were playing Wellington, which was also the place where John Day joined us . . .

'Would you like a toffee?'

'I beg your pardon!' said Geoffrey.

'Would you like a toffee? They're jolly good. I've eaten half the bag.'

John Day proffered the crumpled paper bag of sticky sweets with an engaging smile.

'No, thank you. I never eat between meals,' said Geoffrey stiffly. 'Do sit down.'

John flung his lanky 6′ 3″ frame into a chair.

'I'm about to be called up in a couple of months, but I don't think I'll like it, and I want to do something I'll enjoy, before it's too late, so . . . I'm here for the job of ASM, please . . . Are you sure you wouldn't like a toffee?'

So went the story of John's first meeting with Geoffrey, who was so taken by this 'gormless, spotty youth' that he hired him on the spot. John got the job of assistant stage manager and took to it like a natural. He even lived in the theatre for a few weeks, cooking stews in the prop room, until there were complaints from the front of house.

His cheerfulness under such circumstances was typical. With a laugh like a corncrake and permanently dishevelled hair, John seemed unable to sit still or keep silent for a moment. He was passionately involved in the moment, even if he was only chopping carrots or loading up a car. He was committed to living life to the full, and would laugh like a drain or burst into tears of grief or frustration at a moment's notice. He hurled himself at life like a bouncy puppy, and was still only when he was asleep. A very loving man, he continued to be boyish in his manner even as he grew older, and never lost his ebullient energy.

The company was playing a season at the Wellington Baths while trying to get enough money together to return to India. It was a varied season of plays: *A Streetcar Named Desire*, *Arms and the Man*, *Beauty and the Beast*, *The Merchant of Venice*, *She Stoops to Conquer* and *A Midsummer Night's Dream*.

We must have been very hard up: home was a one-roomed shed behind the theatre across a courtyard leading to the stage door. It was quite warm and cosy, with a gas fire and candles, and Mother cooked porridge and sausages on a tiny stove – I liked the doll's house feel of the place. There was no running water and we used the lavatory in the theatre, which was no fun in the middle of the night, but every two days Mother would take me and her 'smalls' to the public baths, and that was quite an adventure.

For a few pennies we got a small bathroom with a gigantic tub filled almost to the brim with steaming hot water. Mother would lower me into the steaming tub and then scatter in her panties, stockings and bras. Then, having first tied up her hair in a scarf, if it wasn't a shampoo day, she would get into the tub herself, joining the flotsam, and proceed to wash us all vigorously with a large bar of Lifebuoy soap.

Those days were the highlight of my week. Mother loved a good wash more than almost anything, and it put her in a jolly mood. She would sing to me and joke and tickle. I watched her across the floating clothes as the steam rose around her flushed face, humming to herself.

It was during one of these bathtimes that she broke the news. 'Daddy's going to send you on next week as a changeling boy in *The Dream*. Would you like that?'

Would I like it? I was thrilled. I had, in fact, already made my stage début. At a few months old, wrapped in a spare cloak and lying in a basket, I was carried on to the stage, again as the changeling boy in *A Midsummer Night's Dream*. Mother was playing Titania, the company was on tour, as always, and it must have saved having a babysitter.

This second appearance, however, was to prove much more memorable. Although I was playing the same part, I was now, of course, able to walk and felt, at the advanced age of five, confident and ambitious. A small ethnic costume was made: the red turban and gold anklets I remember with pleasure. I was all blacked up, including my little bare feet. John Day rode out into the country on his bike and returned triumphant with a real bulrush. This was to be my spear. I would place it on my shoulder and march up and down beside the sleeping Titania, protecting her from bad actors. Oberon was out to get her with his magic flower and make her fall in love with Bottom, who was my father. Titania, on this occasion, was my sister – but it all made sense at the time.

I don't remember rehearsing, but I do have a memory of sitting on John Day's lap, going over and over the line that I should exit on. Peaseblossom and Cobweb were to lead me on, but they had to leave the stage because Shakespeare said so, and my mother, playing Puck, was not in the scene and so couldn't help. I was to march up and down several times, guarding the sleeping Titania, until Oberon came on, then I was to go 'Oohh' and run off.

I can still recall the feeling of the wooden stage beneath my bare feet, the warmth of the lights that blinded me at first and made the audience shadowy figures in a dark pit beyond the footlights, and the yellow and pink gels that smoked softly from the heat, creating a barrier of safety. Secure in my bright new world, I proudly put the giant bulrush on my shoulder and commenced my march, up and down, up and down, guarding my queen for all I was worth. Up and down, up and down, I felt most important. The lights dimmed, and on and on I went, up and down. I heard a voice. 'BooHughaaowf!' it said. That was not my cue, so I carried on. Suddenly there was Oberon looming over me. He leant over me and hissed, in my ear this time, 'Booger off.' I had been so absorbed in my part that I had missed my exit line.

I fled from the stage in tears of mortification, and could not be consoled even by the treat of a pickled onion from John, who had been elevated to actor and was now, as Lysander, sporting a dashing short toga, tan make-up and blue eyeshadow. It was at least three years before I could be persuaded to tread the boards again – and my second attempt was not much better.

John was called up at last. He left with tears and great, chest-racking sobs. Jennifer was heartbroken. He had become her closest friend, and she adored him with his daft pranks. We heard within a week that the thought of spending two years with the army had sent him 'funny', and that he had thrown himself out of the first-floor window of his barracks dormitory with a dramatic cry of 'I can't go on! I want to end it all.' He narrowly missed the concrete below and landed in a bush, and so escaped injury, but the authorities decided the army would be better off without this crazy individual, so they kept him locked up in a padded cell for five weeks. Then he was discharged, to their mutual relief. Two weeks later he turned up with a large home-made pie for the company, which he unwrapped with a flourish from his suitcase of socks and underpants.

John was back, and he was to remain with us for years, coming out to India on the second tour. He was very gay, but was also in love with Jennifer and would do anything for her. When he finally left the company he set up house with a nice chap and ran an antique shop in Dorset. Then he fell in love with a married lady, whom he later married himself. For the next ten years they were together: the happiest couple I have ever known.

The season at Wellington Baths went on for months. John came, and went, and came back again. James Gibson joined the company, and Brian Kellett was establishing himself as second lead in all the plays. Geoffrey was trying to collect a cast that would follow him to the Far East. Despite the trauma he had witnessed on his previous trip a few years earlier, he was still smitten and determined to return to India, with Malta, perhaps, as a stepping-stone. But it was to be months before he could organize the funds and the bookings.

In the meantime we toured . . . It was the post-war era, and things were tough. My memories are pretty bleak. I remember earache and measles in Ireland and always being in strange, smelly rooms waiting for my mother to come home after work. I remember a Christmas on some farm or other, being looked after by a young girl and being taken to see the goose have its last swim in the icy pond before they wrung its neck. In my first nursery school I had to wear brown bloomers with too tight elastic round the legs that cut into my fat little thighs. The tiny low toilets we used were full of paper, never flushed, and the walls had drawings and smears of shit left by naughty or desperate children. Once I was given a penny by my father and spent hours choosing between a gobstopper and a liquorice sherbet; and once we stayed with a fierce landlady who had a small son my age who bullied me when I was alone with him, but who I liked a lot. His mother made us polish the dining room table legs with heavy wax and old socks.

I remember the cold dampness of cheap digs on tour – a different town, a different bed, a different landlady to look after me every week, while my parents were working at the local theatre. I was not powdered or pampered. Someone was left to 'keep an eye on me', I was always lonely and, it seemed to me, always cold.

Like looking through a telescope from the wrong end, I see this small plain child with a round face and deadly straight blonde hair, four or five years old and very shy. She appears in black and white, no colour, and no sound, just images of the past. It is like looking at an old film.

One night in particular stands out. We could have been in any provincial town in England. The house was across the street from the theatre and was divided into rooms to 'let' to the visiting theatricals (the landlady would have her own flat and would rent the other rooms out, with one bathroom to be shared by all).

In my memory, it is night-time. I am in bed at the top of the house, the light is shining on the landing through the half-open door into the darkness of the bedroom. The bed is lumpy and narrow, the blanket is scratchy against my chin. My face is wet – I must have been crying, yet at the same time I notice, without emotion, that the light on the landing can make different star shapes or crosses depending on how tightly I close my eyes. The socks are not keeping my toes warm and the hot-water bottle wrapped in a dishcloth has become a sorry tepid dead weight.

A door bangs in the street below. I creep out of bed, tiptoe to the window and, pulling aside the net curtains, peer down at the illuminated sign of the Palace Theatre Stage Door. Beneath the yellow streetlights stand a group of people. They have just come out and are laughing and talking together. There is a woman in a white coat wrapping a long scarf around her shoulders – it's Mummy, her dark hair coiled up into a tight bun (to fit under the wigs in the show). The play must have finished. Daddy joins her and puts his arm around her shoulders, chatting to the group. There is more talk and laughter, some goodnights to the stage door keeper, and the group heads off to the corner pub further down the road. I watch until the street is empty. Presently the stage door man comes out and locks up the theatre for the night.

I shiver at the window and go back to bed, curling up with my gollywog, Jack, which Grandma made for me out of old stockings and knitting wool. Pulling up the blankets, I fall into a kind of half-sleep, warmer after the chill of the window. I am woken by soft, swift footsteps coming up the stairs and the familiar rattle of bracelets. I turn round, still with my eyes shut, and there is Mummy, smelling of April Violets mixed with greasepaint. She bends over and kisses me. 'I know you're asleep, darling, but this is "just one to be getting on with" . . . I love you, darling baby.' Another kiss, and she is gone.

Mary was never gone. Mary was always there – in the park, in the train, at the foot of my bed. Reliable, steadfast and faithful to the end. At the age of twelve I was to walk away from her and break her heart; but when we returned to India the following year, with me aged six, she was to become the centre of my universe.

Before we embarked on the return to India, Geoffrey managed to pull together a company for a short but ambitious season in Malta, playing sixteen shows at the Knight's Hall in Valletta. It was to prove an invaluable trip. On the second night of the season the Governor of Malta came to the show with his guests, Earl Mountbatten of Burma and Countess Mountbatten. They came backstage after the show and invited the company to lunch. I was too young to go, and sulked for the duration. But the rest of the company was in high excitement. At the lunch there was talk of the company returning to India, and Lady Mountbatten promised to remember them to Nehru. A lasting connection with her was established, and she later became patron to the company and attended shows all over India.

This was the more remarkable given the minor hitches that occurred in Malta. Lady Mountbatten saw five of the shows that Geoffrey put on, and, after one visit backstage, left behind a small blue hat in the dressing room. When Mother found it, she thought it just the thing for her comic role in *Hay Fever*, which they were to perform the following night with the Mountbattens in the audience. Just before curtain up, and in the nick of time, a note came from Edwina: had she by any chance left a small blue hat in the dressing room . . . ?

More embarrassment was to follow. At the end of the season there was the usual problem with money. The hotel had not been paid, and Geoffrey was carted off to jail for a few hours. Lady Mountbatten was called on and Geoffrey was released. I don't know whether she stood bail or paid the hotel bill, but he was indebted to her for ever. She was a true and very gracious patron, and did indeed pave the way between Geoffrey and Nehru, who also became a patron and help to get Geoffrey out of many tight corners. I never heard Geoffrey praise anyone as highly as he did the Mountbattens. That they and Nehru should spend time and concern on Geoffrey's bunch of 'tatties', as he called us, was always a mystery to me. But he was in his youth: dynamic, witty and very convincing, and he was providing something unique – Shakespeare alive on the school stages of the Far East. He returned to England, raring to go.

My happiest memories of those years in England were the occasional visits we made to Elmhurst, the family house I was born in. I remember the warm brightness of the place, milling with people and full of cooking smells. And I remember Grandma.

She was small and plump and her cheeks were soft and downy and smelt faintly of face powder. She was very short-sighted, had been all her life, and was always losing her glasses, which were usually on her head. To her dying day she was ashamed of her wedding photo, because she forgot to take off her glasses for it and Pop hadn't noticed. She would not have it framed and displayed on the sideboard with all the other family photographs in their shiny silver frames. I have the photograph; it's framed now. She and Pop look very young.

The night before we left, we saw the coronation of Queen

Elizabeth II on our next-door neighbour's black and white television. We had to close all the curtains in order to be able to see the picture on the screen. Auntie Babs, who owned the television, made trifle and jelly. I remember thinking the young Princess too pretty to be Queen and I remember her little boy Charles playing with her golden coronation bracelets on the balcony when she came out to wave to the crowds below. And I remember tears from my mother, because she was leaving for India in the morning and must have felt some premonition that she would not be back for a very long time.

For Mother, this would be the last time she would see Grandma, lovely, soft Grandma, defiant in her youth but cuddly now, the perfect grandparent to the children, lively as a cricket, full of jokes and patience, until six o'clock when she retired to bed with a full bottle of port.

We sailed to India on board the S.S. *Jaljawahar*, a small steamship named after Jawaharlal Nehru. The company that boarded that day was headed by Laura and Geoffrey; then came their two daughters (Jennifer was nineteen; I was a plump six); lanky John Day, who was nineteen; Frank Wheatley, seventy plus; Wendy Beavis, who was twenty-something; and Brian Kellett whose age no one knew but who always looked fourteen. Then there was the small American girl, Nancy Neal, who didn't last long and who was in love with Conor Farrington, a tall, dark, dashing Irishman, who was very romantic and was always writing poems and plays. He had joined to see India and invested some money in the first tour, which he never got back. He did not really get on with India, and was one of the first to return.

I took to the water at once, finding my 'sea-legs' and revelling in the gentle rolling of the ship. Brian was as sick as a dog, and would be so on every voyage for the next nine years, but I was a natural sailor and loved to watch the rise and fall of the horizon from the top bunk in the little cabin I shared with my parents.

For the first time since I could remember, Mother was with me all the time. She put me to bed after reading a chapter or two of *Tom Sawyer* or a scene from a play; she was there at mealtimes; she played with me, winning at cards and deck quoits; she swam with me in the small canvas pool that was erected once we were in warm waters. There were no shows and few rehearsals, and for three weeks the company frolicked in the freedom of life on board. There were parties and fancy-dress shows and, for Jennifer, numerous flirtations with the handsome, white-uniformed young officers who gathered about her like bees round a honey pot.

The sun blazed down as we steamed towards the East. Geoffrey was smiling and happy to be on his way back to the land he loved so much. With his knobbly knees tanned beneath his shorts and his thick brown hair blowing in the salt breeze, a pipe in his mouth and a glass of beer in his hand, he stood swaying on the deck to the rhythm of the waves and described to me the wonders of the country we were sailing to. Then, having drained his glass, he would take my hand and lead me down into the bowels of the ship, where, like a boy with a prized new toy, he would show me over the engine room. He would describe every piston and detail every nut and bolt, shouting over the din of the great roaring beast. I would endure this with patience but not a lot of interest, waiting till he had satisfied himself with a job well done and we could climb the steep steel ladders out of the darkness and into the blinding brightness on the lower deck.

At Port Said we went ashore, and I had my first impressions of the colours and smells of my new life. There were men and women in flowing garments, palm trees and dancing monkeys, fruit stalls piled high with pineapples and bananas and exotic fruits that looked like poison, wide streets of amazing beauty, leading to narrow alleyways deep in stinking filth. And all the time the warm air surrounding me like a blanket of comfort, all the time the vast bright sky banishing for ever the small grey life we had left behind, of cramped terraced houses and digs smelling of damp and bacon.

After a week at sea Geoffrey could not resist offering a show, and *Arms and the Man* was played on the poop deck in the middle of the Red Sea ('Very grey, the Red Sea,' remarked Mother), and *Macbeth* later in the first-class lounge as we reached the Indian Ocean. Conor got so carried away trying to kill off Macbeth that he managed to bring down half the wall light-fittings, plunging the lounge into darkness.

At last, there it was, rising out of the mist and monsoon rain on the shore of our promised land – the Gateway to India. The dark stone monument built to commemorate the visit of George V and Queen Mary in 1911 stood proudly, looking out on to the Arabian Sea. Behind it was the Taj Mahal Hotel, a delirium of ornamental nonsense, like an extravagant wedding cake. From the water it looked out of all proportion, with no central entrance: the builders mistook the plans sent from Paris, and built it back to front, so it faced a small road with its back to the sea.

I neither knew nor cared about any of this on that first sighting. I stood on deck, peeping through the ship's rail in my white cotton frock and leather sandals, gazing with calm interest at the land that I would make my home. All around me grown-ups were bustling about, giving orders and peering through binoculars, as we anchored in the bay, waiting for the tide so we could berth. For Geoffrey, this was the moment he had longed for. He wrote about it in his diary:

On June 25th we sighted India once more. There were the familiar sights I had missed for so long. The Dhows with triangular sails tacking across the Bay of Bombay, the noise, the bustle of the harbour, the crowds of people waiting with flowers and garlands . . . And Mary, with tears streaming down her face.

Mother took me down to do the last of our packing. I was a little sad to be leaving our makeshift home on board, but Geoffrey's brother was coming to meet us off the ship. 'You'll love your Uncle Phil, Foo,' Mother reassured me. 'He's a great character. He owns a shipping company in Bombay and is very well off!'

Then we were docking. The shouting dockmen heaved on huge ropes and, as if by magic, the ship glided into place alongside the quay. Gangplanks were lowered, and luggage offloaded; coolies swarmed about, sweaty and incomprehensible. Finally we got into the customs house, surrounded by indescribable chaos and heat, overcome by the sheer excitement at having landed. In the enormous dark shed little tables had been set up, where customs officials were stamping passports and marking luggage. They had already been on board the ship, and had refused to let in the various daggers, swords, shields, spears and guns that were part of the props we carried, thinking we might be a small revolutionary party about to set up shop. It took three days to convince them to the contrary. By then we were installed at Green's Hotel, Byculla, and Mary was back with me.

June 1952, 30th

Arrived in Bombay . . . again . . . But trouble with customs and tax. Every bag searched, customs on board. Mary appeared MARVELLOUS! What a difference it will be now. Foo thinks she's 'absolutely wonderful'. We are all invited to come back for dinner on board ship tomorrow by the ship's officers. I won't be going. We have our first show the next day, Macbeth matinee,

and Twelfth Night in the evening at the Convent of the Sacred
Heart.

Mother's diary

When we arrived in Bombay for the second time, my small,
dreary, black and white existence in cold England was over; I
was back in India, revelling in the heat, the smells, the colours.

There was always something astonishing to look at: astounding
opulence next to medieval poverty; girl-mothers with wizened,
crippled babies; grossly fat babus sporting diamonds and living
in palatial villas in magnificent compounds. In the streets the
smells of spiced food hung in the air, mixing with incense and
the stench of sewers and decay. And all the time there was the
colour of the place: the blinding sun doing nothing to dim the
oranges and blues of silk saris and turbans, or the garishly painted
posters of film stars that smiled down upon the traffic and the
chaos. Thin cats and mangy dogs would wander along with
skinny babies among the rubbish on the streets, and the sacred
grey brahmin cows, sometimes garlanded, always careless of
danger, sat in the middle of the road chewing the cud as cars
and bicycles manoeuvred around them.

The time of day I grew to love most was four thirty in the
afternoon. At this point the day would start to wind down . . .
the temperature would almost imperceptibly start to drop, the
sleeping dogs would wake from their siesta, and the children
would be given tea ready for the evening stroll in the gardens.
In the cities, the little white babies would be powdered and
dressed in their cottons, and taken to play in the scented gardens
of the Raj, while the ayahs sat chattering together watching their
precious charges with eagle eyes, scolding them and kissing them
better in a protective circle of care.

The light would very slowly start to fade, changing from the brilliant angry white of midday to the pale yellow glow of early evening. Then, quite suddenly, at about six thirty the sky would turn amber and pink. The jasmine would break out and fill the air with its heady perfume as the giant globe of the sun suddenly disappeared into the sea, like a stone plopping into the water.

The fan would be turned to no. 4, medium speed, the mosquito net firmly tucked under the hard horsehair mattress. The crickets would start to rub their legs, producing a shrill sound, and the mosquitoes would come out to feed. The frogs, quiet all day, would stir themselves and start to croak in the pools behind the dak bungalow. In the distance the ever present pye-dogs would start barking to one another, setting up a chain of sound that would continue long into the night and only stop when dawn crept back and they were exhausted and satisfied, a good night's guarding done.

This was my India, the one I will always remember. Man and beast cheek by jowl; life and death always apparent – and no embarrassment about either. Wedding processions would wind through the dusty streets, with the garlanded groom, his face covered by a veil of jasmine flowers, being led on horseback to collect his bride, while a gaily dressed band in turbans blew trumpets and beat on drums to clear his path, and the relatives followed, singing and cheering around the decorated horse.

Such moments would be celebrated with an open and abandoned display of joy, but sorrow would be equally felt. Through the same streets quieter groups would come, carrying a shrouded body on a simple frame, covered in white and heaped high with loosely strewn flowers. They would make their way to the burning ghats (a place, by water if possible, where the dead are cremated on funeral pyres). Sometimes there would be gentle singing, giving thanks for a long and happy life, but if the body was only small – and too often it was tiny – then the tears and grief would pour out for all to see. There was nothing reserved or half-hearted about life and death in India when I was a child.

Mary was at the centre of this revolution in my life, and it was through her that I experienced my India. She wore a 22-carat gold chain round her plump neck and glass bangles on each small wrist. Her African curls had been smoothed into submissiveness with coconut oil, then pulled back and joined at the nape by a bun of tightly coiled false straight hair that did not remotely match the front curly bit – a sort of reverse toupee. She would wash this false hairpiece once a week and dry it in the sun, somewhere out of sight, while she waited in the shade, her sari covering her head and the bald evidence.

I would often tease her by stealing the damp, drying hair and running away with it. She would chase me, her head still covered in the sari, screaming abuse in wailing Konkani until I relented and returned the dreadful thing, which she would pin back on, securing the bun with long, black steel hairpins, before pretending to cry in order to draw me near. Thereupon she would smack my bottom, before the kissing and cuddling would break out. And so would end the ritual of bun stealing. She had the most remarkable patience and, apart from her sulks, which the family came to dread, was the most perfect nanny a child could wish for.

Mary wore a spotless white sari that I used as a hammock, sitting in the fold between her legs and swinging to and fro, with the back of my head nestling against her warm bosom. She had teeth stained red by years of betel-nut and tobacco pan. She must have been addicted to the tobacco: I cannot remember her ever being without a chew firmly lodged in her cheek, and she could spit the red liquid up to three feet with deadly accuracy.

She had a little silver box to hold the pan leaves, betel-nut, cloves and tobacco, and inside that was a smaller one for the deadly white paste. She would show me how to first choose only from the softest, smallest white leaves at the pan sellers in the bazaar. 'Always get him to give you extra, Foo, baba. Always ask for extra more.' She would then instruct me on the making up of the pan itself, spreading the white lime paste thinly all over the inside of the leaf, drizzling on the crushed betel-nut, then adding a tiny dab of red paste. Finally, a layer of tobacco, and the leaf would be rolled into a perfect triangle and secured with a clove. This she would pop into her cheek, saying, 'Not for you, darling. Tobacco not for you. You can have meeta pan [sweet pan], but me Mary only have tobacco one, darling. Not good for your tummy, baby. Mary's tummy don't mind.'

In Bombay she would take me to Marine Drive, the three-mile crescent bordered with palm trees that led down to the beach. Across the road from the water were stately mansion blocks of flats for the wealthy residents of the city. Malabar Hill overlooked Marine Drive, and from there at night, with the lights of the city shimmering by the sea, the crescent resembled a string of diamonds, and so it was called the Queen's Necklace.

Down to the beach Mary would take me almost every evening after tea, as soon as the heat had gone from the day. The air was thick with the sweet salt from the brown sea, the smell of roasting peanuts, traffic fumes and sweetmeats being cooked by vendors crouching over their small charcoal fires in the sand.

We would go by taxi, and one rupee later we would be on the sand, taking off our chappals and splashing in the waves. Or we would go the longer route, stopping off at the Botanical Gardens on Malabar Hill. Mary would sit under the giant banyan tree, feeding the monkeys titbits, while I played on the swing and slid down the banana slide, made into the shape of a shoe.

We would then walk down to the beach, making our way slowly down the hundreds of steep steps, till, this hazardous journey accomplished, we would arrive at the bottom. My white cotton dress now marked from sliding and playing, and my new Bata sandals scuffed, but my energy unabated. I would want to run across the damp sands. Mary would be breathless and, holding my hand, would insist on looking for 'nice place to sit'. Having found such a spot, she would gingerly lower her considerable weight on to the little embroidered cloth bag that she always slung over her shoulder on these expeditions. She spread the bag like a tiny cloth on the sand as a cushion and, taking off her chappals and placing them neatly side by side, she would sit and watch as I paddled in the shallow waves.

As it grew darker we would walk along the Chowpatty Beach, and Mary would buy one anna's worth of warm peanuts, kept hot by a small lota of coal placed on the pile of shelled and salted nuts. The nuts would have been measured out to the exact anna, using a brass measure, then poured into a rolled piece of newspaper that was twisted into a tiny and exquisite cone, all in a flash of the fingers. Cold drinks to accompany the nuts were not allowed. 'Very regrettable, Foo Foo, baba, but definitely not allowed by Mummy.' The generous helping of Bombay Belly was no doubt the reason for this ban on the ice-cold drinks in garish yellow and green that were sold at the neon-lit drinks stalls. Soda water was the only one allowed, and hot sweet tea. These I could partake of, but neither did I ever want.

If I plagued Mary long and hard, pulling the end of her sari, she would sometimes dig into her little cloth bag for a few annas, and I would get a ride on one of the small fly-blown ponies, garlanded with flowers and brightly coloured ribbons, that trotted up and down the beach. Tiny screeching children were held on to the saddle by the pony wallah, who ran alongside with one arm round the child and the other on the pony's rein.

When my turn came I would be hoisted on to the saddle in a flash and off we'd trot. The few annas' worth of ride under way, I would clasp the hairy mane of the mouldy little beast – being plump, and not at all brave, I would by now be in terror of my life, notwithstanding the fact that I had begged for this ride in the first place. The thrill of the bump, bump, bump, my little legs doing the splits across the back of the animal, and my body lurching from side to side in the saddle, was a dangerous dance of delight. The jingle of the bells, the splashing of the shallow waves under the tiny hoofs, the spray of water in my face, as we trotted along in the wind, made these Chowpatty rides on the beach a highlight of my first memories of childhood in India.

As the sun set we would wend our way back to the hotel by taxi, or sometimes, if it was very hot and the taxi queues were very long, we would get a horse gharry. The horses were ancient, almost as old as the carriages, which were Victorian, large and black, with giant wheels and leather upholstery. We would clop through the streets of bustling traffic, the gharry wallah banging the bell on the side of his horse whip, as the extravagant neon lights of the city came on, one by one.

With the fading light, I would grow sleepy and snooze against Mary's shoulder, and we would arrive at the hotel in the dark. Mary would order supper on a tray before taking me to our room to bathe. This was a ritual that involved covering a flannel with Lifebuoy soapsuds and scrubbing me to within an inch of my life – all this within an empty bathtub. Only when I was foaming with suds would she rinse me off under the tap, using a lota (a water-pouring vessel) to make me squeaky clean. Then came the Johnson's baby-powder session, not to be under-estimated in the warding off of prickly heat spots and heat rashes. I would be smothered in the stuff, then put into white cotton pants and a vest before supper.

Supper arrived on a tray and was taken on to the veranda, if there was one, or under the fan. It was invariably fish fry and chips;

if I was unlucky, rissoles or veg cutlets with peas. Mary would have a plate piled high with rice, crowned by whatever curry was on offer. This would be followed by jelly, cold sago pudding or the occasional fruit salad – all relics of the fast-fading Raj.

We would eat in silence; Mary's food was important to her. Mummy would come in on her way to a show or a party at whatever club, school or theatre they were at that night. Then it was teeth cleaning and SooSoo. 'Have you done SooSoo, darling?' Mary would ask before the light went out every night of my childhood with her. 'You won't sleep, baby, if you need to go SooSoo.' So off to the lavatory and, a pee later, I would be in bed under the fan, sometimes, depending on the mosquito alert, under a mosquito net, one white sheet to cover me, the lights turned off, and Mary would let herself down, to lie at the foot of my bed until I went off to sleep.

She would tell me stories until she fell asleep and started to snore, at which I would kick her gently with my toes, resting on her belly for comfort, and she would wake, saying, 'Sorry, Foo, baba, Mary tired.' Then she would resume the story, or start again from the beginning. All her stories came from the Bible, so she had an infinite variety, though they were often confused, combining Adam and Eve ('Adow and Iva') and the Garden of Eden,which she placed firmly in south India, with the folktales of the Ramayana, featuring Francis of Assisi.

I loved listening to the elaborate tales, as the fan creaked its soft wind over us. Above us, as if by magic, lizards stuck to the ceiling and stared down at us, immobile, with eyes frozen and tails slowly twitching. Some were only babies; some had no tails at all. 'Why don't all the lizards have tails, Mary?' I would ask in the darkness. 'Because big lizard he fight baby lizard, but good ones 'scape and leave only tail behind! Now go to sleep, baba.' And she would snore softly again, while I drifted into a contented slumber.

★

So, that's done. I've cut your nails — with great difficulty. They were always like iron and are now more like gnarled cold iron and getting to the bit that's twisted in a fist and growing into the palm of your hand is no easy matter. You frowned a lot, but seemed to know what I was doing, or am I just making that up in order to feel better?

You have a bloodshot eye, probably from poking it with your long nails. It must be dreadful, dreadful, dreadful not to be able to move. I wonder if you know that you can't, and if so, are you used to it by now? Moving the one arm, fist clenched, index finger extended, sometimes at random and sometimes in a sort of a rhythm, compared to the rest of you that doesn't move at all — could this be something of a triumph?

I think not speaking must be the worst, for you anyway. The cruellest possible end. Dying is acceptable, if a little inconvenient sometimes, but to be struck dumb and then paralysed, that surely is one of God's most extreme tortures.

The silent days here bleed into weeks and now years . . . you're not going anywhere, are you, darling? I thought it was only a matter of time, as they say, but you're not in a hurry for the end, and I'm glad.

In the first months I prayed for it to come, to release you and me, and anyone else who cared for you, but I'm used to it now, and the dread of losing you has returned. The feeling of security in having you there, even in this absurd way, is strangely reassuring. I don't think you want to go, and even if you could speak and told me to pull out the plug, I still would not be able to consider such a thing. A kind, well-meaning person asked me how I could let this farce continue: 'I wouldn't let a dog live on in that state!' All very well, but you're not a dog, and 'There are more things in heaven and earth, Horatio . . .'

CHAPTER FIVE

THE POWER BEHIND
THE THRONE

The company was thriving. It seemed in those early years we were on an extended summer holiday. The actors were all young, India was welcoming and full of hope for the future. There was little money to be made, but our work won tremendous appreciation, and it seemed in those days that we never stopped laughing. The fit-ups were full of practical jokes and banter, the endless journeys by car, plane, truck, train and ferry were undertaken with enthusiasm and accompanied by songs and picnics, and there were love affairs going on all the time. The atmosphere was closer to that of a scouts' outing than a professional theatre company on tour. Working ridiculous hours and living sometimes in absurdly uncomfortable accommodation for very little remuneration, this merry band trailed around India from north to south, east to west; there was not a town, hardly a village that was spared.

Leading the way, from one mad escapade to another, was Geoffrey, the bully with a heart of gold, the mad adventurer willing to go anywhere at the drop of a hat if there was a hint of playing a show for a few rupees, and often leaving in his wake a trail of debts that he felt justified in not dealing with – justified because he was spreading the Word and lifting Shakespeare out of classroom textbooks and on to the stage where he belonged.

Beside him was my mother, the power behind the throne. During this, their third tour of India, she was at her most severe and beautiful best. Calm, unflappable, aloof, although she seemed at times to be a little absent-minded, she was in complete control. She reigned over us in cool, crisp cotton.

She was always immaculately dressed. She would disembark from the train that had steamed over the plains of the Punjab for five days looking as if she had stepped out of a beauty parlour. The rest of us would be crumpled and sooty, unwashed and the men unshaven, the third-class journey on wooden seats having taken its toll. But Mother would have showered in a toothmug, changed into a pristine pair of slacks and blouse, tied a turban round her sooty hair, put on her make-up and sprayed on cologne. Finished off with the trademark white-rimmed sunglasses and dainty gold chappals, she was prepared to arrive at the next date. The fact that the next date might be in deepest Kerala made no difference to her: she turned herself out the same for Nehru as for the sisters at the local Bleeding Heart Convent School. Always the Leading Lady, always the maternal confidante to this varied bunch of travelling players.

On the drawn-out train journeys, sometimes taking two or three days, the routine never varied. After choosing who slept on which bunk, the bedrolls would be put out for the night, canvas sleeping-bags with two compartments at each end: one for a pillow, one for a blanket. The centre already had a thin mattress and two small, thin sheets, the sides flapped out and under to reveal a proper made-up bed, which could be rolled up when not used and fastened with leather straps and buckles. I had a blue bedroll with very thick leather straps. I was very proud of it and kept my cuddly toys in the pillow compartment.

Once the bedrolls were in place, Mother would get out the

picnic: Spam and bread and butter was a big favourite; cheese and onions another. This was washed down with beer or whisky and soda. These late-night snacks, as the train pulled out into the dark, were times of great enjoyment and relaxation – for however well or badly the last dates had gone, the next stop was bound to be a triumph!

The snacks were part of the service Mother provided. Where she got them from was sometimes a mystery, but they contributed to a comforting, if unnecessary ritual – since they were only supplements to vast amounts of tea and toast, curries and omelettes that would be ordered at one station, delivered at the next, and then collected at a third, further down the line, where 'they did the washing up'.

Then, before lights out, Mother would get out her Flit gun and spray the corners of the berths and floor to discourage cockroach fever. As soon as it was dark, they would steal out to collect the odd crumb; if you put the light on in the middle of the night, the floor would appear to move for a moment. Flitting done, we would take it in turns to use the tiny bathroom off the compartment. As often as not, it had a keyhole loo in the floor, and the cat learnt to use it.

I would be put into my nightie, teeth cleaned in soda water, and would climb on to my bunk, ready to settle down. I would fall asleep with the moon shining in through the bars of the open window, the cool night air blowing the sheets, and listening to the chuggity, chuggity, chug of the wheels as we steamed our way through India.

On one particularly long, hot journey, John, who was leaning out of the door to catch the passing breeze, fell out of the train. It was not moving very fast and he didn't let go of the door, so he managed, after a few heart-stopping seconds, to haul himself back in. Mother, as she bandaged his bleeding head, could not resist: 'Come let me scarf up the eye of pitiful Day.' We were not a superstitious lot, and a quick 'Enter Lavinia ravished' was said as the antidote to quoting *Macbeth*.

In those years I was the company trophy. I was spoiled and teased and included in all the trips, the picnics, the horse riding, the swimming parties. And half my life was spent on trains or buses, making midnight departures, being woken and dressed to travel. I could sleep anywhere, anytime, I was never car- or sea-sick, I was the perfect travelling child. I would curl up on my top bunk and listen to the grown-ups talk, until I fell asleep.

The imprint of my nomadic years is still with me. I like nothing better than to pack my bags and set off to somewhere else: it matters little where that somewhere is, it's the going that counts. I find no comfort in sameness and, if I haven't been away for a while, I will start rearranging the furniture, altering my environment and the position of things. To be in a tent or a five-star hotel is equally attractive; only dull predictability holds any threat.

The journeys always started the same way. From Bombay to Tokyo, by train, camel cart, bus, ship, elephant or taxi, they started with excitement and ended in a play. All the luggage had to be loaded, the usual officialdom had to be appeased, someone would turn up late or have lost their luggage. But the purpose of the journey hung in the air.

Every day Geoffrey would repeat his mantra at the early-morning meeting. 'We are all here because we love the world and want to be everywhere before we die. We want to see all sorts of people and meet all sorts of friends. We want to show them our plays, the best plays in the world – the plays of Shakespeare. And because to perform these plays in all sorts of places and on all sorts of stages calls for an almost impossible degree of concentration and nervous energy, and because to arrange constant travelling is a constant source of worry in these officious days, I want you all to keep fighting fit. Do yoga, laugh a lot, and always breathe deeply. And when you have a problem, go for a walk and SING at the top of your bloody lungs . . . that will do it!

'Now, then, what do we rehearse today? And are there any questions the company want to air?'

While Geoffrey adored the travelling and footloose life free of possessions, Mother's attitude to being on the road was more qualified. She had her own approach to dealing with the chaos of India and the uncertainty of constant touring, and became expert at imposing a sense of normality and continuity wherever we went. In half an hour she could transform a tatty room in a guest-house into a cosy lived-in apartment. Out would come the throws and the family photographs; cushions would be covered and flowers arranged in drinking glasses beside the beds, books would be laid out and 'things' littered all over the room 'to nicen it up'.

As the months of travelling turned into years, the essential few bags for costumes and clothes expanded to include tin trunks and boxes of books, bedrolls with pillows and sheets, heavy leather cases for ornaments and tablecloths. The four or five taxis needed to transport us all gradually turned into an expensive ten and the number of rickshaws needed in small towns rose to fifteen.

'Bloody women!' Geoffrey would explode at some point on every journey. 'What in Christ's name do you need all this damn *junk* for? I spend a fortune on coolies to carry books you never read and clothes you never wear. I have one suitcase and I run the sodding outfit!'

Mother paid no attention to his outbursts, and the caravan of possessions grew steadily larger. Sometimes she would sneak a tip to the coolies or rickshaw men who laboured, sweating, under almost immovable boxes of books. They would salaam and bless her, as she turned to me with a 'Shhh. Don't tell your father.'

'I never tell him anything, Mummy, you know that,' I would reply. I never disobeyed her; no sensible person would dream of questioning her gentle commands. She never raised her voice and there was no hysteria, just quiet control. While Geoffrey was a firecracker, liable to explode at the slightest hint of trouble, she was calm and collected – though in reality she was every bit as forceful as her husband. She rarely lost her temper, and only once did she do so with me, when she took a Mason Pearson hairbrush to my bare bottom. Whatever it was I did, I never did it again.

Mother's apparent coolness could be misunderstood as lack of feeling, but to her it simply wasn't the done thing to let anything hang out, let alone all of it. A woman of infinite patience, she was especially good with children. 'Quality time' was a term that had not yet been invented for working mothers, but I experienced it with mine. When she was with me her concentration and commitment were absolute: nothing could distract her for the allotted time, however long the story, or the walk, or the bedtime ritual on her rare nights off.

She would read to me for hours – Mark Twain, Zola, Kipling, Chaucer, *Don Quixote* and Shakespeare's sonnets. Nothing childish except Pooh Bear, he was allowed, but definitely not Noddy or Enid Blyton. As I grew up, comic books were banned, but I did get *Just William* past her, which may explain my tomboy attitude to life in those years. 'Tatty love stories will fuddle your brain, darling . . . If it's not well written, it's not worth reading,' she would say, giving me a hug. She, like Mary, was forever hugging and kissing, unlike my father, who restricted himself to a stiff pat on the head now and then.

I realize, looking back, that at this time in my life I was completely happy. Mary was my Mary. I worshipped my big sister, placing her firmly on a pedestal from which she was never to topple. Mother was Mother, and my father was Geoffrey, and he was something else. From my earliest years he treated me as an equal. He never talked down to me or altered his tone. He would ask my advice about tour dates and shows long before I was equipped to know the answer. If he got into a tight spot about money or conflicting dates, we would go for a walk and he would sound me out, and even if he didn't take my advice, he pretended to, which made me feel important.

I was the only one, apart from Mother, who stood up to him. And later on, however much we disagreed about something and tried to manipulate one another, we would come to an understanding based on mutual respect. I believed he really did value my opinion, even as a small child, and we had years of a very truthful and close relationship. But I didn't think he loved me very much. I did not mind. I had more love than I needed.

You were never much of a toucher. So it's been hard getting used to giving you the odd cuddle, and holding your one good hand. I'm still half afraid you'll jump up and shout, 'Stop being so bloody namby-pamby and pawing like a dog.'

'Canoodling in public is a disgusting modern habit!' you would say. 'You don't have to SHOW us how much you love someone by groping them in front of the rest of us! We might be having our tea, for God's sake, and there, in front of us, are two people twisted up together. It's revolting!'

Geoffrey was very Victorian in his attitude to affection, and how to show it. I can remember him holding Mother's hand only once, and that was at night when there was no one else there. But he dearly loved her and looked after her every need as best he could, showing his devotion by never letting her out of his sight, keeping her by his side and bullying her every day.

Although he decided early that she was the one for him, a letter sent when they were courting reveals how matter-of-fact was his behaviour. In 1930 he was leaving the Merchant Navy and was to meet her in London.

Merchant Navy, Bear Inn, Llaounderry, May 1930

FRIDAY. My Dear, Received your letter. Am a bit worried about your suit, my pearl. I hope it has arrived by now. We arrive London about 3 pm Sunday. I have booked a room at the Strand Palace. I suggest you travel to London on the 1.0 something pm train, arriving Euston around 9.50. Or if you can find a better one, then come on that. If you arrive before me, tell them to give you the room booked by me. Bragg's the name. Wire me at the above address, Saturday, containing time of arrival at Euston.

Love G.K.

P.S. I'll take you to Hamlet. Bring your new suit if it has come.

Not a love letter written by Byron, but then that never was Geoffrey's style. Of all the hundreds of letters my mother kept, from her early school years to her death, there is only one love letter from him that I can find. It's very short – very sweet and heartbreaking for me to read now. There's no date:

Wyndurst. Kendal. Wed. In Bed.

Darling xx Darling xx Darling Girl xxx

I'm so tired, dear, and excited. I'm going to see you tomorrow, I hope. Oh I do hope and I know you'll come, so

61

I'll just say Goodnight, my Laura, with hundreds of
sweet little kisses xxxxx God bless you treasure x
Goodnight xxx

With boundless energy, Mother sailed through the travelling and performing the length and breadth of India, juggling everything with consummate ease. Then she got religion.

We first met Father Patrick Arango in Bangalore. A lovely man, intelligent, witty and very wise, he was extremely ambitious and exceptionally well read. He was to go on in later years to become a bishop and spend a lot of his time in Rome consulting the Pope about his various missions for young orphans scattered all over south India. Father Pat and my parents spent hours sitting on the veranda in the evening arguing about politics, life and literature. Geoffrey was always involved but would often get bored and stomp off to do his letters or have a drink with the boys.

Dear Mother

Our lives have been so full of incident these past few
weeks. Peter's departure, Foo's tooth ache, Mary in
hospital. I wish you could hear her adventures in the
hospital!

Father P Arango (a priest who reminds me so much of our
Pop) took us to a Chinese supper last night. He's one of
the grandest persons we've ever met (!!!!!) He's helped
us a lot, and come to dinner with us many times. He even
took a rehearsal of Candida the other day!

Yesterday, Shakespeare's birthday, we played
Othello, and he came to that and brought some of his boys
from the seminary next door. He's only been to one other
play of ours, The Merchant of Venice, and he's seen that

twice! He never goes to films. Dinner time. I hope it's a
good one. I'm hungry.

Love to all, Laura. XXX

Mother took the whole business more to heart than Geoffrey. She began first by going to mass, then in the space of six months, converted to Catholicism.

She played the part to perfection. A great many mantillas joined her wardrobe. Rosaries, a small crucifix and a Bible became her bedside companions, laid out afresh when we unpacked in a new place. Soon she became impossibly virtuous and took to bestowing forgiving smiles even when there was nothing to forgive. She hummed a lot around this time, and many a row ended with Geoffrey bellowing at her about her 'bloody daft saintliness' when in his opinion she was 'as wicked as a witch' and had 'evil thoughts'. This line of attack was intended to goad her into her old self, but for a while she was not to be goaded.

The embarrassment factor for me, however, became almost unbearable. I was used to Mother being glamorous and witty at the centre of any group. She was my role model of the perfect mother, and her sudden transformation was appalling. Gone were the snazzy P. K. slacks and Dietrich sunglasses, to be replaced by baggy skirts and frumpy bush shirts, worn loose and *outside* the skirt. Her lovely brown curls were bunned up and covered in scarves, her silver bangles went, and a large cross hung around her neck. She stopped her lifetime habit of Pond's Perfect Pink lipstick and covered her usually rosy cheeks with too much powder. Even her lavender eau de Cologne and April Violets perfume languished at the bottom of her suitcase – and that was the most alarming of all: she not only looked like a missionary, but she also no longer smelled like my mother.

Worse still, she started taking me with her to morning mass on Sundays. I did not mind the mass; it was her behaviour that made it an ordeal. Even as a child I realized that it was out of proportion to the event. She genuflected at everything. She knelt far longer than anyone else and in places where no one else did at all. She smiled and nodded in a knowing fashion at any nun or priest who caught her eye, as if they had a secret of some kind, nudging me to do the same. When she went up for holy communion, I would say a heartfelt prayer that God would not allow her to go the whole hog and prostrate herself before Him in front of the altar.

Halfway into this religious obsession, Jennifer was persuaded to join us on Sunday. This only made matters worse, as she soon developed a habit of fainting dead away in the middle of the service. She was always a bit of a fainter, but this was uncanny. Almost always on cue, just before the sermon, up to the pulpit would go the priest and, thump, down would go Jennifer between the pews, out cold, arms and legs sprawled between our feet and cassocks. She was not a small woman and extricating her was no mean feat. Several of the devout would help us to carry her out. By now the combination of sister and mother would have turned me red with shame, and I would stand at a distance while she was patted and watered on the steps of the church, her arms and legs flopping limply around her helpers. A taxi or tonga would be hailed and back we would got to the hotel . . . until the next Sunday, when once again, kneeling between us and looking sweetly at the holy tabernacle, plop!, down she'd go again. In the end even Laura admitted defeat and reluctantly agreed to leave her behind.

Geoffrey had his own opinion, as usual, and goaded Jennifer with it. 'It's because you're bad!' he chuckled. 'God looks down and sees your rotten soul. He's appalled at the state of it. He sees all your sins. He has seen you with ALL THOSE MEN! He knows . . .' And he would roar with laughter.

Geoffrey could not care less about the state of anyone's soul, let alone that of my sister. But I think he had an inkling of what she was up to. I, meanwhile, wished that I had thought of it first.

In fact, Geoffrey had been a convert to the Catholic Church for many years, but, unlike Mother, his reasons were not simply religious, but rather more complex. His admiration for the nuns, priests and missionaries, who covered the Far East with their splendid schools, was tremendous. He also owed them his livelihood and needed their approbation to a certain extent. His love of pomp and ceremony made him admire and enjoy the ancient and theatrical traditions of the Latin mass, and he had a very strong sense of moral values – even if it was a little hard to discern sometimes. He believed passionately in good and evil, and his puritan attitude to sex married perfectly with the teachings of the Church. Confession came in handy too.

He maintained that human beings had a soul and that they needed to look to something other than themselves, *some* sort of god, in order to be released from self-centred pettiness. His religion and beliefs, like so much of himself, he kept private, though he always, always ended every letter with 'God Bless'. It was not surprising, then, that he reacted with such scepticism to Mother's religious fervour.

After about two years of this, and for no apparent reason, Mother suddenly returned to her level self again. The holy pictures were left inside books or in the suitcase, the Bible and rosaries were joined by family snaps, and her beloved pipe lay once more at hand for the smoke before bedtime.

Her friendship with Father Pat, however, continued all her life as a strong and stable influence. Letters went between them every week for years to come. But, as Geoffrey said, 'Thank God your potty phase is over.'

Can't kiss you today, Daddy, I've got a cold. And what's more, so have you. You have been wheezing away like an old broken instrument.

I've been organizing your funeral. I feel you deserve a well-staged affair, since you are giving me ample time to plan it. So I've decided to bury you in Dorset, on the coast, overlooking the sea, with a great big tree, yet to be chosen, planted near you. Or on top of you – whatever it is that comes with this particular service. I have spoken to the undertakers, who are not the usual grim-faced and depressing bunch, but jolly and positive. They will come and get you and look after you and do things to you that will make us all feel comfortable. Well, that's the idea – only time will tell. I will go down and look at the plot. That way I won't be caught out and have to decide things in between rehearsing a play and grieving.

And we don't want a repeat of YoYo's torturous journey into Hades, with the undertakers stealing Mother's gold bangles, making her up to look like an old Chinese tart, then locking up her ashes over the weekend so she missed the flight to Bombay with you and the family, who were off to scatter them on the Goan Sea. The ashkeeper or gravedigger had taken the weekend off and left town, and the key to the ash safe went with him. You and the three grandchildren were booked to fly out early on Sunday morning with Mother. I was in a show so unable to come. We waited in vain outside the man's house until the early hours of Sunday morning but he failed to return and you flew off without her! A pointless exercise, but the tickets were paid for and booked, and off you went, leaving me to a deal with the remains on Monday morning. After a great deal of high-voltage aggression on my part, YoYo was dispatched to join you all by 'special courier'. Apparently, ashes of 'human origin' cannot by law be 'shipped', they have to be accompanied by a live person! So off she went, sitting on the lap of an out-of-work drummer, a nice young chap in leather trousers, with earrings and a pony-tail. He must have sat patiently with her for the nine-hour flight to Bombay. But how did he go for a pee? Did she go too? Or did he ask the passenger in the next seat to 'kindly hold on to this for me'?

He arrived in Bombay without a permit to land, so YoYo's grandson had to go through customs and collect her. All this ended in her being scattered on the sea in Goa, at sunset, as her firstborn daughter had been some years before. But what a fiasco to get her there – and she didn't want to be in India anyway, towards the end of her life. So I've decided you're staying here.

The Love House, Baga Beach, Goa, India
11 Feb. 1992

My Dear Felicity

First I want to thank you for all you've done for us. You must have felt as terrible as I did and you conquered it bravely.

Yesterday the ashes were scattered on the waters – I could not feel sad – that was not YoYo at all – oh dear.

Now it is all over I feel desperate – It has been too long too long and I've been a brute to her, a selfish brute – and I'll never forgive myself.

YoYo was alive this time last week. Makes you think about it.

God Bless Us Everyone.

CHAPTER SIX

THE FIRM

Now look here! This is getting beyond a joke . . . Today, as soon as I started reading to you, you let out a blood-curdling groan. I could not believe the groans were connected to my reading, but, having tested it out, it would appear they are. Either you don't like Byron; you hate my reading to you; or you react to . . . what can you react to, but the poem? This is so frustrating. Can you understand, after all? Or is everything through a mist and you don't know what you're doing?

This will drive me mad in the end, it really will. I shall pull out your plug and let you die in dignity. You keep all your smiles, well, the one you did once, for other people. Other people say you hold their hands tight or look meaningfully into their eyes, but I never seem to be here when that happens, and I get the feeling that you don't want me here any more. Years of trying to get a sign from you have failed, until today, when you seemed to be playing bloody hell with me for reading to you. Do you blame me for not getting you better? Or not making you dead?

I was always the one you looked to in the last ten years of your life – for the car, the air-fare, the hospital. Maybe you think I'm holding you prisoner here. What a lot of questions. And none answered.

Life is a bit of a bugger at the moment. Everything is against us. Your feeding tube has to be changed. That means a trip to the hospital, a minor op and a general anaesthetic. The gadget in your belly is corroded and must be removed and a new one put in. 'It's not very nice, Miss Kendal. It's gone infected. Not very nice at all,' says lovely Sister Mary, getting me to sign a piece of paper that blames me, not them, if you cop it . . .

Oh, and the other thing is, they have started leaving out your false teeth. They no longer fit properly, apparently, and the nurses are afraid you'll choke on them.

False teeth always remind me of Frank, whose dentures were a source of constant drama . . .

Frank was one of the oldest members of 'the Firm'. He joined the company on the first tour, when I was a baby.

```
We are up in the hills, came part of the way by bus, the
rest by pony, and Mary and Felicity in a sedan chair,
like the Queen of Sheba! They jibbed when they saw Mary
and only more coins would induce them to take her! Frank
Wheatley is going to join us. He is a young, 60-ish
English actor.
```

Mother's letter

Frank Wheatley was indeed over sixty when he first met the company and was travelling around with his one-man show. He introduced himself to us and complained that his bookings were suffering from the competition. He suggested that he join us, or go in the opposite direction. Geoffrey wrote in his diary:

I like Frank. He is an ugly looking specimen, but robust and strong, he walks and cycles everywhere, he has a deep voice, and we could do with another man – and he is game to join us.

As I grew up I liked Frank too. He always dressed in old-fashioned colonial style, baggy cotton suits, always grubby, the same sola topi, and on his shoulder an ancient Assamese shoulder bag, embroidered and frayed – this in the days when no man would dream of such a thing. He smoked the very cheapest cigarettes and, till the very last puff, they would hang out of his moist, thick lips.

At seventy-five he retired to the Grenville Home, the old actors' goodbye house, but he got bored, and so wrote one day asking Geoffrey if there might be a job for him with the company. My father wired him back to come, if he paid his own passage, and so at seventy-six he joined us again, taking over all the older parts. Frank made our kibbutz-like group complete, with ages ranging at that point from seven to seventy-six.

He became the butt of many a joke. He was loved, but not well loved. None of the younger members wanted to share a room with him. He was an 'old queer' (my father's words) and, although he wasn't, even at his advanced age, beyond touching up the odd young man, the main objection to cohabiting with him was his truss. He had a hernia and refused to have an operation to fix it. Instead, he wound many yards of often unseemly bandages round his stomach. Being of a certain age and also a bit of a miser, he only had two of these contraptions and when one was being washed by the dhobi, what was left could be unattractive to a roommate. Many rupees changed hands as the actors bribed each other over who would be put with Frank at the next location.

He had no teeth and very little hair, but his actor's vanity was still very much in evidence. He had a bald pate that he would place on his own bald pate and he had two sets of dentures – one for juvenile parts, all pearly white, and another set, all cracked and yellow, for the occasions on which he played a *very* old person.

One of my least favourite jobs when I later became props

person was in *The Merchant of Venice*, helping Frank to do his quick-change out of his Old Gobbo and into the costume of the Duke. I had to be in the wings with his costume and a box of make-up that also contained his best teeth. He would rush off and, with shaking hands, tear off his 'bald wig', take out his 'old teeth' and rub off his red nose. I would help him change costume and on he would go, glorious and proud, smiling with his shiny dentures and tossing his glossy Duke's wig, to hold court for Shylock and Portia. I would be left to tidy up what was left and gingerly carry back to the dressing room his horrid bald pate and sickly, spittle-covered false teeth.

Having him in the company was none the less comforting. His age meant that he was always around. He was a grandparent figure: not affectionate in any outward show, but a great one for stories. He loved to eat above all things, and he would take me for ice-creams and snacks in the bazaar. Nothing was too much trouble in order to get something extra to eat. We had many, many times when the food was dreadful or not plentiful enough. All I had to do was wait and eventually Frank would come and find me, and we would be off in a rickshaw scouring the town for a café or sweet shop.

And then there was Brian.

Brian was a *proper* actor. He had joined the company in 1947, having already acted with the Birmingham Rep, and, although young, had a gift for character parts ranging from comedy to tragedy. He could pass for a schoolboy or a wizened old man – he was a genius with the make-up palette and nose putty.

He was Mother's best friend, her ally and confidant, and was small and attractive with thick brown hair and piercing blue eyes. He had 'come out' long before it was the fashion and was a most attractive and amusing person, with tireless energy and a wicked sense of humour. He was the mainstay of the company for many years. His letters home during the first months were not promising:

> I am now in my tenth month in India and will return home
> in a month or so . . . I love the hot climate, but it would
> be good to have a good East wind and cloudy sky and time
> to crouch by the fire. Here in Calcutta there are riots,
> burning fires in the streets and transport in disorder.
> There are times I wish I was at home.

In fact, he was to stay with us loyally for nine years without a holiday – longer than any other actor.

Poopsie was another matter.

Poopsie was a thief. No doubt about it, God rest his soul. I loved him . . . but he was a thief. He stole from anyone. Most of the time it was trinkets, money, small pieces of jewellery to flog in the bazaar, a few rupees from someone's wallet, and, occasionally, larger sums from the company's till. He was never caught red-handed and was very adept and cunning, but the evidence was always there, and although he would fix you with his innocent brown eyes if ever he was questioned about his actions, he knew that we knew.

He was christened Marcus Murch, but we called him 'Poopsie' because he had a poopsie kind of laugh. He first acted with us as a pupil of Sherwood College, Naini Tal. We were short of an actor to play the priest in *Hamlet*, and would always get in a student, or the local talent, to help out. Poopsie was rehearsed and drilled in his speech over Ophelia's grave, which runs: 'Her obsequies have been as far enlarged as we have warranty . . .' Poopsie's version was a little different. On the first night he started off grandly: 'Her obsequies have been enlarged . . .', dried up, and, looking dolefully into the grave, said solemnly, 'She's had it!'

This was not a good start, but he got better, and when we left the hill station it was agreed that he would join us later on, after his exams.

He was one of sixteen children adopted by Miss Murch, an extraordinary woman, who went out to India as a young missionary schoolteacher. She was a true English eccentric, a confirmed spinster who could not resist an orphan baby. She had little money and lived off various charities, but she was a powerfully persuasive character. She would stride across the hills of Naini Tal wearing a white sari, tied too short, and a flowing cloak, and carrying a staff-like stick. As she was nearly six feet tall and heavily built, she made an impressive figure. Marcus had been left on her doorstep in a cardboard box when he was a few weeks old. At that stage she already had eight boys and three girls and was known as the local saint with the stick, but she took in Marcus without a second thought.

She would browbeat the heads of the top public schools to take on 'her children' and give them the best education for no payment but for the thanks of God. She obtained passports for them by going directly to the Prime Minister, got a house donated to her 'cause' by the local millionaire, and brought up her family with joyous enthusiasm. She insisted on being called Miss Murch, except by her children, who had to call her Mummy, and was one of a dying breed of English ladies married in one way or another to the Far East. She was a glorious celebration of woman, with a strong Christian faith and endless energy.

When she found out that her Marcus wanted to join the company, there was little Geoffrey could do to stop him. Miss Murch had told him: 'My boy wants to leave school and join you, Geoffrey. I hope that's all right. He'll finish his exams next month, then I'll bring him to join you. I'm so pleased that's settled.'

Poopsie was small and very strong, had the body of an athlete and never kept still. His hair was thick and wavy, and over his handsomely hooked nose his eyebrows gently met. His teeth were the brilliant white of Colgate ads and his eyes were wild.

We all loved Marcus, but he did on occasions lose his marbles, going completely berserk and hitting and scratching like a thing demented. There was hardly a member of the company he had not grappled to the floor on some occasion or other. Miss Murch said he was from warrior stock, which might have explained it. She had never found out directly who had abandoned their baby to her, but she did discover he came from a warrior tribe in the mountains, Pathans perhaps, and he must have been illegitimate, as being a boy they would otherwise have treasured him. He certainly rode with graceful abandon and his character was untameable. But he was also most definitely a thief, and this did not fit in with the tribal pride of a Pathan.

He was funny and tactile and madly exciting. He would spend hours singing songs with me while he played his guitar, or swimming with me in pools and rivers.

He had a wonderful baritone voice and would always be singing at the most inappropriate moments. Mother was forever saying, 'Dear Poopsie, do shut up, we can't hear ourselves think.' But she was also his protector and champion. Many a time when mutiny was growing in the ranks over the latest petty theft, she would hold a meeting and explain that 'it's only because he's an orphan, we must give him another chance'. And so it went on . . . for years.

Sometimes Poopsie would put a waltz on our gramophone during fit-ups and sweep Mother into his arms. They were both great dancers and they would glide around the hall, swooping and whirling, like Fred Astaire and Ginger Rogers, while all about them actors continued to set up for the show, paying no attention. I would watch in awe at Mother's grace and beg Poopsie, 'Dance with me please, Poop.' He taught me how to waltz and cha-cha and do a mean tango.

He was a good actor too. His voice was deep and powerful, and he had a pure BBC accent. Feste was probably his best part, but his most unlikely success was as Miss Prism in *The Importance of Being Earnest*. He padded out his bottom and added an ample bosom, grey wig and small glasses to become the Edna Everage of his day. He was, in a dreadful way, completely convincing.

Mother's map of India, painstakingly drawn in Indian ink, indicated all the places the company had visited by 1956. An index at the side showed how many times they had returned to each place. We were then four English actors, an American, an Irishman, my parents, my sister and me. Fluff the Rabbit only lasted a month: a stray cat ate him in Allahabad. But he was replaced by two mice, and later the regrettable cat Sheba.

Mary was also part of 'the Firm', and in addition we had Mangatram, the luggage boy, helper and general dogsbody. He was devoted, but did not always see eye to eye with Geoffrey's artistic intentions. Geoffrey was passionate about dispensing with realistic settings and using simple backgrounds with only the barest furniture on stage, way before it was considered fashionable. 'Shakespeare said, "When you hear us talk of horses IMAGINE that you see them!" He was right. What do we need all those bloody French windows for? It's all pretend, anyway, and if you come on to the stage, the audience will believe what you tell them, not a load of scenery waggling about.'

For the most part, the sets, or lack of sets, worked very well. A plain background of black curtains, a blue sky, borrowed furniture with our own props, our portable footlights and the one, very precious spot – supplemented by whatever lights happened to be available – completed our fit-ups.

In his first week with us, however, Mangatram decided to take matters into his own hands. We were performing *The Importance of Being Earnest*, and the set was covered as usual with the blacks, the sofas and chairs placed correctly, with props and lights ready to go. The company went off for a snack, returning just in time to make up for the performance. Brian went on stage to check something and discovered, to his mystification and horror, that all the furniture had been moved. The sofa now faced upstage, the two chairs were angled away from the audience, the side table was placed out of view in front of the sofa and the ottoman halfway into the wings.

He came rushing into the dressing room in a panic. 'Someone has been moving all the things on stage,' he cried. 'Is this some kind of a joke? Where's Mangatram? I need him to help put it all back. We only have half an hour.'

Mangatram was found sitting outside with a cup of tea, very pleased with himself. 'Brian, sahib, I helped make the set-room look much better, yes? Now it looks like a room in a house, yes?' 'NO!' said Brian firmly. 'Come and help me put it back!'

In India, a certain amount of realism was always necessary.

On rare occasions Mangatram would partake of one bottle too many of toddy, local spirit made from God knows what. Then he would become a man obsessed and take the odd swipe at Mary. This was followed by her resigning, and him being threatened with the sack. But it was always patched up, and always happened again.

He and Mary shared a room during the several years that he stayed with us, and she was a little in love with him – understandably. He was tall and handsome, had a whopping great moustache that he curled up at the corners, and insisted on wearing a grand white uniform with brass buttons and shiny Bata shoes. The shoes made him walk with a limp, but he loved them and would polish them for hours in the morning, sitting outside and drinking tea with Mary.

Mary's affection for Mangatram made her worry a great deal about her weight. She was so large that she could never walk far without getting blisters between her thighs. Occasionally she would embark on remedies for her size. She would down Epsom salts and get the local leech wallah to apply his little black devils to her back. Then she would go to bed, cover her face with her sari and moan for a few hours.

Despite his smart appearance, there was nothing that Mangatram would not do, except sweep – that was below his caste. He refused to even pick up a broom. On more than one occasion Mother swept the stage, while Mangatram stood by, looking worried. Occasionally he was hauled in to pad out a scene. When we were a witch short for the three weird sisters in *Macbeth*, Mangatram would be swathed in one of the black witch costumes with a very large hood and taken on stage with his back to the audience, where he had to stand looking at the cauldron, while one of the other witches spoke his lines. He looked absurd, with his moustache and leather shoes, and it is a mystery that we ever got away with it.

In *Henry V* his job was to hold up the flags and point them on stage during the 'Once more into the breach' speech. He liked being involved in the show, but sadly he let the exposure go to his head. At one performance he decided that four flags were not enough, collected up all the French flags and held them out too. It was clearly time for him to step down.

After Mangatram eventually left to return to his village, where he had a wife and three children, he was replaced by Azarool. Azarool was a tiny thin man, a sad replacement for the glorious

Mangatram. But he could lift luggage like a wrestler: in his skinny, sinewy arms he had the strength of ten men. One of his duties was to keep a sharp eye on the sixty-odd pieces of luggage we carted about. He took to marking all the tin trunks with the company's name, but he didn't find it at all necessary to put the letters in order, so we travelled as Haskspernana, or sometimes Shakpeeraan. No one seemed to mind. And he never lost a bag.

Like his predecessor, he drank toddy, only he indulged rather more often. He would only drink off duty, which made the mornings a bit grim. Many a journey was embarked on with Azarool swaying in the breeze, surveying with sadness and bright red bloodshot eyes the mounds of luggage to be shifted. 'Silly bugger's drunk again,' was all Geoffrey ever said. He was a strangely kind employer and, for all his shouting, very generous. Azarool, however, did not get the smashing white uniform: it was too big, and by then we were hard up again, so he had to do with a plain grey bush shirt, shorts and sandals.

We also started off with a young dhobi to iron the costumes. He came complete with wads of cloth that he put on the floor as a work table and an enormous coal iron. But he grew homesick after a few months and went back to his village, so we got in the local man who worked at the hotel in Poona. He was very pleased to help and took great care over the task – rather too much, in fact, so that at the half he was being hurried along by anxious, naked actors. John took charge and sorted the costumes in order of appearance, and the show started. Nothing more was thought about it until, halfway through Othello's first jealousy scene, the dhobi appeared with his bundled-up iron on his head, said to Othello, 'All done now, sahib. I am thanking you,' and walked across the stage.

*

Above Mother, Jennifer and Geoffrey in England before I was born

Left My parents on their wedding day at Gretna Green

Below The actress who took over from Mother when she stopped acting in *White Cargo* to have me

Above Mother in *White Cargo* pregnant with me and already a little plump

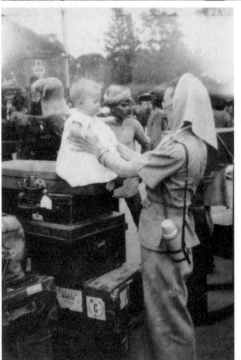

Left My first visit to India with Mother – me sitting on our luggage

Right With Mary in a train – not first class!

Below On a railway station in India – Mary never wanted her photograph taken . . .

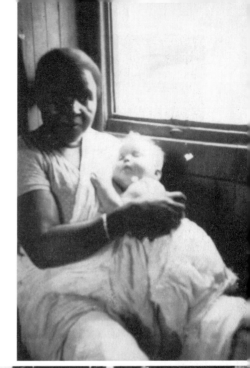

Docking in Bombay Harbour, with me at the front

Our tin trunks of costumes and props being loaded on to a camel truck

A heavy schedule for Shakespeareana

Geoffrey all dressed up for *Charley's Aunt*

After *The Merchant of Venice* in Bangalore with (*left to right*) John, Peter, Mother, Brian and Poopsie at the back and Jennifer, Anwar and Wendy in the front

John being a camel

Jennifer and Brian as Viola and Sebastian in
Twelfth Night

Frank in one of his suits and with the hunting
stick he always carried

A wooden stage on bricks! Fitting-up in Bangalore with Jennifer, Poopsie and Brian at the back, and Shashi and Peter in the front

The palace at Udaipur

Geoffrey, still dressed as Shylock, greeting Lady Mountbatten backstage. Peter and Brian in the background

Nehru in the Gaiety Theatre, Simla, with the flag of India covering the Viceroy's coat of arms

You're not looking well. Your eyes are gummy, and you appear more twisted and stiff than usual. Nowhere to park the sodding car. And it's raining. It's been raining for hours, gentle English rain, small pencils of smog-filled water, dribbling out of the grey sky. Not like the monsoon rain of India, the rain of my childhood that I loved so much.

Geoffrey shared my enthusiasm for the monsoon and wrote about it to Jennifer, before I was born:

ENSA H.Q., Bombay

Dear Impresnik,

You sod pot – you haven't written to me for two weeks – I've been away, miles away from anywhere and when I come back there is no letter – what are you doing? Swotting I suppose – being top in everything.

Laura will tell you about the Yank camp, by the Lord it was lovely – I take back everything I said about the Yanks. I must have visited about a hundred camps, but nothing like this. I had a touch of Bombay tummy – a hellish thing, worse than . . . I went to the bog 69 times in one day! I'm alright now. The sky is quite cloudy today, almost English. The rains here though are best. It absolutely pisses down to be rude about it – if you even think of crossing the road your clothes are as wet as if you'd jumped in the river. I'm sending you a parcel.

Love Popeye

On the first day of the monsoon, the skies exploded in a magnificent waterfall of solid warm wetness, pouring out as if from a bucket. The heat was suffocating for weeks, and the nights unbearable. When the rains finally came, we would all run outside into the downpour – children, adults, dogs. We would splash barefoot in the large brown puddles that formed in seconds on the hard-baked earth. Standing with my face upturned to the heavens, I would drink in the sweet water, letting my clothes soak till I was dripping with cool relief.

I would run and find Jennifer. 'Fufu, Fufu, the rains are here! Come on, let's go walking!' She would drop what she was doing and, taking my hand, she would say, 'Come on, little Fatty Foo, let's see who can get wettest.' And, carrying our chappals, we would march bareheaded and umbrellaless into the nearest town or bazaar, or along the country roads, where there would be monsoon snacks – quite different from the ones offered in summertime. Now there would be charcoal-baked corn on the cob rubbed with chilli, salt and lime juice, piping hot bell puris stuffed with garlic and vegetable curry and dripping in salted yogurt, spiced lentils and steaming sweet coffee. Even at the remotest village in India these monsoon snacks represented their rains and relief from the summer.

Hours of walking later we would return, sopping wet. Though thoroughly soaked, I would be content in the knowledge that tonight I could sleep. What relief, after the relentless build-up of humid heat during the months before, when even the cicadas slowed down to a croak and a thin cotton sheet was too hot as a cover, when just my arms touching my sides had been unbearably clammy. I would take a midnight shower half asleep and return to bed still dripping, letting the fan dry the water on my body, and for a few blissful moments there would be cool respite, before the sweat started once more to stick my thighs together. But with the monsoon came sleep.

Jennifer had the most glorious smile, and when she laughed she showed all her teeth, white and shiny and perfectly straight. On tour as children we would share a bedroom, and she had what was almost a fetish for personal hygiene. We would brush our teeth and sponge our faces, and she always brushed and sponged longer and better than I did. Being thirteen years my senior, she would sit me on her knee and sing me snatches of opera, telling me the stories of *La Bohème*, *La Traviata* and *The Barber of Seville*, launching into the appropriate aria when she got to the cue.

I called her Fufu, Jennifer being a mouthful, and she called me little Fatty Foo, a nickname I took rather too seriously until, years later, looking at early photos of myself, I realized that it was perhaps a little unkind. Plump perhaps.

Maybe that nickname was the only small sign of sibling rivalry, something we seem to have bypassed in our relationship – although she did ask my mother to promise faithfully that, as soon as I had finished breastfeeding, I was to be given away (a promise I believe my mother made, for some reason). But I adored Fufu without conditions. Love I reserved for my mother, Jennifer got something else. And she responded with fierce love and protection. She was volatile and passionate in work and at play, far too close to my father for her own good, and insecure about her talent and her strength. She was forever finding new causes to obsess her. She had intense beliefs and was overwhelming in her commitment and protectiveness to anyone or anything she got attached to – be they animals, orphans, birds or beggars.

I knew I wasn't pretty, I knew Jennifer was the pretty, clever one, but I was not in the slightest bit jealous. I loved her completely and my plainness was not her fault. Time and again she would put me first, adjusting her needs to mine.

She was a most beautiful woman in her youth, but sometimes weak from asthma, coughs and colds. By contrast I never caught a thing: I would eat all sorts of unspeakable rubbish with no ill effects and sail through fevers in a few days. Jennifer was different.

But then Jennifer was good. 'You're a bad little bugger, Foo, and you're as tough as old nails,' Geoffrey would say, if ever I crossed him. Jennifer would burst into tears and throw things or slap his face if there was a disagreement, and he would slap her back – quite often, as he did Mother – but he never struck me in his life.

But for all my admiration of her, I never wanted to be like her. She was definitely the favoured one, but I was happy being me. She had a need to be admired and loved that seemed to me a weakness; her constant generosity of spirit sometimes left her exhausted. She had no inner calm and spent herself pleasing other people, unable to keep any part for herself. Her confidence in herself was very frail. She had more talent as an actor than I ever did, but she had inherited none of Geoffrey's bravery and bluster.

Jennifer told me everything. Mother told me nothing at all. Mother was not the type of person to have any intimate discussion with anyone. Her finishing-school manners had taught her to cover her underwear with her dress or skirt when she laid them out on a chair, and she had never in her entire life gone alone into a chemist's to get her sanitary towels, preferring to send Geoffrey off with a large carrier bag in which to conceal them, which he would fling at her, laughing. 'Silly bloody woman. Why can't you get your own?' It never occurred to me to broach any intimate subject with her at all.

So it was that I remained in blissful ignorance until one morning when, at the advanced age of eleven, I ran into a company meeting, shouting, 'Come quickly, there are two dogs stuck together. Bring a stick or some water, their bottoms are stuck together!' It was not Mother but Jennifer who led me out amid hoots and gales of laughter to explain in rudimentary terms the well-overdue facts of life.

She took me into her bedroom. The dogs were not stuck, she

explained, and proceeded to amaze me with details of bodily functions that I found quite fascinating and not a little silly.

'Are you sure? Are you really sure?' I kept saying. 'You're not teasing me, are you?'

'Not at all, and there's more to come,' replied Jennifer earnestly. 'You know the towels that YoYo and I have every month?'

'Do you mean the big things you loop on to an elastic belt?' I said, with a horrid premonition of what was coming.

'Yes. Well, one day, you'll get to use them too.'

This information did not have the desired effect, and I ran from her bedroom in tears. This was too much, on top of all the complicated stuff about the dogs and babies; the sentence of the elastic belts and the thought of my father having to go to the chemist's for me every month was intolerable. I had always wished I was a boy, now I knew that I was right.

It was a few years before I finally came to terms with the inevitable and started to enjoy being female, but by then I was falling in love a lot and it all seemed worth it.

There was another baby between Jennifer and me, whom my mother lost during the war. They had been staying in the family house in Barrow, and Jennifer, a small child, was asleep in her cot. My mother woke to an explosion of sound and light, then found herself in darkness, with the cold night air rushing through the bedroom. One side of the house had gone: the wall where Jennifer's cot stood. In the dark she rushed over, thinking to throw herself after Jennifer, cot and all, but the cot was still there, with the child still and safe.

My mother grabbed her daughter. The family gathered to find that no one was hurt. They went down to spend the rest of the night in the bomb shelter. But in the morning my mother lost her baby. She never mentioned the baby to me until a year before she died. By then she was eighty-five and very frail, and we were driving to see the hip surgeon in Harley Street. She said it had been a little boy, and that she had never told anyone about it. How different were the reactions of the women of her generation, compared to the outpouring of emotions and personal problems that is thought almost essential to our state of mental health today.

I had often asked why there was the thirteen-year gap between my sister and me, and was always given 'the war' as the answer – and, although even I could see that the maths didn't quite work, I never inquired further.

Another seizure. I was 'called in'. And now I'm here. You look as white as a sheet.

They have been giving you oxygen. I can tell that by the cylinder standing by your bed with the pale-green plastic mask hanging limply by its side.

You don't look well, darling. I think you are on the way out this time. As I sit here your breath seems to stop for an eternity, then, with a shudder, you're off again, wheezing and puffing. And what a pong. Jesus, it's awful.

But now that it's nearly over, I am not relieved. I thought, I honestly thought, that I would be relieved, after these four years of watching you go. But I'm not. You seem to be having a struggle and it's making me feel afraid for you. I want you to go swiftly, I want you to glide away, to go well. After all this time of practising, I want you to do this, I want you to give in gracefully. Please?

They have put you in a black and white checked shirt that is not yours and does not suit you. It's on back to front and you look ridiculous. Your nappy needs changing, under your pink sheet, the whole thing is absurd.

For the first time I wish you were dead, out of this ridiculous situation. What a frightful thing to end up like this, after your life, after all that yoga, all that walking and being fit, all that braveness and laughter, all those chota pegs at glorious sunsets. Why is this the way you want to end it all? What can I do, my dear? What can I do?

Three days later. You old bugger. You're still here!

'He had another stroke,' was the verdict. 'But he seems to have come through it rather well.' So you are not going on the boat to Hades this time. You are a remarkable piece of man.

I came across one of your early diaries the other day. I knew you loved India, but I had no idea you loved it so much.

Christmas Day, 1956, Ootacamund

It is all here, in India . . . where else in the world can you go to every clime and still be in the same place? No frontiers to cross, no currency regulations, no passports needed. It is all here in India.

The eternal snows of the Himalayas, the Central jungles, the mountain streams, turning into giant rivers, the deserts, the romantic royal cities, the tropical south and the cool hills, the white beaches of Goa and the exotic east coast. All here. The multiple creeds of Hindu, Muslim, Christian . . . the Parsees and the Jews, all living in harmony. This country is blessed by myriads of Gods, all looking down upon us. One can feel it as soon as one arrives. It is here for everyone . . . and the blessing is India.

That is why India is my home.

Okay. You win. I'll cancel the plot in Dorset.

CHAPTER SEVEN

THE PROMISE

The Maharajah seemed enormous. His colossal belly strained the ruby and diamond buttons on his brocade astrakhan coat, and his head, swathed in a fuchsia puggaree, seemed impossibly out of reach. I held the jasmine and rose petals in my by now sweaty six-year-old hands and, going on tiptoe, extended my arms in a futile attempt to garland this giant.

The company had just finished performing *Arms and the Man* for him and his family at the palace and, as a special treat, I was allowed to stay up late and pay this tribute to our patron. But our patron was standing up and talking to the cast, and I was down below and unnoticed. My heart was thumping and for what seemed like an eternity I waited for a miracle. The grown-ups were laughing and I wanted to cry, but I didn't dare give up. Suddenly a vision in turquoise silk and gold jewels bent down and whispered into my ear, 'Let me help you, sweetie.' In a waft of Mitsouko I was gathered up by two thin strong arms, and the Maharanee of Udaipur lifted me up and allowed me, blushing, to garland her husband.

We were staying at the palace at the invitation of the Rajah. His staff had met us at the railway station in Udaipur several days earlier with red carpet treatment and a luxurious convoy: a truck for the luggage and props, several limousines for the actors and a very old, silver Rolls-Royce for my parents. Our scruffy band of actors piled into this exotic caravan and rode in state through the dusty streets of the once splendid Mogul city, now run down and crumbling. The drive up to the palace was still magnificent. We sped past the pillared gates, up the long, winding driveway, through breathtaking gardens that were still tended by dozens of malis. Watering the ornamental flower beds with goatskin water carriers slung on to their belts or sitting on their haunches, cutting the rolling lawns by hand with small scythes, they salaamed our incongruous procession — even without their master the Rolls was worthy of a salute — and went back to their work.

It was early morning and misty when we arrived at the palace. Parking under the ornate portico, we were greeted by a distinguished-looking gentleman in full burrah sahib gear, complete with cravat, white poplin shirt and shiny brogues. He was a member of the royal family and treated our motley crew as if we were honoured guests, rather than as travelling actors for hire. He led us through the central courtyard and along a vast, balconied corridor to our quarters. The east wing of the palace had been opened up for us. After Independence, the princes had been persuaded to sign over much of their power in return for their title and a pension that could not compete with their former riches. The family, having to cut down in order to survive in these relatively straitened circumstances, had shut up most of the palace and now lived in only a small part of it, though still in comparative splendour.

Only a few years after our visit they would turn their home into the luxury hotel it is now, with air-conditioning and television. But when we were there the furnishings in our rooms, although old and threadbare, were still splendid: art deco lamps, Victorian mahogany wardrobes and carved bedposts. Glorious carpets, now faded, covered the marble floors. Each bedroom had an ante-chamber, beyond which was a bathroom with an Edwardian bath-room suite and 1930s lamps. The smell was musty and the atmosphere decidedly spooky, but to our band of actors, used to cheap digs in England, this was opulence few had dreamed of.

The part of the palace that remained in use was the same as it had been for hundreds of years and certainly the same as it was during the Raj. One day we were taken on a guided tour by the Rajah himself, omitting the ladies' suites, which were out of bounds to men. A vast central courtyard led to living accommo-dation, puja rooms and halls of 'audience'. 'Jali' screens of carved stone or marble stood in front of the women's quarters, and also at the end of some of the state rooms, to enable the women to watch what was going on without being seen.

There were hunting trophies everywhere and billiard rooms with dozens of tiger skins on the walls or strewn on the floor. The stuffed heads of buffalo, deer, wild boar and cheetah seemed to stare down at us in amazement. There were cabinets full of jewelled ornaments, silver lamps, gold trays, ivory tables and a gun room full of all manner of weapons. The palace was adorned with large oil paintings of past and present family – the place was like a museum, crammed full to bursting with heirlooms. My favourite was an electric train made of silver. It ran the full length of the banqueting table on a silver track, stopping in front of any guest who wished to help themselves to one of the spicy delicacies piled high on its silver carts.

The setting for the performances was similarly extravagant. *Arms and the Man* was one of two shows given to invited audiences. A shamiana (an open-sided, ornate tent) was erected on the enormous stone balcony overlooking the lake. Persian carpets were laid under this and sofas and easy chairs placed in rows for the guests. Bearers in full traditional dress, with turbans and white gloves, attended to the refreshments of chota pegs, spicy pakoras and salted cashews for the seated royals.

The show was played out under the stars on the balcony, against the backdrop of the lake, surrounded by mountains. In the middle of the lake was the now famous water palace, a beautiful pale ghost of domes and carved marble balconies, shivering in the moonlight, that seemed to float on the water.

I was told the palace was built in the seventeenth century by the then ruling king for his favourite wife, so that he could visit her by boat away from the court. I had been taken to look at the water palace earlier in the day by one of the servants, who had rowed me over in a small boat. Mary, who was terrified of water, refused to come and stood waiting by the landing stage until we returned.

The building is now refurbished and part of the main hotel, but in those days it was empty and derelict. As I stepped gingerly over the damp weeds growing through the floors and wandered through the abandoned rooms of cracked marble, the servant told me bloodcurdling stories of revenge and jealousy and death, of how the Ranee was discovered with her lover and the Rajah had him hacked to pieces and thrown into the lake; the Ranee was then left to commit suicide by eating crushed diamonds. Real or invented, his stories made a lasting impression. I was pleased to get back to the mainland and to Mary's ample bosom.

As I was to discover, the exquisite water palace with its grim history was typical of a residence where beauty was often accompanied by strange, even gruesome, secrets, and where treasured possessions – be they people, pets or objects – were kept like museum exhibits.

Before we gave our command performance we had been given several days to settle in and make ourselves at home. On our second day Mary and I went exploring. While Mother settled down to write her letters 'home', we wandered round the back of the palace through the rose gardens, where Mary plucked a rose and twisted it into her false bun with a steel hairpin. Whether in a park garden, a tea plantation or a royal palace, her habit was always to 'steal' a flower every day for her hair.

At the back of the palace we came across dozens of stables. The number was impressive, but even more astonishing was their curious size – they looked as though they belonged to some giant. Most were empty, but in the dark of several others we could discern large pale sheets covering mysterious objects.

An old driver was polishing the silver Rolls in the courtyard. 'Oh, yes, so you've come to see the pets?' he inquired. 'Come, come, I'll show you Rajah Sahib's collection.'

He led us into the dark stalls and whisked away the sheets to reveal a collection of priceless cars. There were Bentleys, Bugattis, Fords, American limos, Italian sports cars, gleaming, in mint condition.

'Rajah Sahib, he no drive all of these . . . but all must be kept tip-top and in readiness to go,' explained our guide. 'Rajah Sahib he *no* drive, he just check up every day. Every day he does check up! He comes to look at his pets.'

Then he explained the mystifying size of the stables. 'These garages are elephant stalls. We had *so* many elephants, now we only have one, chullow, come with me, I'll show him.'

We went through another courtyard, past what seemed to be hundreds of horse stables that looked minute by comparison – empty now, no Arabian steeds, no stable boys, just dust and weeds, the days when a Rajah had hundreds of horse and dozens of elephants long gone. Beyond the stable block in a clearing stood the sole remaining elephant. He was chained to the ground by one foot and was being fed grass by a tiny boy.

'He's very friendly,' said the driver. 'Azrul, show your tricks.'

Azrul shouted 'Ooot, ooot' and nudged the elephant's trunk with a small stick. At this, the elephant twisted his trunk around the waist of the little mahout boy and plopped him on his neck, where he looked down at us and laughed. We were later to be given a ride on this old chap in the howdah that he was to wear when he carried Her Majesty Queen Elizabeth II on her first state visit to India in the sixties.

We left the elephant to his breakfast and continued on our sightseeing walk. Beyond the main building at the side of the lake, set in dense undergrowth, was a sinister-looking building with steps up the side leading to a balcony. There were no windows or doors that we could see, and, as we climbed the steps, squirrels and insects scuttled away, and monkeys chattered in the trees above. The balcony ran round the top of the building, which was no house but deep pit, like a gladiator ring, some fifty feet square with tunnels leading down into an arena.

At the far end was a carved pavilion – I found out that this was where the Rajah and his guests would sit and watch the spectacle below. They would have been out hunting the night before and might have caught two tigers, or a tiger and a wild boar. These animals would be released into the ring through the tunnels, and, being trapped in a confined space, would fight each other to the death. The wild boar nearly always won.

The pit had not been used for many years. Rusty iron gates hung lopsided from the tunnel entrances, and the ground was deep in grass and weeds. Only snakes and the odd rat inhabited the place now. It was hot on the balcony and the midday flies were buzzing, so we made our way back through the gardens of preening peacocks to the cool rooms and lunch.

The image of this outwardly beautiful death trap has stayed with me ever since. My attitude to animals and indeed my attitude to humans must certainly have been influenced by these early experiences of India. I grew up with very little sentimentality about life. Suffering, poverty, pain and sickness were part of everyday existence, something to be dealt with, not avoided or brushed under the carpet. Our approach was realistic: the show must go on, you did what you could to help in any given situation, but you didn't waste time or emotion on the vast sea of suffering that made up a great deal of India.

Unless, of course, you were my sister Jennifer. Jennifer, the 'softie' in our family, was forever adopting stray cats and dogs, rescuing crippled birds or taking in small beggar children to wash and feed. In one instance she installed two tiny beggar girls in our hotel, planning to get them housed and fed, only to come home from the show one night to find them gone, and also all the company's cash. This fazed her not one bit, and she never tired or gave up her missionary inclinations. But, life being as it was, she was often in tears – she was a tearful sort of person and I grew used to her emotional explosions.

So it was that, the next morning, when I saw Jennifer in tears, I thought little of it. Nor did I take much notice as she flounced out of the room, blubbing about 'men being cruel and horrible'.

We had just had breakfast and I was in my parents' room, waiting for Mary to collect me. Mother sighed and went back to her script and I went back to playing on the floor with my cloth dolls in miniature Indian dress, when a message came that there was a present for me.

Presents were not something we went in for much; they were reserved strictly for birthdays and Christmas time, so I was more than a little excited. I rushed to get Mary, who was in our room finishing her morning tea, and together we went in search of the 'present'.

First I was told it was in the stable block, which was somewhat bewildering. We went out and asked the drivers if they knew anything about a present, but they pointed to the kitchens. This was getting more and more interesting, like a game of hide and seek, and by now I was bursting with anticipation. At the back of the palace the kitchen block opened out on to a yard full of women chopping onions and sifting rice, grinding spices and washing silver cooking vessels.

Amid all this hubbub were children playing and one of them had a baby deer, a tiny creature on the end of a piece of coloured string. He was stroking it and feeding it milk from a baby's glass bottle and teat. 'Oh, Missy Baba, this is your present,' said one of the cookboys.

I couldn't believe my eyes. My very own live Bambi – about a week old, small, bony and still wobbly on stick-like legs. I gathered up my precious bundle and staggered back to our rooms with him, where he promptly peed on the floor.

There followed some negotiation about his accommodation. Mother reluctantly agreed that I could play with him for a few hours every day and help feed him milk from a bottle, then he could sleep on a rug in my bedroom if he didn't shit on the floor and provided I could get to sleep. He did shit on the floor and I couldn't get to sleep, so Mother put her foot down and he had to be returned to the cooks' yard at night.

He became quite tame in the remaining week of our stay. He would follow me about in the garden and frolic along the endless corridors of the palace in the hot afternoons. I called him Raju and loved him completely.

The 'present', however, was what had upset Jennifer. Raju was the consequence of a hunting party that had gone out the night before with the Rajah and a few of the actors. They were after tigers, but failing to bag any had ended up shooting a deer just before dawn. They had not seen the baby hiding in the dense jungle, or they would not have fired. When they went over to collect their trophy, this little chap had been standing over his dead mother. Rather than abandon him to his fate they brought him home.

Jennifer was a vegetarian and passionate animal lover, so the episode of the slain deer had sent her into a major outbreak of anguish and horror. I, on the other hand, was not much moved. I was a hard-hearted little thing, and already my experience of India and the poverty of people meant that animals came way down on my list of priorities.

I spent an idyllic week playing with my Raju, and when the time came to say goodbye I don't remember shedding any tears. Even at that age I was already used to moving on and leaving behind friends and places, going on to new adventures, new faces, new bedrooms. But I had been so happy with my little companion that I managed to persuade my mother to get me a kitten for Christmas. She promised – something she was good at. She never forgot or broke her promises, but this was one I came to regret that she kept.

We were leaving for Delhi. We would stay at the Cecil Hotel, one of the most beautiful in the Far East at that time. My parents knew the owners and got a special deal on the rooms. We said goodbye to the palace with many salaams and piled into the train that was to take us overnight to Old Delhi Station. The company was doing well, my father was riding high and even making a small profit, and I went to sleep that night on the top bunk, dreaming of kittens and Christmas and listening to the grown-ups chatting and laughing on the seats below.

I woke, as usual, with my ears full of engine soot, to the sound of orders being placed for tea. I was sad to have left my baby deer behind, but was already growing used to the idea and becoming excited about what lay ahead.

It was early morning and the train had stopped at a tiny country village. Geoffrey took me for a walk along the platform to gaze at the wonders of the workings of the engine. The engine hissed and belched out its steam on to the platform, and the driver smiled down at me through his pan-stained teeth. 'Teekhai, Missy Baba?'

'Bilkul teekhai!' I replied.

'Sahib, the train will be moving off to be departed soon!' he warned Geoffrey.

As we hurried down the platform to our reserved coaches, the first whistle went. 'Up you get, little Foo,' said Geoffrey, pushing me up the steps from the low country platform. I clambered aboard just as the station master in his blue cotton uniform waved his torn green flag and blew his whistle. The train was already moving off as Geoffrey casually hoisted himself aboard with a well-travelled air.

Inside our carriages, usually reserved for 'Shakespeareana' but this time for some reason booked for 'Mr Shakespeare and His Ladies', Mother was passing round the tea. Tea and toast was a staple treat on Indian railways. 'T-n-toost, sahib?' was the cry at platforms all over India. There was sometimes T-n-cake, but Mother would never allow that. 'Fly-blown, darling, don't touch it.' Fly-blown was a caution often used by Mother – pre-cut fruit, salad and cake were all susceptible to fly-blown, darling. So it was always T-n-toast.

I launched into the toast. Jennifer was deep in conversation about the need for us all to learn Hindi. Brian was not so sure it was a problem. Frank was visiting from the next compartment. His old hands were having a bad day and half his tea was spilling over his cup. 'What the hell, I'll do what the natives do,' he said, slurping from the saucer.

The train gathered speed and I settled on the bottom bunk

underneath Mary, who was asleep on the one above, her sari pulled over her face. I balanced my toast on my knee while I drank the hot, sweet tea, and looked out through the bars of the open window at my India. In the north the land was dry, the villages were in the open, and the main job for bullocks was the working of small wells and irrigation plants. But as we continued south the land would turn greener, the trees would change, and the hard-caked earth would give way to lush paddy fields. The horizons stretched for ever, the sky an endless canopy of space. The country here in the south was richer, with palm trees, streams and pools. The villages would appear in a clearing of hacked-away vegetation and the bullocks would be ploughing the fields, while herds of buffalo soaked in the small rivers and streams. And everywhere there would be children, scattered like peanuts all over the land, playing outside mud huts or on their way to school, shouting and laughing at the train as it passed, stopping to watch and wave.

The warm breeze in my face brought with it the familiar soot particles from the engine, landing on my toast and in my eyes. I looked out at the country I loved, enjoying its colossal size and the fact that, however remote the place, there were always people.

That evening we arrived in Delhi, the great walled city of the Mogul Empire, scattered with tombs, forts and mausoleums, many decayed or built over. Some scholars say that there are seven cities on the sites of Old and New Delhi, some say more. The history is rich and stretches back centuries. At one time Shah Jahan, the ruler who built the Taj Mahal, reconstructed the Old Delhi, restoring large bazaars and streets leading to the fortress. As there is no wall on the eastern side where the River Yamuna flows, Delhi was sacked regularly over the centuries, the last time being in the eighteenth century when the Persian ruler Nadir Shah looted treasures that included the Peacock Throne and the Koh-i-noor diamond.

In 1911 the British moved the capital from Calcutta to Delhi. At the time, Lord Hardinge, the Viceroy, claimed that 'the change will strike the imagination of the people of India as nothing else could do ... it would be accepted by all as the assertion of an unfaltering determination to maintain British rule in India'. The following year Edward Lutyens was appointed to supervise the planning of the new city, to be located south of Old Delhi. He crowned his design with the magnificent Viceroy's Residence, now the home of the President of India.

Our group of travellers, arriving at the bustling Delhi Station, were to stay at the Cecil Hotel, which was at this time one of the best five-star hotels in the Far East. My father had befriended the owners during the war, and now returned with his company on a regular basis. We were given a special rate and always squeezed in, however full the hotel was; once, on a later visit, when four of us had yellow fever, we were housed in the swimming pool changing rooms! On this occasion we were accommodated in splendour in the centre block.

As the line of taxis from the station unloaded the ten actors and their luggage, I rushed off with Mary to unpack, taking in with glee the flowers and fruit laid out in the rooms, the eider-down quilts, the exquisite chintz furnishings. This would be a Christmas to remember. We supped that night in the great dining room: there were sweet trolleys and flaming puddings and life was simply marvellous.

Hotel Cecil, 1957

Dear Mother

 Here we are in Delhi. It is very, very cold and we are having a wonderfully successful time. All the seats are

sold out for all the shows, and we have had to put on more
matinees to accommodate the demand.

Tomorrow our patron, the Countess Mountbatten, is
coming to see The Merchant of Venice. She is staying at
Viceroy House with our other patron, Nehru. He has
already attended two shows and this time came back
stage to meet us all. He has very tight security all the
time and there was someone standing guard at every exit
and entrance onto the stage. This took a bit of getting
used to, but it worked out well, except for the time I
was waiting for my cue and the kind guard opened the door
onto the stage for me way before time, trying to be
helpful, but leaving the actors on stage alarmed and
bewildered by the door opening during their scene, when
no one was due to come through it! But Delhi is a
glorious city. Please send me some make-up sticks of 5
and 9 when you can.

Bye bye darling. X
Mother's letter home

Lady Mountbatten came backstage after the performance to
meet the company. She captivated Brian and John by remembering them from Malta. Everyone was very proud that our
famous patrons took the trouble to visit the schools and see our
shows, and when Geoffrey was also invited to lunch with Nehru
at Viceroy House he was beside himself with excitement.

On the day of the lunch he had to give a morning performance
of *Macbeth* at a Jesuit school, which didn't finish until twelve
thirty. As the company packed up, Geoffrey dashed out on to
the bustling Delhi streets to hail a taxi, but the taxi got lost and
Geoffrey was half an hour late. 'Bloody terrible it was,' he
complained. 'Awful! I hate being late and a great crowd of people

were kept waiting because of me. I had to battle my way to the throne room, all sweaty and still covered in some of Macbeth.'

Geoffrey had first met Nehru ten years earlier, just after Independence. Geoffrey was constantly having trouble with things like income tax and railway connections. 'Always go to the top chap' he always said, and that is how he met Nehru, who invited him to a meeting to discuss his tax difficulties. They talked of England and the theatre, and Nehru admitted that it was a pleasure to meet someone who did not want to bore him with politics or parties. They got on well, and these two unlikely men had many luncheons together until Nehru's death. Indira, his daughter, would often be the only other guest. 'She was often beside her father,' Geoffrey commented. 'She was quiet, but obviously very bright.' It was with Nehru's help that our Indian company members got passports, as the usual route could some-times take years and involve endless red tape, queues and form-filling.

Our four-week season in Delhi was a triumph which is more than can be said for Christmas Day, however.

Although our shows generally played to packed houses, there was rarely any spare cash. The company was paid a pittance, and the journeys over the vast distances of India swallowed up most of the profit. Presents, therefore, even at Christmas, were usually tokens. But a kitten cost nothing, so I reminded Mother of the promise she had made only a week earlier at the palace in Udaipur: that I could have a kitten for Christmas, because I had had to leave my little Bambi. I was horrified to learn that she had forgotten, or was pretending to have forgotten, about my longed-for little cat. Moreover, she even suggested that it was not 'a good idea to tour a cat, Foo'.

Broken promises are part of growing up, but this was my first lesson and came, of all people, from my mother, who *always* kept her word. I went to bed in tears, and even the thought of other toys from the bazaar and a wonderful Christmas dinner in the big dining room, with turkey and Christmas pudding, did nothing to cheer up my little heart, aching for a tiny kitten to love and to play with.

'Shut your eyes and go to sleep, Foo,' my mother comforted me. 'Things will look better in the morning.'

'I'll never believe you again and I *won't* go to sleep!' I cried. But, of course, I did.

The next morning I was woken by a hissing, spluttering basket, wobbling and shaking at the bottom of my bed. My heart pounded. I *loved* my mother – she had not forgotten after all! I scrambled to untie the basket and, as I did so, a large cream and black monster leapt out, spitting at me. It pounced on my head, fixing its sharp claws into my scalp, biting and scratching. My mouth was full of fur. It all happened so quickly that I had no time to defend myself. I felt no pain, just surprise, as I heard Mary scream out, 'Ay, ay, ay! Gow, gow . . . ooot, ooot!' The beast was dragged off and my mother was called. She rushed in to see blood pouring down my face and my new pet crouching under the bed with its ears back, its tail swishing and its great blue Siamese eyes staring out from the darkness.

This was my 'kitten', this huge, nine-year-old, battle-scarred Siamese tomcat! There was a lot of washing of wounds with Dettol, but, while my mother was sorry, she also seemed strangely determined to keep the creature, explaining that he was 'only frightened and would grow to love me'. But our first meeting set the tone for our relationship. The cat never loved me, in fact he hated me for the next five years of his life – and I hated him. I could never touch him without being attacked, whereas with Mother he was as gentle as a lamb, lying like a baby on his back in her arms, purring loudly.

She had found him on Christmas Eve being chased by a dog, his owner having gone back to England and left him at the hotel, where he became wild and uncared for. I pleaded with her not to take him with us when we moved on, but she had named the savage Sheba, and Sheba came with us; Mother's word was law. He travelled in a basket with us for the next five years, scratching me whenever he got the opportunity. He never got lost, but stayed contentedly at the foot of Mother's bed wherever we were, making the occasional foray out to beat up native cats. No one liked the beast except Mother, but he was a remarkable traveller: he even learned to use the keyhole lavatory on trains and he always knew, by some sixth sense, when we were about to leave and presented himself, ready to be packed up in his basket.

When one morning in Darjeeling I found Sheba stone-cold dead, I was strangely moved. Jennifer told me that I jumped up and down, crying happily, 'Sheba's dead! Sheba's dead!' But I remember being unnerved by his cold hard body, and missing him on the long journeys. He had been my enemy for five long years, and I missed his aggressive, surly presence.

Christmas was not over yet, and there were more humiliations in store. But first the whole company assembled in Jennifer's room to exchange gifts. Having been patched up and fussed over, I was beginning to feel better. There were little ivory elephants, small beaded bags from the bazaar, the latest *Plays and Players* magazine sent from England for Jennifer, and a book of poems for my mother – the usual modest gifts. The actor John Day, with his customary exuberance, had found some very expensive wrapping paper, and he 'shared' this by wrapping up a present, delivering it to be opened, then taking the precious paper back outside the room, wrapping up the next gift – and so on. I was given a little cloth doll dressed in a sari, some beads and a box of Cadbury's chocolate. But the real treat lay ahead: Christmas dinner, with all the trimmings.

It was to be a black-tie affair, with a band and dancing, and, because it was Christmas, I was to be allowed to join the grown-ups. There was only one dinner suit between the company and that was a costume worn by my father in one of the shows. This had been mentioned to the manager, who said it was quite all right, the company was welcome and must, of course, come to dinner. Form was always important to the British Raj in India.

That night, dressed in as much finery as we could muster, we presented ourselves in the dining room to be seated. We were shown to a large table at one end of the vast restaurant. As we sat down, champagne was served. Then, with tremendous ceremony and politeness, a screen was erected around our table to mask us from the rest of the diners. The bearers served us immaculately, the band played, but we stayed behind our screen.

Geoffrey, for all his bluster, behaved impeccably at moments such as this. Without the slightest trace of embarrassment, he graciously took his place at the head of the table, sporting the one and only dinner jacket, joking and laughing as if it were the most common thing in the world to be cordoned off in a dining room at Christmas. His easy leadership and sense of humour endeared him to his actors, and any upsets he caused through his fiery temper were short-lived and forgiven. Whatever his failings, there was never any doubt of the love and loyalty he engendered within his company, and on this occasion everyone joined in the joke and had a wonderful evening.

But my little girl's ego was bruised. I felt shy and embarrassed to be an outcast. I saw no fun in being screened off, and I did not want a big fat cat that bit me. Halfway through dinner I asked to be excused and retreated back to my bedroom and

Mary. I remember very well getting into bed, relieved that Christmas, in all its glory, was now over.

The Cecil Hotel in Old Delhi is now a public school. The once glorious gardens where I walked with Mary are now sports fields, the large high-ceilinged rooms are classrooms, and the great dining room where we suffered our humiliation is used for assembly. Gone are the flags flying over the entrance, the liveried staff and cosmopolitan guests. In its heyday the hotel was like a small town with rooms that included balconies, dressing rooms, drawing rooms and sometimes servants' quarters. In the days before air-conditioning the rooms were cooled by punkahs. There was nothing the hotel could not supply, but if anyone complained about the food or the service, they were never allowed to return.

The visit to Lahore was not long after Sheba the Terrible was adopted. Mother had trained the beast to wear a collar, walk on a lead, and to keep quietly to his basket when the ticket inspector came into our train compartment (Geoffrey was never one to waste his money on fares for the cat).

In Lahore we stayed in a large guest-house run by a genteel old lady. The house was a tall colonial residence, once very grand, with large gardens in an enclosed compound shutting out the dusty streets of the city, where women in full purdah walked, covered from head to toe in what looked like large tents, with tiny laced peepholes to look through. Gaily painted tongas bowled along, pulled sometimes by bony, fly-blown ponies, sometimes by sleek and polished horses, and accompanied by the sound of the tonga wallah banging his bell against the horse shaft to warn people and animals away from the big, brightly painted wheels.

The lady of the house was grey-haired and wore long, soft,

flowing dresses and beads. She taught me to play Patience on a tiny card table inlaid with ivory using minute cards. She was a retired teacher and spent many hours telling me stories of old India. I was told that she was the young English girl who had been dragged through the streets of Amritsar, which in turn sparked the terrible Massacre of Amritsar, when the British opened fire on an unarmed crowd. She would not leave India and had stayed on, surrounded by English bone china, Edwardian furniture and her memories. She never married and now opened her house to passing Europeans to make ends meet.

The house was old, with few servants, but full of strange and interesting things for a child. Lace cloths covered every chair and wooden surface, there were paintings of the Lake District and Roman ruins, tiny glass objects were displayed in cabinets, and grandfather clocks chimed the hours away. It was a wonderfully creepy place, with corridors and staircases leading off long balconies. At the top of the house there was a large nursery, with teddy bears and dolls, old and worn. A tiny cot with a lace mosquito net stood in the corner and an old train set that did not work was set up on the floor. I slept with Mary in this strange room, on one of the larger children's beds, while Mary camped on the floor. Who the nursery was intended for I never knew, since our hostess was a spinster. But no one knew much about her and no one was very interested in her, apart from me – there were plays to perform and bookings to make, and the weeks in Lahore went very quickly.

Jennifer's birthday party was celebrated with Jimmy blowing up 121 balloons and Mother taking me off to the bazaar and spending all her savings on a pair of 22-carat gold earrings. They were lovely, with a sun and moon and stars hanging down in delicate clusters. 'Don't tell your father how much they cost,' pleaded Mother.

The next day I heard a bellowing from my parents' bedroom. 'You stupid bloody woman!' roared Geoffrey. 'I would have given you the money for Jane's present! I'm not a miser, for Christ's sake!' He was in a jolly mood, and not really angry at all. 'Come along, we'll go and get her something else as well.'

Back to the bazaar they went, with me in tow, and a small gold chain joined the moon and stars earrings. 'You know I don't agree with buying presents,' he said to me sternly on the way back. 'But birthdays are different!' I wondered what on earth I could give her that could match the golden treasures she was getting.

That night, while everyone was out at work, Sheba had a fight with the local cat in the garden and, after some bloodcurdling noises, came hurtling into my bedroom and hid under the bed. I bent down without thinking to see what had happened, and the terrified cat leapt out at me and savaged my face in a spitting, clawing, biting rage. I managed to shake him off, and stood up with blood pouring down my face. My head felt as though a hammer had hit me, and I cried out in pain for Mary, who screamed when she saw all the blood and rushed into the bath-room for towels. Hours of mopping up later, I was asleep on Mother's bed, bandaged and sore.

More drama followed when the others got home. Jennifer screamed at Mother that she was mad and bad to keep the monstrous Sheba and I feigned sleep during the ensuing row, but after a while 'woke up' and pretended that I did not mind, that it was not the poor cat's fault and that I did not want Sheba to be left behind. All that really concerned me was what to give Jennifer for her birthday. Poor Mother, tired and guilt-ridden, tried to soothe me, kissing and holding my wounded head and arm that Mary had wrapped in large torn strips of sheet.

'Darling, I'm so dreadfully sorry about Sheba, but I tell you what. *You* can give Jennifer the gold earrings. They can be from you, sweetheart. How's that?' 'That's fine,' I said, snuggling up on her bed. 'That's fine. Thank you, Mummy.'

I went to sleep feeling sore, but happy that things were sorting out. I had a glorious present for my sister and the hairy horrid would be left behind, I was sure of that. The birthday party was a breakfast full of balloons and surprises. A cake had been made, and Jennifer was almost in tears, she loved the gold earrings so much. 'Oh, Foo,' she kept saying over and over again. 'Oh, Foo.'

We stayed another week in Lahore, with the company playing almost every day, and my card skills improved. We waved goodbye to the lovely old lady and got into the spanking new tonga with the fat white horse that Geoffrey had by now made into his own personal transport. Off we went to Lahore Station. I was sad to leave; I had liked the old lady. But I was even sadder to see Sheba's basket, with Sheba inside it, loaded on to the luggage truck.

CHAPTER EIGHT

EARLY STAGES

Darling, you smiled! A great big open-mouthed, toothless, silent scream of a smile. Not at me but at Kunal, who is here to visit you from India. Kunal, your first grandchild, Jennifer's eldest son, your favourite. He is here for your birthday – eighty-eight tomorrow – and when he came into the room you stared at him and smiled. Maybe you are on the mend. Maybe you do know what's going on.

Kunal had not seen you since your stroke. 'It's pretty grim,' I told him. 'He doesn't recognize anyone and can't communicate at all. The only reaction was months ago, when I read him a letter from your sister, but since then there's been nothing that one can be sure of, so don't expect him to know you.'

So I told him on the way in this morning, and now this smile. It was over in a second, but it was there, it was definitely there.

So. Happy Birthday, darling. The family have just gone. We all gathered round you with champagne and balloons, home-made cake was sent up from the kitchen, and we had a sing-song and blew out the tiny candles – your grandchildren and your one remaining daughter. No more smiles today, but that one you gave Kunal was like a miracle.

We tried you with some ice-cream, but when I gave you the first spoonful you started coughing, and Kunal started panicking that I'd killed you. Until your new teeth come, I think it's a bit dicey. Your mouth is all squashed without teeth and I'm afraid of your choking. The new teeth, according to the Sister, will 'cost an arm and a leg'. Well, Mother had two false hips off me, so I think I can stretch to a set of dentures for you.

Your birthday will not be celebrated tomorrow, on the day itself. We stopped marking it when Jennifer died thoughtlessly on the same date. It was fifteen years ago now. She was in hospital and gravely ill. The whole family was together in London to be with her, and we planned to take you for a Chinese meal, then swing by the hospital and share your birthday round her bedside. But she died early that morning, and we never celebrated your birthday again.

Was it really fifteen years ago? I am now the age she was when she died, and the last years have gone so fast, and my memories of her are still fresh and vivid, but much less frequent. How sad, the steady, slow forgetting of a life.

I was a tomboy and one of my favourite pastimes was climbing the tall tamarind trees. Tiny lizards would scuttle away through the dense dry grass at the foot of the tree and insects would buzz around my head as I climbed. Then, as I got higher and higher, reaching out to pluck the long brown tamarind fruit, monkeys would stare and chatter in the branches. Sitting wedged in a chair of branches, I would eat the sour tamarind until my teeth were set so on edge that I had to stop.

Hours and days would be spent in the countryside all by myself, climbing trees or wading in streams, playing with the half-tame goats or just sitting in the shade, waiting for the time to pass until the grown-ups had finished working or Mary called me in to eat or nap.

When it was the kite season I would go to the bazaar and, for a few rupees, purchase one or two small brightly coloured paper kites. They were made of the finest tissue and were extremely delicate. The village boys had taught me how to fly them, and I would find my way to the roof of whatever hotel or house we were staying in and fly my kites for hours. Sometimes there would be kite fights. The trick was to buy bright pink or green finely ground glass and sugar powder from the bazaar, then to pull the kite string through the powder. It would stick to the string and if you were skilled you could slice through the strings of other kite flyers and win points in the street. My pride and joy was a red and yellow wooden string-holder with two handles, and I would spend hours carefully winding and rewinding the fine, coloured, glassed string, being careful not to cut my fingers, and mending my treasured kites.

Because I spoke Hindi I could easily find playmates when I was very small, and usually ended up playing with the servants' children, who always ran about the compounds behind the kitchens. We often played Bones, a fiendishly complicated game that involved tossing old bones into the air and catching them precisely in the correct order. Mary would take me to the local meat seller and we would get a dozen or so goats' knuckles, then Mary would clean them and dry them in the sun. New ones were not at all the thing to have; very old, worn bones that looked like polished ivory were best, and I would barter several new bones for an old worn one.

I had a collection of cloth dolls bought at railway stations. They were all Indian women or men in traditional costumes, and the better ones could be dressed and undressed in their little coats or saris. They were all adults, however, so I longed more than anything for a baby doll. But baby dolls were simply not available in India, so I made do with my sari'd ladies, performing grown-up stories with them from the plays I knew.

It was a magical childhood, no doubt about it, and apart from a year or so when my little friends from the servants' quarters went to school, I was never lonely or unhappy. The days would be solitary sometimes, but there were also days of long journeys full of chatter. I liked being on my own and living in a world of make-believe. Besides, the company was around, an extended family who petted and teased me.

The biggest tease was James Gibson, who appointed himself my firm friend – and torturer. 'Oh, Jimmy, *please*!' Mother would object, as he inflicted yet another prank upon me, but her pleas were in vain.

Once he lifted me effortlessly under one strong arm and took a running leap into the deep end of the marble pool in Ajmer's palace gardens. I emerged at the surface clutching him tightly round the neck, spluttering and shrieking at the top of my lungs. I could not swim and was terrified of deep water.

'You're such a *coward*, Foo. Come on, let's do it all over again.' And with that, he yanked me out, laughing, carried me to the edge of the pool and held me over the water until my high-pitched screams shattered the afternoon peace. 'Oh, James,' Mother said again. '*Must* you?'

Jimmy's teasing was an established part of my relationship with him, which split into equal parts of devotion and terror as to what gruesome thing he would do to me next. Mother's refrain 'Oh, Jimmy, not again' accompanied most of our activities and indeed much of what Jimmy did.

Jimmy had joined the company in Wellington, playing an Englishman as his first part. His thick American accent never left him, even as Jack Chesney in *Charley's Aunt*, but he was an ardent company member and hurled himself with great enthusiasm into a wide variety of parts. His playing the Prince of Morocco blacked up, with Shashi Kapoor cast as Gratiano, paled down, was typical of my father, who observed political correctness long before such a thing was considered important. He had a very genuine lack of prejudice when it came to nationality. 'All actors are the same,' he would cry. 'What the hell does the colour of their skin or the shape of their eyes have to do with it? Are we pretending to be someone else, or are we not? Typecasting is a bloody abomination!'

One of my early non-speaking parts was as Jimmy's small servant boy in *The Merchant of Venice*, a part invented by my father. He doubled Gratiano with the Prince of Morocco, and I was blacked up to match him. I would simply follow the Prince on, take off his golden slippers and, placing them in front of me, stand looking out front, not moving for the duration of the scene, until the Prince, in a huff at making a bad choice of casket, thereby losing out on Portia and her fortune, strode off with the little page-boy in hot pursuit. Small pause, little page-boy rushes on again having forgotten Prince's slippers, says 'oh' at the audience and, clutching the forgotten gold slippers, rushes off again to the sound of gentle laughter – if he got the timing right.

Very impressed with the red pantaloons and the small embroidered waistcoat and gold turban, I enjoyed the first few performances immensely. But after a week or so, the long scene in Belmont began to pall and although Jimmy was always sweet to me, joking and teasing me in the wings, once we went on stage he was fully immersed in his role and little Foo did not exist.

One particularly sweltering afternoon in Ajmer, the sun sending hot daggers of light through the cracks in the blackout curtains, I was standing on the stage of a boy's school as the little page-boy. Sweat was trickling down my chubby legs inside the pantaloons, and I was wishing I could be an ordinary little girl and not dressed up like a dog's dinner and told to stand still. I was lost in my wrath and self-pity, completely absorbed by aggressive thoughts, when suddenly I noticed that Jimmy had stopped speaking. I looked round, to a glare from Jimmy and muffled giggles from the boys in the front row. Then I realized, to my horror, that a large pink bubblegum bubble was fully inflated in front of my nose.

Shame of extraordinary proportions descended on to my tiny frame. I wished most sincerely to be swallowed up, made to disappear. This emotion was replaced in an instant by the panic of conflicting decisions. Should I pop the bubble, which might stick to my blacked-up face, run off stage, ignore the whole thing, or suck in the offending article, hoping that I could swallow it and not choke to death? In the end I removed the gum with my hand and kept it in my sweaty little palm until we left the stage. I was very unhappy. Not only had I behaved in the most atrocious manner by going on stage chewing gum – and bubblegum at that – but I had let down Jimmy and spoiled his scene by getting a laugh as his page. He was not amused, and neither was Mother. She waited until the end before silently giving me the 'look that froze the heart' in the dressing room.

I learnt to swim shortly after this episode, partly, I'm sure, to impress my friend Jimmy and try to gain back a modicum of his respect.

It was in Ajmer, however, that we saw one of the most eccentric remnants of old India. We always stayed at the Master's house, as guests of Jack Gibson, a remarkable man who had been headmaster of Mayo College for many years. His home was an imposing white building on the edge of the vast grounds of the college, which was a public school built for the princes of India. All the imported refinements of England were firmly in place at this establishment – even the tradition of caning was upheld, although Gibson was not as fond of it as his predecessors had been. He would sometimes excuse himself from luncheon, which he always took with the company, and bound down the veranda, where some unhappy lad would be standing, clutching a note detailing crime and punishment. 'Sorry about that,' Gibson would say, as he returned. 'Horrid business, but it seems to work!' And with that, he would launch into conversation again. I looked forward to our visits to Gibson's house; he was a real Etonian pukka sahib, who had adopted India as his own; a confirmed bachelor, tall and striking-looking, with floppy grey hair and a crooked grin, made so by the ever present pipe. A lover of music and English literature, he would sometimes treat us to Mozart and readings after dinner. Mealtimes were ablaze with passionate talk of politics or poetry, interrupted now and again by him bellowing for the cook, or throwing his home-made bread to a guest at the end of the table with a call to 'Catch!' He was a close friend of Geoffrey, and they corresponded all their lives.

At the stroke of four, cake, cucumber sandwiches and bread and butter would be trolleyed out on to the veranda. Freshly brewed Assam tea would be poured from a silver teapot through a Georgian sterling strainer; there would be doilies, embroidered napkins and delicate fine bone china. Everything was just so. One summer afternoon, however, this ritual proved the prelude for an astonishing experience.

After tea and gossip, the company piled into tongas and cars to drive the short distance to the old palace for the treat of the visit. The Rajah was playing polo, and we were his invited guests. We disembarked and walked through the empty palace, now used only for functions and festivals. The privy purse had been cut to a minimum, and the Rajah and his family lived in a large house on the outskirts of Ajmer.

The day was cooling as we made our way through the courtyard and out on to the polo fields behind the palace grounds. Armchairs and sofas had been placed on rugs beside the pitch and we settled ourselves for the match. Out came the Rajah and his team at full pelt, in their jodhpurs, boots and helmets, their polo sticks flying. The other team rode out with much brandishing of sticks, and the two teams then proceeded to circle each other at speed, with a further impressive exhibition of daring and dexterity.

Only one thing was missing from this extravagant display: ponies.

The Rajah, no longer able to afford his stables, had continued, undeterred, with his favourite sport by mounting the teams on bicycles. He carried on in this fashion for several more years, until even that economy had to be reined in. And so this bizarre game was played out in all seriousness in front of a hotchpotch of travelling players and an old English schoolmaster as if we were regal guests and heads of state at a royal tournament.

The game was played at a terrifying pace and with considerable skill, more skill, it seemed to me at the time, than was required for the conventional form of polo – after all, you don't fall off a horse if it stops. The orange and yellow turbaned teams pedalled like maniacs, shouting commands and encouragement, and seemed at times to almost float across the green turf. Then, with a crunch of metal and a buckling of wheels, the players would collide in a heap – only to disentangle in a moment, remount, and be back off in full cry as if nothing had happened.

In the fading light, the hills of Rajasthan turned deep purple and twinkling lights appeared in some of the windows of the deserted palace, throwing an eerie light on to the misty field. The mosquitoes came out to feast and the Rajah's team were winning, at polo, if nothing else. It was a strangely disturbing evening, watching the decline of the princes of India encapsulated in this odd game: polo with no ponies, in the fields of a palace no longer lived in, played by a prince without a kingdom.

★

These were the glorious years. Although the Raj was over and the country was transforming, the romance of old India was still living, along with hope for a new future. We divided our time between palaces and schools. The work was hard and the travelling constant – incredible journeys between the north and Cape Comorin and the backwaters of Kerala – but the excitement kept everyone going. All the actors enjoyed swinging between the hugely diverse audiences, some more extraordinary than others.

Our most glamorous bookings were, naturally, those that came from the Maharajahs – although they did not always work out as planned. At one point we were invited to visit the Maharajah of Gwalior, a great favourite of Geoffrey, who thought him the Most Regal of the lot. We were to play for him, then join in a tiger shoot the following week. Mr Pierce, the Education Minister, had warned Geoffrey that we were becoming too popular with the princes and that the tour was causing some distress among the ministers. The visit would almost certainly be cancelled. It was.

Our next royal visit was to the Maharajah of Travancore. Travancore was one of the princely states that became part of the state of Kerala in the south. Our hotel was on an island in the river, and the Maharajah's chief dirvan sent his barge to take us to supper and the show. The barge was decorated like a coronation coach, with liveried crew in silks and turbans. We lay on quilted silk cushions and felt very grand. The dirvan met us before the show, dressed in a silk dhoti, a large gold cummerbund, an enormous turban and little gold earrings. I was most impressed.

Then, after a few months of slumming it in the south, the Maharajah of Mysore sent a message by courier. He had chosen *The Merchant of Venice* to be performed at his private theatre, which he had had built for his wedding and which turned out to be a miniature version of a West End theatre, complete with proscenium and boxes in the balcony. It was decorated in lavish baroque style – gold and silver with velvet curtains and plush seats. There was a glass fountain in the courtyard of the theatre, and the doors had glass panels, engraved with the word WEL-COME, like a Victorian pub.

The Maharajah chain-smoked and had a servant beside him at all times, holding a silver ashtray on a long stand. Into this he would flick his ash. Then, when he had finished a cigarette, he would hand the end to the servant, who would stub it out and instantly produce the next cigarette, which he lit with a gold lighter.

During the performance the court ladies were secreted behind a screen in the auditorium, where they giggled and whispered audibly. The Rajah sat in his white brocade in the centre seat, surrounded by his palace officials, who wore immaculate stiff turbans and remained motionless throughout the show; there was not a sound, not a smile, not a glimmer from the Big Man, and his subjects obediently followed suit. For the full two and a half hours of the play, the actors got no response at all.

When the company finished, with some relief, we were all ushered into the auditorium to meet our host. He bade us goodbye in a hushed, tired whisper and, still without a glimmer of a smile, walked slowly out of his theatre and into the courtyard. As his officials bowed their heads almost to the floor, he drove away in his pink and gold Rolls-Royce.

One of the judges of the High Court had been in the audience and he responded more positively. He was so impressed by the play and its message of justice, that he booked the company to perform *The Merchant* the following week in his courtroom for his lawyers and clerks.

The visit to Mysore was talked about for months with great

hilarity. But I was still on the perimeters of the workings of the Firm, still spending my days with Mary playing in the jasmine-scented gardens of India without a care in the world. But my life as a little memsahib was soon to be interrupted by school time.

The question of how I might be educated loomed larger and larger, prompted partly by our regular visits to the Loreto Convents. These institutions are scattered across India. There is a Loreto School for Girls in every city, some towns and all the major hill stations. At that time they offered a most exclusive and very expensive education to the daughters of the British Raj and the aristocracy and civil servants of India.

We had played at every one of the convents, where the nuns were always welcoming; they became close friends and patrons of the company. But as I grew older they became increasingly concerned. 'Where will your little daughter go to school?' I would hear the nuns ask my mother, over and over again. 'Why don't you give her to us? We'll gladly take her on.'

Mother would not think of losing little Foo to boarding: having left Jennifer in England during the war, nothing would induce her to leave me. But the constant worried inquiries about my education became embarrassing and she started 'having a go' at Geoffrey. His ideas on anything were always left of centre and his response was typical. 'Formal education is a lot of bollocks!' he shouted. 'I should know, I've been in thousands of schools. If you know the works of Shakespeare and Milton, and the Bible, if you can read, if you have travelled the globe with your eyes open, what more can you require? Unless you want to be a bank manager or mend bicycles!' He thundered on: 'I am giving her the best education in the world, and teaching her a trade. I'm giving her her freedom. Freedom from wanting things. What do you want her to go to school for? She'll learn sod all!'

Mother persisted, as usual, until she got her way, and Geoffrey capitulated – in his own style. He finally agreed that I could go to school – not just to one convent but to all of them.

And so it was. Whenever we stayed anywhere for more than a few weeks, I would go to the local Loreto. The books would be the same, the holidays and the syllabus would coincide, I would make a lot of friends and, best of all, the nuns would not charge a single rupee. To this day I don't know how he swung that one, but Geoffrey and his troupe were much loved by the Loreto nuns, and I was made to feel most welcome.

There was, however, the issue of school uniforms. Each school had a completely different outfit to adapt to the wildly varying climates and conditions. A heated battle with my father ensued. I refused point-blank to set foot inside a classroom unless I had the correct gear.

'It's only a costume, Foo. Why don't you go in civvies and be different?' pleaded Geoffrey, not wanting to watch his hard-earned rupees disappear on a dozen different gymslips. 'That's the POINT,' I said stubbornly. 'It's the wrong costume and I want to look the SAME.' I was already feeling that I was the odd one out too often for comfort, and I would not give in this time. 'Come on, then, you little monkey,' sighed my father. 'I'll get you the right stuff . . . and a new tin trunk to carry it in.'

We set off for the shops in Bangalore's Victoria Crescent and returned an hour later with a big silver trunk painted with garish motifs and sporting my first very own lock and key. Into this wonderful shiny box, I lovingly packed my new uniforms: the red and white woollies for cold Simla; the grey and blue pleated skirt and cardigan for Naini Tal and the navy gymslips for Darjeeling, with tie, blazer, woolly gloves and beret. A horrid khaki cotton dress for Karachi was joined by a sweet gingham job for Bangalore; Bombay was smart beige and yellow; and so on. I padlocked my treasure and hid the key in my luggage, feeling very grown up and the proud possessor of so many important things. The trunk then joined my already considerable luggage: the boxes of books, suitcases of clothes, bags of toys and many cages and baskets that transported my growing menagerie of birds, white mice and the dreadful Sheba.

And so my formal education began. Every time we moved on, I joined a different class in a different school with different girls. I got more and more used to 'catching up' and, although the first few days were horrid, I was a cheerful child and at that point did not take myself too seriously. I made friends – though not long-standing ones. I liked being with my peer group and loved learning. When things got too tough, I had the alibi of being underprivileged and the ultimate get-out of being able to move on.

I especially enjoyed my schooldays in Bangalore. The most anglicized city in India, Bangalore was established as a British cantonment in the early nineteenth century and during colonialism was in the princely state of Mysore. After Independence there was no wholesale repainting of street names, as there was in much of India. Queen's Road, Kensington Road and Brigade Road are all as they were. It is solidly middle class; it has slums, but far fewer than most cities. Being above sea level, the climate made it retirement heaven for the ex-military officers and civil servants. It also had the largest Anglo-Indian community in India.

I went to the Sacred Heart Convent in Bangalore, where Mary would bring my lunch to school every day, hot from the hotel kitchen. There would be rice and dhal, and a sweetmeat, all placed in a tiffin carrier with each item of food in its own compartment and the whole wrapped in a cloth. This she would lay out in front of me on the log dining table on the school veranda, and then go and chat to the other ayahs who had done the same for the twenty girls in my class. It was here that I took my first exam – to my utter astonishment, and that of everyone else, I came first.

Laura recorded the incident in a letter home:

'Homestead', Residency Road, Bangalore

Dear Mother·

  Mary has come out of hospital. It was one of those POOR ones, but beautifully run by nuns, for people who can't afford to pay. We thought she had an appendicitis, it turned out to be only a stoppage or bad constipation. 'Joojar didn't done it for five days' in Mary's language! What a relief. It's good to have her back.

  Foo has just come in beaming with her school report! First! No one is more surprised than she is! She thought she would be tenth! This is so much better for her than it was in Karachi, when the only tests she did she was top in Urdu and bottom in English.

Karachi was indeed the scene of some of my most inglorious behaviour at school. It was also memorable for the wildlife we encountered.

We had booked into the Farook Hotel. It was small and clean, with simple rooms and stone floors. The food was terrible, and Mary took to cooking my meals on the small kerosene burner she toted around for the cat's daily stewed mutton.

The kerosene proved useful in more ways than one. Jennifer and I woke one night in a panic. We were used to mosquito bites and even the odd bedbug, but this was something else. Our arms and legs were covered in angry red welts, map-shaped and raised, which didn't just itch but made you feel as if a million little flies were biting your skin. We stripped the bed and saw a few fat bugs crawl lazily into the mattress creases.

Jennifer was almost mad with rage. 'This is terrible! We can't sleep a wink. How can we catch them? Get Mary, she'll know what to do.'

Mary was woken and came in looking worried. 'What's the matter, darling? You ill, Foo, baba?' We showed her the bite marks and she started shaking her head. 'Oh, they very bad, very bad. Can give you fever. You must not sleep with these.'

She inspected the beds, with more shaking of her head and sucking of her teeth, then disappeared in search of a remedy. She returned with a bottle of kerosene and a spoon, then proceeded to pour drops of kerosene into the mattress. As dozens of brown flat bugs began to emerge, she scraped them out with a spoon. Jennifer said she was going to be sick, but I was all eyes. It was fascinating.

Half an hour later, the room full of the smell of kerosene and the burnt-almond odour of dead bedbugs, Mary had done. 'Most dead now, but best is not to sleep on this mattress any more,' she pronounced. Defeated, we got out our bedrolls and slept that night on the floor.

Bugs and insects became a part of the everyday, along with snakes in the bathroom and monkeys stealing things through the windows. Yet I felt completely safe: you just had to keep a look-out, that was all.

The company was playing in a successful season at a large open-air theatre, and I went to school at the convent in the city. Mary would take me in a tonga every morning and collect me in the afternoon. I did well and was made class prefect, given a badge and the task of keeping order in the classroom when the teacher wasn't there. I was to patrol between the desks and report any misdemeanours.

The prospect of being dressed in a little brief authority went entirely to my head. I was soon the leader of a mini-fascist movement, holding meetings and choosing members. I would lead my gang out into the hot dusty playground at break and we would chant 'BBSG', which stood for 'Banging "B" Side Girls'. 'B' side girls were taken from poor families who couldn't pay school fees. They had their own classrooms and a different uniform. The teachers and facilities were the same, and some of the bright girls joined the 'A' classes, but they were identifiably different by their dress. Three or more of my gang would link arms and, chanting away, accidentally on purpose 'bang' into a 'B' side girl.

Eventually, this regrettable behaviour was noticed by the staff, and my prefect badge removed. As well as undergoing the shame of losing my status, I had to stand in front of the entire class to have my hand hit several times with a wooden ruler. My teacher was, quite rightly, livid, and the force of her third stroke broke the ruler in two. The pain was dreadful, but nothing compared with the public humiliation.

My enthusiasm for bullying having been extinguished, I decided to try sainthood instead. Sumi, who sat next to me in class, presented me with an opportunity. She was thin, with two long, braided plaits, and she collected small picture cards of saints, which could be bought at the tuck shop for an anna a card. This became my new project. We set up a saint swap shop and made quite a killing, eventually selling rosaries and all sorts of religious bric-a-brac for a few annas more than we had paid for them in the first place.

Our enterprise meant that we had to spend every break in the chapel. We needed to convince the nuns that we were serious about spreading the word and that that was the reason for our setting up shop. If a nun came into the chapel, Sumi and I would bow our heads humbly and mumble Hail Maries, or gaze longingly at the Bleeding Hearts of Jesus looking down at us from the altar. I used to wonder why Jesus was so very white, with blue eyes and blond hair. I think if he had been depicted as being more shepherd-like, I might have been convinced, but to me his image seemed miscast and too soppy. Sumi, however, was a very devout little girl and when I mentioned such doubts to her, she would have none of it.

I enjoyed my Holy period. I prayed quite seriously and the money I made from the swaps was used to get more religious stock. I even had a go at trying to stop Geoffrey from swearing, but that was not very productive. So I concentrated on being 'good' at school and was sickly sweet for the rest of the term.

The time came to move on. I did the end of term tests, coming, as Mother reported, top in Urdu and bottom in English. But by then I had succeeded in convincing the nuns of my holiness, and as a parting gift they gave me a small white Bible. This joined the other books in my tin trunk and I never took it out again. I simply moved on to the next phase, leaving behind my friend Sumi and my role as Saint Felicity.

Dear Mother

   Felicity was baptized today. She was received into the church. You would have loved to have seen her. She looked lovely, really lovely, all in white with a white veil. Three of the nuns from her school were there and Jennifer and Mary and some of her school friends. We all went to tea at the convent afterwards and she had a long iced cake and presents from everybody, just like a birthday!

For a few years this unusual experience of the education system seemed to work for me. But Geoffrey was right. Apart from Hindi and Indian history, which I loved, I learned 'sod all'. And the uniform situation turned into a nightmare. As I started to grow, they were always too big or too small, or I ended up with combinations of both. Replacing every article every year became prohibitively expensive, so I constantly resembled Alice in Wonderland between bites: blazers down to my knees over a skirt that showed my knickers. It was agony. And it certainly did not help my concentration to think that I looked like fat bag lady beside the delicate, wealthy and beautifully groomed girls of the convents.

Then one day I was literally thrown on to the stage. I must have been about nine years old and going to school at the Convent of Mary and Joseph in Byculla, Bombay. The company already had *Macbeth* in the repertoire and my father thought it a good idea to set me to work on Saturdays. That way he could incorporate the Macduff wife and son scene that he had had to cut for want of a small boy to play the son.

I had been rehearsed painstakingly for weeks, Mother and Jennifer taking me through my lines again and again till I was sick of them and knew them backwards. I was quite precocious and could recite by heart the first three scenes from *The Merchant of Venice* and *Macbeth*, having heard them all my life as I slept or waited backstage. Mother had taught me her old-fashioned method of learning lines, which was to write out the play in an exercise book, with your cues on one side and the lines you had to speak on the other – a technique that I am sorry to say I still use.

The first night, or rather afternoon, approached. We were to play a Saturday matinée at the very convent school that I was attending. Under my father's supervision the set had been delivered that morning by rickshaw; the metal trunks full of props, furniture, lights and costumes had been unpacked and placed at the side of the classroom.

Most of the audience were already seated: the rows of eager students murmuring quietly, each one clutching a school edition of the play in anxious expectation of the great English tragedy; the line of nuns, gently fanning themselves with programmes. Footlights shone on to the empty stage, smoking a little with the heat, 'Shakespeareana' painted on them in bold black letters.

Backstage the actors were making their last-minute, ritual preparations. Our dressing room was in fact a classroom (the hall, being used mainly for assembly and speech-giving, did not boast changing facilities), where Mother had draped blankets over a clothes-line to divide the women players from the men.

Bowls of water, mirrors and towels had been supplied by the convent along with school desks on which the company had carefully set out the contents of their make-up boxes. All around the scent of liquid paraffin and cold cream mingled with cigarette smoke, dusty costumes and cheap perfume.

Jennifer, half dressed as the first witch, made me up, Mother being far too busy getting ready to play Lady Macbeth. Fidgeting nervously in the damp, sticky heat, I sat while she smeared thick greasy foundation on to my face. She grinned down at me. 'Don't worry, little Fatty Foo, it's going to be fine. There's always a first time for everybody!'

Mother kept an eye on this procedure from the mirror where she was applying 'hot black' to her eyelashes. (Before false eye-lashes were invented, actors employed this method: you melted a pea-sized glob of black wax stuff in a teaspoon over the flame of a candle, then applied a tiny amount to each eyelash with a paintbrush, drop by drop, until you built up a fringe of by now hard wax. The trick was not to inflict third-degree burns on your eyelids. It was quite a skilled operation and my mother was an expert: from the front the result looked natural and very effective.) 'Jane – teach her to put her wig on properly . . . no duck-tails at the back,' she called over from her school desk dressing table. 'You must always anchor a wig firmly at the temples and the nape,' she instructed me. 'You never know what will happen during a show, and your wig must be part of you, never a hat.'

Jennifer finished my make-up, nos. 5 and 9 mixed to a pale tan, brown eyebrows where there had been none, a little shading round the chin. With my wig firmly in place, I was ready for the costume. Here again came training from my mother. '*Never* put on your costume before your make-up and your wig. Only amateurs behave in that disgusting fashion!' So, after the make-up, on went the little tunic, the kilt, small leather belt complete with sporran, tiny dagger in holster, criss-cross garters up my legs over my tights – and, placing my beret at a slant on my head, I was all set.

'Good luck, darling,' said Lady Macbeth, leaning over me with a whiff of April Violets perfume. The long black wig and red velvet dress had transformed her from the Mummy I knew into a stranger. Her hands, pale with wet white and bejewelled, flitted across my firmly cemented wig – and she was gone, leaving me to wait for what seemed a thousand lives before my scene.

The dressing room was silent now except for a half-hearted gin rummy game. I sat quietly, a cold feeling moving slowly around in the pit of my stomach. The play seemed to last for ever. Actors came and went, were killed or conquered; quick changes happened all over the classroom, costumes flying; and no one seemed to pay me any attention as they passed by in different stages of blood, sweat and concentration. From the stage came my father's voice, strong and passionate. Finally, Wendy, who was playing Lady Macduff, came off, dressed as the third witch in full hag make-up and black gown. Tearing off the witch's costume, she revealed a green one underneath. She cleaned off the old hag, did a fast re-make-up and, taking me by the hand, led me to the side of the stage.

Standing well back in the dim light, so as not to be seen by the actors on stage, I let go of Wendy's hand and tried to remember my first line. 'As birds do, Mother.' Yes, that was it. That was all right, then: I knew how to begin, the rest would follow naturally.

Still ringing in my ears were my father's notes, barked at me from the auditorium – notes I had heard him give to the actors many times before: 'Don't forget, Foo, *breathe*. More breath is what you want – breathe deeply before you go on stage. Don't dither, stand with your feet firmly and *grip* the stage. Keep your head high, your eye up, and don't creep around the flat to enter, enter from a distance, go on with *power* . . . don't fidget, remember your stock in trade is your voice and your body, be strong with both – don't ever use a gesture if a word will do. And don't chatter in the wings, it takes away your power. Take a deep breath, *relax*, go on, and the stage is yours, Foo!'

It was very dark in the wings, very different from the morning when I had happily rehearsed with him in the centre of the sunlit stage while the company fitted up the set around us. It was very different too from going over my lines with Jennifer and my mother. This was somehow serious and I did not like it at all. A mere three yards away from me was the pool of light in which I would soon stand. This pool of light seemed a strange and terrifying thing, a dangerous place, somewhere I would be swallowed up. I suddenly felt as if I were stranded on the top of a big dipper – my head hurt, my legs turned to stone, and in my tummy was a cold lump of horrible, sickening fear. I tried to remember my father's words. Relax. I tried to breathe deeply, but it only got worse. I tried again, but my fear now turned to undeniable panic. Every part of my body prickled, every line spoken on stage brought my cue nearer and nearer. Escape was the only solution. I had to go, and I had to go now, before it was too late.

We were standing stage right, but I knew from the morning that behind the Big Blue on stage left was an exit – and freedom. The Big Blue was an enormous sky-blue cloth that travelled with us. It needed an entire trunk to itself, it was so large, and took two or three of us to fold it and pack it. It was stretched across the back of the cyclorama and covered a multitude of sins.

I crept away from Wendy. Upstage behind the Blue I could see a tiny chink of light stealing through the exit door on the other side of the stage. Our cue came. Wendy winked at me and went on stage, expecting me to follow. I looked once more at the chink of light, I looked at my 'mother' on stage waiting for her son to join her . . . I could not, my legs would not, I had no choice but to bolt – and bolt I did, behind the Blue, towards the light, committing as I went the worst of all possible sins by making the Big Blue billow – so destroying the otherwise intact illusion that this was not, after all, a small convent school in Bombay, but the Scottish castle of Dunsinane. I ran anyway and got to the door. It was locked, the latch stiff, I pulled hard . . . it gave way and I pushed open the door – the sun was blinding, the air was hot, and I was free!

A hand got hold of the scruff of my tunic. 'Don't be such a bloody little fool!' Macbeth roared. 'Get on that stage!' He picked me up and threw me on, where I landed at the feet of my by now panicking 'mother'. She looked at me with undisguised relief and asked sweetly, 'And how will you live?' 'As birds do,

Mother,' I croaked, as if nothing had happened. My wig was firmly in place, secure and professional – but I've been running towards that chink of light ever since.

CHAPTER NINE

PROPS WALLAH

Dear Mother and Dad

We are in Simla, in a beautiful little theatre running
a sort of repertory system. Gaslight one week,
Charley's Aunt the next. Very soon the rains will
really start and the season up here will be over. Simla
has been really great and the people here more friendly
than anywhere else. It's impossible to walk down the
Mall or into the town without someone introducing
themselves. And the autograph hunters are in perpetual
attendance.

Last week we were honoured with a visit from the Prime
Minister Nehru, who saw a performance of She Stoops to
Conquer. Not many of the old Royalty visit here now,
instead innumerable film stars, many of them attending
our shows and inviting us to parties and social
functions. Doing repertory means that I am ALWAYS busy
with my paintbrush. But it's only for a few weeks, so I
don't mind.

Love Brian

During the Raj the entire government moved itself up to the hill station of Simla for the hot summer months. In this tiny town on the side of the hills, with the Himalayas in the background, 150 or so government officers and their wives lived and ruled the British Empire. They created a world of garden parties, tennis parties, theatres and picnics, a miniature version of the counties of England with all the paraphernalia. Everything was shipped over from England, including grand pianos that were carried up by coolies. The cool air was a wonderful relief to the ladies and the children in their heavy clothes and hats: Viceregal Lodge was very formal, abiding by strict protocol.

Simla became the centre for great entertaining and gala evenings. One letter from a memsahib of the day describes it as 'the Cheltenham of India'. The Gaiety Theatre was built just off the long mall leading to the top of the hill and the bandstand pavilion. It is a perfect replica of a Victorian theatre, complete with boxes, small orchestra pit and gallery. It was built in Queen Victoria's Jubilee Year, when the whole of Simla celebrated with great ceremony and bands playing.

The novelist and traveller Emily Eden wrote in her journal:

Simla, Saturday May 25th, 1839

The Queen's Ball 'came off' yesterday with great success. Between the two tents there was a boarded platform for dancing, roped and arched with flowers and then, in different parts of the valley, wherever the trees would allow of it, there was 'Victoria', 'God Save the Queen' and 'Candahar' in immense letters twelve feet high. There was a very old Hindu temple also prettily lit up. Vishnu, to whom I believe it really belonged, must have been affronted.

We dined at six, then had fireworks and coffee, and then they all danced till twelve. It was the most beautiful evening; such a moon and the mountains looked soft and GRAVE, after all that fireworks and glare. Twenty years ago, no European had ever been here, and there we were with the band playing, and observing that the St Coup's Potage à la julienne was perhaps better than his other soups, and that some of the ladies' sleeves were too tight according to the overland fashions for March, and so on, and all this in the face of those high hills, and we one hundred and five Europeans being surrounded by at least three thousand mountaineers, who wrapped us up in their hill blankets, looked on at what we call our polite amusements, and bowed to the ground if a European came near them . . . I sometimes wonder they do not cut all our heads off and say nothing more about it.

Kipling played on the stage, which was used mostly for amateur dramatics, including a lot of Gilbert and Sullivan. Below the central royal box, the Viceroy's arms were painted in gold leaf and the Union Jack hung underneath.

The government continued the tradition of moving to the hills in summer after Independence, but transferring the nation's administration to the hills every year became a bit too expensive, so the summer that we played at the Gaiety was the last time that Nehru and his entire cabinet made this trip. He came to quite a few of our shows, the first being *Arms and the Man*, which he had seen several times before, but which seemed to be his favourite. His seats were, naturally, in the royal box in the centre of the dress circle above the Viceroy's coat of arms. Geoffrey thought this not very appropriate, so he tacked the Indian flag over the offending article. Many years later, when we were shooting a scene for the film *Shakespeare Wallah* in the theatre, I was moved to see that the flag was still there, now faded and dusty, but with the same tacks holding it in place.

I looked forward to Simla: it was a date that always went well. The atmosphere was relaxed, the climate perfect – sunny and warm, but chilly at night. I enjoyed wearing pullovers and socks and having blankets at night. I loved the breathtaking views of the hills with tiny houses perched on the sides and the plains down below stretching into the distance, while behind the Himalayas rose, proud and colossal. There were pine trees full of monkeys and the houses had to have netting and bars on the windows to keep them out. Brian wrote home about them:

YMCA, Simla

Dear Mother and Dad,

Just a few hurried lines to tell you we are STILL in Simla. We were to move on, but stayed for a further week, and are playing The School for Scandal until next week. I am glad to stay longer, I have made such good friends here.

The rains have now started and it's cooled down considerably. The monkeys can be rather troublesome here. It's not possible to go out and leave a window open or, at night, you take the chance of a rude awakening. These monkeys can be quite vicious. The other morning when I tried to chase one that was about to pounce on my toothbrush, he looked at me and bared his teeth, then took the toothpaste as well! Later on his mates came in through the half open door and within minutes there was soap powder all over the bathroom and off they scampered, taking my bath towel with them.

Love Brian

Brian was not the only one to have encounters with the monkeys. One hot sunny afternoon John and Jennifer decided to visit the Monkey Temple, perched on top of a hill way above the mall. It was a long trek to the top, up a narrow path rising steeply through the trees. I persuaded them that I could make it too and, taking some nuts for the monkeys (a disastrous move) and some sandwiches for our lunch (an even worse mistake), we set off on our hike.

It was a beautiful climb, the snow-capped Himalayas in the distance gleaming in the sunshine, Simla down below growing smaller and smaller as we climbed, until the bandstand pavilion in the mall was a tiny speck. The trees shaded us and we arrived at the top in good spirits. The temple was almost derelict and there was no one about, no sadhus or keepers. There was evidence of recent pujas – offerings, garlands, cracked coconuts, empty fruit skins and dry rice – but no humans, just monkeys, monkeys every-where. They swarmed over the old stone temple roofs; they lay in the sun grooming each other for nits; baby monkeys scampered in and out of the temple doors and squealed in fun up and down the pillars. It was a strange sight, almost as if the monkeys knew that this was their house and no one would shoo them away.

We sat down to drink the tea from our flasks and eat our sandwiches. No sooner were the sandwiches exposed in their brown paper than all hell broke loose. The trees above us came alive with screaming, chattering monkeys. The babies stopped playing and bounded towards us. Jennifer gave one of the smaller ones a nut from her pocket and in a flash a big angry male had walloped the infant, taken the nut and eaten it, and was baring his fangs at Jennifer, demanding more. John, never the bravest of men, was surrounded. 'They're hungry!' he cried, an absurd understatement. 'They want food!' 'Well, give it to them,' I pleaded, more acutely aware of the physical danger. 'Let's give it all to them and go back now!'

The hooting monkeys were getting more aggressive and they

seemed to be doubling in number every minute. We threw what we had on the ground. I kept a small piece and tried to feed a baby monkey. This was not a good idea. With a war-like yell, a forty-pound bundle of angry Indian monkey flew at me, attaching itself to my head, holding on tight and screaming abuse. My mouth was full of monkey hair. I couldn't see or breathe. John, brave at last, leapt to my rescue and prised the beastly thing off. I turned to run for my life, but John caught my arm and, holding on to Jennifer, said in a voice strangely unlike his own, 'Look them in the eye! Look them in the eye!'

The absurdity of trying to obey this command by looking several hundred crazed monkeys in the eye did not, at this point, strike us. So we three foolish Western people backed slowly down the hill, while attempting to keep control by eye contact. Daft as this sounds, it might have worked. We were followed for a while, but once we were down the hill and round a bend, the monkeys gave up on us and we ran for our lives, shaken and bruised, but glad to have escaped intact.

Typically, given our cavalier attitude to life, my bites and scrapes were bathed in Mother's Dettol and forgotten about. No mention of rabies or doctors, we just carried on as usual.

You are getting thinner and stiffer . . . a husk, a husk of a person, with a slightly bloated tummy and legs that are now so rigid they stick out in front of you, giving you the appearance of a surprised chicken when you are propped up in the big padded armchair beside your bed. And the only movement is your scraggy arm, which sometimes moves up to your nose and down again beside you. Up and down, up and down.

'Up and down, up and down, I will lead them up and down.' Puck was the first big part I played, the year we visited Mount Herman School.

Mount Herman was a favourite date for all of the company. We reached the hill station of Darjeeling by the night train from Calcutta to Siliguri in the foothills. Then we changed on to a narrow-gauge 'toy train' that looped and twisted its way round the hillside, with those passengers who couldn't afford the fare perched on the roof. At Goom, some 7,400 feet above sea level, there was a pause for hot, sweet tea and a stretch of the legs, and for people to wrap themselves in jumpers and shawls, then the little train would take off for the last lap. Puffing its way through the trees, it slowly chuntered down to Darjeeling at 4,000 feet. By now it would be late in the afternoon of the second day, and memories of the hot sticky plains would melt away at the smell of the pine trees, and the sight of the Himalayas and the ever present mist on the hillside.

Mount Herman, originally built as an American missionary school, became one of the better co-ed public schools in the hills. The grey stone building sat on the side of a steep hill overlooking the Himalayas and the border with Tibet, a few miles below Darjeeling. It was my favourite Loreto Convent. St Paul's, the posher and more exclusive boys' school, was much higher up the hill, seemed always to be covered in mist or cloud, and had a severe and serious atmosphere compared with Mount Herman, where the teachers were jolly and the pupils noisier. There had been several heads over the years, but Mr Swift, a portly Australian, was the one I remember best. His wife Gloria taught in the school. They had living accommodation on the top floor of the north wing, and late at night the company were always invited to partake of Mrs Swift's home-made chocolate cake and scones, Horlicks and Ovaltine.

We lived in teachers' rooms in the north wing of the sprawling grey stone building. The rooms were small and prettily furnished, with chintzy curtains, rugs, big armchairs and flowered eiderdowns on the beds. Small fires burned in the tiny Victorian fireplaces during the winter and the view of the Himalayas – gleaming white snow-caps in the sun – was breathtaking. On a bright clear day we could see Kinchinjunga, soaring into the clouds.

They were contented times. I went to the Loreto Convent during the first few years we visited. The shows went well and the nuns loved the company, providing high tea afterwards and sitting while the actors ate their fill, telling slightly risqué shaggy-dog stories.

Do you remember any of this?

The small hall at Mount Herman where we did the shows on a tiny wooden stage with a tatty green front curtain? The evening snacks with the headmaster and his wife, ravenous actors eating her home-made cakes late into the night?

My childhood was landmarked by treats of this kind: a cup of hot chocolate or a Chinese meal was something very special. Living as we did in hotels or guest-houses, meals were provided, with no choice, and spending our limited resources on food of any kind except the odd peanut or snack was frowned on by Geoffrey.

The Mount Everest Hotel, perched precariously on the hillside off the mall, became a pivotal point of the week. If I was very good, I would be included on a company trip for lunch with Brian and Poopsie or Jennifer and John. And, if I was not at school, I could join them for a hot chocolate at the ice-cream parlour at the top of the mall. Then I could walk up Observatory Hill for a browse in the Bata shoe shop and on to the chemist's for toothpaste and liquid paraffin, hairpins and cotton wool. Mother once met Sherpa Tenzing at the chemist's on the mall, and went into swoons of rapture, getting his autograph and embarrassing the daylights out of me. Sometimes we would have lunch at a tiny Chinese restaurant before the taxi drive back to Mount Herman and Mother's habitual nap before the evening show.

On rare occasions someone would go to the races at Lebong, the smallest and highest race course in the world. One of the nuns at my convent, Mother Marie Antoinette, a four foot nothing little saint-like person, once rode around this race course in full nun's habit. She taught me French and biology, giving up on my French after a few lessons. She would take the whole company into the small school chapel on every visit we made and talk to God in a loud, firm voice, telling him in no uncertain terms to 'Bless dear Geoffrey and sweet Brian, to look after dear little Felicity, make us all a lot of money and protect us from harm.' She would go on for quite some time; it was a ritual she never broke, and even the most heathen of the cast went with her and bowed their heads.

She was a remarkable little woman. She had joined the convent at eighteen and given away her dowry of a considerable fortune. To mark the occasion of her seventy-fifth birthday, she took herself off to the race course and went riding around it, galloping at full speed, with her nun's habit blowing in the wind. 'I had to do that once more before I die,' she told the astounded jockey, whose horse she had taken. 'I used to race as a girl, but I haven't lost it, have I?'

It was here that I played Puck, a performance that was to contribute to my already steep learning curve.

Geoffrey was adding *A Midsummer Night's Dream* to our repertoire of eleven plays. I was page-boy in *Merchant*, Macduff's son in *Macbeth* (a part I had now mastered) and Lucius in the dreaded *Julius Caesar*. I was also expected to polish the brass and help on fit-ups at the weekend. In *The Dream* I was cast as Puck, a part Mother had played in England, and my costume was modelled on the one she wore: green body and tights, green make-up and fly-away wig, leaves and ivy sewn around one leg and some of the torso and over soft green ballet shoes.

It didn't take me long to learn the lines. The prospect of being in a play for more than a few moments was daunting, but as I didn't have a choice I tried not to let it worry me. I helped with the costume-making, dyeing tights and cutting out and sewing on the green plastic ivy and leaves. The wig was an old blonde one also dyed green and sprayed to stand up on end. It made me look like a surprised punk, caught in a gale-force wind, but I was impressed to be following in Mother's footsteps.

I had been rehearsed for weeks in between shows and school and was confident of my lines. It was taken for granted that I would start work sooner or later, although this was a bit sooner than I had anticipated. I was only twelve, but the part had to be played by someone and we had run out of actors.

I took the day off school and, after helping to fit up the small Mount Herman stage, started to get ready for the show. I was told how to make up: a green face with fly-away eyebrows and eyes with brown wings at the side. My hands had to be made up too. I squeezed my little round body into my costume. My chest was still flat as a pancake, much to my disappointment, so I looked like a boy. On went the wig and I was ready, way too early.

I sat at the school desk that was my dressing table and decided to go through my lines. Everyone else was still making up. My first line was . . . my first line was . . . I couldn't remember my first line! I went over to Mother, who was turning herself into Hermia.

'What's my first line?' I croaked, heart thumping.

'Don't go through your lines before you go on, darling, or you'll panic and forget them,' she said. 'Your first line is "How now, spirit! whither wander you?" Now calm down. You'll know every word, as long as you don't think about it just before you say it!' And with that she went back to her make-up and wig.

It was all very well for Mother to be calm; she was always calm. I, on the other hand, was in a cold sweat. There was still half an hour to go, so, against her advice, I decided to run through the entire part in my head. I went to the side of the stage and started. I knew all the long speeches, I knew the moves, I knew the middle of every scene – but the first line kept escaping me. I was by now in a blind panic. We never had a prompter during a show and there was no one who could help me if I missed an entrance. Puck had eight entrances, from different sides of the stage, and I could not for the life of me remember them in order. What was I to do? I dared not ask Mother. No one was paying me any attention and I felt utterly shipwrecked. Plus the dreaded 'curtain up' was getting closer.

Desperation gave me an idea: since we didn't have a prompter I would do the job myself. There were still fifteen minutes to go. I got out my battered copy of the *Complete Works* and wrote out on separate pieces of paper each and every cue, followed by the first line, then the exit, then the following cue, first line, and so on. I pinned the relevant bit of paper at each entrance, with an arrow pointing to the next prompt. By now I was hot and sweaty and my green face was gradually dripping off, to reveal a glowing pink, but at least I could face the next two hours; there was a fighting chance that I would be in the right place at the right time and not disgrace myself by being 'off' or 'drying up'.

The show went well. After the first few minutes I began to relax and even began to enjoy myself. By the last line of the play, Puck's 'And Robin shall restore amends', I was a hardened pro.

No fuss was made of my early effort (nor any mention made

of my DIY prompt system) and I didn't expect any. But that experience may have had a lasting effect. To this day impromptu speaking in public fills me with terror, and I am never happy in a part until I know what is coming next.

So now I was nearly twelve and a working member of the company. My initiation had been painful, but I had done it. I had not let anybody down. And, more importantly, I had enjoyed the feeling of power when I got a laugh. Soon after this I was given the part of young Gobbo in *The Merchant of Venice* – and then I found out how to make people laugh.

'She did well, didn't she, YoYo?' was all that Geoffrey said of my Puck performance, but he evidently decided I was ready for responsibility. Soon afterwards he made me the official counter of luggage. I was given a book and in it I had to itemize each and every bag, trunk, bedroll, basket and bundle. There was one column for personal bags and another for costumes and scenery – including such oddities as the 'footlight box', the cat basket and the trunk for cauldron and skulls. Geoffrey wrote in his diary:

One of Felicity's most important jobs is looking after the props. As we can't carry props for 15 plays, Felicity is responsible for borrowing what we don't have on any given day. At six she was helping, at eight I gave her her first salary book, now, at eleven, she gets ten rupees a month, which she writes down in her little green book.

She goes to the local convents when she can. Felicity is learning to be responsible for finding props and looking after the ones we carry. There is no finer school for anyone to learn the art of backstage work, regardless of whether she will be an actor or director. At the end of the show she returns the borrowed items with thanks to those who kindly assist us. This is teaching her to deal with different people all the time.

This was all very well for him to write. I had to go, legs atremble, with my 'list' to the headmaster's study, or to some terrifying Mother Superior, or the Officer in Charge. It was a nightmare, but by the time I was twelve years old I had learnt to ask, if not demand, the props and extra mirrors and tables we needed for any given show. I could not return empty-handed: it was the prop wallah's job and I was the prop wallah. From a shy and timid beginning, I became a little tyrant and, if it had not been for Mother's firm hand, I would have grown unbearably bossy and rude and would no doubt have lost us a few dates in the process.

The list, which I had to present to the relevant person in authority, was always the same and had been printed up by Geoffrey:

Shakespeareana

STAGE REQUIREMENTS

1. Dressing accommodation.
2. Washing water.
3. Drinking water.
4. Six small desks or tables.
5. Six small stools or chairs.
6. One straight-backed armchair.
7. An electrician.
8. A dhobi for pressing costumes.

Please have these ready on the stage two hours before show-time.

Thank you.

I was also in charge of making scrolls and letters. Parchment was achieved by singeing the edges of a piece of paper with a candle, then 'smoking' it with the same candle to make it look old. I had to paint the crowns and caskets gold and silver; and hammer bottle-tops flat, making a hole in them with a nail, then paint them silver and sew them on costumes to make armour. Props such as the three caskets for *The Merchant* had to be kept painted, crowns and swords polished and unbent after every show. On *Macbeth* nights, I helped to make up the witches' cauldron with salt and methylated spirits, mix blood for the various murders and set out the drums and thunder sheets.

The more I proved my capability, however, the more my workload grew. Next I was put in charge of the prop trunk, prop bags and the footlights, despite my protestations that the footlights were not strictly speaking props. I was shown how to set out the prop tables on either side of the stage and how to read the list of props for each play from the prompt copy. I knew most of it already, having helped to fit-up all my life, but now it was my responsibility, and the grim realization of my curtailed freedom was beginning to dawn on me.

At the beginning and end of every journey, I had to tick the number of pieces. This was a dreadful task, as they were forever being altered and half the stuff divided between hotels and theatres. I had sleepless nights, terrified that something would be lost or stolen and that Shylock would not have his dagger and scales to claim his pound of flesh.

After a few weeks of this insomnia, I refused to continue. Geoffrey relented and responsibility for the props and scenery was handed over to Frank Wheatley, while I still had charge of the personal belongings. That was fine by me: no one possessed anything of any value, so mislaying a case would never be as disastrous as losing costumes or make-up. Frank meanwhile made a great deal of his new position and held us up for hours while he slowly counted and re-counted the twenty-odd pieces of gear, then, with shaking hands (his hands always shook), licked his pencil and ticked off his list.

'Get a bloody move on, Frank!' Geoffrey would exclaim in exasperation. 'We can't wait for you to dither about like this. I'll give the job back to Foo if you're not careful!' Frank took no notice. Frank never took any notice: he was completely unflappable. Only on one occasion did I ever see him getting even the slightest bit distressed, and that, of course, had to do with his teeth.

We were playing *Julius Caesar* at a convent in Kerala. The school had no stage, so we were performing on a flat and very polished floor, with the audience sitting in chairs just a few feet away from us. I was now playing Lucius, Brutus's boy servant, a part I hated, partly because I had to sing a song to him in the tent scene and felt embarrassed by my less than presentable prop harp with its loose string, but mainly because, after the dreadful harp episode, I had to fall asleep on a gold painted cloth which gave off fumes that made me faint. The quarrel between Brutus and Cassius goes on for an eternity and I would undergo a series of panic attacks. All this made me dread the bookings of *Julius Caesar*, but the performance that afternoon was to be one I enjoyed – and poor old Frank was the cause.

The Reverend Mother was enthroned in the centre of the front row. Octavius Caesar, our dear Frank, had not on this occasion fixed his false teeth in properly and, on the line 'Defiance, traitors, hurl we in your teeth!', he hit the 't' in the last word so hard that his own dentures flew out and landed on the polished floor in front of him. He bent down instantly to retrieve them, but, as ever, his hand shook, and instead he flicked them across the shiny floor, where they came to rest at the feet of the Reverend Mother, who, without a word, bent down and put them in her sleeve, then carried on watching the play as if nothing had happened. It was so awful that nobody laughed.

Frank found it hard to speak for the rest of the scene, and I was sent round after the show with a tea-towel to retrieve the offending objects from the Reverend Mother. It was to be many years before I was to encounter the glamorous side of showbusiness!

CHAPTER TEN

NEW BLOOD

Your cough is better and you look more rested, though you still frown when I touch you and stroke your hair.

Tried to read from Kim, but halfway through a chapter you groaned and sighed, which was disheartening and which I took as criticism, so I've stopped. Showed you a lovely photo of YoYo in India; you seemed to focus on it for ages. No groaning and sighing then!

Last night I dreamt that she came back and lay beside you on a big white bed under a punkah. She was looking very lovely with her hair all soft and curly. She was naked, and sweetly old, and she lay down beside you and stroked you in the most loving fashion. You seemed peaceful, and happy, and cool under the sheet. It was a beautiful dream. I woke up, made a cup of tea and read till the early hours.

She seems to be about more and more, my mother. I hope that does not mean that you are going to join her. Not now. After three years I've just found something for you to do, God damn it, a way of spending time with you and not feeling anguished and depressed. Working here in your room, at this little wooden table, trying out the odd idea, scribbling away. This is good, I've got used to it. So don't leave me just as I've found a way to cope.

This place is costing a fortune, such a shame, because I'd so much rather give it to you to spend. You always liked a bit of cash. As a little girl in India I was given a small salary book to write down my weekly pocket money. A small blue book bought in the bazaar in Hyderabad. Rupees and annas at the top, a new pencil and rubber, and the first rupee to make a note of in the top column, under 'in'. Across the page you wrote 'out'. Then came a lecture about the 'out' never ever being more than the 'in'. Coming from you, even then I felt it was a bit rich.

Money had always been tight, but was beginning to get tighter. The days of the Rajahs were fading and, after a bad flu epidemic that closed hundreds of schools and lost us a lot of bookings, the company was under strain.

At length we managed to secure a few days' performing at a girls' school. There was no stage in the great hall, but the headmistress was determined to provide one. So, with the help of some rather weak string, she tied together several dozen flat-topped desks and covered them with a tarpaulin that she secured at the sides. It looked perfect. The show was set up and, although Brian had some misgivings about the structure, we started the play.

Everything started all right, but the Indian string was not up to the rigours of performance and the heels of the actors' boots kept getting stuck in the inkwell holes on the desks. As the tarpaulin loosened, the whole contraption became less and less steady. Finally, when Frank disappeared between two desks, Geoffrey decided to give in, and the second half of the play was performed on the flat in front of the 'stage', much to everyone's relief.

It was not unusual to play on stages tied together, or indeed on desks, but that was the worst example. Open-air performances held their own horrors. Candles blew out, cauldrons were extinguished, mosquitoes attacked with a vengeance, frogs croaked, dogs barked and backstage there was the chance of stepping on the odd snake in the inky dark.

We moved on next to Rajasthan, to perform in a cinema in Ludhiana. It was monsoon time and cold in the north of India. Most of the company managed to get free accommodation, but Mary and I slept in the box of the cinema. I would curl up in my bedroll halfway through the last film and go to sleep with the songs of Vijayantimal ringing in my ears and the flickering of the screen on the seats above my head.

We must have been stone broke. Apart from a few nights sleeping on railway platforms, things had never been as desperate as this before. Mary would sleep beside me, snoring as usual, and I was very sniffy about the whole thing, complaining bitterly every morning when we gathered to wash in the ladies' lavatory. We stayed only a week or so, while the rains poured down outside, but Ludhiana was most definitely a very low point in the history of the company.

The next date proved even worse. We visited a town called Muzaffarnagar, north of Delhi. A large marquee had been erected to house an audience of over 600. We played *Henry V* to a full house and endless curtain calls. I was playing Boy, a part I fancied myself in tremendously, as I had to be carried on dead and floppy and always supposed the audience to be heartbroken at the sight of me. Besides, getting a reaction for doing nothing was very gratifying.

The next night was *Saint Joan*, and it was packed again. But Geoffrey was worried. 'I can smell a rat here,' he said. 'I should have seen the takings by now.' The organizers turned up as we were getting *Othello* ready on the third day, to explain, with downcast faces and much wagging of heads, that no money had been made at all so far.

'It is a very regrettable, Mr Kendal,' I heard one of them say.

'We are very sorry about this unhappy turn of events, but we have not collected from the audience what they are owing and, due to this most erratic situation, we cannot pay your fee.' The man smiled and wrung his hands. 'I am very sorry.'

'What the bloody hell do you mean?' roared my father. 'Every sodding seat was sold!' 'No, no. We sold only 200 seats, sir, and that has to pay for the advertisements.' 'What advertisements? There are no advertisements! Christ Al-bloody-mighty!' raged Geoffrey, becoming apoplectic.

Just then Poopsie turned up, dripping wet from the recently started monsoon rains. 'Can you believe it?' he cried. 'There's a boy over there trying to set fire to our ticket stubs in the pouring rain!'

We raced to the scene and, sure enough, hundreds of used ticket stubs were crammed into a bucket, spilling over the side and on to the ground. The little man looked at Geoffrey. 'Oh, dear,' he muttered. 'I shall take these items and dispense with them elsewhere.' And with a smile, he collected his brimming bucket and left.

'Right, everybody. Pack up,' barked Geoffrey. 'We are leaving this God-forsaken joint immediately!' We packed in haste and later the same day we were all on a train, third class this time, back to Delhi.

Mother's letters home during this period were growing plaintive:

Kishore House, Daisy Bank, Simla

Dear Beula,

How I wish I could send you some coins, but I haven't drawn my salary for three months now, the firm has needed it! We have to stay here an extra week to settle

the tax question. Geoff is sending a wire to Nehru and he
may go and see him in Delhi. Tomorrow we play a cigarette
factory, so that will make up a bit. Jimmy sent me a pair
of BEAUTIFUL nylon tights from America. Dear Jimmy,
he is so generous. I've told him the next thing to send
is a millionaire. These tights are just what I need for
Ariel. They cost four quid in dollars! Sorry, I'm
feeling a bit over coin conscious at the moment.

Love to all, L.

There had always been cash flow problems, mostly because the organizers did not pay the agreed amount. This happened most often in south India. Once Geoffrey stopped the show after a season of packed houses and no payment. The students who had put in their rupees nearly started a riot, so half the money for that show was handed over. After the show the organizers left town.

During these times of virtual poverty we travelled third class. Unable to book in advance, we had to push and shove to get seats on the narrow wooden benches and even narrower wooden bunks above. Frank insisted on a window seat as a rule, but, when it was dreadful third, at every station tied-up chickens and children would be handed across his lap through the open windows; he soon gave up and sat in the middle.

There were 'passengers' even in the lavatories, and the floor was covered with chickens and children. Night travel was the worst of all. The light would blaze brightly all night, so even if we were lucky enough to secure the top bunk, it was almost impossible to sleep under the glare of the unforgiving light. Mother came up with a solution. She delved into the paint bag and, with a pot of black paint, covered up the offending light. We would arrive the next morning filthy but rested.

A short phase of peevish anger engulfed me during this period. I had had enough adventure. I was fed up with being hard up, with midnight journeys to godforsaken towns, playing to students sometimes my own age, who did not work and who were free at the end of the day to play games. I was sick of living in the ever changing rooms with, as often as not, smelly bedbugs waiting to devour me. I wanted desperately to be a secretary, to learn to type and work in an office with filing cabinets and phones to answer. I would dream of living in a small house with an upstairs. A garden was not out of the question, as long as it wasn't tropical, and a lot of the time there would be snow. My name would be Brown or Crawford and I would be *normal*. I took to having princessy tantrums and behaving in a very shabby fashion to Mother, who was already feeling the strain of the last year.

But even at our lowest ebb, there was light relief. John Day was often at the centre of it and his daft practical jokes kept us going. He was particularly naughty before his return to England. He viewed this departure with a mixture of excitement and dismay, since we were now his family and he was still, as he always would be, a little in love with Jennifer. He was the brother she never had, and their close friendship was to last all their lives. But for his last fortnight he was naughty, and on one occasion managed to surpass himself.

On the morning of John's misdemeanour, Geoffrey had pontificated during rehearsal, as usual, giving the actors a lot of notes on how never to laugh on stage under any circumstances. 'Sheer amateur indulgence!' he scorned. 'No one will think you're funny, except you. So try not to corpse *ever*! Now, come along, you load of pansies . . . let's try and run through *Twelfth Night*.'

That evening, halfway through the play, Geoffrey, as Malvolio in his yellow stockings and cross-garters, picked up the letter planted for him. But, as he bent down to do so, John, who was playing Andrew Aguecheek, collapsed on the floor, helpless with the giggles. I was playing Maria and was 'concealed' behind a screen made to look like a bush, as was Brian, who was padded up and playing Toby Belch. I had no idea what the matter was and tried to hush John up.

'The letter, the letter! Look at the letter!' John spluttered. I had only just dropped the letter in Malvolio's path and could see nothing funny about it. 'There's nothing wrong with the letter,' I hissed, but John was off again, tears streaming down his cheeks. For the next few minutes Aguecheek has no lines, which was just as well, as he was incapable of speaking. When it came to the moment at which Malvolio spies the letter, John was lying on the floor behind the 'bush', and at the words from Malvolio, 'What employment have we here?', as he took up the letter, John gave a groan and left the stage on all fours.

Brian and I stared at one another, bewildered. Then Geoffrey opened the letter. Out tumbled, pinned to one of its corners, a great long condom. Malvolio's next line, 'By my life, this is my lady's hand', was drowned by squeals of pure joy from the students in the audience.

To my utter amazement, Geoffrey was not in the least angry. He gave a small smile and went, with his letter and condom, in search of the culprit. Behind the 'bush' he found only a cowering Toby Belch and Maria, so he carried on in search of John, who was now quaking in the wings. 'Come on stage, you silly tart,' Malvolio whispered, still in character, then went on to play the scene, condom and all.

The kids loved the show and applauded longer than usual – but we were never asked back to the school again.

I was growing up with theatre law replacing the usual 'No elbows on the table' and so on. Although Mother was adamant that good manners were essential for young ladies, as she learnt at finishing school, I would get 'Never put shoes on a dressing table', 'Never whistle in the dressing room' and 'Hold your costume off the floor till you go on stage' in place of encouragements to help old ladies across the street and be kind to animals. In India the old lady would probably be a beggar and most animals in the East have no rights whatsoever. So I was learning fast, but not the same set of rules as most young girls.

Geoffrey, meanwhile, drilled me in good practice on stage. The list of practical advice that he wrote out for actors still makes me smile – and still holds good:

Practise getting on and off. You look silly if you dither; stand with your two feet and grip the stage. That is your power.

You have to keep fit, not by violent exercise, which is bad for the voice. Yoga is best. Breath is what you want. The best is yoga, a little and often.

The curtain always goes up and always goes down. What happens in the middle is your affair.

If you really dry up look hard at another actor. The audience will know it is him.

Enjoy being nervous. If you are not nervous before you go on, it is best to take another job, you will never be an actor.

In love scenes, remember – the audience must be thrilled, not you.

Drink cold water before you go on, never alcohol. It may make you think you are giving a great performance, but you won't be.

Listen to the whole play, not just your bit, and do this every night, however long the run.

As often as possible, rehearse in the shoes you will wear. If you wear spurs, rehearse in them.

Soon after John's departure, Frank wanted to go home again. He had stayed for nine months and had hurt his leg falling over a stool, which he claimed 'that imp, Poopsie, deliberately placed in my path,' (Poopsie was always teasing him, and they were not the best of friends).

His passage back to England was arranged for the following month, when we would be in Bombay. In the meantime Geoffrey set about recruiting new actors. We took on two new actresses: Sonja Frankenborg, a pretty German girl whom we met in Madras, and Coral de Rosario from Bangalore. Coral was very good at playing young men and old women, and between her and Mother, who for a short while played Oberon, the plays continued – with some degree of chaos – when a major catastrophe overtook us.

Frank lost his 'best' teeth. Not only did this mean that you could not understand a word he said – a drawback for an actor even as old as Frank – but it also meant that he could not chew, and eating was what he lived for.

Things looked very dim indeed at the morning meeting when this was announced. The naughty boys in the company tried not to giggle as Frank explained that, as was his custom, he had put his teeth on the bedside table before he went to sleep. The guest-house had run out of soda water so, afraid of dysentery from tap water, he had wrapped the full set in his hankie. When he woke up both the hankie and the teeth were gone.

The servants of the guest-house were summoned. They knew nothing of the teeth. The bearer who had brought in the morning tea had not seen them, and no one seemed to know what had become of the fabulous chompers. Frank was almost resigned to reverting to his 'second' cracked set, when Poopsie mentioned how much a full set could fetch in the bazaar. This threw Frank into a frenzy of suspicion. He called all the servants, bearers and sweepers and offered a mighty reward to anyone able to reunite him with his beloved dentures. A search party was set in motion, with much shouting and 'deco'ing and that evening, finally, Frank's teeth were proudly placed in front of him, gleaming white, on a dinner plate along with the brown Windsor soup.

'Big teeth found in rats' nest in gutter on roof-top, sahib. Rats take teeth to roof-top, thinking teeth food, sahib. Now here they are back for your usage. Spanking clean. Thank you, sahib.' Given Frank's lack of hygiene when it came to anything, let alone his teeth, the mind boggles at what the rats thought they had captured. But, without a moment's pause, Frank whipped out his understudy pair, plopped in the gleaming set from the plate, and fell upon his Windsor soup.

So Frank left, and Coral and Sonja were now a fixture in the company. When Peter announced soon after Frank's departure that he really had to go back and earn some money, casting became critical. Another man was needed.

Jennifer suggested a young actor, Shashi Kapoor. She had already met him briefly in Bombay. They had had a few suppers together months earlier, and he was as smitten as she. This opportunity to work together was, Jennifer said, 'fated', and Mother wrote home:

> The new boy is going to be brilliant as Laertes and
> Sergius, and Jane is very happy, she is coaching him on
> his lines. After all, the poor boy has to learn nine
> parts in a few weeks! I must say, they make a very
> attractive couple.

There was no hint in those first days of what was to come.

CHAPTER ELEVEN

GOODBYE TO MARY

'Worship at my feet.' Thwack! He hit her shoulder and a fresh bruise joined the little blue cluster already appearing on her bony arms. Jennifer giggled, bent down and touched his sandalled feet in a salaam of obedience. 'That's better! You must learn to be respectful to your man . . . you Belighty memsahib.' Shashi took my sister's face in his hands and kissed her hard, paying no attention to me, as I sat on my bed in the room I shared with Jennifer at the Sunny Fields Guest-house in Bangalore.

As an eleven-year-old, still in convent school, plump and painfully shy, I worshipped him, this tall, beautiful Indian actor that my sister had fallen in love with. He was funny and glamorous, the most flirtatious man I had ever met. He combined flattery and bullying with such attractive skill that he was almost irresistible. He was too thin, but it made his huge eyes, fringed with thick long lashes, seem even more beguiling. His flashing white teeth and wicked dimple were used quite deliberately to get his own way with both men and women, and the swagger of success was with him long before he became the number one Bollywood superstar.

Shashi was the son of a great and grand Indian actor, Prithviraj Kapoor, who had his own itinerant theatre company, very similar to my father, except that Prithviraj travelled with enormous scenery, a cast of hundreds, cooks, cleaners, wives and children. When they went by rail, they hired most of the train, whereas we were lucky to get two compartments.

Shashi's father was playing the well-known Indian classical play *Dewar* at the Royal Opera House in Bombay, and Jennifer and Wendy decided to see the show one evening when they were free. Shashi had a small part in the play – he was eighteen, and still learning his trade. Before the performance, Shashi peeped out through the tabs to look at the audience and size them up – a habit a lot of actors have, and few admit to. He saw sitting in the fourth row of the stalls a young girl with long fair hair. She was dressed in a black and white polka-dotted summer dress with a halter neckline – daring – and she was pretty, laughing with her girlfriend and fanning herself with her programme. Shashi, according to Shashi, fell instantly in love.

After the show he raced front of house to introduce himself and asked the girls bashfully if he could offer a guided tour backstage, thinking it would be an unusual treat for Jennifer to meet the actors in costume and little imagining that that was how she spent most of her life. But Jennifer and Wendy pretended they knew nothing about the theatre and were overwhelmed and delighted to be taken to meet the cast. The next afternoon I was sitting in a Chinese restaurant, watching Jennifer and Shashi fall in love over their noodles. They would stay together till she died, through thick and sometimes very thin. She never did anything half-heartedly, my sister, it was all or nothing, Love or War. And she had met in Shashi the man she wanted for ever.

It was not long before she had arranged for Shashi to join our company. John, Frank and Peter had gone back home and we had a lot of shows booked in Bangalore: *Arms and the Man* and *The Merchant* were planned for a season of two weeks at the local cinema. Jennifer came up with the answer to this crisis – she wired Shashi, who was in Bombay.

He came on the next train, clutching copies of Shaw and Shakespeare, and for the following five days Jennifer tutored him, until he was ready to take over as Gratiano and Sergius. He had never acted in English in his life and was shaking with nerves, but he carried it off with great success and was reluctantly welcomed into the fold by my father, who was never keen on any boyfriend Jennifer had. His caustic remarks had seen off many a gallant lad – and a few elderly gallant gentlemen. His possessiveness of her was absolute. He pretended that it was for her own good, or the good of the company: she being the leading lady, next to my mother, he didn't want to lose her. But it was more than that. Having left her during the war, I don't think he could bear the thought of her ever being away again. She felt something similar – she did, in any event, spend much of her life living and working with him.

But in spite of her love for her family, Shashi was everything in the world to her. Knowing of Geoffrey's jealousy, she included me as chaperone on most of their early dates and outings. I was to be the errand runner and confidante, a role I fell upon with a passion. I was a stooge for jokes; I was the safety net for flirty times in the bedroom when they hugged and talked and planned the life they would spend together.

I came to rely on this partnership that included me, and when they naturally moved on to a more private relationship, I became sulky and moody. I would weep with bitter despair if I was not included on a visit to the cinema or a late meal. Quite unfairly, I began to feel rejected and unloved, and Jennifer could not understand my behaviour. She found it hard to exclude me, if it was going to entail great tantrums and sulks, so I started tagging along again, and she divided herself between her new love and

Me, Jennifer, Shashi, Brian, Mother and Frank

Just before we left for Singapore, with Mother going through her
religious phase, dressed all in white

Aged thirteen, playing Viola

Jennifer and Shashi in Bombay just before I left for England

Above On location for *Shakespeare Wallah*

Right Ismail, Jim and me

Below right Leaving for Berlin with Shashi
and his father, Prithviraj

Practising on my bike for *The Mayfly and the Frog*

With the great Sir John

With Alan Badel in *Kean*

With Tom Courtenay in *The Norman Conquests*

Right Just married, outside the Chelsea Register Office with Drewe

Below Charley continuing the family tradition in the television series *Edward VII*, playing my daughter, Charlotte, opposite my Princess Vicky

With Geoffrey at Bombay Harbour after I was married

Visits home to India with Jennifer and family

her demanding little sister, who insisted on being part of her life. No one ever wanted to lose Jennifer.

Within six months Shashi was working hard, playing in every show. They were both happy and in love, but, despite Jennifer's best efforts, a rift was growing between Geoffrey and Shashi. Already there was talk of marriage, and the possibility of Jennifer leaving started a family storm brewing that was to erupt catastrophically before very long. But then we were invited out of India for the first time in many years – to play a season in Singapore, sponsored by the Shaw Brothers.

With high spirits we planned the trip. We had cholera shots and small pox shots (a precaution that filled me with terror when I was young), we were all kitted out with new white trousers and shirts, the scenery was repainted painstakingly by Brian, and we were bursting with excitement. The company had now played to a million people in India during the six years of its continuous tour and consisted of ten people, among them Jennifer, who was now twenty-four, and Shashi, who had just turned twenty. This cheerful, motley crew set sail to take Singapore by storm.

This was to be goodbye to Mary. By now I was working in some capacity on most of the shows – if not on stage, then helping with props, time-keeping and the wardrobe. I felt quite independent, and Mary had no real function apart from that of a maid. I was out at the show every night, so her usefulness was over. I had mentioned this to Mother perhaps a year before, but Mary's devotion and loyalty were such that she did not have the heart to let her go – and Mary wanted to stay with us for ever.

But now we were leaving India and so, with upset and tears, she was given a cash bonus and told that she would not be rejoining us when we returned. The whole company was depressed; she had been such an integral part of the troupe and family. Jennifer pointed out that if I really wanted Mary she could stay on and at least do the ironing, but I was growing up and I did not want an ayah. Mary's time had come, and I was already seeing myself as a teenager, ready to join the adult world. I was adamant: I did not want Mary any more. I got my father to agree – which was not difficult, as he saved a salary without Mary – and her fate was sealed.

The week before we left we spent in Bombay, preparing for the new tour, doing up the set and costumes. The atmosphere with Mary was tense. She hardly spoke and did a lot of silent crying, wiping away the tears with the corner of her sari, her red eyes fixed on me beseechingly. We were the only family she had ever been close to and, as far as I remember, she had no new job to go to. And even a glowing reference coming from a bunch of touring actors would not amount to much, not for the big posh jobs with the burrah memsahibs of India.

Finally, this interminable week passed, and at last we were boarding the ship to Singapore (the same vessel, incidentally, that had brought us to India in 1953, now renamed). Here chaos erupted: Jennifer realized she had not taken out all the appropriate papers for the dogs she travelled with; and three of the Indian actors were turned back at emigration for not having the right visas. Shashi, Poopsie and Coral had to stay behind and follow on by plane. Feelings were running high, with Jennifer in tears and Geoffrey sprinting from one crisis to another in a state of high agitation.

Mother, as always under these conditions, stayed absurdly calm and remained sitting down. She always *sat* when things got hairy, even if it was only on the luggage, and she took on the air of a saintly martyr. Mary had come to the dock to see us off and was standing, weeping, at the side of the gangplank, the hysteria about dogs and passports and visas raging around her.

At last it was time to board. The ship was full and we were the last in the queue. Mother hugged Mary and went up the gangway, while I hung back with Jennifer.

There was much confusion, but in the middle of all this I had never been happier. I was leaving India for new adventure; I was leaving my babyhood in the form of Mary; my real life was about to start. There would be dollars and chocolates and wonderful clothes. We might at last make some money and serious shopping would result. I was going to be working more and might even start smoking! All these foolish fantasies. None, apart from the smoking, would come true, but I was full of myself and glad to be so. I gave Jennifer's dog a kiss, said goodbye to Shashi, Poopsie and Coral, gave Mary a quick hug and run up the gangway, joining the rest of the passengers all leaning over the rails. There was shouting and calling as the crew got ready to depart.

'Darling, you didn't say goodbye to Mary, not properly,' Mother said, as she looked over the railing of the ship to see Mary standing rooted to the spot, gazing up at us. 'I did, I *did*,' I lied. 'It's not too late.' Mother pushed me to the steps. 'Go and give her a kiss, you horrid little girl.' Jennifer joined in. 'How could you be so heartless, Foo!' I looked stubbornly ahead, refusing to budge. The boys on the quay were now moving people away from the side of the ship, untying the gangplank steps and letting loose the giant ropes holding us to the dock.

Suddenly, it was too late. We were off. The ship slowly started to glide away from the side. Mary put her sari over her head, covering her mouth, and still she stood, staring up at us, not waving or moving. I looked down at her and, for a single moment, felt my heart would break. But it was only for a moment, and then I waved at her and turned away to continue my life without her.

My compulsion to move on, to leave places and people behind

without a backward glance was to be demonstrated again and again.

The last time I saw Mary was on a visit to India after I was married. She was old and grey and could hardly walk. She came to Jennifer's flat for tea, bringing with her a little German girl that she was looking after for a few weeks.

She had lost her glorious smile. In its place was a shadow, and her eyes were dim. She was sweet to me, but I was a stranger to her now. After all the years of giving love to other people's children, no family would in return look after her.

After Mary left, I was elevated to being 'one of the girls', thereby sharing a room with Jennifer, Coral or Sonja. Jennifer was my preference, but, depending on her love life, she sometimes chose a single room. Geoffrey, despite his Victorian upbringing and sarcastic pronouncements in public, was remarkably liberal-minded about people's sexuality – which doubtless contributed to the happiness of the company, who were able to entertain their lovers (of either sex) long before it was fashionable. The only rule was that whatever went on, went on behind closed doors. He would turn a blind eye to discreet affairs, but he loathed sexual flaunting in public. He even ignored Jennifer's active love life – she was a very modern woman – which seems remarkable, given the jealousy that he was to exhibit in Singapore.

On the ship, however, Jennifer decided to share a cabin with me, which I loved. It reminded me of times when I was little, and she would cuddle up in my bed and sing me snatches of opera. During the day she was a snazzy, sexy lady, but, like Mother, she had a positively Victorian bedtime ritual, which I would lie on my bunk and watch. First her long hair had to have a hundred brush strokes, then there were four minutes of vigorous, frothy toothbrushing, a great deal of sponging and powdering, and washing out of smalls. Finally she would be ready, her face shiny with cold cream, her hair in plaits and ribbons, and her toilet completed. Swamped in a voluminous, full-length cotton nightie, she would climb into bed with a book.

I stared in disbelief. 'Do you do all this in front of Shashi?' I asked innocently and was startled when she climbed out of her bunk and into mine and burst into tears. She then proceeded to share with me her agony about Shashi. I wasn't really interested and found the turmoil surrounding her love life rather tedious. I was very fond of Shashi, but then I got on well with most adults, and, if he made her happy, I approved. But the tears and tantrums that accompanied their relationship bored my little head, and I listened with only faked interest as she poured out her anguish.

'Daddy has told me that it isn't Shashi he objects to, or the fact that he is Indian, or that he is younger than I am . . . it is just that he doesn't want us to leave the company. But Foo, Shashi has his own country and his own life, and he doesn't want to stay with us for ever, touring Shakespeare. And why should I give him up for the sake of Daddy's company? I wish he would understand that all children grow up and want to leave. It isn't that I don't love Daddy, but it's such a dreadful situation and it could have been so wonderful!'

I nodded mutely, so she wailed on. 'I am made to feel selfish and inconsiderate, just because I want to do the perfectly normal thing of getting married. If Mummy and Daddy objected to Shashi as a person, I could understand, but I know they don't. It's just my going, and I know it would be the same, whoever I wanted to go off with. It's all too ridiculous and Mummy's gone berserk again and has started crossing herself at mealtimes and covering her chest with sacred hearts!'

I had noticed this holy nonsense making an unwelcome

comeback and agreed that it was pretty embarrassing. 'Anyway,' Jennifer said, gaining strength from her outburst, 'anyway, Shashi's family are wonderful and they will accept *me*. So I'm not going to feel guilty any more. We will play the tour for the fixed time, then I am leaving to marry Shashi, and that's that!'

She kissed me and got back into her bed. I stayed on the top bunk, watching the moonlight on the waves, and feeling sorry that Jennifer couldn't stand up to her father like I could and that, when she needed Shashi most, he could not be here to help her.

The voyage passed uneventfully, without the usual excitement of a show on board. Down to half his cast and worried about Jennifer, Geoffrey was in no mood for frivolities and it was a sombre journey.

CHAPTER TWELVE

SINGAPORE

We arrived to find the missing three already landed and Jennifer's Tibetan terrier in quarantine, where he would stay for the duration. There were a lot of tears and visits to the kennels and I was getting more upset than I realized by the constant moods surrounding me. I kept a low profile, sneaking out for long walks alone, eating lots of chocolate and smoking Marlboro cigarettes.

There were press conferences scheduled by our sponsors, and one long piece, headlined 'Felicity's Good Life', talked about my vagabond lifestyle and how I was working full time at barely twelve years old. This had the undesirable effect of prompting a visit to Geoffrey from a health inspector, who said that I would not be allowed to take part in the plays, as I was under-age and it was against the law to employ child labour. His news tipped Geoffrey over the edge. A minor volcano of emotions erupted, with Geoffrey shouting so loudly that Mother left the room.

I don't know what happened next, but I do remember playing the first season, so I can only imagine that Geoffrey either bribed the inspector or lied about my age.

As was so often the case with us, the booked tour turned out to be a disappointment. The shows were full, but somehow

Geoffrey never made any money. So he took on further bookings, which exhausted the company and did little to help the ebbing morale. The Shaw Brothers owned and ran most of the cinemas and several large fun-fairs. One was called the Great World and it had rides, restaurants, stalls, shops, magic shows and food halls. Also within this theme park was a large, open-sided hall with a rickety stage at one end. Chinese wy yangs (travelling shows) performed there normally, and we were booked in for two weeks to play *The Merchant* twice nightly.

The dressing rooms were sheds at the back, overlooking the café kitchens and the bucket loads of dead baby piglets, potatoes and gutted chickens that were piled high outside the entrance. The view meant little to me, but it sent Jennifer into a frenzy of upset. Everything seemed to be against us. The rains came and the roof of our 'theatre' was corrugated iron, so no one could hear a word most of the time. It was a dreadful two weeks, rescued only by the wonderful food and the fascinating place in which we were staying.

We booked in at the York Hotel in Scotts Road, run by Mr and Mrs Soffelt. The place consisted of two large, cream-painted Edwardian villas set in spacious grounds. A winding driveway led past pillared gates and rhododendron bushes to the balconied entrance of House No. 1. House No. 2, where the owners lived, was reached across a wide lawn and hidden by bushes and trees. It was the smaller villa, but no less imposing, with a wide veranda and columned entrance – a typical colonial residence.

Geoffrey had characteristically wangled a deal on the rooms, which had high ceilings and simple furniture, a happy mixture of Edwardian oak wardrobes, Chinese lacquered tables and modern lamps and divan beds. Our special arrangement did not include the slap-up breakfast they did for most of the guests, but large pots of steaming coffee and tea in thermos flasks were deposited on our veranda every morning, along with three dozen boiled eggs and bread and butter. Whether this came as part of the deal or was simply a sign of the soft-heartedness of the owners, who adopted the company as their own after a week, was never revealed. I think it was the latter.

Mr and Mrs Soffelt were an elderly Danish couple who had lived in Singapore all their lives. They had both been captured and tortured in a Japanese concentration camp, and this had so affected them that they now lived as virtual missionaries, letting out rooms for less than half of what they should cost to the semi-poor – a category into which we certainly fell. The inhumanity to man and beast that they had witnessed had made them decide to dedicate the rest of their lives to looking after stray animals: this was their way of doing some good, after the dreadful experiences they had had. They had no children, so the strays they adopted became their family, with the guest-house providing the money they needed to run this menagerie. The Chinese as a nation are not very kind to strays, so there was no shortage of animals to which they could minister.

Mrs Soffelt had once been a beauty, but no evidence of this remained. She was a tall woman with long legs, tanned by her years in the East, a tan that failed to cover her alarming varicose veins. She dressed in printed cotton frocks and flat brown sandals, wore a large man's wristwatch and was always in a hurry, her hair in a state of constant collapse. She wore combs to hold up the greying brown locks that curled in an unruly fashion, but the style she started out with in the morning, of rolls and coils, was by mid-afternoon a haystack of pins. She still applied make-up, in a style frozen in time: her eyebrows were pencilled into an arch of permanent surprise; her cheeks were rouged with the same lipstick with which she achieved a perfect pouting bow that lasted only until lunchtime. She never seemed to be still, giving everything her full if hurried attention, her large grey eyes beaming out care and concern for the world about her.

Mr Soffelt was a little different. Equally kind, he was quiet and slow, handsome, with a head of thick white hair and an even thicker accent. He looked after the financial side of the business and was not much in evidence until evening, when they would both stop work and sit on the lawn or veranda in front of their house, dispensing gin and tonic and talking to some of their guests, all the while surrounded by their animals.

There were some thirty dogs of all shapes and sizes and temperaments – some friendly, some considerably less so – roaming the lawns and corridors of the house. There was also a kaswaree bird (a small version of an ostrich) that had been given to them when its owner left Singapore. The bird was on its way to the zoo and Mrs Soffelt protested that it had been running free all its life; to be cooped up now would be too cruel. It never ventured out of the grounds for some reason, and it never attacked adults, but anything nearer the ground was fair game. I was petrified of the damn thing. If ever I went out alone it would suddenly appear from behind a bush, fix me with its eyes and, letting out a bloodcurdling hiss, would charge at me full pelt with lowered head and huge flat feet flapping on the path. At the very last minute the ghastly creature would swerve and plod off as if nothing had happened.

These attacks aside, I loved staying with the dogs and Mrs Soffelt, who would sometimes take me on her daily dog-feeding journeys downtown. Lee, her old Chinese driver, would pile buckets of sloppy food and baskets of home-made dog biscuits into her ancient little Ford, and we would set off for the docks. At the sound of her car, cats and dogs would appear as if by magic from mounds of garbage and out of alleyways. She would dole out her slop with a great ladle into the road, checking to see whether any animals were hurt. If some needed help, they would be blanketed up and taken to the vet, or driven home. She was so in tune with them, and so fearless, that none of these wild things ever growled at her or bit her. Dog biscuits were always at hand and she was forever throwing them out of the car window at strays, narrowly missing unsuspecting pedestrians.

One morning we found the tiny body of a little brown puppy perched on top of a rubbish heap. It looked so vulnerable and perfect, I lifted it off, thinking I could bury it in the garden rather than leave it to rot like an old cabbage. As I carried the little bundle over the garbage, it opened its eyes. 'Mrs Soffelt, he's alive!' I cried. 'Well, bring him home, then,' was all she said, slopping out her buckets to the growing crowd of dogs. I carried my small brown puppy back to the guest-house, nursed him back to health and called him Rubbish. He stayed with us for the next few years.

Not many people would put up with the combination of a crazy kaswaree called Jack and thirty-odd half-wild dogs as part of their accommodation, but we were no ordinary travellers, and before long the Soffelts had adopted us along with their menagerie, taking us under their wing and waiving bills when things got rough. And things were about to get very rough indeed.

CHAPTER THIRTEEN

MUCH ADO

The atmosphere in the company was getting worse. The usual camaraderie, the jokes and repartee were becoming thin on the ground. The Firm was breaking up and the strained silence accompanying the fit-ups was evidence of the situation. Money was in short supply, so there was little opportunity to escape into the town. Some of the company would try and cheer themselves up with a movie or a Chinese meal, but most of the time we were forced together, day and night.

Worst of all, it was clear that Jennifer was planning to leave with Shashi sooner rather than later, and Geoffrey's possessiveness was approaching fever pitch. Even on stage the situation was becoming intolerable for my sister. Her father was not going to accept her departure from his company and into a new life with any grace whatsoever. He was so antagonistic towards Shashi had he would only speak to him through a go-between – usually me.

I knew this was not a personal reaction to Shashi himself; Geoffrey had been the same with every boyfriend Jennifer had ever had who was serious enough to represent the possibility of her leaving, or having a life apart from the family. His behaviour was nothing new, but to Shashi it must have seemed intolerable.

When, one morning at breakfast time, Geoffrey said to me,

'Ask the man over there if he thinks he and my daughter will allow us to book some plays in Penang next month,' I knew things couldn't get much worse. At the next performance Geoffrey managed to get through the entire play without once looking at his future son-in-law – not an easy task when you are sharing a stage. It was most unlike him to be so unprofessional. After this particularly hostile display, Jennifer decided that things were unbearable. She announced in a shaky voice at the morning meeting that the following weekend she would be flying to Bombay with Shashi to get married.

Geoffrey went white and left the room. A few moments later, Mother followed. I did not understand my father's objection, nor Mother's refusal to take my sister's side. After all, they were both actors. Shashi, like Jennifer, was a second-generation theatre person; we felt India to be our home; and, until he decided to marry into our family, we had all adored Shashi. But I did not want to lose my sister and so, with conflicting emotions, I would listen long into the night to my parents' vitriolic objections to this love match.

Geoffrey and Laura argued, it seemed to me, all night, every night, from the moment they knew Jennifer was going until the morning she left. Recrimination, blame, insults about the couple and each other: they never stopped. Geoffrey's jealousy had caused a catastrophic personality change. His sense of humour deserted him entirely and he started to drink heavily. I was sharing a bedroom with them for some of the time, and would beg them in tears not to row, and, more than that, not to call Jennifer a tart and a fool. This kind of language was not unusual, but it was the way they talked, the way they shouted, the way they both drank five and six too many whiskies.

As Geoffrey got more and more drunk, he would become more and more objectionable, shouting so loudly that he set the dogs barking. This would be followed by Mother's shhh, which made him even more livid, and he would become violent, usually towards a table, but more than once towards her. It was a terrible time, a dark and sad time in the family: not kind, wise or loving. I was ashamed of my parents and their tawdry behaviour.

The hotel guests never complained, and, now that a date was set, the company grimly got through the next fortnight, waiting for the storm to blow over. But for me it was a time of great disillusionment. Both my parents were falling from the very high pedestal on which I had placed them, and Jennifer, who had been beside me always, was leaving.

The morning of Jennifer's departure came as a relief. None of us had slept a wink the night before: Jennifer, because she was crying; my parents because they were rowing, each blaming the other for the loss of their child. It was as if she were going away for ever, and in Geoffrey's mind that was what he had decided. Banishment was his punishment. 'I never want to see her face again,' he had yelled at Mother the night before.

And when we stood on the veranda that morning and Jennifer, red-eyed, threw her arms about his neck, her tiny shoulders shaking with sobs, he stood, stiff and straight, his arms plastered to his sides, looking ahead and silent, until I pulled her away from him and hugged her into the waiting taxi. The look of bewilderment on Shashi's face at this appalling behaviour is something I will never forget.

I watched the green Mercedes taxi drive away with my darling sister weeping in the back seat, and turned away with an aching heart and a feeling of confused unhappiness.

I've been going through some of your letters and filing them away in some vague attempt to keep in touch with you. There's a lot about Jennifer dying. Funny how real death numbs the senses: these letters are more moving now than in the fresh shock of her horrible death. Not that the funeral was any better – a gruesome experience if ever there was one. I remember it now as a kind of appalling dream.

It took place in a little chapel in Golders Green, but with no religious ceremony to go with it. A confused priest was unable to help as he was not allowed to be priest-like: Jennifer being agnostic, Shashi Hindu, my parents converted Catholics and me a converted Jew, none of us wanted to take responsibility for the wrath of the wrong god raining down from the heavens. So there we all were, early in the morning, except YoYo and Beula, who had refused to come, thank God.

It was misty and drizzling when the small coffin in cheap wood, covered in flowers and carried by her two sons, was placed on the plinth for the short, confused and unsatisfying ceremony. The chapel was packed, and among the crowd were some very well-known faces that I was surprised to see. The sense of grief and floods of freely flowing tears made up for the lack of occasion. The service, if you could call it that, consisted of my reading the sonnet 'Shall I compare thee to a summer's day?' and Geoffrey reading another sonnet followed by the last words she wrote, scrawled on a piece of paper and given to him at the hospital two days before she died: 'The readiness is all.' Quoting Shakespeare to the last.

I remember feeling glad that I had not gone to see her at the icebox place, where she had been dressed in red – a colour she never wore and one that did not suit her. And feeling sorry that we had been persuaded to go for the gold plastic coffin handles (all the better to burn) because in the event they simply looked like gold plastic. I laid a single rose on the coffin and stepped down to join the crowd of weeping mourners. Then, with Mozart's Concerto No. 21 heartbreakingly amped through the morning mist, a remote-control sent the coffin, flowers, handles and all wobbling off through a hole in the wall. As it disappeared, a skimpy green velvet curtain juddered over the coffin exit, for all the world as if we were in a magic show. And that was it for Joe public.

For the family, however, the fun had just begun. We were ushered backstage to observe the incineration, this being a vital part of Hindu custom. Being present at the moment of burning is spiritually important for the living and the dead, so Shashi had arranged for us to join Jennifer in what was to be her last journey.

We left the plush seats, the carved pews and beautiful stained-glass windows surrounded by flower arrangements, went into the vestry and from there through a little door into the 'reality zone'. This was a large oblong room, rather like a garage. The floor was littered with hammers and old tools stacked in boxes, rubbish bins overflowing with bits of wood, old plants, plastic cups, lengths of wire and cardboard.

Trying not to step on the planks of wood and debris on the floor, we picked our way to the far end of the room, led by the sweet and, by this time, perplexed priest to where Jennifer's coffin, now denuded of flowers, was perched on a metal trolley. Two garage mechanic types in overalls pushed it, with us following, round a corner to the wall with what must have been eight or ten oven doors at coffin height, reminding me chillingly of the gas chambers. The trolley and its passenger were pushed in front of one of the doors and, without a second's pause, one mechanic opened the door with a long steel pole, while the other shoved in the coffin at tremendous speed, using two huge metal chopsticks to guide it into the middle of the furnace, where it burst into flames.

Then, bang, the door was shut and it was all over. Jennifer was gone. We picked our way out slowly, and in my case unsteadily, over the rusty nails and planks of wood, saying 'thank you' as we went. To whom and for what? But we did. I can't remember what happened much after that except that it was cold and it was only September.

How very different it would have been at a Hindu ghat. In Bombay it would have been by the sea, the funeral pyre piled high with sandalwood and scented logs. The body, wrapped in a simple white cotton shroud and then adorned with jasmine, marigold and roses, would be placed by the menfolk gently on top of the pyre, then covered with perfumed oil and more flowers. Prayers would be said and the eldest son would light *the fire as the sun set on the same day that the person had died. There would be open, uninhibited tears of grief, and acceptance of the cycle of life and death. To some I know it seems a macabre way to end, but compared with the shyness and embarrassment evident in European culture, it seems preferable and certainly more healing.*

Jennifer had left the company and the strain continued for months. We went across the causeway to Johor Baharu and into Malaya. In Sibu matters came to a head between Geoffrey and Laura in what came to be known as 'the cheongsam episode'.

Generally, Mother's loyalty and devotion were astonishing. I never heard her criticize her husband in public and even though they rowed like cat and dog, they always made up and presented a united front. But while she was cool and composed on the surface, underneath there lurked a demon temper and a jealous temperament. She would brook no rival, and once marched up to a young actress and, in front of the whole company, told her in no uncertain terms that if she continued to 'make eyes at Geoff in that soppy manner', she would be sacked. In Malaya this side of her personality burst out again.

Geoffrey did have a tendency to frequent pubs and bars, and in Malaya bars come equipped with pretty girls with long black hair, exquisite figures and dazzling smiles. We were staying in some seedy hotel with an all-night bar and juke-box that seemed to be on automatic. Geoffrey started taking longer and longer over his nightcap, lingering in the bar with the ladies of the night who entertained the customers.

One night I was woken by great thuds coming from the next room, where my parents were having an almighty row. This then gave way to the sound of Mother crying. I knocked sheepishly on the door in my pyjamas and went in. I was told to go back to my room by a wild-looking Geoffrey, while Mother dashed into the bathroom, but not before I saw that her nose was pouring with blood. I learned the next morning, after a sleepless night, that, fed up with Geoffrey's behaviour, Mother had somehow procured for herself a skintight, red satin cheongsam. Squeezed into this dress, slit up to her waist, and wearing her hair piled up on her head, black eyeliner to emphasize her already oriental features, and red lipstick, she tottered down to the bar on high heels. Perching herself on a bar stool, she proceeded to smoke from a long cigarette holder and ply her trade. Geoffrey, being of an equally jealous disposition, blew several gaskets and ended up giving her a bloody nose.

For a few months after that he became her slave and, when he complained or started his shouting, she would simply touch her nose and give him a look, and he would stop in his tracks. They continued to row – it was a way of life for them – but she had made the point that he had gone too far. She was devoted to him and could play him like a harp when she felt so inclined.

This unseemly episode seemed to be one more step in the decline of the company. Things had changed, both within and without, and the good fortune and high spirits that had been so characteristic of everything we did seemed to be evaporating.

In the beginning the company was eccentric, but extraordinary and brave, and the work surprisingly good. We filled a unique position, with Geoffrey and Mother regarded almost as national treasures. As travelling players we had no caste and no position in the society of the land. We seemed to cross the divide. We were neither burrah sahibs nor missionaries, but an impoverished bunch dividing our time between posh public schools, army clubs and small educational establishments, with the odd foray into local cinemas and theatres.

We criss-crossed India, trailing with us costumes, pets and

servants, prepared for anything from dak bungalows to dormitor-ies in schools, or, as often happened, spare hospital beds – insects, snakes and scorpions were in plentiful supply. We experienced the glory of India, the glamour and the wealth, but were not the privileged. We were mostly on the borderline of poor, living as the people did, rather than as visitors. We belonged. We could fit in anywhere and the touring never stopped. There was no such thing as a holiday; we stopped only when the bookings failed, there were riots, or the schools were shut.

But as the years of touring continued, so did the world. The climate in India began to change, movies and television began to take the place of theatre, travelling became more expensive and, as the tourist industry grew, it became less possible to live on the shoe-strings we were used to. Actors wanted a proper wage, and the links Geoffrey had with the past were dying out. The modern world that Geoffrey and Laura had left behind in Europe was beginning to intrude. Geoffrey sustained the com-pany until Jennifer left – after that it was a slow but definite decline. The numbers were cut back and we entered a truly shabby period. Nothing seemed to work well, and I was growing up and straining at the family leash.

I found time for day-dreaming and falling in love. This I started to do regularly, whenever we stayed long enough for me to see the same boy twice. It was always a rushed job. Sometimes notes would be exchanged or, blushing up, I would accept a chocolate or a book, but these early encounters were always entirely platonic, until a boy in Coimbatore held my hand for a brief clammy minute. After that I became desperate for contact. But our moving on always seemed to coincide exactly with the escalating ardour, and so I remained very innocent of boys and what they were until I was an overblown fourteen. Then I fell headlong down the bottomless pit of first love.

His name was Janis Duler and he was the catch of the bunch: a champion swimmer, tall, blond, perfectly tanned and very James Dean in a smouldering, Yugoslavian way. His father, an engineer, was based in Bombay with his wife and two sons. Janis was the elder brother and both went to a Càthedral Boys' School along with a group of boys whose parents were posted in Bombay.

At Breach Candy swimming club he was the leader of a teenage group of revellers, a mixed bunch of visiting foreign kids, Indians and immigrants. *Summer Holiday* was showing at the Regal Cinema and the pop stars of the moment were the Everly Brothers; the mood was for sunbathing, listening to the latest LP, going to beach parties and falling in love.

Janis sent his younger brother to ask me if I'd date him: I was over the moon. We did a lot of heavy, moody dancing, and the next day, after school, he gave me his ID bracelet. For one headspinning month I 'went steady'. We swam and picnicked at the pool and beach. Everything was perfect – until one night, when I failed to come up to the expected standards of passionate abandon. My convent school upbringing and Mother's puritan ideas about sex let me down; at the crucial moment I went into retreat. After some fatal fumblings, he drove off, never to return.

The next day a note was delivered. Would I send back his ID, please? Mortally wounded, I wrapped it in a scarf he had given me, and back it went. I sobbed into my T-shirt for a week and listened non-stop to 'Only the Lonely'.

Meanwhile, the backlash from Jennifer's departure continued. It would be a year before the family was reconciled to the fact that she had gone.

She married Shashi in Bombay in a Hindu wedding, sur-rounded by Shashi's relatives and friends. She wore the red bridal costume, complete with mendhi on her hands, and her head was covered in the duputha of a modest bride. The ceremony was traditional, with flowers and chanting, rituals and blessings. She was deeply in love with her new husband and with India, and she felt a profound sadness that her own parents, who had brought her to this land with such joy, should withdraw their good wishes for her marriage.

I think that I would never have forgiven them, but she knew them well and hoped that time would help. And she was right: it did. In the meantime we were a depleted bunch adrift in Singapore. We managed to limp on with various cut versions of the texts. I played some of Jennifer's parts – very badly – and Sonja took over the rest. The nature of the company was always to be positive, and it wasn't long before there was singing and joking at the fit-ups again. But Geoffrey would remain in his taut, strained mode for a while yet.

The lack of funds became acute, to such a point that when Brian read about a talent show at one of the big cinemas with a cash prize for the most dreadful monster, he and Coral decided to enter. She went as the Hunchback of Notre-Dame and won first prize and he went as Dracula and came second – all this with make-up and costumes constructed from our show. Coral was the most convincing, with her putty nose, humped back, big old boots and blinded eye, while Brian made a very dashing Dracula, with silvered hair, white gloves and fangs that dripped stage blood. They donated their winnings, some several hundred dollars, to the company, and the hotel bill was paid – this was the kind of loyalty that Geoffrey engendered. But we still did not have enough for the fare back to India.

Undaunted, Geoffrey organized a show at a small concert hall. How he got it for free I don't know, but we painted posters and drew leaflets and walked the streets of Singapore for the next few days, handing them out to unsuspecting pedestrians. The show was *She Stoops to Conquer* and the admission was advertised as free. To everyone's surprise we played to a full house, then, to the audience's surprise, Geoffrey made a speech at the end of the play, declaring that we were stranded and needed our return fare. Hats would be passed round by members of the cast and we would be most grateful for any contributions, however meagre. It was at moments such as this that I wished to belong to a completely different set of parents. Humiliation sat heavily on my shoulders. I did not see the charming side of the situation, nor Geoffrey's ingenuity in organizing it and bravery in dealing with it.

The audience was very generous, but not quite bountiful enough for us to get to India. So we went to Borneo instead. Travelling deck, we loaded our costumes and luggage into the hold and took our place on the covered deck, where there were rows of marked out and numbered spaces about the size of a single bed each. This was where we were to sleep.

When we boarded to take up our allotted deck space, the purser, with a worried look, summoned the captain. With a great deal of embarrassment and mopping of sweaty brows, it was explained that we could not board after all. There was a rule from olden days, still in existence for the steamship company, which stated that white men may not travel deck or cargo.

After the usual explosion from Geoffrey, a compromise was reached. He would pay for a single cabin, and we would all have to use its lavatory and bathroom; meals were to be taken in the dining room, not with the other deck passengers, standing in line for rice and fish in the galley. Mother would take the cabin and we would be fed with dignity – as Europeans, not as riff-raff – but at different mealtimes from the 'real' passengers. Yet again we were the misfits. But by now I thought it was fun and, apart from eating at very weird times, the passage was a happy one.

The weather was warm and, apart from waking up with damp hair from the sea spray, it was ideal. This sort of adventure I loved and I joined wholeheartedly in the fun of it.

After a typically eventful tour of Borneo and Sarawak, Geoffrey's good humour returned. He loved Sarawak; we played with some success and Poopsie, Brian, Sonja and Coral had a ball. We were once more in a land that was starved of entertainment, and valued for turning up at all. We were overwhelmed by the sheer beauty of the place: the mountains and waterfalls, volcanic lakes, rivers and jungles, unspoilt and undiscovered. It was a happy time and a healing time. We finally returned to India refreshed.

Then Jennifer had her first child, a glorious little boy. She brought him to Delhi to meet his grandparents and the rift between them was healed overnight. It was not long before she joined the company again and played in some of the shows, although her return was only temporary. Shashi also joined us for the odd guest appearance, driving the schoolgirls into a frenzy. He was fast becoming one of the biggest stars of the Bombay talkies, with producers begging him to take on additional films and work double and triple shifts.

With Kunal, Jennifer's little son, we all went to Hong Kong for a tour of the schools. It was a tremendously good visit and some money was made – enough to pay back some loans and continue, yet again, on to the next place. We returned to India, then to Malaya, we toured India once again. Some of the old rhythm was returning.

But another departure was upon us. Brian had finally decided, after nearly nine years, that it was time to go home. His departure was one of the saddest for Mother, who had come to rely on him both on and off the stage, and we missed his quiet presence, even more than the ebullient characters who had left before him.

His small handsome face always had a calming effect, and after all the years he left a gap that was never quite filled.

He had hardly changed throughout the years he had been with us, keeping his Peter Pan good looks, his thick brown hair and short-sighted blue eyes. He was invariably smartly dressed, and his deep voice, booming out of his small frame, was often a surprise. A few months before leaving, he had fallen over a small step in the dark one night in Darjeeling. His hip was cracked, and we had to leave him behind in Mount Herman School, unable to travel. He returned to us some weeks later, and we said goodbye. His lovely blue eyes were sad, and now, with years of Indian experience behind him, he walked towards the plane that would carry him home. The slight limp that was to be the legacy of his life in India was scarcely apparent as he boarded. He had first joined Shakespeareana when I was a toddler, and his leaving marked a sea change. With Brian gone, and Jennifer only visiting, the company was never to be the same again.

But we were soon to be joined by someone else, who was to take Brian's place as friend and colleague.

On a sweltering summer night in Cochin during a performance of *Candida*, we noticed three white sahib types in dinner jackets in the front row. It turned out that they were British tea planters from the plantations ninety miles away and had ridden all the way over on motorbikes to see the show, dressed in black tie, as it was an evening performance. One of them, Ralph Pixton, was very keen on the theatre and came again and again during our stay, always the ninety miles by motorbike – though not always in dinner jacket!

He was tall and very pukka sahib, had a great sense of humour and an even greater taste for adventure. He had no formal drama training, but asked if he could join us. Geoffrey could never resist people who offered themselves to him, so Ralph gave his notice to his plantation bosses – who thought he had had too much sun – sold off his belongings, and joined us in Poona a month later. Four weeks after that he was playing Polonius, Antonio, Oberon and Petkoff, with a few more parts in rehearsal.

Ralph was extremely laid back and suffered from none of the nerves and neuroses common to most actors. While this easy-going trait undoubtedly stood him in good stead for our vagabond lifestyle, it gave him a bumpy ride at the outset.

The crisis came one evening during *Hamlet*. I was a pubescent Ophelia, to my father's ageing Hamlet. It was not one of the company's most artistic productions, but Ralph, on his second night as Polonius, was doing fine. All went well until the scene where Polonius is supposed to be hiding to spy on the couple, and Hamlet demands of Ophelia, 'Where's your father?' Although Polonius doesn't enter here, he is supposed to be listening. By some sixth sense, Geoffrey knew the man was 'off', which indeed he was . . . Ralph was in the dressing room, oblivious to his calling.

Without much ado, Hamlet dropped Ophelia's hand, strode into the wings and, at the top of his voice, shouted, 'Where the bloody hell are you? You stupid fat fart . . . you're FIRED!' He then made a flourishing re-entrance and, looking daggers into my eyes in case I laughed, continued with 'Let the doors be shut upon him, that he may play the fool nowhere but in's own house. Farewell.'

Geoffrey's fury was spent by the next scene, and Ralph, being Ralph, forgave him the public insult and settled down to become one of the most dedicated members of the Firm for the next three years.

CHAPTER FOURTEEN

SHAKESPEARE WALLAH

For some reason, this week you are under a pink bedspread, but I hardly think, at this stage of events, it's an issue worth raising! I feel today that I can't stand this for you any longer. And yet your eyes sometimes seem understanding and at peace, your cheeks are rosy and your skin warm. And although there is no language, even body language, which seems the saddest thing of all, sometimes while I hold your one good hand, you clasp mine tight, sometimes you pull away, always at random, a seemingly meaningless gesture of moving the arm that works. Or you turn your head to look, then, just as I get to an interesting bit of gossip, your eyes shut. The dead arm twisted and limp, still breaks my heart as I hold it. I don't want to be like this with my children – I don't want them subjected to this confusion.

To mourn or not to mourn. That is the bloody question. Are you dead or not? You are in a way, though of course not physically. I look and think of you now as someone other than the father I had before. This is a shadow of what was, merely a shell, a precious shell that must be treated with care, but an empty shell. You have long since gone. You came into this world with all the paraphernalia that you need now: the liquid food, the nappies, the nursing. It was done then in celebration. How very sad that when it ends up the same way, at the end of a paltry eighty-eight years, it is done out of pity.

Should I take you to the top of a mountain and let you go in the open air, like the Red Indians? But what about the nappies? Here nappies are laid out in neat bundles at the foot of the bed, while the old crumpled people, who were once in charge of their own destinies, crouch over radios or stare blankly at television screens, surrounded by flowers and get well cards. Photographs of loved ones comfort them from the small bedside tables, and mushy food is lovingly prepared and spoon-fed three times a day, until it's bedtime, and the pink for girls, blue for boys, candlewick bedspreads are turned down for the night.

I met Ismail and Jim when Shashi was working on his first film for Merchant Ivory: *The Householder*, a beautiful and delicate film, shot in black and white on a tiny budget. It was to be the beginning of lifelong friendships and partnerships between Ismail Merchant, James Ivory and the writer Ruth Prawer Jhabvala, with Jennifer and Shashi coming into the group as part family, part partners in crime. Jennifer dragged me along with her to any social meeting when I was in Bombay, so I got to be one of the gang.

Passing me a damp, salted crisp (called 'chips' in India), Ismail leaned across Jennifer and said, 'One day I will put you in my film, Foo . . . wait and see.' The matinée was about to start and we were in the large air-conditioned Metro Cinema in Bombay – there for the air-conditioning, I think, as much as for the film. Packets of Ashok's chilli chips and ice-cold bottles of Coca-Cola were being handed round. The thin paper straws always gave up before the last sip by sticking together at the end and the chips were soggy from the humid Bombay climate, but the air-conditioning cooled wonderfully, and just going to the cinema was an event.

'Here, take more chips,' insisted Ismail. 'Take, take!' He shook the packet. 'I will make this girl a superstar,' he said again, with his infectious laugh. 'You will see.' The lights dimmed and I thought no more about it. Ismail was full of fantastical ideas, and I was fourteen, in the middle of my first love affair – though 'affair' was scarcely the right word – and I did not care to be a film star. Ismail's flattery was taken as the quip I was sure it was meant to be. His sweeping statements were already an ongoing joke and we would tease that he was to be the next Cecil B. De Mille. Little did we know how we would eat our words. At this point he was a bouncy boy with a lot of energy and enormous ideas to go with it, but he was just our Ismail and no one took him seriously. Only time would tell how powerful his methods of persuasion would become.

Ismail, Jim and Ruth made a formidable team. Ismail was the loud, ebullient one, Jim the intellectual, witty one and Ruth the silent, brilliant one, who would sit observing everything and occasionally making a comment that would have us bent double with laughter. Jim and Ismail would have glorious slanging matches and Ruth was always there, quiet and astute. The meals together became a binding force. Ismail would cook, or we would go to his father's house in downtown Bombay, where his mother would prepare food fit for the gods in her tiny kitchen, but, in true Muslim fashion, would never come out to join the guests.

Being with the group became the highlight of my visits to Bombay. Much younger, but included, I remember talk of making a film, to be called perhaps *Shakespeare Seller* or *Shakespeare Wallah*, but never took it seriously. They were to use some of Geoffrey's early diaries and journals. Ruth would write the screenplay, my parents would play the two leading actors who had a company touring India, and I would play the young love interest, Lizzie, who falls for an Indian playboy, but is sent off to England to make a career for herself.

It was to be shot in black and white, on the shortest of shoe-strings. I was to be paid forty rupees a week for the duration of filming – the equivalent of about two pounds nowadays. I don't remember agreeing to do it; in much the same way as I started working for Geoffrey, I was there, the work needed to be done, and so I did it. I was a very teenage teenager, spinning with self-absorption. Ambition of any kind was to come much later.

Jennifer and Shashi went to New York for *The Householder* opening and sent back letters and photographs of the buzzing capital. They stayed at the Ritz and visited all the sights. Jim and Ruth had a small apartment in the same block as Greta Garbo. I was agog. 'Do you ever see her?' I inquired. 'Oh, yes. Sometimes. Rarely,' drawled Jim. 'What is she *like*?' I asked. 'Well . . . she's like . . . Greta Garbo,' he replied. 'An older Greta Garbo.'

I was still touring away from Bombay most of the time, but in between a contract was set up, a script written, and dates set to start shooting. There did not seem to me to be anything unusual or especially exciting about any of this. I had always been given a part, told to learn the lines and get on with it as best I could. I expected to do the same in this case.

The contrast, then, of Jim's gentle and observing direction came as something of a surprise. He took notice of what I was doing and guided me to make choices. I was not used to this approach – in fact I was not used to any approach at all. I had been thrown on stage to get on with it and work out if it was all right in front of an audience. Jim's painstaking direction was very impressive, but a little unnerving at first. I already knew the brilliant cameraman, Subrata Mitra, from *The Householder* days. He was slower at lighting than anyone on earth, but he had worked all his life for Satyajit Ray and was a brilliant artist. I nicknamed him ToTo, a name that stuck, and we became very close.

His care and talent helped my little round face, and Jim's

wisdom my performance, but for all my small concerns I still wafted carelessly through most of the filming. I had known these people for years; they were family, not employers, and the rest of the cast consisted of my parents, my brother-in-law and a few actors that I knew, so there were no nerves to be overcome. It was not until right at the end of filming that I became aware of how much this film would mean to me. Although I had enjoyed every minute of it, I had not taken it quite seriously enough. Then came the last few scenes, where Lizzie was to break down. This called for real acting and real tears – no messing about here – and I realized on my way to the location that morning that I really cared very much indeed. I wanted to act well, but most of all I wanted to please Jim and prove to him, in this scene if in no other, that he had been right to cast me.

It was a little late in the day, but I think I got in under the net. And I discovered something I had not known I could do: I could cry real tears if required. It was a trick, or a talent, call it what you like, that my mother had acquired, Geoffrey not at all, and Jennifer only on occasions. Years later, when I was in the Actors' Company, Ian McKellen asked me how to do it, and I couldn't tell him. I was worried for years that he thought I'd deliberately kept this trick a secret, when the truth was that I had no idea how I made myself cry.

The filming was fun and every day there was a new disaster or triumph. The budget was so tight that we hardly had a schedule; we just adapted to the weather and would race around the hillside below Simla, hunting for a cloud to do the cloud scene. If it rained, we shot the rain scene – and so on. Ismail would shout 'Action!' at the top of his voice if there was so much as a ten-minute break or pause; and the ding-dong game of his shouting commands at Jim, and Jim ignoring him completely, began.

It could not have been a happier unit, and after filming we

celebrated my eighteenth birthday, with Ismail cooking curry supper for the entire cast and crew. We were staying in a small hotel in Kasauli, a tiny hill station below Simla that still retained its old British Raj retirement home charm. There were villas named 'Stratford Cottage' and 'Honeysuckle Home' and 'Kismet' along the lanes, and the old club house still had Colonel this and Major that listed as members in the dusty billiard room.

Staying at the hotel was the young daughter of the Holz family, who used to run the Cecil Hotel in Delhi. She was on her way back to England to marry David Lean, who had met her when he was filming in Agra the previous year. The circle of life was to loop with me years later, when I went to a birthday party for her husband David Lean in the company of his old friend and colleague Robert Bolt. Sitting next to her at dinner that night, I thought how strange life was. Here were these two young women, both brought up in India, with these two much older men, both extraordinary in their work – and we had met all those years ago on a hillside, because her parents did hotels and mine did acting.

After two months the film was nearly finished and the last shot was taken on a dusty trunk road outside Bombay. The crew were down to cameraman, make-up chap, Jim, Ismail, Shashi and me, the jeep we travelled in was the set, and we only had enough raw film for two takes on each set-up. The small scene was completed in an hour and a half, and with hugs and relief we finished filming.

We set off back to the city in the jeep piled high with camera and make-up, costumes and picnic box. Shashi was soon back to his usual routine of filming day and night on several block-busters at once. Ismail flew to New York to set up another project, Jim went into editing, and I returned to Geoffrey, Mother and what was left of our company.

For the next six months or so I continued to tour with them. We visited Malaya again, Borneo, and then went on to Japan, returning, as always, to India. I was restless, waiting for something to happen, though I didn't know quite what. I was biding my time, growing away from the security that touring had given me, doing the props, setting up and moving on in a daze, performing our now tacky, edited versions of the shows that gave our audiences a 'taste' of Shakespeare – when once it had been a banquet!

Finally we returned to Calcutta and to one of our regular and favourite hotels, the Fairlawn. It was a colourful and lively place, owned and operated by Mrs Smith, whose family had kept the place for forty years. You entered through the garden and open verandah full of green and red plants to come upon a bright, spotless home from home. There were cosy loungers covered in cushions, brightly painted furniture, flowers, patterned drapes and interesting knick-knacks. Full board was compulsory and all the rooms had baths, which made it very popular. Reservations in advance were necessary, unless they knew you.

It was in this much loved haunt that I learned one day that my wait was over. I got a wire from Jim and Ismail: the film had been accepted at the Berlin Film Festival and, after that, would go to the London Film Festival. Would I, could I, get away and join them there? If so, I was to wire back. Shashi would pay my fare, they would pay for the hotel, all they needed to know was that I could make it.

Before telling Geoffrey, I wired back that I would be there. Then I turned to face the music. No sooner had the expected repercussions started about my leaving, than I fainted dead away under the dining room table. Coming to in the bedroom, I remember thinking to myself that this was how Jennifer coped so often. This is not like me, I thought. I have never fainted in my life. I shall stand up and be a man, and fight this fight in a vertical position! But no sooner had I got to my feet than my legs gave way again. My head was aching and I started to sweat. Mother was fussing about, looking worried, and there was no sign of Geoffrey.

'You're not well, darling. You're not well,' Mother repeated again and again. 'I'm all right,' I insisted – the fear of being unable to go to Europe in four weeks was already beginning to dawn on me. 'I'll be fine, it's just the upset,' I argued. 'Or I must have eaten something funny.' But I had not eaten anything unusual and by evening my temperature was 105° and I was wafting in and out of a not unpleasant haze. Once the doctor told me what it was and that I should be well in two or three weeks, I gratefully succumbed to the illness that had made it impossible to argue about leaving or anything else.

I had contracted paratyphoid, and concern for my health diluted the concern over my departure. Geoffrey came into my bedroom once a day and laid a shy hand on my brow. He didn't speak much, just did a lot of grunting. Mother nursed me with flannels and sweetness until the fever passed some two weeks later.

By that time the tickets had arrived, the date had been set. Jennifer would meet me in Bombay, arrange some clothes and fly with me to Berlin. I was on my way.

CHAPTER FIFTEEN

HOMEWARD BOUND

Fairlawn Hotel, Calcutta
11 June 1965

Darling Fu,

We heard the plane pass over – it was good to know you
are on your way to Jennifer and the children and that
Shashi and Jennifer will be going with you. What joyful
preparations Jennifer will be up to for your grand
experience!

But, oh Fu – you can't imagine how much we miss you!
Daddy and I took Chook for a walk, and he couldn't
understand why he couldn't go into your room, so I got
the key and showed him you weren't there. We'll look
after him for you, he'll be all right . . .

I meant to give you some money, darling, but alas I
know it will be needed to go towards the hotel bill.
'Twas ever thus! I don't expect you to write long
letters, darling, but just short ones . . . often! Be
good, do well.

All my love, Mummy

I felt sick. The long bout of paratyphoid had left me weaker than I realized. And despite my protestations to Geoffrey and our blazing rows, now that I was finally on my way from Calcutta to my new life alone, the prospect of the journey to Europe without my parents' blessing seemed less and less inviting.

The plane touched down with a bump at Bombay's Santa Cruz Airport. Walking on to the hot windy tarmac, I felt faint. I could see Jennifer waving to me from the visitors' balcony in the distance. I ran the last few yards to meet her and she hugged me to her. 'Darling, *darling*. I am so excited for you!' She seemed a little hysterical. 'I've started collecting things for your wardrobe,' she went on. 'I've got samples and swatches for you to look at. The posh tailor at the Taj will have to make the clothes, our little family dersie [dressmaker] won't be able to follow the *Vogue* patterns I'm using. I've already ordered the material for a suit, and I've got some wonderful raw silks which we can get embroidered and beaded for the première gowns – one cream, with seed pearls, perhaps, and the other black with a heavy gold on the bodice? I hope the tailor can manage in time, we only have a few days. You fly out on Sunday . . . Shashi and I will follow two days later, so I can bring anything that isn't finished.' She rattled on about shoes being 'a problem' and handbags being 'easy'. Mahammed, her driver, collected my suitcase and, piling into her small white car, we set off for her apartment in the city. 'You've lost weight, Foo. You don't look well, darling. And you smell funny. It must be the remains of the fever . . . I'll put you on my juice diet – that should help.'

Her love for me was always maternal. She took my hand and continued: 'Anyway, as I was saying, it will be a rush, but I'm sure I can manage to get you fitted out with the basics. Shoes are being copied from some of mine I got in Paris last year (isn't it lucky we have the same shoe size?) – I mean, I can't let you go off to a film festival in sandals and a cheap cotton dress, can I?' This babble continued all the way into town. No mention was made of my parents, or of their hostile reaction to my leaving. There was no need to explain my hurt and confusion. She knew already; she had been here herself a few years earlier. Besides, I was too numb and she was too excited for either of us to want to discuss what was for both of us a painful wrench.

The next few days were spent in a flurry of fitting. Silks and accessories, handbags, shoes and gowns – only the very best would do, all paid for by Jennifer. In this very typical fashion she was generously helping me to leave my parents and India with some style and confidence, helping me to step away from the family and on to the stage in England. She was helping me to gain something she had wanted for herself. She hated the term 'housewife' and the decision to give up her work haunted her all her life.

But for all Jennifer's valiant efforts, this particular little frog could not be kissed into a princess. 'I wish I was pretty,' had been my mournful cry as a child. 'I wish I was pretty, like Fufu.' By the time I was due to leave for Berlin, Fufu had done all she could. The juice fast had helped: I no longer looked ill or smelt funny. My cases were packed with tissue paper to protect the new clothes. I boarded the plane to Germany wearing the new green travelling suit with a cream silk blouse and tottering on high heels.

But I was under no delusions. I knew that the transformation had not quite 'taken' and that I appeared, to say the least, eccentric. My body was still scrawny from the typhoid, but illness had not altered the shape of my face, which remained positively plump. My hair was long, dark and unstyled. I wore far too much black kohl around my eyes in a vain attempt to look as doe-like as the Indian film stars. My speech was most definitely tarnished with a lilting Indian accent. I hadn't a clue about what was hip, in dress or attitude. The suit so lovingly made for me was too big and at least three years out of date; the many bangles I wore placed my taste very firmly on the bazaar side of the street. Nevertheless, armed with my new wardrobe and staggering in my badly made shoes, I was prepared to have a go.

What a weird little person I was.

At eighteen I had already had ten years' experience working, but had never gone for a job interview or been properly employed outside the family. I could hold my own with princes and heads of state, but was tongue-tied with my peers. I spoke two languages (albeit one of them Hindi, and of little use). And although I knew the major works of Shakespeare and Shaw by heart and had a good working knowledge of the classics, I could not spell for toffee.

My nature was outwardly sweet and a bit fey, but this masked a will of iron and a selfish determination to succeed at all costs. I had never seen a live play performed by professional actors, apart from Indian shows and those of my father's company. And here I was, fully intending to become a leading actor on the British stage. This bundle of contradictions boarded the plane knowing too much already, and not enough at all.

I don't remember the flight to Berlin. I slept most of the way. A car met me at the extraordinarily clean airport and whisked me off to an even cleaner four-star hotel. I could not believe the lack of refuse in the streets, the swept-naked pavements, the roads that were smooth and pothole-less. The air itself seemed to have been sanitized. A severe culture shock was taking place.

At the hotel James and Ismail had already checked in. Madhur Jaffrey, the Indian actress who was in the film, was joining us later. I had a shower and joined the 'team' in the lobby. I had not seen Jim or Ismail since we had finished the film, months before, and, seeing them again, I suddenly felt safe.

'Foo, you look wonderful,' cried Ismail. 'Come . . . we are going to your first press conference.' The days that followed were crammed with activity. Two or three films were seen in a day, with lunches, press calls, meetings, dinners and premières. There were film stars all over the place, along with models and critics. No one paid attention to me, and I was happy to tag along, silently absorbing this brave new world. Every now and then Ismail would drag me from a corner and shove me into a group of journalists, saying, 'You must meet our STAR . . . Why don't you take her picture? You don't understand! This girl is going to be a big star, you mark my words. Forget Julie Christie!'

Knowing Ismail so well, these extravagant statements did not convince me – or anyone else for that matter. But I loved him for making them. The time between functions was limited, but we managed to see the Berlin Wall, which did not shock me, and some raunchy nightclub acts that did. Although the days were full of fun and jokes, and the camaraderie between us all, once Jennifer and Shashi arrived, was strong, both my clothes and my emotions were at odds with the times, and I was still not at ease in this new and rarefied atmosphere.

The days of first-class travel and visiting princes' palaces had taken place when I was young; the last years in India had been a financial struggle, and anything but luxurious. We never seemed to have any money but, in India, that did not seem to matter. Now I was in Berlin and didn't have any money, and it mattered a great deal. I was living among people who did: there were film stars all over the place, limos and galas and millionaire types flaunting their wealth. I felt like a little beggar girl who was being shown life the other side of the city wall. Eliza had been taken out of the gutter and was being paraded at the tea party, and the joke was that I couldn't speak 'proper' either!

And even though I was the same colour as those around me, I felt very foreign. I had no feeling of coming back to my roots. I missed the squalor, the animals roaming in the streets, the noise, even the filth. This place was too *clean*, and the food too tasty. Something was wrong here. It didn't feel real.

I loved the hotel and the room service, however. The flowers on the trays, the white towels and deep bubble-filled baths were a wonderfully new experience. This I could get used to. If only I could stop feeling as if I had come from outer space, stop reacting with surprise at the efficiency and speed of things, I might perhaps grow to like this world.

I tried to convince myself, but at the end of each day I collapsed into my large, down-covered bed, eating the chocolates that were laid on the pillow by the maid and promising myself, I can go home if I don't like it . . . I can always go home. I would dream of railway journeys, of palm trees and vast horizons, rocking myself to sleep as if I were still a child on a train, steaming across the dark plains of India. But I knew I must not give up. I would be in England the following week; then I would really know if I could stand it.

My spirits were not lifted when the awards for the festival were announced. The Best Actress Golden Bear was won by Madhur. At the end of this hectic week, and feeling vulnerable and out of place, this was the first of many blows to push me gently into growing up. I loved and admired Madhur's beautiful performance in our film and I certainly had no delusions or expectations about winning myself. But I played the lead; she took a smaller role and it was, to all of us, so unexpected.

Jim and Ismail were extremely sweet to me as they took me into their room to 'break the news'. And, perhaps because they were so conciliatory, I felt more upset. Had I in some way let them and the film down? My emotions were hard to disguise, and, looking back, I hope I concealed them from 'M', as we called her, because she deserved her prize for her delicate work.

With Jennifer and Shashi, I said goodbye to Berlin. Wearing my green suit, now a little tight round the waist from a few too many frankfurters and cream buns, I was on the flight to London at last. The sky outside the window was grey, we bumped along the air corridor in the little plane, and for the first time since leaving Calcutta I missed my mother. She would have made me feel better about missing out on the award; she would have put a short, sharp stop to my sneaking feeling of jealousy. She would have understood why I felt as I did. She could see through my act of sweet little daft thing; she could understand my ambition and would smooth everything into perspective with a few soothing words.

We were nearly there. As the announcement was made – 'Fasten your seat-belts please, we will shortly be landing at Heathrow' – I secured my belt, smiled across the gangway at Jennifer and took a deep breath. Below I could see tiny fields and even tinier houses. It was grey and the fog was swirling past the window. I could see a winding river and some factory-like buildings. A 'green and pleasant land'? It didn't look it. Oh, well, I thought again, I can always go home. I pictured Mother's face, hoping to draw strength from her image. Then, taking my ambition in both hands, I prepared to set foot on my native soil.

My native soil was decidedly chilly. And Heathrow Airport a let-down after the immaculate efficiency of Berlin and Frankfurt. But the fact that all the natives spoke English was an immediate novelty – even though some of the accents were a cockney too dense for me to follow.

Jennifer, Shashi and I made our way to Paddington. Jennifer had decided to explore London at a later date and whisked me straight to my Aunt Beula's house in Olton.

'We have to take you to Elmhurst, Foo,' she insisted. 'I bet you don't remember any of it. It will seem much smaller than when you were last there and six years old.'

I did remember Elmhurst. I remembered the large lawned garden with a tall Victorian swing and the vegetable patch at the bottom behind the fir trees. I remembered the tall laburnum tree with the long green pods and I remembered the doctor coming and making me vomit so that I wouldn't die from poisoning when I had mistaken them for green pea pods and helped myself to a few.

I remembered the big white house, steps up to the door with the stained-glass windows, and the smell of lavender wood polish. But my memories were blurred and patchy.

My grandma was more vivid. She had short white curly hair, was plump, soft, kind and funny, and a great cuddler. She would sit me on her lap at every opportunity, and loved reading to us and playing games, 'Spot the Leg' being the favourite. She wore thick beige stockings with small, highly polished brogues. She would stuff a stocking and fix a shoe on to the end, then place the false leg in between the genuine articles or to the side of them as she sat in a chair. We would have to spot the false one – in one pull – or the game was lost. 'Spot the Leg' was a game that never ceased to amuse us. It would end in giggles of delight as my cousin and I tried to pull off the 'false leg'.

For the first five years of my life she was the perfect gran, and my visits to her at Elmhurst were the happiest of times. She would feed me and play with me in her warm home with the garden and swings outside, the large eiderdowned beds and flower-filled rooms.

But Grandma was not going to be there. She had died years before, when I was still a child in India. Mother had cried bitterly for a few days and there had been a terrible row, in which she remonstrated with Geoffrey: 'I should have gone to see her before she died. I asked you to send me, but all you ever think about is your precious company and the next date!' For once it was Mother who was shouting, and Geoffrey trying to be reasonable. He didn't join in, and let her rant and rave against him for days, until she had spent her sadness and her grief. I did not understand the meaning of death and Grandma was by then a distant figure to me, so I did not miss her at the time. Only when I returned to the house did I feel her loss.

The train from Paddington steamed into the countryside. Small hills, I thought, very small, and the horizon seemed unnaturally near. 'Oh, look, Foo, English cows!' shrieked Jennifer, as if I had never seen such a thing in my life before. The large brown and white animals fenced into small green fields looked like toys dotted perfectly about a miniature landscape. I realized how very far away I was from my bony, half-starved Indian bullocks, wandering freely about the streets and roads. And there were no people to be seen anywhere in this manicured landscape. Even in the remotest parts of India there are always people. It is impossible to go more than a dozen miles without coming across small village huts, farmers in the fields and children playing in the clearings. This tidy land with no sign of life was very odd to me.

The street lights were coming on as we approached Leamington Spa. Pressing my face against the cold glass of the window, I stared out as we passed rows and rows of tiny houses, washing blowing in the wind in tiny yards. This is what Geoffrey had left behind; this is what he had hated. 'Small houses and small minds, they go together. The world is yours, but not if you live in a row of small houses!' 'Well, I won't then,' had been my reply. 'I will live in a great big one!'

We stopped for a while at Leamington Spa. Looking out on to the station as the fog settled, I began to remember being here before. I remembered the damp fog, I remembered the small houses seen from trains and buses, and I remembered not liking any of it very much.

I was getting decidedly gloomy, when an announcement was made that high tea was being served on the train. At this I brightened considerably. We made our way to the buffet car and I felt much more positive about everything after scones, toasted teacakes and strawberry jam.

We talked about the times in Elmhurst when I was small and we would share a bed up in the little bedroom at the top of the house. 'You'll love Beula, Foo,' enthused Jennifer, anxious to reassure me. 'She's just like Mother, except that she can cook. Shashi's a little in love with her, aren't you?' she teased. 'That woman is wonderful,' he responded. 'I wish I'd married her instead of you, and her cooking is the best in the world.' Shashi flirted his way into every woman's heart, and, as he sat opposite me in his beautiful, tailored suit, I felt very grateful to them for making this journey with me.

As the train pulled into Olton Station, however, my heart began to pound in the most alarming manner. I had been anything but excited on the journey, and although I was greatly looking forward to seeing my family, I felt shy and unsure of how I would cope with living here. But as soon as I saw the station sign OLTON I could hardly contain myself. I recognized the station! I could see the corner shop and the post office, just as they used to be.

The train squealed to a stop. I can't recollect how we got to the house, but, standing in the driveway on the gravel path, smelling the pine trees and the damp grass, the sense of coming home became a reality. I looked up at the first-floor bedroom window where I had been born. It was the same; nothing had changed in all these years. I was back among the smells of my childhood, the sounds of my childhood – the songs of particular birds, the distant hum of traffic. It was like suddenly hearing a song from the time of one's first love. Long-buried feelings flooded over me. Suddenly I wished my mother were by my side. This had been her home too.

'Your eyes were wide open and as big as saucers,' Mother used to tell me, rather too frequently. 'The night you were born your daddy was playing *White Cargo* at the rep. I was staying with Beula and Mother at Elmhurst. Two weeks before you were born I helped deliver Beula of a baby girl. The doctor was late and I was so big with you that I smashed the hand basin with a bucket, getting hot water. Then a fortnight later, in the next bedroom, you were born, and your eyes were as big as saucers – and wide open. I *know*.'

I would tease her that although I was born in Olton, I was really Indian, having been conceived in India on their last tour with ENSA. 'Foo, darling . . . oh, FOO!'

My mother's sister rushed down the steps of the house and hugged me to her as tightly as she could, and I felt in that moment as if I had never been away. Any fears about not feeling welcome and, worse, not feeling at home vanished in the space of that hug.

A week of festive pub-going and eating followed. I was to live at the top of the house in the same room I had shared with Jennifer. I was taken shopping, to the girls' night out in Solihull, and initiated into helping with the washing-up, something which, even at our most poverty-stricken in India, we never had to do. However far down the line we were, washing and cleaning was always done by someone lower. I found it most enjoyable, chatting with the women, tea-towel at the ready, or Fairy Liquid on the go. I became a dab hand at washing-up. Props I could do. It was getting a job I wasn't so hot at.

CHAPTER SIXTEEN

MADE IN INDIA

'But I can't even get an interview, let alone an audition, and I'll *never* get a job,' I wailed down the phone to Ismail in New York.

'Why are you so impatient, why don't you see this will take time, why don't you people LISTEN? Constantly I think of you and realize that it is hard and difficult for you to make approaches to people and nobody seems to take promises seriously . . . I have been in Losey's office many times to remind him to see you, but what can I do from here? Until the film is out and is shown to an agent who will send you on the rounds, it will be difficult. But I cannot understand why you are so impatient!'

'I'm impatient because I've been here now for months. I've written fifty letters, had ten replies, all saying "not interested", and I'm getting fatter by the minute on Beula's apple pies.'

Beula was the aunt from heaven. She welcomed me into her home, and if it had not been for her, feeding me apple pie and hope during that first dreadful year in England, I would have given up after a month.

'Be brave, Foo,' Ismail insisted. 'I will be coming over shortly. I will see you get the best agent in town. Everything will be fine, you'll see. You must *trust* me. I will see you soon.'

Letters were my lifeline during that year – letters from Jim and Ismail and my parents. In their different ways they kept me sane and kept me going. I wrote back every day to one of them, then waited impatiently for the post to bring a reply.

I wrote to Jim, who was in New York, asking when the film would be shown and complaining about the cold. He replied with typical good humour:

August 28, 1965

Dear Phoo

What a depressing picture! There you are huddling in the rain on some barbaric beach where nobody speaks English and there is nothing but melancholy sounds of wind and waves, birds, the creaking of peasants' cartwheels . . . I have just seen a short on Britain and Wales . . . that is where you are, isn't it? You must not stay there, it's very bad.

It isn't going to be a pushover for you, Phoo, at least not without the film to show. It would have been better to wait for a print of the film before applying yourself to the many who turned you down. The film has just gone through customs and as soon as I see that this print is alright I will order another one which will be dispatched to the British Film Institute for the London Festival and for you to show. First Robin Fox must see it, then you must contact him. Then Lindsay Anderson will see it. Ismail has been operated on and spent a week in hospital, but I wouldn't be at all surprised if he is in London to do the distribution in the next few months, so once he is there, he can help you. You know how good he is at that sort of thing.

. . . So please be patient and hold tight. I know
something must come of this.

Much love Jim

The next post brought one of the first lively letters from
Geoffrey:

Dear Jane and Foo
    You are a couple of bright buggers! I take you all
round the world to the most glamorous of places, and you
end up in Solihull!!!
    Personally, I'd rather be in Blackpool, all by
myself, with a few quid to dispense on oysters and stout
and other gay things!

Mother added a postscript:

Darlings, don't mind daddy . . . he just misses you! We
tried to shield you from the competitive world you
insist on joining, but anyway . . .

God Bless, Mummy

I didn't 'mind' Daddy, but his letters were sometimes a little
short on sympathy and my confidence was already pretty shaky
beneath my youthful show of self-assurance. I was secretly afraid
– afraid of not getting work, and even more afraid that if I did
I would be a total wash-out.

I pinned a lot of faith on the film coming to England and
showing people what I could do. Consequently, the next letter
from Bombay sent me reeling into the kitchen for a double
helping of apple pie.

Bombay, 30/7/65

My dear Foo

Yesterday we saw Shakespeare Wallah.

I am at a loss to see how it has been shown anywhere.
The story is incomprehensible, best bits cut out, worst
bits left in . . . two hours of unrivalled misery . . . an
insult to India.

The title is too apologetic to think of . . . who knows
what a 'Wallah' is if they are not told? At the end the
ship sails off backwards! Four people cannot carry a
coffin, your Ophelia is far too long, and why is that
silly scene of mine and Laura's left in when the rest is
cut? Without a doubt your sister is the best, the only
one who comes alive, a real pro.

This is not to say that you are not lovely. But you are
much better when you are scruffy and greasy. The last
two scenes are the best, the one with you and Shashi and
the one with you and me in the theatre. Of course, by
that time, Jim had grasped that people in the theatre
have guts.

But you are damn good, though Shashi is wasted. The
only shot worth seeing is the shot of him by himself,
when everyone else has gone to bed, a real winner. He
should go into films in English with foreign directors
who know how to exploit him.

You should be very glad that M got the award and not
you. Much harder for M now they will expect too much from
her. Jane should have got it, if anyone, she is such an
incredible actress. She acts with her brain and
therefore everything else works in unison.

We have absolutely no work. No one wants us at all.
Bombay is really horrid in the rain, houses are falling

down all over the place, one fell down just behind the
garage last night killing six people. Motor cars splash
and the servants chatter and people screech about booze
[Bombay was dry] and their many rupees . . . the city of
dreadful day.

   You say the film is being shown to an agency, so you
can get an agent . . . be careful of agents, they are not
to be trusted.

   We may come to England soon, no point in stopping here
any longer. Your mother and I had a vision once, we made
the vision come true . . . as near as any vision ever did
come true. And then . . . Maybe I should make a film. I've
had a wonderful training seeing Shakespeare Wallah.
Oh, and what about the music they swanked about so
much?? Bloody hell, it never stops! But I must.

                                                   Love G.

The music for the film was written and edited in by the great
Satyajit Ray, Jim's guru and adviser. It was one of the best things
about the film and was beautifully used. Not for the first time
in his life, Geoffrey was completely wrong! Five years later he
saw the film again. 'Bloody wonderful,' he said. 'I was wrong.'

   But he was not wrong about my hating the cold or about my
not fitting in. The first few months were torturous. The food
made me blow up, the weather made my hands and feet cold all
the time. I loved the family, the house, the comfort and being
made to feel so welcome, but, although I had been born in the
house, it was not my home. I had never polished a table that
wasn't a stage prop, and I had certainly never hung washing out
to dry. These things were fun at first, but no substitute for real
work. I appeared to be a native, but I knew nothing of the habits
of middle-class England in the sixties. All the English people I

had known were either mad actors, which didn't count, or burrah sahibs living the life of the Raj.

A young Indian girl arriving fresh from Bombay would be forgiven for taking too long to work out the change in pounds, shillings and pence. I just looked stupid. I could not get used to going 'up' to London, when it was clearly 'down' on the map. I could not relate to the orderly queuing system – such behaviour would be almost suicidal in the East. I had lived in a time-warp of protection, half fading British Raj, half forties theatre lore.

It was not just the money and manners that threw me – the morals were even more of a minefield, as I soon discovered.

'What about a goodnight kiss?'

'What about a goodnight kiss?' I thought to myself in horror. Had the boy gone mad? I had only met him three hours earlier. Surely he could not be serious.

'Um, err, I don't think so,' I mumbled, reaching for the door of the little sporty number he had parked in the darkened driveway.

'Oh, come on, don't be shy!'

He fumbled with my arm, pulling me back into the car.

'I'm really sorry,' I heard myself say in a prissy voice. 'I'm really sorry, but I don't know you well enough.'

I got out of the car feeling sick with embarrassment and lurched into the house.

That was my first encounter with the Swinging Sixties, and I was out of date. *Darling* was the latest hit film; the pill was being downed by the tonful; free pot, free love and freedom for the youth of today were all the rage, but I had been brought up in a very different culture. I could swear like a trooper with the company and I could listen to vulgar jokes too. But when it came to my behaviour, as a young girl I was purely Victorian.

At my first party in London I was asked if I smoked, and I replied only occasionally, and only Craven A.

It was sad really. I missed a lot of fun. It was not until I met my first husband, Drewe, that I let my guard down. Before that I was rather gauche, wittering on about getting a good night's sleep, or inventing a boyfriend in India – anything to avoid contact. Wide-eyed and amazed, I watched the 'with it' girls dating and sleeping with whomever they chose at the drop of a hat and the popping of a pill. Mother's morals had been firmly imprinted, and it took me a long time to catch up.

My parents went on tour, which lifted Geoffrey's spirits. His letters became more frivolous and full of wit again. He wrote from the S.S. *Maharajah*, describing their exploits and state of health: 'We are all incredibly tanned and fit! I hope you are enjoying the washing-up!' In a sense, his good humour and affection was harder for me to cope with than his brusqueness. The telegram he sent me for the first birthday that I ever spent away from my family filled me with homesickness:

25 SEPT 65
FELICITY KENDAL. ST BERNARDS RD OLTON. BHAM.
FARE WELL, THOU ART TOO DEAR FOR MY POSSESSING
HAPPY BIRTHDAY GEYO.

Jim's letter on the same occasion was a bit more heartening:

September 1965

Dear Phoo
    Happy Birthday. Now you are 19 and in one year you will become famous, think of that.
    Who would have thought of it, a year ago in Simla, as we rested after our labours at the Gaiety Theatre.

Jennifer says you have a ticket valid to New York. It
would have been marvellous to have had you there during
the film festival – you're a nit-wit for not telling me.
Why on earth didn't you say something? Why do you stand
on your pride? You still have to stand on some sort of
teen-cum-oriental form of special courtesy? Don't do
these things anymore.

Of course, you can't help it. You've lived in India so
long you've become de-westernized and a bit backward to
boot. You must have lessons in behaviour. Now, a proper
western girl would march right up and wave the ticket
under our noses and say: 'Look here . . . Good to New
York.' But you acted like a little Indian bride. Too
awful. Well, Losey and Lindsay Anderson and others like
that will knock this out of you and you will be brassy
and just a bit hard, and that will be good.

Love, Jim

The requests, demands, inquiries about my returning kept on
coming in varying forms. Mother would plead; Geoffrey would
make loaded suggestions:

My dear Foo,

Now this is only a suggestion and I am not trying to
bribe you or something like that. But if you would like
to come to Hong Kong, we will wait for you. Poopsie,
being Indian, has not got his passport. After six
months of trying it seems there is some hitch . . . So if
you could come and join us for the shows in Hong Kong let
me know definitely the dates and I will arrange flights
and bookings etc.

This was always his way: to promise travel when he had no way of paying for it. Once in Hong Kong, I knew for sure that I would have no return fare and only the prospect of further shows to try and pay my passage back to London. He added further pressure by suggesting that such a tour would not 'prejudice' my chances of work in London, but increase them, as 'managements are more impressed by people who have a job, than by people who want one' and concluded with a typically heavy hint:

> Anyway, let me know what you decide, and I hope it will
> be the best for you.

Sitting in Solihull with no prospects of a job, the film not yet opened (and scorned by Geoffrey anyway), I felt keenly the impact of his insinuations about the dubious wisdom of my move. No doubt he was still reeling from my desertion and had convinced himself that he was acting in my best interests, but I felt his lack of support to be tactless and hurtful – and there would be times over the coming years when it would grow more tactless and hurtful still.

I did manage to keep in touch with the reasons I had come to England, however, courtesy of Jennifer and Shashi, who took me to London to see some inspiring shows, one of which was Olivier's *Othello*.

This was a play, along with *The Dream* and *The Merchant*, that I knew well – I could recite great chunks of it by the time I was seven. It was one of my favourite plays, and I remember reading it in tears during my teens. I had only played Bianca once or twice, when we were short of an actress, but I loved it dearly.

I must have written to Geoffrey describing the production in London, and he replied with enthusiasm:

Dear Foo

   I note what you say about Olivier . . . you know I have
an idea that he is right. You see, if you analyse Othello
without any preconceived notions, you will find that he
is not such a wonderful 'hero' after all. 'Noble moor'
may be said in sarcasm, the list of characters was not
written by Shakespeare you know! Othello is really a
bit of a pompous ass, together with being a bit of a
fool. He is a professional soldier, a mercenary and a
foreigner. Colour is a great thing to him, rather like
it is here. He has a streak of one-upmanship which is
most unpleasant. I, together with all my predecessors,
have glorified him, because of being mesmerized by the
words. But that is not always right; and I really
believe that Olivier may have got the right idea . . .
Actors are very clever, but few can resist a glorious
line.

   Now Scofield is good! I saw him years ago as Marlow in
She Stoops at the Birmingham Rep. He was a very young
man, and it was obvious then.

Reading letters like this was very cheering. It was like being
back at home and talking about the theatre as we always did,
and it was as if the distance and disagreement had not come
between us: we shared a common passion.

Many years later I was to play Desdemona to Scofield's Othello
in Peter Hall's production at the National Theatre. And in a few
months' time I was to go through the agony of auditioning for
the great Olivier. But, of course, I didn't know any of this, which
is just as well, since I would have taken the next plane home if
I could have foreseen it.

Before long Jennifer and Shashi had to return to Bombay, and now I was on my own. I carried on writing endless letters hoping for an interview or a meeting with an agent.

Dear Phoo

I wish I could come to London, but I can't, we just don't have the money.

Ismail will be there, so I hope the film will help get you work. Don't be so keen to go back to India until you've really tried. We all miss India, but there are advantages to working elsewhere, especially for you, now, when you're young.

Enclosed are some negatives for you, which will come in handy. They are in little bits, so someone will have to painstakingly tape them together. All our still negatives are in a dreadful state. Have some contact sheets made and then enlarge the ones you like. Don't just choose pictures of yourself that make you look the way you'd LIKE to look or imagine you look in some rosy idealised way. That may not always correspond to the way other people see you, nor would it necessarily be the way agents and directors may see you. So make an interesting selection. Ask Jon to get them done for you, don't go to some hole in the wall photo store. Remember Mitra's [cameraman] dictum: Give me some BLACK! Don't let them palm you off with grey prints.

I wish you every kind of luck in the Festival and wish I could be there. Please write me everything that happens. Of course Ismail will escort you . . . ! What a question. Whoever did you think he would escort, Princess Margaret?

I am writing in a rush. Be brave and I know everything will be very good, you will see.

So . . . chin up and remember the line from the film
. . . Let life imitate art! . . . AHEM.

Much love Jim

I tried to be brave – in fact, I was brave! There was really nothing to be afraid of except for the brutal fact that if I failed to get work, I failed to get money, and without money I would have to return to my parents to continue touring and being employed by my father. Not a possibility I could easily stomach.

But I tried not to convey my determination never to return. As the film was about to open, I got kinder letters, wishing me well. The messages were mostly from Mother, but I knew my parents well enough to realize that this meant the frost was thawing and Mother was signalling Geoffrey's forgiveness – although she could not resist ending with a bit of emotional blackmail (a strategy that she was never to give up):

We shall be thinking of you, darling . . . I've been painting the props this morning and making scrolls . . . poor imitations of the ones you used to make! I am looking after all your props, but they do get the worse for wear. Oh Fu, I hope it won't be too long before we see you again.

Poor Daddy, he does miss you darling.

In December *Shakespeare Wallah* opened at a small cinema in London. The week before this, I attended the festival opening with Ismail. He looked handsome and young, dressed in his national white chooridar trousers and black astrakhan jacket. I wore the black creation Jennifer had made up for me: full-length raw silk gown, embroidered with golden mangoes and Indian sequinned braid. Long black satin gloves, very high heels, a big tasselled gold shawl and long shiny earrings completed the outfit. All that was missing was the fairy on the top.

Pictures taken that evening show me standing beside Ismail and smiling up at a dapper James Fox, who was suitably attired in a lounge suit! Despite my appalling lack of judgement when it came to appropriate dress, a week later I sallied forth again, this time for the première of the film itself. On this occasion I was got up in Jennifer's creation No. 2: floor-length cream satin with pearls and beads hanging from the tiny tight bodice. Again I went for the long earrings, and too high heels, the opera gloves and the damn silly gold shawl, but this time I added an extra bit of magic. On to my small, pushed-up left breast I glued – God pity me – a single gold sequin. And adorned in this manner I set off with an unperturbed Ismail to the première of my first film.

After the showing, Ismail propelled me through the crowds of good and great talents. I was introduced to critics, to producers, to Joseph Losey and John Schlesinger. Then Ismail took my elbow and, marching me up to a tall, dark, handsome man, introduced me: 'Mr Fox, I want you to meet your new client.' The tall dark man shook my hand graciously. 'You will take her on to your books and you will see – she will make you a lot of money.' Ismail was laughing, his charm turned on to the full. He added, 'I will come to your office and we can talk some more. I also have a few projects that I want James to do. So, we will meet tomorrow, yes?' A bemused Robin Fox smiled back as Ismail turned to me: 'This man is the best agent *in the world*. And he is yours!'

My shoes were killing me and I didn't believe a word of it, but the man was very charming and, as he said goodbye, his big hand squeezed a gentle understanding of my embarrassment. 'Oh, Ismail, I wish you wouldn't,' I pleaded. 'What do you mean?' Ismail laughed. 'This man will be your agent, you will see!'

The film was reviewed as 'a classic', 'important', 'brilliant', 'charming' and 'special'. I was described by Felix Barber as 'a pretty, round-faced girl', by *Harper's Bazaar* as having 'a rare quality and a candid charm'. Patrick Gibbs from the *Telegraph* said I was his 'young actress of the year', and, while the *Guardian* called me 'sensational', Alexander Walker, who loved the film, didn't mention me at all!

So Ismail had done what he had promised. He had put me in a film; he had taken me to Europe; I had got the good reviews he had predicted. And his final prophecy came true as well. Three days later, despite the sequinned breast, I received a letter from the Grade Organization, asking me to join as Robin Fox's client. Ismail had finally got me an agent.

CHAPTER SEVENTEEN

RESTING

Soon I was going up to London every week to meet directors and casting agents. After my earliest, tentative visit I wrote to Jennifer, pretending I was confident . . . and happy. She replied in her usual encouraging way:

Darling, Darling

Your first trip to London seems to have been quite successful. I'm sure you'll get something – you are unusual, if nothing else. You must not give in. You must persevere – no matter how long it takes – you have the time and you will get something. You mustn't worry about money . . . we'll look after that.

You say you have no clothes. Would you like another suit? I could get something made here and it would be more unusual. But it might not fit. I do miss you terribly, but I'm glad you're there. And I know you'll be doing your bit in the house.

I need Gucci diary refills and I've lost my black YSL scarf. I will send some money for you to get my replacements.

Last night at one of Shashi's premières I wore my long

sheath dress and evening gloves. One film star person
asked me if I'd forgotten to put the rest of the dress
on, and Shashi's heroine asked if my fingers were cold!
　　Darling, I'm so glad you're there.

　　　　　　　　　　　　　　　　　　Love, love, love, Jennifer

Oh, God, no, I thought. Not another suit! But I was short of
clothes and had not yet got the knack of shopping in large stores.
All my clothes in India had been made by a dersie from a picture
in a pattern book.

I wrote back that I was not sure about anything else made in
India, but my protestations were useless.

Darling
　　I am making you a cloak, I think it will come in handy.
I suggest the silk the same as your green suit . . . with
a different lining?

　　Do you need another suit? What about something à la
Kashmir with embroidery? Like my kaftans? With gold
buttons perhaps? The tailor has your measurements
and he could copy anything to your size, it could be
very nice. But have you got fatter? Let me know by
RETURN!

　　I think I could get you a quite stunning outfit and
also include an extra shirt in the same raw silk as the
lining to the cloak? Made with the slightest flare,
yes? Not straight. By RETURN let me know. Perhaps you
could send me a kettle in a parcel? Prestige do a good
one with a copper base. I'm ill in bed . . . write to me
now, this moment.

　　　　　　　　　　　　　　　　　　　　Love, J.

It was dawning on me that Jennifer's eccentric style of dressing did not suit me. She could get away with flowing silks and elaborate colours: she was beautiful, tall and slim, and she was married to a handsome Indian film star, for God's sake, so she had an excuse. Her glittering jewels were real diamonds, not bazaar concoctions made of paste, and her personality was larger than mine. She looked like an exotic bird with marvellous plumage when she took to the streets of grey England swathed in her Indian silks; I just looked ridiculous. But she clearly saw me as taking on a role that was no longer possible for her.

My dearest darling

Your dog is full of fleas. Thank you for leaving him for me to look after! He is sulky and bites people (not me). Please send me some Parasites revcod cleaner. I believe it's only a few shillings. I can't get it here.

Poopsie has been staying and my perfume has gone missing, and something is missing from the safe too. I'm sure it's him because in my usual mean, spying fashion I read one of his letters from a girlfriend asking him for perfume and thanking him for a present! Anyway, there's nothing to be done. That's just Poopsie.

I am pretty lonely when Shashi is away. I do everything alone here. I miss you. You have to be successful for both of us. Go to London, sell yourself, but get a job! Go and live in sin, but go and MEET people, don't get stuck in a house, go on the streets.

Love, J.

Advice and support kept flooding across the water in letters. 'Don't ever get a job via the casting couch, Foo,' insisted Shashi in a brotherly fashion. 'Be a strong girl and you will be something in your own right very soon.'

But with the constant stream of letters encouraging me to do well, the pressure to succeed increased. Ismail was back in New York now that the film had opened in London and wrote telling me that he was 'constantly thinking' of me, that I was a 'fine and wonderful actress' and congratulating me on engaging Robin Fox as my agent. (He seemed to forget that I had not managed to engage anyone, and that he had all but insisted that Robin take me on.) 'I am anxiously awaiting PHOO appearing as a star anywhere,' he continued, and told me that he would write to Kenneth Tynan about me; he had already written to Malcolm Muggeridge, who was now awaiting my call.

I had only just received and digested Ismail's letter, when he phoned to repeat his instructions. 'You must contact Malcolm Muggeridge. He will be wanting to see you. I met him and told him about you, and he wants you to telephone him. You must do it now!'

'Oh, Ismail. What on earth does he want to see *me* for?' I longed to contradict, but experience had taught me that it was useless with Ismail. You ignored him at your peril. Doing what he said was always the best way. So I took down the phone number in silence.

'Malcolm Muggeridge has heard about you. He is very interested in India and he will help you to promote your career. He is living out of London, but you must go and see him.'

'All right, Ismail, I will, I promise. Thank you. I'll let you know how I get on.' Fat chance, I thought, but I kept mum about that. By now I was desperate, and anything was better than sitting waiting for the phone to ring or the post to come. So I rang Malcolm Muggeridge.

To my surprise, he did seem to be expecting my call and

invited me to lunch at his house the following week. 'Go to Charing Cross, telephone me from there, and I'll let you know how to get to me,' he said.

To this day I don't understand what on earth possessed him to waste his time and food and wife's cooking on a nineteen-year-old, out-of-work actress, but off I went to Charing Cross on a cold December day. The snow was thick and beautiful in the countryside, and I was cold, as always, but quite excited at the prospect of meeting this interesting, clever man. I arrived at Charing Cross and, as directed, phoned his number. 'Mr Muggeridge, I'm at Charing Cross, it's about twelve thirty, what should I do now?'

'Get a return ticket to Robertsbridge,' he said. 'I'll meet you at the station.'

As I boarded the train I suddenly felt very apprehensive. What on earth was I going to talk to him about? This was a busy, intelligent man with a very intellectual television programme – or at least it seemed so to me. The last one had been about the meaning of God – not easy terrain for a Bombay girl. I shall be tongue-tied and appear silly, I thought. I wish to God I hadn't listened to Ismail. What am I doing here? But my fears melted as soon as I walked through the ticket barrier.

'Over here!' shouted a jolly little man in tweeds and a funny hat. 'Over here!' He greeted me with a warm handshake, bundled me into his small Austin and drove me to his home, where his wife was cooking us a scrumptious lunch. We sat chatting about India in his book-laden office, overlooking snowy fields. I could have stayed for ever. I can't remember exactly what we talked about, but the time flew by, and before long I had to go back to the station. He waved me off with his hat, got into his little car and drove away.

No work came directly from our meeting, nor did I expect

it to. But the fact that he had invited me to lunch and that I was able to hold my own with this clever man gave a boost to my confidence, which carried me through the next few months and the uphill struggle to fit in and to get work. I was deeply impressed by his kindness and generosity in giving up his time for me, something which, until then, I found the English strangely reluctant to do.

Finally the news I had been longing for arrived. I had got an audition. In a panic I rang Geoffrey for advice.

'What should I do?' I hollered down the phone. The line to Bombay was crackly, and Geoffrey was a bit deaf, so I had to shout. The first three minutes of a long-distance phone call were 'cheap time', and I hated spending longer than this on Beula's phone.

'It's impossible to advise you. It all depends on the chap who is listening. I never did auditions. If it wasn't obvious who was good, I wouldn't try! Now listen, we plan to come to England, unless you decide to come to Hong Kong. I've written you a letter about it. You should get it in a few days. We are off to Assam,' he continued, oblivious to my anguish. 'Still going strong, even at our age! It will take us five days to get there by train, and we are doing nine shows all in different places with long journeys in between.' Then, at last, came a word of encouragement. 'Good luck with your audition.'

This was not helping me in my hour of need. 'Can I talk to Mother, please?' She came on the line with a lot of love and 'We miss you, darling.' She was cut short by the operator: 'Three minutes gone, do you want to continue?' 'No,' I said with a sigh. 'Bye, bye, Mummy, love you.'

And up to my bedroom I went, to try out my speeches in front of the mirror.

Geoffrey's letter with his real feelings about my audition arrived the next day:

Dear Foo

   You are completely *mad* having an audition . . . every
amateur can do that . . . you have made a film and can
obviously act . . . if people can't see that at once,
they won't see it at an audition. Look at Jane, they let
her slip through their fingers. They should come to
you, not you to them.

  YOU HAVE NO PRIDE!

'Thanks a bunch, Geoffrey.' I muttered, when I read the letter.
How could he be so cruel? I comforted myself with the excuse
that he was like this because he wanted me back to tour Hong
Kong for no money, then went upstairs to my room to practise
for my very first audition.

I had been told to have three pieces: two classic and one
modern. For my first, I had chosen Saint Joan's last speech. I'd
heard Mother doing it for so many years that I knew it by heart,
although I'd never played it. The other two pieces were Viola's
'Make me a willow cabin' and then, to blind them with my talent,
Ophelia's 'mad speech'. That should amaze them, I thought. I
knew that none of these could be construed as modern, but the
most recent play we had ever done was *Charley's Aunt*, so I had
to choose from the classics.

As in so many things, my choice of pieces was a stab in the
dark. I was trying hard to learn the traditions of a foreign country,
but my abysmal ignorance of my homeland and of the world of
British theatre was to result this time in one of the most humiliat-
ing episodes of my life.

On the fateful day Beula woke me with a cup of tea and a
good luck card. Trying not to think of Geoffrey's letter, I got
dressed in my little green suit (appalling choice: all actors with
any style dressed tatty in those days), struggled into my stockings,

coat, gloves and scarf, and raced down the road to the station, my long jangly earrings swinging against my cheeks.

I got my return ticket to Bristol. While waiting on the small, windy Olton platform, I decided to check the letter from Robin giving me details of where to go:

Dear Felicity

　Val May will audition you for his next season at Bristol Old Vic. Your audition will take place at The Duke of York's Theatre in St Martin's Lane. Be there at 11.30 am. Go to the Stage Door entrance. Good luck.

　Telephone me when you have finished.

Robin

I relaxed. I had allowed myself plenty of time. The train pulled in as I stuffed the letter back into my bag and, finding a window seat, settled down for the journey.

I had not been to Bristol before, but I knew it was the place for budding talent. The theatre was flourishing, and Val May had a reputation for encouraging young talent. Some of the most exciting actors, like Peter O'Toole, Judi Dench and Ian McKellen, had all played there. It was the place to be – if I could just get into the company. The stuffing had not yet been knocked out of me, and I had the confidence that, given the opportunity, I would be able to convince Mr Val May of my talent.

It wasn't until we were pulling into Bristol Station that I began to feel a cold, heavy sensation growing in my stomach. 'Fill your belly full of AIR! . . . Breathe . . . it will calm your nerves.' Remembering Geoffrey's advice, I stepped off the train, and, with a good half hour to spare before my allotted time, I got into a taxi at the station.

'The Duke of York's Theatre, St Martin's Lane, please,' I told the driver.

I was met by a puzzled 'What theatre, love?'

'The Duke of York's,' I said, getting out my letter. 'It's in St Martin's Lane.'

'Sorry, love, there is no Duke of York's Theatre that I know of.'

He asked another driver waiting for a fare, and he couldn't think of a St Martin's Lane either.

By now I was getting worried. 'Are you sure?' I asked, desperate for this not to be happening to me.

'Sorry, love. You'd best find out who gave you that address and ask them if they know what they're doing.'

I gathered my coat and back into the station and I went to call Robin from a phone box.

'You are WHERE?' he asked.

'I'm in Bristol and it's now twenty minutes to my audition and NO ONE KNOWS WHERE THE THEATRE IS.'

'That is because, my dear, the Duke of York's is in London, as is St Martin's Lane, as everybody knows.'

'Well, I don't. How would I know that they audition in a different place?' I could feel the tears of frustration at my foolishness pricking my eyes. 'But what shall I do?' I gulped. 'I'm due on in a few minutes?'

Robin took charge. 'Get on the next train to London and phone me from the station when you get there. I will try and get you a later slot. Goodbye.'

I put the phone down feeling like a fool. Not only had I messed up this chance, but I now looked a complete idiot to Robin Fox, one of the best agents in London. He must have been wondering why he took me on. *Oh shit*, I said to myself. Then another dilemma struck me. I had only my return ticket to Solihull and ten pounds. Stupid bloody woman! Would I have enough cash to get to London and then a taxi to the theatre? Don't think about it; just do it, I told myself. I managed to persuade the ticket office to change my ticket, and within half an hour I was on the way to London.

At Paddington I rang Robin. 'You're here. Good,' he said. 'They'll see you at the end of the day, after the last appointment. Have something to eat and be there at five thirty. Now, can you manage?'

I got myself to St Martin's Lane an hour early and parked myself at a Kardomah Coffee Bar to wait. All thought of Saint Joan's plight or Ophelia's craziness had been banished during the last few hours. Now I was tired and hungry and my ego was anything but intact. I downed a cappuccino.

At last it was time to go to the theatre. I went in and explained how I had come to miss the eleven thirty appointment. My story, though I tried to make it sound kookie and sweet, fell on stony ground.

'What are you going to give us?' said the disembodied voice from the stalls. I told him. 'Oh, well, start when you're ready,' was the weary reply.

So I did. I was into the second half of Ophelia's 'mad speech'. 'I would give you some violets; but they withered all when my father died.' I was acting madly, using the stress of the last few hours as fuel. It was going well; I was convincing; the wait had been worth it; I was on my way . . .

'Thank you. Would you jump? Jump ahead to the last piece. Thank you.'

Gosh, I thought, I'm so good he doesn't need to see the rest. I launched with gusto into Saint Joan's speech before she is taken off to be burned. My mother used to make me cry when she did this part, and I had learnt it by listening to her. 'Light your fire!' I cried. 'Do you think I dread that as much as I dread the life of a rat in a cage? MY VOICES WERE RIGHT!' I bellowed, my own voice straining into a squeal.

'Can you come to the end, please?' The voice in the darkness was tired, and not in the slightest bit impressed. I stood rooted to the stage, my mouth open in astonishment. The grim truth descended on me like a bucket of icy water. I was to stop. I was not good. I was to go away and not bother this tired man any more. I was of absolutely no interest whatsoever to him or to his theatre.

As I walked out of the stage door into the bustling London streets, on my way to Robin's office, I was in a state of shock. I had only a few pence left, so I walked to Regent Street, the words 'Can you come to the end, please?' ringing in my ears.

I climbed the stairs to Robin's office in the grand Grade Organization building and begged to see him. He was in a meeting, but his second-in-command, Ros Chatto, ushered me into her office and sat me down on her plush green sofa. 'How did it go?' she inquired. I had managed to keep control of my jangled nerves all day, but now the waste of it all overtook me, and I sat weeping into my coffee. Ros was most sympathetic, and more coffee was brought, along with some tissues.

'Please ask him to let me try again!' I begged unreasonably. 'It was because I was so tired and so upset at the mix-up. I know I can do better next time,' I sobbed. My excessive mascara was now running around my eyes, making me look like a demented panda bear, and the obligatory sixties false eyelashes were peeling away with my tears. 'I'm not used to auditions, but I will get good at them, I promise.' I tried to convince Ros, but it was a promise I was never able to keep.

Robin came in and with the sheer power of his charm made me feel that it was not a lost opportunity. There would be many more jobs, and no, he certainly would not ask for another meeting. He was in the middle of setting up Stratford and a meeting with Olivier at the Vic in Waterloo. 'Don't even think about this again, Littly. Everything will be all right, I promise.' He was so convincing that even when I blushingly asked to borrow the return fare home, he made it into a joke so as not to embarrass me.

Back in Elmhurst I shared my traumatic day with Beula. She had made me one of my favourite suppers: sausage and mash, followed by apple pie and cream. I ate so much of her loving comfort that I had to change out of the green skirt and into something loose. We watched telly by the fire, and not for the first time I was desperately homesick.

I knew I was on to a loser with my audition, but I had no one to talk to about it who knew how to help me. I had been so know-it-all with my parents before I came to England, scorning their offers of help as to how to go about getting a job and dismissing them as old-fashioned and out of touch. I had arrogantly chosen my set-pieces without advice, and they were the very worst selection I could have made. Any director of any experience would be sick of them by now. Plus the fact that these great speeches are mostly mangled in the mouths of novices. No wonder he had wanted me to come to the end.

But this was not yet clear to me. I was to go through many more painful hours yet, squeaking my way through auditions on the stages of London.

My dear Foo

    Thank you for your letter. Undated! I hope you can get a job at Stratford, but I should not go to the other reps, they really are a bit of a comedown, you know. I had to work in that horrid place, with people who had no

idea what theatre was, because I could never get
anything else.

I am busy writing my book, but YoYo will persist in
purifying the bloody thing. She thinks I will be up for
libel, but it is very hard to write a book and be kind to
all and sundry. I will rewrite some and keep *all* the
people out of it!

You will be surprised to learn that your drunken
father no longer imbibes. I just cannot stand the
society that drinks in India and I refuse to listen to
such a lot of ignoramuses.

God Bless. Good Luck, And be careful of those
REPTILES!

The audition for Stratford was no better. I was on Ros's sofa
again within days, again with the tissues.

'What can I do? I've seen the girls that do get the parts, they
aren't better than I am, but they have a way of seeming to be. I
will not go to drama school, I know more about the theatre than
they can teach me. Why should I go backwards?' I complained
bitterly.

Ros fixed me with her large blue eyes. 'One thing is clear to
me, Littly. Your career is not going to be meteoric. But you will
have one . . . eventually. I promise you that.'

Mother wrote to me with similar words of comfort and
wisdom:

Darling Fu

Sweetheart, I've told you . . . auditions are
terrible! Especially for you who went right into
practical experience with big audiences. You didn't
have any experience of personal recitals on your own,

ever! Poor wee Fu. You're very courageous and all will
be for the best.

   Don't get downhearted. There is terrific competition
in England and you will have to learn to cope. I wish I
could grow wings and fly over to see you, Fu. Now cheer
up, you're only nineteen, there's plenty of time. You
have done amazingly well so far.

This last comment is a bit bewildering. I hadn't done a thing,
had failed to get anything but an agent, and that was through
Ismail's influence — but, unlike Geoffrey, Mother was always
positive. And at the time I seized on her words gratefully.

*Darling, the play opened last night to good reviews — or so I'm told.
My confidence can no longer stand the critic's point of view, written
in hot blood and read by trembling actors in the cold light of day.
Any graceful comment or compliment skimmed over in the search
for the slightest criticism, which will burn itself into the brain and be
remembered for ever. In a week or so this madness fades, and I can read
whatever is written with a more detached attitude. Anyway, the audience
has already told you if it worked . . . And it did last night, that's for
sure.*

   *I wish you could see it. I know you like this one, and I play the part
as Mother would have done, or at least I try to. Oh, bloody hell, I wish
you could speak to me. I want to talk to you about this play, and about*
The Seagull, *which starts rehearsing next week. I can't remember what
you felt about Chekhov. You never played him . . . maybe not your
style.*

   *I remember you liked me best in the classics. Long frocks, wigs, large
emotions and leading parts— those pleased you. I remember opening* The
Second Mrs Tanqueray *for the National at the Oxford Playhouse
before we came into London. At the first preview you said my voice was*

weak, and I later read the local review. The critic remembered seeing Mother on the same stage years ago, and commented on how I reminded him of her, but sadly did not have her beautiful voice . . .

I am so tired, and I won't be able to see you much for the next few weeks, rehearsing and playing at the same time.

CHAPTER EIGHTEEN

HOMESICK

Throughout my first Christmas in England I was miserable and homesick. The family did everything they could to make me feel welcome and loved, but I felt out of place. I had been firmly turned down by Stratford. Even when the family included me in a big Rotary Christmas dinner bash, the slip of paper inside my Chinese fortune cookie bore the immortal words: 'You may not be a star, but you need not be a cloud.' I still have the paper in my make-up box. Along with the tiny key chain with a skull on the end that Jennifer gave me as a first-night gift when I was plonked on the stage by Geoffrey, it's the only thing that I superstitiously hold on to. It makes me smile now to remember how seriously I took myself, and how upset I was by this message of doom.

Letters came from Bombay, describing their plans: it would be turkey as usual, with the imported Christmas pudding from Fortnum's, then a swim after lunch or a sleep. The children would miss me, Jennifer wrote, and it wasn't going to be any fun without me doing the tree. Shashi had planned to get Jennifer a 5-carat diamond, but she wanted a flat instead. All this gossip and chatter was mailed to me almost every day, with the intention of cheering me up but in effect making me wretched with homesickness.

Jennifer phoned me on Christmas Day. 'Happy Christmas, darling. Can you hear me?' The line, as usual, was crackly and unreliable; as often as not you were cut off mid-sentence, and no easy conversation could take place at the top of your voice.

'I miss you all. Did you get the scarf I sent you?' I bellowed.

'Yes, darling, it's gorgeous,' Jennifer shouted back.

'But the money is for you, not to spend on me, you naughty girl. By the way, you must write more to Mummy and Daddy. They are fighting a lot nowadays and Mummy seems very depressed.'

I felt guilty now, as well as lonely. The letters and pleas for me to return that Geoffrey had been sending me weekly were probably the cause of this upset. I wasn't replying, putting off the evil moment of confrontation that I knew was due.

'I will write, I will write tonight,' I promised. 'Are you all right, Fufu?' I used my baby nickname for her. 'Oh, and I wrote to John Neville at the Nottingham Playhouse yesterday, so I'll let you know if I get to see him. I asked him to see the film, if he could manage it, or to send someone from casting.'

'Darling, you must not get so low, your letters are full of negatives,' said Jennifer, and then asked me how the meeting at the Aldwych went. I told her, loudly, that it was a very definite no, but she refused to allow me to be downcast. 'Darling, you *will* get work,' she insisted. 'But you must keep nagging people. Now have a nice Christmas and write to me every day. You must tell me all the news immediately, and when you get a job you must *cable*. I love you, and don't fuss so! Goodbye.'

She rang off. But she had made my day with just one small word: *when*. Not *if*. I left the small telephone room and returned to telly and family by the fire. I had been cheered no end, just hearing my sister's voice. When I got a job, I was to cable her . . . It will be all right, I thought, it will be all right now.

On Boxing Day I got a call from Geoffrey. 'Are you bloody well coming or not?'

I had been so thrilled to hear his voice that this anger came as a surprise. I had written many times that I would most certainly not be leaving England until I got a job or ran out of money, and that I was not going on a tour of Japan when I had hated the last one.

I reacted without thinking. 'No. I'm not bloody coming. I've told you that already. Why did you go and book a tour with me, when I told you not to?'

I had stood up to his bellowing all my life, but for some reason this was more important to him than before. 'Look. This is a damn good tour. I stand to make some decent money and I'll send you back to England first class. Don't bloody let me down now.'

'I'm not coming,' I said calmly. 'Can I say hello to Mummy?'

The phone went dead. I stood in the small telephone room, willing this not to have happened. I could hear the family Boxing Day noises coming from the drawing room. A feeling of utter loneliness swept over me, a feeling of sadness and shame. Why were my parents so odd? Why couldn't they let me go? Why was my father so selfish and cruel? Self-pity washed over me, and I sat on the floor feeling very sorry for myself. My cousins called to me to send their love to Laura and Geoff, and, as I have done so many times since, I went out to continue the celebration, pretending everything was fine and happy. Only my aunt knew that something was up, but she was wonderfully perceptive during the years I lived with her and never once made me feel embarrassed or strange.

The next week was full of festivities. Rotary dinners, chaired by my uncle, card evenings, parties – I was included in everything. I was scooped up by my mother's family and enveloped in kindness.

This did make me happy, but the nagging upset of the phone call, which I felt I could not share with anyone, was still with me.

The day after New Year a letter arrived. By then I was beginning to hate my father. No one here was put to work at thirteen, I thought vehemently. No one here was without a home; no one here was expected to devote their life to the family firm. And on top of that he didn't love me anyway, I concluded. I was only important to him now that Jennifer was gone and he needed a young actor.

I was bitter, and Mother's letter to me did nothing to alter my opinion:

```
Darling.
  I am reading and re-reading your letters about Japan.
You are quite wrong, you know. Daddy literally cries
when he reads your letters, Fu. Then he goes into the
bathroom and blows his nose . . . then comes out and
pretends he's angry with you for not coming to Japan.
  You understand him, don't you? He really does love
you, Fu. And he can't help but wonder if you're all
right.
  We are going out for Chinese supper in Kowloon. Do
write.
                                    Love, Mummy
```

In Hong Kong, the Kendals, as they now called themselves – Shakespeareana was dropped when I left, for a reason I never found out – met up with Ralph Pixton, who was now practically running Radio Hong Kong (for this service he received the OBE). He had booked some shows for them and offered them his flat to stay in. Poopsie, who was also in tow, was put up at the YMCA as Ralph's flat was only small.

They worked Hong Kong, left on another tour of Borneo, and went on to Malaysia, and all the while letters came flying back to me in England: loving, funny, upset, encouraging, complaining. The ones that were especially upsetting were forgotten and not mentioned in the next. The umbilical cord was stretched but not cut. Although I had no wish to return, neither did I want complete separation, and these letters were still a lifeline to me. I looked for them every day, however rude they might be about my feeble ambitions.

Some of Mother's letters details Geoffrey's upset. He had started drinking again, always a sure sign of distress with him:

Darling Fu

  Daddy had promised not to sit and booze all day with Ralph – who can drink all day long and it doesn't affect him – but it has a disastrous effect on your papa because he KNOWS he's being such a fool . . . and it makes him snore! He has promised to pull his socks up. I'm so glad . . . before it goes too far!

Geoffrey obviously didn't keep his promise for very long, as her next letter outlined one of their most absurd conflicts of will:

Darling Fu

  Oh dear, do you know what I've done? Last night your dear papa was snoring again and making unbearable noises . . . he must have had a few too many on the quiet.

  Well, I took a pillow and gave him the wollopingest great WHACK I could muster! He's never been quite so shaken! I then FIRMLY stated that I'd had quite enough of this and was going to ask Jane to arrange an air

> passage for me as soon as possible. That did it! He's
> been wonderful ever since!
>
>   Today I had to mend the pillow. I'd burst the stuffing
> all over the place. Darling, I miss you. Daddy is trying
> to send some money.

It was now 1966. I hadn't told anyone, but I was down to my last nineteen pounds. I read the job advertisements in the paper when no one was looking and contemplated trying for a job in a pub or a café. But the shame of not being able to work out the right change at speed, since I still had a problem with shillings and pence, was very daunting. The family in Olton had offered again and again to help tide me over if I needed to borrow money, but with no prospect of a job I had no means of repaying them, and Geoffrey's habit of leaving a trail of debts like Hansel and Gretel's line of crumbs wherever he went was a big deterrent to the idea of owing money. And my foolish young pride would not let me tell Jennifer how hard it was for me.

I was faced with the dilemma of confessing that I had lied about how much money I had left, or trying to get a job that I might not manage to keep. There was always the possibility of washing-up in a restaurant or pub – no knowledge of any kind needed for that – but my heart sank at the thought. My Eastern upbringing made me recoil in horror at the loss of face, sinking to the lowest work, reserved for the lowest caste. What a very Eastern little person I still was. I had a lot to learn.

Then out of the blue I got a phone call from Shashi from his film location in Uganda. The line was terrible, but I managed to grasp that he was sending over two thousand pounds to me in England. 'For you to use, take whatever you want and don't be shy, it will help you.' He asked me to then put the rest in the bank so that Jennifer could have access to it whenever she visited

Mother and Geoffrey in Goa

Geoffrey and Charley in Goa

With Jennifer

Happy times with Drewe and Charley on the steps of the Love House

In Malta

With Charley on the Serpentine in London

An English picnic with Ismail and Jim, and Drewe behind a flower

Jennifer at her most beautiful and happy with Shashi and their three children

Geoffrey and Mother in Jennifer's flat in London

Filming *The Good Life* with Dickie

Larking about after rehearsals with Paul, Penny and Richard

The *Good Life* girl

With Jennifer and Geoffrey in Chelsea

Geoffrey in my kitchen just before his stroke

me. 'I trust you, as long as you promise not to get silly presents for Jane and the kids!' he laughed. 'Your sister wants me to get her a big flat, so I am working harder than ever.'

The line was getting worse. 'Thank you so much, Shashi!' I shouted. 'Thank you! Give my love to everyone.' And he was gone.

My guardian angel had stopped in. After six months of scrimping every penny for the tube fare or a new pair of stockings, I had enough to go to London as often as I needed to for interviews. I could afford the stockings and even a proper meal at a café.

But I had to admit that Geoffrey was right: my horizons had shrunk. I was now obsessed with small things, such as shillings and pence. I was worried most of the time; I was losing my free spirit and becoming timid. I was watching *Top of the Pops* rather than visiting museums; I was reading the *Daily Mirror* rather than Chekhov. My wildness was wearing off, but in its place came mediocrity. I was joining 'the little grey people', as he would describe half the world, the ones who are 'afraid!'

From a world full of new places, new faces, noise and animals, sweat and curry, with life and death as part of the everyday canvas, from a world of chattering actors, servants and the constant vibrant sound of India, I had reduced my sights to mundane isolation. I missed the stimulation. I even began to miss the rows, the ever present noise, the upsets and rudeness that had made my life so secure until now.

I wrote every day, pages and pages, pouring out the words I would have said. Letters became a vital anchor, and I wrote daily to Jennifer, pages full of the fears that I needed to share. Each day was spent waiting for a letter or a phone call. In between I went for walks along the roads of Olton, down to the convent where Jennifer had gone to school, around towards Solihull and back again up the hill. Rain or shine, I'd walk. And every day the pounds piled on. It seemed that the more my confidence in what I was doing ebbed away, the heavier I became. I grew secretly frightened and less sure that I was right to continue with this apparently hopeless venture of trying to get work with no proof of any training, except what Geoffrey would call some 'cock a mamie' story about a touring company in India.

I wanted to see more shows in London, but the train fare had to be reserved for interview times. I got as much support as was possible from Mother's family, but I'm not sure they were convinced that it was the wisest path for a nineteen-year-old with no education to be here, trying for a job in a world she knew nothing about. My parents were seen, I think, as the odd ones in the family; and, since they never had a bean in their pockets, they were not much respected, although they were greatly loved. And now the vagabonds' daughter was here – but how long should she stay?

Geoffrey had consistently lived by his creed, which ran: 'I will never be a respectable citizen with a house, an insurance policy and all the other possessions that this fear-struck world seems to think necessary.' But this was not a view shared by many people in Solihull.

CHAPTER NINETEEN

FAILING STAR

Robin Fox had at last fixed me up with another audition. I had phoned Bombay, reversed charges, and spoken to Mother on the crackling line. Geoffrey was out, and with great excitement I told her the news. 'Good luck, darling. I'll tell Geoff when he comes in,' she said. 'Write and tell us what happens. You haven't written to us for ages!'

Four days later, with a week still to go before my audition, a letter came from him. I had sent him copies of a new photograph I had had done for *Spotlight*, the directory of actors and actresses.

My Dear Foo

    I have long suspected dormant insanity in our family, being stronger in the females of the species. Now I know I am writing to the latest example of the phenomenon.

    In your last letter we found three photographs of what looked like the most stupid of all the a-go-going asses we see nightly gurning on television. Later I was told that they were meant to be you, and that armed with these caricatures you hoped to storm the citadels of the London Theatre. My dear pathetic stupid girl, you

really are quite a nice-looking, healthy specimen of
English womanhood, you are intelligent and you are good
company, and good fun and quite good at your work about
which you know a lot and you have some very good pictures
in the film and taken by ignorant Chinese boys in
Singapore – all these show you as you are – then why, in
the name of all that is insane, go and have pictures
taken that make you look as daft as anyone else? Are you
really crazy? And have you been kidding me all this
while? TEAR THEM ALL UP.

Laura tells me that you are seeing Sir Laurence
Olivier, and that he is going to see the film – poor man,
he will be the only one that will know that my first line
of text is incorrect, and he is about the only living
actor that has played Puff (and damn good he was). Of all
the shots they took, they would, in their abysmal
ignorance, use the one that has a textual error, and in
about the best known line of Sheridan's . . .

The audition for Olivier's season at the Old Vic in London
was for a job that I really wanted. This was where I did not need
a repeat of that toe-curling episode in St Martin's Lane, so I
decided to stay the night before in London. I had the address
and details on a postcard, and Ros Chatto, fearing no doubt
another collapse on her sofa, had sidestepped the possibility by
inviting me to lunch:

Felicity,
Your audition is on Wednesday at 12.15 pm at 10a,
Aquinas Street, SE1, which is the offices of The
National Theatre. Mrs Chatto is looking forward to
seeing you for lunch on that day.

I was still living at home with food and comfort provided, but I was down to my last fifty pounds, and the nightmare of returning to India as a complete flop, unable to get a job of any kind, was becoming more and more likely.

I had found a very cheap hotel in Earls Court. Breakfast was not included, but I was offered 'a nice sunny room' for thirty bob. 'That has a bathroom on the landing and you can have tea when you wake up,' the fiercely permed lady at the desk told me.

The nice sunny room turned out to be in a basement at the back of the building, and smelled of damp and fried bacon. The window that the sun had never seen was small and high, overlooking a brick wall three feet away from the window. As I put my overnight bag on the bed, I noticed it start to vibrate slightly, the window rattling in unison. An earthquake in London? Surely not. As the vibrations and rattling increased, accompanied by a low rumble from outside, I realized that my nice sunny thirty-bob room was practically in the underground train tunnel.

Oh, well, I thought. Be positive. It could be a palace tomorrow. I left my bag and went outside to find some supper. After a fry-up at the Golden Egg I felt much better and decided to have an early night.

Going into my room, I noticed that my suitcase had been opened and several items placed neatly on the bed. I rummaged quickly through my things to see if everything was there – it would be a strange thief who left things so tidy – and it was all there, except for my travelling iron. This was a minor catastrophe. The cotton blouse I was to wear in the morning was creased by packing and so was the green jacket of the fatal suit. The skirt no longer fitted me: one too many of Beula's apple pies had made zipping it up out of the question. So I had brought along a new pair of bell-bottom slacks. But without an iron I would look decidedly creased.

I went upstairs to the permed lady. 'Something has been taken from my room, from my bag. Have you seen anyone go into my room?' I asked.

'No one but me,' she said sternly. 'No one but me and I have confiscated your iron!'

'Well, can I have it back please?' I came over all pukka. 'I need to iron a blouse for the morning.'

'Do you want to burna down my lovely hotel?' she shouted at me – she was Italian. 'You can have it back when you leave. Go to the dry cleaners if you want pressed clothes.'

I wasn't up to arguing with her. The aggressive side of my personality was definitely under par, and I slunk back to my room.

After a fitful night in my shuddering bed, I got up early, ate the pot of yogurt I had smuggled in and, dressing in my sad-looking blouse, I set off for Waterloo. I was hours too early, but at least I was there. I walked up and down the river, going over my lines. Then, looking much more like my contemporaries who made scruffiness into an art, I knocked on the door of one of the Nissen huts that were office and rehearsal rooms for the Vic.

The casting lady led me to meet the great man. He was charming, dressed in cord shirt and braces and much taller than I had imagined. His two hands shaking mine were warm and reassuring. He introduced me to Kenneth Tynan, dapper, thin and smoking hard – I had no idea who he was. The casting lady said a few nice things about me, then they all sat down.

Kenneth Tynan had reviewed *Shakespeare Wallah* for the *Observer*. He loved the film, and described me as Buckingham's daughter: 'Also their Ophelia is charmingly played by the dumpling-faced Felicity Kendal.'

I might have worked on stages all over India from the age of nine, but I was totally unprepared for the trauma of auditioning for a great actor. I lacked the emotional nerve. I launched into Ophelia's madness with a sinking heart, then swept straight into Saint Joan. The sun was shining through the windows of the Nissen huts and, in the bright daylight, standing only a few feet away from one of the gods of the theatre, I felt gawky and vulnerable. My legs began to shake uncontrollably inside my bell-bottoms, and by the time I got to Viola my voice, once quite strong but weakened by lack of practice, had deteriorated into a high-pitched squeak.

I got to the end. I knew that I had failed miserably. Olivier thanked me, as if I had been perfectly wonderful, Tynan stuttered something witty, told me how much he had liked the film and wished me great success in the future. They were so nice, but I walked out certain that I had failed yet again. With my tail tucked firmly between my legs I got on the bus to visit my emotions on my long-suffering agent. Perhaps, I thought, I will *never* get a job; perhaps I should give up and leave these poor people in peace?

Ros took me to a small Italian, where she filled me with red wine and courage, and by the time I was on the train to Olton I was determined not to go back to India without at least trying for another six months.

A letter from Jim in New York crossed in the post with my heartbroken note about my failure.

So, you will be meeting Olivier next week? Let me wish you better luck this time. Jennifer wrote me that you were very shaky for the Old Vic in Bristol? Keep your chin up. You have to be determined TO HAVE YOUR OWN WAY . . . it's the only way to get on in life. To add to

your gloom, the distributors here are suspicious of our
film. They say it's not commercial. One thing is that
they all like it very much and sooner or later we will
have OUR own way . . .

  A word of advice from an older colleague and friend.
Do not despair.

He went on to add practical help to his words of encouragement, listing the telephone numbers of people I should call, including Verity Lambert at the BBC, the painter Eden Fleming, the director Clive Donner and Lady Reed.

I phoned John Day, who offered sympathy and an outing to see a show. He also sent a note full of condolences and advice:

Dear Foo

  I am so sorry, the wretched things should be done away
with . . . nobody who is any good can possibly be so at an
audition. But that isn't any consolation for you. I
feel sure it wasn't meant. And your other news is very
exciting. If you have impressed Robin Fox he will
surely do something for you. Anyone who saw the film
can't be put off by a bad audition, really Foo, it was an
enchanting performance.

  Do let me know what happens, and don't get depressed.

                          Love, John

P.S. If you ever have to write to Olivier again, do spell
his name correctly. I before E! Otherwise you will look
completely ridiculous!

Geoffrey's response was of course more abrasive, but intended to make me feel better in its own way:

My dear Foo,

I am sorry about the Olivier audition, but I told you
what the buggers are like in that God-forsaken joint!
That reminds me of a story. Once, when Olivier was
leaving the stage door after a show, a beggar woman
asked for a few bob for a drink. He was at his grandest
and said, ' ''Neither a borrower nor a lender be,'' quote
William Shakespeare,' and walked off. The
beggar woman shouted after him, ' ''Fuck off !''
quote Tennessee Williams.' I don't know if it's
true!

We have left Hong Kong, I am in my shorts on deck and
the world is mine again!

The ship is heavenly . . . you would love it . . . a
cargo ship with only eight passengers. And Big Blond
Norwegian Officers, mad to go! Why aren't you here?
Can't you feel the call? You will end up as I said in a
damned awful house with a brood of kids and no
birthright . . . You know the Old Vic was started by a
woman [Lilian Baylis], a Catholic too of all things,
and she used to pray, 'Please God, send me some actors
and send them cheap!'

We are planning to sail to the UK. You need not speak
to us if you are too grand by then, and we will not in any
way embarrass you, I hope, with our colonial manners
and dress. And if we do any shows we will not allow
anyone to know that we are linked with the famous
Kapoors or the Kendal tribe so you will not be sullied by
us unsuccessful actors. So have no fear . . . YoYo can be
your ayah and I will be your chauffeur if you like, if
that is not aspiring too high.

This witty banter did not amuse me; I found it hurtful and sarcastic. It was not remotely true, he did not *want* fame, he wanted more money, as always, but only, as always, in order to travel further and do more plays. But I was still struggling to make ends meet and unsure of my future. The thought of this giant eagle landing with nowhere to stay and no money, Mother with all her suitcases and him full of opinions, was daunting, even if it only was for a few weeks. Much as I missed them, I wanted them to leave me to find my feet alone. But the next letter was full of his particular brand of humour and made me realize that a short, sharp dose of his high-voltage energy and his no-bullshit approach to problems was what I really needed to recover my sense of proportion.

My dear Foo

I am enclosing an Irish sweepstake ticket for the race run this month. See if by any chance of the love of God it has drawn a horse, if so, claim it, and you shall have half. Don't forget, one day I may get something for nothing!

I found the missing swords today, but not the spotlight (Poopsie probably sold it for strong drink in the sweatshops of Assam somewhere).

I don't really want to leave India, but my India is no more, so there is no point in staying. They have mixed up patriotism (which is a silly word if you are not in love with the soil and beauty of the place) with loyalty to the ruling class – which is completely criminal. Therefore, our Utpal Dutt, who is a true Indian and loves the place, is in jail, while scoundrels who love power and themselves, and would sell their birthright for a mess of pottage, are lauded as heroes. No place for me.

Utpal Dutt was a member of the company for a short while, several years before Shashi joined. He was already an established Bengali actor in Calcutta and was a passionate Communist. He was tall and heavily built, with a rolling gait and large, hooded eyes. He was not handsome, but his personality was electric. Jennifer fell head over heels, and at one point there was talk of marriage between what we called the beauty and the beast.

He was a beautiful stage actor with a magnificent voice and would have been a pillar of the company for years, with Geoffrey's blessing, but his political views had no outlet in our work, and he left to start his own company in Calcutta, where he wrote and produced great plays, all with a stirring political message. But this was India, and no sooner had the red flag appeared in Act Three than the police stopped the show and he was carted off to jail. He was sent there with predictable regularity, and this was his life for the next few years. Jennifer was heartbroken and sobbed a lot on the train journeys, but Jennifer was always in love, so no one paid her much attention. Utpal married, Jennifer met Shashi. Years later, in the film *Shakespeare Wallah*, Utpal, who was by now a well-known actor, played the Maharajah in one of the best scenes in the film.

Ghandi spoke of 'Truth' as the one power . . . and that was the last bit that was ever spoken here, I'm afraid. Very sad! And a great experiment that was never given a trial.

History will weep over the ashes of the delhi as it will glory over the ashes of the Mahatma.

I wish I had been born an Indian. There would have been no bloody Pakistan then. The border would have been erased on the 16th of August, 1947!

CHAPTER TWENTY

HOME ALONE

The first few years in England before I met Drewe were the loneliest of my life. I was shocked by the isolation I felt, sitting on a crowded tube train or walking the bustling damp streets of London, with no smiles, no salaams, no one calling out to beg or sell, no eye contact, just the constant roar of traffic and the impression of people going somewhere as fast as they could without wasting time.

Despite growing up as the only child among adults, with no definite address or friends my own age and with a constantly working mother, I never remember feeling lonely in India. In the remote hill stations of India or on the plains, comfort and security lay in the people about me and the very countryside we travelled through. I was now back home, among my own people, and I felt stranded and alien.

There were pockets of comfort for me, though – all directly linking back to India. John Day was in Somerset, at the end of the phone, and wrote to me with constant encouragement. When I moved to London, there was Brian and, sometimes, a visiting Jimmy Gibson. They both fed and watered me, they both paid for seats to see shows, and Brian found me my first digs.

He had a wealthy Indian friend, Nicky, who was an antique dealer. Nicky was small and dapper, a natty dresser, with cashmere coats, Savile Row shirts, Gucci shoes, smart suits and, on his left hand, a sparkling diamond. He lived in a tiny house in Shepherd Market filled with priceless *objets d'art*; these were constantly being replaced, as he made a habit of selling all his stock. One day we would be eating off gold plates on a brocade Victorian sofa; the next week it was a green *chaise-longue* and Wedgwood willow pattern.

He charged me almost nothing for a sweet small attic room in his house. He was a meticulous landlord. Payments were made every week over the kitchen table. His notebook would have logged any extras I had incurred, and he would insist on such tiny repayments as an extra blanket or chipped mug. Then, business completed and the paltry sum of five pounds and a few shillings handed over, he would arrange to whisk me off to the theatre, where he treated me to the very best seats and a slap-up meal at an exclusive restaurant.

He became a close friend after these early Eastern hospitalities. I lodged with him for over a year, until at last I felt brave enough to branch out on my own and rent a tiny, one-bedroomed flat in a 1930s block in Chelsea. Between Brian's care, Nicky's home and Jimmy's excursions round London, I began to find my feet.

One aspect of life as Nicky's lodger confused me for months, however. Almost every time I went home, some man or other loitering around Shepherd Market would stop to ask me the time.

I asked Brian what it was about English men in London, and was it, by any chance, a pick-up line? 'Oh, yes,' he replied, quite amused. 'Shepherd Market is where all the high-class tarts hang out . . . didn't you realize?' It had never occurred to me that with my exotic scarves and heavy eyeliner I might look just a little lively. I was not remotely put out. At least they thought I was expensive!

I continued to try for films, plays and television. Then, at last, I got my first job.

It was a small part in a television series called *Love Story*. Ursula Howells was the lead, and I played a Greek Cypriot waitress in a long dark wig and no shoes. I had to slink about and do a lot of sweeping and eyeing up of the Greek boy in love with Ursula. I didn't get him, as I only had three lines – she did, and I ended up dancing forlornly on the kitchen table for some reason I forget.

I was dreadfully bad and not a little miscast, but it was a job and, to my great relief, all the actors behaved in the same easy manner as our company in India. The country still felt alien and weird to me, but the process of acting was the same. I felt my first big hurdle was over: I knew these people. If only I could get another job, and then another, I would be all right.

Then one morning, when I called into Ros's office for a little of her coffee and sympathy, Robin put his head round the office door and said, 'Sarah can't do the dates for the BBC play, shall we offer Littly to them?'

'Why not?' said Ros.

'Come with me,' said Robin, leading me into his large, masculine office. 'Sit down, dear.' He made a phone call and, in his deep, laid-back voice, I heard him saying, 'I've got someone with me now that I think you should see for the part of the Girl . . . she's just got rave reviews for a new film set in India and with her classical training she would go very nicely with Sir John, I think.'

No one could say no to Robin. He dressed immaculately, had a lady-killer smile, and his thick dark hair and eyebrows gave him a James Bond quality. On top of this, his air of concern and graciousness made him devastatingly attractive. I was soon very proud to be one of the few young actors he had taken under his wing, and, as I got to know him, I realized with some relief that it was not Ismail's insistence alone that had secured me his services, but his shrewd sense about a talent that he felt I had hidden away somewhere. He was to be my rock in a sea of uncertainty for the next few years, until, very sadly, he died of cancer, and Ros took over his clients, me included, thank goodness.

I would do anything to please him, so when he asked me if I could rid a motorbike, I instantly replied, 'Yes, of course.' And so the next day I went to see Lionel, the producer of a television play called *The Mayfly and the Frog*, a two-hander starring John Gielgud. He was to play the recluse millionaire who bumps a girl off her motorbike and takes her to his home, where the only other person is a butler who is never seen but whose voice is heard. A very interesting script, and the first new play Sir John had done for television.

I was hired, on condition that, in addition to riding a motor-bike, I also went blonde and lost half a stone. I went platinum, lost nearly half a stone with the help of some deadly pills the producer gave me and attempted to ride a bike. My answer to Robin had not been strictly true. I had not, to the best of my recollection, ever been on a motorbike. Elephants, camels and horses, yes, even the odd water buffalo, but no bikes. But I wanted the part and couldn't let Robin down, so within a week I was out on a country road being taught to ride a great black beast of a thing. Soon I got the hang of it and did manage to ride at some considerable speed for the filming, the one problem being that when I stopped the bike was too heavy and if there was no one to hold it I had to leap off before it fell on top of me. I only let the side down when, during a long take, I needed help in keeping the giant upright at traffic lights. My legs, short and weak from dieting, kept buckling under the strain of the leaning Harley Davidson, and in the end one of the sparks had to support it out of shot.

I was in awe of Sir John for the first two days. After that his glorious sense of humour and relaxed concentration on the work put us all at ease, and although he was never one of the lads, he never behaved like the star he was.

The voice of the butler was played by Timothy Bateson, who was the subject of one of Sir John's treasured indiscretions. We were standing in line at the BBC canteen, deep into our last week of rehearsal. Looking solemnly at his tray of roast lamb, Sir John turned to Timothy, who was standing behind him. 'Timmy,' he said. 'Are you really going to do the voice like that? It's not terribly good.'

Timmy and I looked at each other in horror, and then burst into giggles. By then we were all a little in love with this wonderful person and his *faux pas* were collector's items. It was nice to have one of our very own.

I was starting to see a lot of shows and was becoming slightly more excited by the prospect of living in England. My letters back 'home' to India were now very young, very naïve and very enthusiastic:

Darling Mummy and Daddy

It sounds as if you are being worked to death . . . as usual!

Have you got the outside cabin? I do hope so.

I have been to see Peter Brook's RSC production of The Dream. It is fantastic, wonderful, really incredible! The woman who doubles as Hippolyta and Titania is really superb [this was the young Sara Kestelman, very

beautiful, very sexy, and at the start of her career].
You would love the production, Daddy, NO SET! Just a
white box. I am so excited!

I gushed on about Peter Brook as if I had just discovered a new
talent, describing the performances and staging in detail, bowled
over by the minimalist approach to costume and scenery that
Geoffrey had advocated and that here, at the Aldwych Theatre,
was used to great effect in a brilliant production.

But though I was settling in, letters from India could still make
me homesick.

Fairlawn Hotel

My Dear Foo
  It is lovely back here at the Fairlawn, the No One
Hotel, as far as I am concerned. We arrived back from
Patna, before that Nepal, have a show tomorrow and I am
buggered. Too much work! So I am eating meat – bacon,
pigeon, the lot! I feel an awful sod and hate the idea,
but vegetarianism is hopeless when all you get is what
is left of what is left, and if I had Indian veggy curry
then I'd die of dysentery . . .
  It is nice to be back here, though the city of Calcutta
is worse than ever, really falling to pieces, dirt and
rats all over the place.
  This is where you walked out on me, you bugger, and
left me with your dog to look after. Funny how you and
Jane both walked out in my favourite hotels . . . the
Fairlawn and the York, Singapore . . . it must be my
standards have always been too low!

*

Ros was on the phone. 'Now this one you *will* get. Sir John wants you to audition for the part of Cecily in *The Importance of Being Earnest* that he's directing for the West End. I'll call you with the details later, but I wanted you to know so that you can have a happy weekend.'

A happy weekend? I was on cloud nine for the whole week. I'd never acted in the play, but I'd done the props and consequently knew it almost by heart. I loved the part, and, on top of this, I'd worked with Sir John and he knew I could act. He had sent me flowers and asked me to dine at his house, so he must have liked me a little. Ros was right; this one I would get.

I could hardly wait for the following week. Geoffrey had sent me a few upsetting letters; he clearly was not giving up on my returning, and I had done nothing yet to impress him: a small walk-on in one telly; and even *The Mayfly and the Frog*, although very grand television, was still to him *only* television. But this he would have to applaud. A play from his own repertory, in London, and directed by someone he admired so greatly. He had to be pleased.

I waited backstage at the Queen's Theatre, clutching my worn copy of *The Importance*. The company manager introduced me to a tall blond actor who would read with me when Sir John was ready. The nice tall blond actor confided to me that he had been recalled, which meant, apparently, that he had got the part of Algernon. 'So don't be nervous,' he said. 'I'll concentrate on you and give you all the help I can, as he's trying to match your Cecily to me. Good luck.' He squeezed my hand as we were called out on to the stage.

As the lights hit us, Sir John called from the darkened stalls, 'My dear Felicity, how nice of you to –' There was a pause. He walked up to the footlights and, looking at the nice tall blond actor, said, 'Oh, not *you*, dear boy, not you, not YOU!'

I think a curtain should be drawn over the rest of this scene. Needless to say the nice blond actor did not get the part. Nor did I. But I was now the proud possessor of another of my very own Sir John stories.

I hated losing Cecily, but my heart was getting harder and my determination along with it. And I still adored the great Sir John.

CHAPTER TWENTY-ONE

PARTNERS

By the time I met Charley's father I had done three televisions and was cast in another two-hander for Rediffusion. The play, called *Gone and Never Called Me Mother*, was half an hour long: a young couple meet for lunch, apparently on a date, but she is actually there to tell him she is going to marry his father.

I remember nothing at all about the script or the job except meeting my leading man. He was dressed in blue denim to complement his tan, his blond hair and his blue eyes. He was hip, and cool, and of the moment, and his name was Drewe Henley. He had a little dog that followed him everywhere without a lead, and his rapport with animals, kindness and gentle nature were very attractive to me after the quantity of male chauvinist swaggering I had already encountered. He drove an old sports car and was very serious about modern art and movies.

I had been in England just under two years and was still a green girl, and I went quite weak-kneed whenever he turned on his charm. Yet despite the temptation that this Adonis presented, I managed to get through the job without becoming involved in anything more serious than long talks into the night and the odd bowl of spaghetti. I was sad to say goodbye when the work was over, but I had discovered that he was married and my morals were made in India.

My next job, a play for the West End after a tour, took me travelling, and a few months later, to my surprise, I got a message in Brighton that Drewe was coming to see me the next day. He turned up looking thin, but still tanned and handsome. Sitting there, with his little dog beside him, he told me he was leaving home and getting a divorce, we would be together, and that was that. Then he drove back to London, and I went to the theatre to perform the matinée of *Minor Murder*.

I had gone along to the audition with the usual shaking legs. No good had come of these ordeals, and as far as I was concerned it was a waste of time, but I still had to go through with it. If I was offered the chance of a job, I was in no position to be grand and not turn up.

The play was based on the true story of two teenage girls in New Zealand who had lesbian leanings and a bossy aunt. In the play the bossy aunt will not stand for their inclinations and wants to separate them, so they hack her to bits in Act Two with a machete-type thing. In order to make this grisly denouement irresistible to the public, they hack her to bits wearing bikinis – one bikini being black and the other white to demonstrate which of the couple is the butch one and which is the softy. I went for the part of the softy – and the white bikini. I did not get it.

But, as there was another girl they wanted to see, I was asked if I would stay on and read the black bikini butch part, so she could audition for the white bikini. I was still acting like an Indian bride, as Jim had put it, and was not yet bossy enough to tell them that if I wasn't good enough to cast, I wasn't good enough to read, and they could find someone else. So I agreed to help out, although inwardly I was angry and hurt. I read the butch part opposite a young actress, Tessa Wyatt, who was to become one of my greatest friends. She got the part of the white bikini, and I was offered the black bikini on the spot. It is the only part I ever got from an audition, and it was a part I did not go up for and did not want.

We finished the tour and it opened in the West End to some goodish, some dreadful and some confused reviews. The play did not fare well, although the two bikinis emerged with some credit. 'These two young actresses are hard pressed to win much sympathy, but their presence gives the piece an unusual twist and they both put up a spirited display of nastiness. Their several scenes are always compelling.' This was the *Telegraph* and Eric Shorter the critic. He was to champion my work for a few years, for which I was grateful. The play, however, closed in ten days.

I didn't mind at all. I knew it was nonsense. And by now I was living with Drewe in a tiny flat in Chelsea. He had turned up with a suitcase one night without warning. 'I did tell you I was leaving home. Well, here I am.' He came in, opened a bottle of wine he had brought with him, and eighteen months later we were married.

My dear Foo,

Yesterday we played Wilhelm Prep. Mr Joshi is now head, and his daughter, Vijaya, is the most beautiful, without doubt, the most beautiful Indian girl I have ever seen. Most attractive, intelligent and glamorous. Lovely.

I have just had a terrible row with your mother. She won't admit she has plucked one eyebrow thinner than the other. She won't even admit she has plucked her eyebrows ever at all!

Tell me about your TV and what of your husband. Is he

```
going to live idle? Can the bugger cook? I'd like to have
enough money to come to Europe and buy a car . . . It's
almost impossible to get a decent drink in India any
more. Beer too strong, whisky undrinkable, gin poison
. . . why, why, why???
   Do you ever go to church? You are a fool not to. My
salaams to the husband man.
                                              Love, G.
```

We were married at the Chelsea Register Office, a stone's throw from our flat. Brian came as best man and, with my new parents-in-law, we walked back to the roast lamb and salad I had prepared that morning. I was stunned by the whole affair and not in the slightest bit ready for the responsibilities of joining my life to that of another.

My parents sent me a telegram:

WHO CHOOSETH THEE SHALL GET AS MUCH AS HE DESERVES! LOVE, SHAKESPEARE WALLAHS.

Hardly encouraging!

In the early months of marriage, it was all too perfect. Like two barmy people in love we would hold hands, hugging and kissing in crowded rooms, in the rain, in the high street – we could not get enough of each other. Oblivious to the world around us, we made plans for our ideal future together. We went to Paris and walked the streets all night in a high of togetherness; we went to Spain and slept on the beach under the stars; we sunbaked on the Dorset coast, reading books to each other. In the winter we made snowmen and pelted each other with snow. It was a fairytale kind of romance, but, like a fairytale, it was unreal.

I threw myself into the 'part' of wife, cook, cleaner, provider, as if it were a job that would last only for the run of the play. I expected rave reviews if I did well, and time off when I was tired. I was badly miscast, and although we were deeply in love, the combination of these two volatile people was doomed from the beginning.

Our first Christmas together we both had Asian flu. An epidemic was sweeping the country. We huddled together, shivering over a single hot-water bottle. On Christmas Day all we had to eat was a bit of old chicken and some toast – but we didn't care, we had each other. And when the hot-water bottle burst in the bed that evening, we dragged ourselves on to the floor and with temperatures of 102° happily went to sleep.

Geoffrey and Laura wrote in their usual double act. She was solicitous:

```
Darling
   I hope you are both getting on. Don't ever think that
Daddy and I are anything but the perfect Darby and Joan
when we are alone. He may go through life shouting at me,
but he's a remarkable man, your father, and I only hope
you two can be as happy as we have always been.
```

He was peppery:

```
I hear you and your new husband have had influenza. We
used to have a canary called ENZA, because we had a cage
and when we opened it, influenza!
   I did not make that up, I just remembered it. I am now so
old that I can remember all my jokes that I learned when I
was a boy, and I tell them and everybody roars with
laughter. I am not sure whether it is because nobody
```

remembers them, or whether it is pity for my dotage.

Are you both on the dole? What are you doing? If you
have no work, are you a snob? My dear, why don't you tell
them all to shove it and start your own company with your
new man?

Poopsie will drive me mad. He has a daft little
transistor and goes to sleep with it playing banal
balls all night, so he wakes unrefreshed and as daft as
ever. Why am I always stuck with these senior
delinquents?

I cannot think of any more rot to write, so I will wait
for the post.

Love, G.

My understanding of marriage was based on the unusual
partnership of my parents, with their loyalty and commitment
the example of how things should be. To apply those rules to
actors trying to make separate careers in London was, at best,
misguided. Before long jealousy was spreading like rising damp
between us. I was madly ambitious by this time and was
developing a harder shell by the minute. I would not be shaken
from my course by distractions such as babies or holidays. If I
got a job, it took precedence over everything else, and, since I
had so assiduously played the part of subservient devotion during
the courting period earlier on, this must have come as an unfair
and surprising change of attitude.

I had married too soon; Drewe was on the rebound from
another marriage. I was twenty going on twelve, had only been
in England for two years and was in no fit state to see that my
very first love affair might not be the one to last. My guilt about
wanting to work and make a career for myself, my almost paranoid
fear of becoming a housewife, didn't help me to think clearly. I

had so many conflicting emotions. And riding high at the top was a stubborn need to prove to myself that I could be independent. After the first hot flush of excitement at housework, the dullness of it was surprising, and I could not for the life of me comprehend why anyone should want someone else to do it for them as a lifetime's work without payment.

Dismally immature and scared of any sort of conflict, I hung on to the fantasy that love conquers all. On the surface we were a happy, compatible couple. My new husband had a blossoming film career, while I was plodding on very nicely being offered the right thing at the right time, and most of it work that I wanted to do. But the love that kept us going in private turned to jealousy when work and other people interfered. Nothing came between us in the end except my work, my ambition and my deep-seated belief that I could have everything. I would not put my marriage 'first' – to me that was a nonsense. The two most married people I knew had worked together all their lives, and it was work that made them strong.

When work was not involved, our compatibility was indeed total . . . until the next job offer, when we would treat each other with resentment and jealousy, only to come together with relief once the cloud of work – and the threat of other people – had passed by. I must have hinted some of this to Mother, who wrote back in concern:

Dear Fu,

I've read your letter to Daddy, who has just banged off one of his letters to you on the typewriter. I don't KNOW what he's said, but I can guess. It's just his way of showing that he cares. Oh, my little girl, say your prayers, trust in God. All will be well.

Love, Mummy

Geoffrey, though, was more direct:

1969

My dear Foo

I was moved by the Holy Spirit to write you a long
sermon yesterday on 'how to be happy, tho' married' . . .
actually, that was the title of a famous book written at
the turn of the century. But mine was better. It was
based on how to stay married in our business – that is,
of course, unless you want to piss on your props and fuck
the profession.

After writing the letter, I thought I'd better wait
till my passions die and read it again before posting
it. I did. And I find it full of sound advice. I will put
it in my will, to be read out and quarrelled over in the
years that follow.

Needless to say, he sent the letter anyway.

My dear,

I am 60 this year and I have been wed for nearly 40 of
those years. I have been a bastard most of the time and
broken all the commandments, and enjoyed doing it – but
I have managed to keep the base of the family intact,
despite being an actor. So I feel I have a right to an
opinion about marriages.

In our business it is very difficult when you have to
work separately. What you think is marital jealousy is
really professional jealousy. I tell you in all
humbleness and humility, as I sense there is an
'atmosphere'. If you try to turn an actor into a
respectable housekeeper, he will sooner or later kick,

and if you try to turn an actress into a housewife, she will kick one day too. So do try to be SANE you two.

Your sister tells me you are worried about not having any offspring. Bloody hell – you are damn lucky! The world is full of too many offspring as it is. Am I damned because I have no son? Do you think I bloody well care?

Don't listen to anyone else, listen to me, for once. Get yourselves a show and do it now. If you have not got the brains, get someone else to do it for you. Marriage is a barmy thing and can only work by giving to it all the time . . . together . . . and in our business, one has to be even more generous, or it will all blow up, and that is bloody silly. Marriage in our business can be quite fun if you will BOTH give and not be jealous of each other's work.

Christ Almighty, we both gave up dozens of jobs to be together and start our own company. You must understand that you will have a lot of opposition, but you must be sure and absolute in your power together, a shield that the nasties of this world cannot possibly dent.

Oh dear, it is so difficult to explain and you are probably both horrified and annoyed and I'm probably wrong, and I won't post this. No, it's on an aerogramme and cost 85np, so I must post it. Oh you two silly sods. Why not come on tour with us and enjoy yourselves and have fun. You'll be too bloody old by the time you have made up your minds.

I write in all humility,

Love, G

But things did not improve. We had been married only a few months, yet scenes fuelled by unthinking jealousy followed by extreme tenderness, and mood swings from laughter to violent temper tantrums, were becoming the norm. I mistakenly thought that it was my work that was causing these upsets, so turned down any jobs that might take me out of town or that were too time-consuming.

When I was offered the chance of joining the Old Vic Company for one play, *Back to Methuselah*, playing the small part of Amaryllis, I thought it perfect. Little did I know that the prospect of my playing a newborn, coming out of an egg on stage, would send Drewe into a frenzy of jealousy about what, if anything, I would be wearing. I tried to reason with him: it was the Old Vic, Clifford Williams was a wonderful director, I would not be required to do anything I did not want to – and, after all, it was a play by Shaw!

When the morning of my first day arrived, there was a lot of sulking in the bathroom. I did not realize that this was a sign of something seriously wrong, so obsessed was I with getting to work on time. I had planned to go by tube, but the tears and pleadings didn't calm down until I was late, so I took a taxi we could ill afford.

At the theatre I was introduced to the large and impressive cast for the play: Anna Carteret, Ronald Pickup, Louise Purnell, Derek Jacobi, Sheila Reid – all young and ambitious and already making their mark. Clifford Williams made a short speech about the play, and the read-through began. Suddenly there was a loud knock at the rehearsal room door. My heart sank as I saw through the glass panel my new husband, wild-eyed, beckoning to the director. There followed a mortifying few moments, with Drewe demanding to be allowed to vet any costume I wore and, worse still, insisting that I should not appear nude. Clifford was nonplussed and not very pleased, retorting that I could wear a bearskin if I chose, and that it was up to me and the designer anyway.

The stage manager was a wonderful woman who managed to calm everybody down and usher Drewe out into a taxi. We continued with the read-through. My face by now was burning with embarrassment. I guessed, rightly, that I would be blamed indirectly for this regrettable intrusion. And I felt a cold fury at the position I had been placed in with my fellow actors: being made to look a complete prat.

I returned home to a half-wrecked flat and Drewe in tears of repentance, begging me to take him to the doctor. 'I'm not well. I'm not well,' he kept repeating, all night long. Suddenly I realized how scared he was, and the awful truth – that his behaviour might be beyond his control, that he might really be ill – began to dawn.

The next few weeks were terrible. Visits to doctors; tests; drugs to calm down; drugs to cheer up; but still his mood swings got worse by the day. I was growing frightened for him. One day, after an agonizing night, we ended up in Harley Street. Here, to my horror, the psychiatrist decided he should be admitted to a clinic for his own safety. I signed a paper that allowed them to take him even if he refused and sat, numbed, in a too large chair in the psychiatrist's room, listening to the diagnosis.

I couldn't cry; I couldn't even think through what I was being told. In voices hushed in sympathy, long words were being used to describe the problem, possible treatments, and drugs and names of clinics. I couldn't understand any of it, but I knew what it meant. I had lost my young husband to manic depression.

For a long time I couldn't, or wouldn't, believe that there was nothing I could do. I felt there must be a cure, a drug, a healer, something, somebody who would show us the way out of this life sentence.

Getting on the train to the clinic at Harrow-on-the-Hill where he was to have his treatment was one of the worst moments of my life. The misery sat in the pit of my stomach like a cold stone. The sun was shining, and I was due at rehearsal that afternoon for *Back to Methuselah* at the Old Vic. I had left our little flat in Chelsea tidy and put fresh flowers on the table, trying to find comfort in the domestic security of our home. I had ironed his pyjamas and folded them carefully in the plastic bag, along with a new book and some chocolates.

I knew that he might not remember much after the shock treatment, but nothing prepared me for the horrifying change that came over him.

I arrived just before the treatment and waited in the hallway, where the patients, some crazed, some depressed, came and went. I sat for what seemed an eternity. At last the doctor came out of his room and along the corridor. I noticed he was rolling down his shirt sleeves. How odd, I thought. 'You can go in now,' he said. 'But do remember, he isn't likely to remember anything for a few days.'

Afraid but hopeful, I went into his room. Electrodes had been applied to his temples, and there was a faint burn mark on either side. His hair was drenched with sweat, and his usually sweet, smiling eyes now stared at me vacantly out of deepened sockets. I panicked for a moment. Where was my husband? Who was this man? Where was the strong creature who had been so passionately angry when we tried to bring him here? A shell sat in the chair, with wild eyes, not knowing who I was. What have they done to you? I wanted to scream.

'It's Foo, darling,' I said. I went and knelt beside him, taking his hand. 'You've had the shock treatment, and you'll be better now,' I muttered feebly. 'Take me home, Foo, just take me home.' He held me in a vice-like grip. 'You have to take me home.'

The period in the clinic seemed to help his condition, although the first weeks were dreadful. He was becoming a shadow of his former self. The smooth strong muscles wasted, the tanned skin hung in folds. He was pale and sick, his haunted eyes and bony shoulders making him seem taller than his six feet. 'I can't remember what happened last week, I can't remember.' Froth induced by the heavy load of drugs collected in the corners of his mouth. 'I'm frightened, Foo. When can you take me home?'

Drewe was a funny man before his illness. He would tell me stories until my sides would ache with laughing. And clever too. He had gone to the Slade as a student, but had left when he got bitten by the film bug and changed course, going to the Central School for Drama. He was too nice a person to be an actor, really – the little germ of arrogance was missing.

I was made of sterner stuff. I would not turn down a job because it didn't suit a holiday plan, or the leading man was too attractive, or my husband wanted me by his side. And I unreasonably expected this attitude not to matter. Coming from a family of actors almost fanatical about the importance of work, I could not relate to a more balanced way of seeing things. And then to top it all there was the illness, and this made the mismatching complete. At a time when he was to need calm domestic security, I would be off to rehearsals or away at night in a play. It was a dreadful shame. It was nobody's fault.

Our son was born from a close love, which lasted on through him and for him. It was just in the outside world that it couldn't breathe.

We walked in the beautiful gardens of the clinic and gradually he got better – well enough to come away with me on holiday that summer. I suspected then it might never go away, but felt I had strength enough for both of us. I loved so fiercely and so well that I thought I could manage anything, I would cope with whatever cards happened to be dealt. I was the tough one of the family. Nothing would alter my marriage or my love. I was twenty-two years old, and completely wrong.

CHAPTER TWENTY-TWO

THE ACTORS ARE COME HITHER

Letters came with advice and concern, and as usual the latest news of the company. Poopsie had either left or been pushed, and Geoffrey decided not to employ anyone ever again. He reinvented the plays as two-handers for himself and Mother but got cold feet for his first show in Bombay in front of Jennifer.

Your sister is coming to our show and I have a cold.
Nerves I think. I know she will hate it . . . I should
never have gone on the stage. I should have been a grocer
and had a mini and a floppy wife, and backed horses, and
smoked Woodbines, and had a cat, and some slippers, and
varicose veins, and read the News of the World, and told
dirty stories, and been a virgin, and never haunted the
low places of the East, and thought foreigners funny,
and ate stews and brought up my family and been proper
minded . . . That would have been the life. Then I would
have a decent haircut and go for holidays and have
money! I have not got a piece left after paying off
Poopsie, but my God it was worth it! Though I do fear my
sanity.

God Bless, G.

Back in London, I was trying to take his advice and act as a team with Drewe, whose health had improved sufficiently to work. We were both offered a season at Leicester, playing in *Henry V*, *The Promise* and *Let's Get a Divorce*. The theatre was run by Robin Midgley, who had given me my first break with Gielgud, and I was happy to work for him again. The director of *The Promise* was Richard Cottrell, who almost immediately became a great friend.

All the signs were good, and the season and the plays went well. But my attitude to work was more ambitious and pedantic than my partner's and before long tension between us spoiled an otherwise happy time. I had brought with me Geoffrey's pigheaded commitment but none of his humour. It was early days for me and I took everything too seriously, giving nothing to my relationship and everything to my work. Away from the theatre, things were still tense.

A year later Richard offered me Queen Anne opposite Ian McKellen's Richard II. I was still stuck on the idea that I should try and work with my husband and create a well-known, working 'team' – a foolish fantasy, since I had now no reason to think we could work well together. I was far tougher than I looked, and, when push came to shove, I looked after my own corner. And, very like Mother, when I was working my marriage came a definite second.

For whatever reason, Richard did not include my husband in the offer. This made a big impact on the already vulnerable state of his health. I took it for bloody-mindedness, but, in order to keep the peace, I turned the job down. It was the wrong decision. The peace was anything but peaceful, and Ian went on to score one of his many early successes as Richard II: a performance so magnificent that I wept with regret to have missed being part of it.

But Richard and I had liked working together, and I wrote him a card begging to be included in one of his next productions. I did not have to wait long. Ian, Richard and Edward Petherbridge were in the first stages of setting up a new company, to be called the Actors' Company. The actors would run it with directors of their own choosing; they would cast it themselves, have a say in all administrative decisions and be involved with set and costume design, touring dates, etc. With high hopes and flying ambitions for the project, I and a team of splendid actors set off with Richard as our leading director.

One night I went to a late meeting that Dame Peggy Ashcroft joined. She came in to give advice and her blessing. I had never met her before and, being in India, had missed most of her earlier stage work. I was instantly impressed by her quiet, gentle manner and the gigantic personality that lurked behind it. She seemed to be a sweet, middle-aged lady in a frock when she came into the room and sat down in the circle of young actors. Then she began to speak. The moment she did so, she transformed into a vibrant beauty, with sparkling eyes and a flashing smile. I very much wanted to work with this person. Just to watch her across the stage would have been inspiring. Sadly, although I saw every show she was in, I never did work with her on stage. But I did do a radio play with her a few years before she died. It was called *In the Native State* and renamed *Indian Ink* for the stage.

But for now I had other rivers to cross. Not the least of these was that I had discovered, to my great joy, that I was going to have a baby. We were about to start rehearsals, so I told Richard with some trepidation. I would be seven and a half months pregnant by the time we finished the tour, and although I wanted to continue, I understood that it might not be acceptable to the rest of the cast. Richard was adamant that I should stay. 'I don't mind, if you don't mind,' he said. 'After all, Annabella is pregnant anyway in the last act of *'Tis Pity She's a Whore*. And you can be as fat as you like as Clara the maid in the Feydeau!' At the next meeting we put the question to the company, who didn't seem to care. Actors as a working group are so bound up in the task in hand that they are often remarkably uninterested in private or public dilemmas. So I started as planned on one of the happiest and most interesting jobs I had had so far in England.

It was a particularly well-matched group of actors that first season. The total democracy we had had in mind was difficult to control, however. The idea was to be as democratic as possible, with no leading actors but a lot of general meetings. The meetings were endless, the most long-winded culprit being myself, who had an opinion about everything. 'Come to the point, Foo,' my great friend Caroline Blakiston said more than once. 'We know you're right, but don't take so long in saying so!' In any case, the decisions were finally taken mostly by those with the strongest will, and the natural way to cast any play turned out to be to give the better actor the better part.

A strong bond grew up between us all, and we cast and acted in the first two plays with great camaraderie. By the third, however, it was becoming clear that, however democratic we wished to be, the audience was not. Charisma and talent divided us on the stage. Some are born great, and that's a fact. Ian's star quality could not be questioned; and when he and Edward Petherbridge stole the show, and the reviews, playing two of the smallest parts in the Feydeau, dreams of total equality began to fade.

By then my corset for Annabella was getting pretty extended. I carried a large shawl in the virgin act, draping it around my belly, leaving it off and letting out my corset for a very convincing pregnant last act. As the maid, Clara, I had a large costume, filling it with padding at the start of the tour and slowly discarding it as I filled out, putting it to the side to balance the bump at the front.

They were happy times. Equipped with an excess of ambition and a lack of finances, we cooked up great curries and stews, taking it in turns to dazzle with culinary skills and venturing only rarely into restaurants. Although the company did not survive the ravages of time, we had struck a blow for freedom and proved, beyond doubt, that we could run the show. Today I would not be so naïve, nor would I wish for anything other than a strong director at the helm, guiding actors and production. But, at twenty-four, it was the place to be, and I was lucky to be in at the birth.

My own baby was growing fast. Like Mother before me, I worked up until the last few weeks. I was fit and energetic, if a little large. As Clara I rushed about in frantic farce fashion, carrying trunks and bed linen with equal abandon. As Annabella I was knocked down a flight of stairs and into a table; Edward Petherbridge became more and more protective as my belly got bigger and wanted to cut the slap and push that resulted in my fall. But I insisted that nothing was changed. The imprint of 'the show must go on' was deeply embedded in my attitude to work and I refused to alter a move because of my state of health. I was arrogantly confident of my technique and my ability to protect myself and manoeuvre the fall to look as if it was dangerous and painful, when I was actually in control and not hurt at all. In retrospect I was a bloody fool. But I was also lucky and got away with it.

The end of the tour was a sad day for me. The job had been the nearest thing to Geoffrey's company, even in the fact that Ian was an actor-manager under the skin. Although there was talk of another season, nothing was definite, and anyway I had another job to go to in a few weeks' time . . . my first baby.

My dear Foo

Buon giorno, Buona gente . . . In case you don't know,
that is the greeting of the Franciscans, spoken first
by St Francis. Good Morning, Good People. Beautiful,
isn't it?

It was a great joy to hear your lovely voice last night
and to speak to you for a brief time. But stupid thinking
one can only communicate over such a distance . . . the
pitiable striving of man!

Delighted to hear of your financial freedom! So you
are living on the dole . . . for the grand sum of £10.65
per week! More than they gave me, I only got £9.10 on my
pension!

I hope to be able to afford to come and see you and your
creation soon, which will be very pleasant. I have
started my yoga again and I am straight and fluid.

God Bless, and if it happens before I write again, you
have my thoughts, prayers and complete concentration!
I hope you like it when it arrives, but do remember no
one else will – they never do.

God Bless, G.

Our little boy was born early in the morning on 23 January
1973. He was the blessing of my life.

The sky outside my bedroom window was a deep indigo blue.
As dawn broke and turned the colour paler, I knew that I would
remember that morning for the rest of my life.

I remember that sweet newborn smell and the gentle weight
of the tiny body lying on top of my chest, so vulnerable, yet
with the strength of ages, the fragile fingers and toes so perfect
and so small, so very, very small. I felt engulfed with calm and
smugness. I had won my battle against the drug barons. I had

not been induced in any way; I was awake and alert, able to savour my baby and hold him, free from the haze of pethidine or drips. At last something that required no audience and no applause had happened in my life. I had got this bit right, and on my terms, and at last I had someone who was more important to me than I was to myself.

The birds were singing as I turned over with my precious bundle in my arms and went to sleep, happier than I had ever been before.

CHAPTER TWENTY-THREE

THE BLESSING

My Dear Foo

  Your letter arrived dated day two of your son's life.
A most graphic letter . . . you should write more, you
know, not letters to me but letters for potty women's
magazines. Yours is what is wanted to counteract the
dismal sadism of horror stories of births and deaths,
that should not be horror stories. Anyway it is grand to
be sane about these things and I am most grateful that
you have achieved that state of purity!

  Poor little sod. I am sorry for it. All that life.
School, puberty, love, hate, decay and then senility
. . . all in the future . . . can't possibly win. Hellish.
So be good to it, won't you. Then there will be all the
sins to enjoy. Pride and sloth and envy . . . and eating
and drinking . . . What HAVE you done?

I plunged into work again – far too soon, in retrospect – but
that's what I did. At six weeks old, Charley started coming to
work with me.

I was in a television series, *The Dolly Dialogues*, directed by
John Frankau, who was to become one of my dearest friends.

I met him two weeks after my son's birth and explained how I wanted the job, but that I was feeding the child myself. Rehearsals would be a problem, so would recording, as he was on a three-hour feeding schedule. John at once set about with pen and paper and drew up a schedule with what he called 'Feeding Breaks' inserted every two and a half hours, and then said, would that do? I took Charley and my friend Joy to rehearsal, and she pushed him in a pram until the allotted time, when I popped into the ladies', fed my son, and went back to work.

Just as my own mother had done, all those years before, I soon learned to juggle my devotion to my work and my child, and to cope with the torn loyalties that being a 'working mother' involved. Taking my tiny son to rehearsals I began to realize what she had been through with Jennifer and me when we were small, and to value the strength behind her professional calm. I realized too that her self-discipline was sometimes misinterpreted as lack of feeling, that she was often misunderstood, and that many of her emotional needs went unnoticed. But to her it wasn't the done thing to let anything hang out; she just got on with it.

I had seen a stark example of the way she covered up what she really felt at the time of her first hip operation. She seemed so calm during the many early visits for blood tests and X-rays – it was all done with an air of nonchalance, in a mist of perfume and wafting silk scarves. Through a touch too much mascara and slightly lopsided pink lipstick, she would smile at the nurses as if it was a tea party and the blood sample or injection a mere side issue. When asked by the hip surgeon if she was on any medication, she replied charmingly, 'Oh, yes, all those little round ones.' It seemed she had no fear at all of the looming operation, of the pain or of the possibility that it might not work.

As the time came for me to take her in, I was very busy in rehearsal and, because she demanded nothing and seemed so at ease with the situation, I gave her only my spare time, which amounted to very little. The day before I was to take her in, she came with me as I drove round London on errands. She was chatty and bright, and at one point I left her in the parked car as I dashed upstairs to collect a parcel. It took longer than I thought, and I went to the shop window to check that the car was all right. Looking down, I noticed through the passenger window that her hands resting on her lap were clasped tightly together, turning the knuckles white. As I stared down, she started to wring her hands in the unmistakable action of distress. I felt embarrassed, as if I had spied on her – she had not wanted me to see this – but also deeply ashamed of my ratty temper during the morning drive and my carelessness in dealing with her.

I rushed down to the car in time to see her face change in an instant from anguish to a beaming smile. 'Are you all right, darling?' I asked, getting into the car. 'Of COURSE I am, Foo, don't you worry about me!' I leant over and held her hands: they were cold as ice.

At the end but only just at the very end, she was so very poorly that I got a glimpse of the old woman she really was. But usually her energy and vivacity, combined with her appearance, gave her the aura of a woman half her age. She was an outrageous flirt, graceful, small, with soft brown eyes and brown hair that only went grey in her late seventies.

Like Mother, though, I also found ways of keeping Charley close to me while I was at work. I finished *The Dolly Dialogues* and went almost straight into another television series, this time playing Princess Vicky in *Edward VII*. In one scene the Princess appears with her baby daughter and, as Charley was still feeding, he was put into a long white Victorian dress. That was his first part, continuing the family tradition of using our children.

Quite soon after our baby was born, the signs returned that our marriage was suffering internal damage, though it was not yet apparent that it was to prove fatal. I shared everything with Jennifer, writing to her about my worries. In an attempt to help, she wrote back inviting me to spend a family holiday in Goa, hoping that the break from work and England would help, and that the idyllic surroundings of sea and sand would calm our fraying tempers.

> We are all going to Goa for a holiday at Xmas. Why don't you all three come and join us? Shashi will send you the tickets and Daddy will arrange everything. Do come. We will sort all this out together.

The prospect of travelling to India at the end of the year filled me with energy, and made the next few months fly past. By autumn preparations to fly home were being made with great excitement. Letters came from the family full of anticipation, Geoffrey's, as usual, full of banter:

> My dear Foo
>
>   Your tickets are being sent to you. If you have the offer to star as the Virgin Mary (a character part for you) and your husband as JC himself, doubled with Judas, tell them to shove it right up as far as it will go, come on the next flight, and prepare to stay at least a month. We will take you to places of interest on a trip and show your husband what life is really like. You will visit Rajasthan, Agra, Delhi, and VERY briefly, the South. Then you can return and slum it in England.

The weather here as always is gorgeous and hot. Jane depressed me yesterday by coming to see our show in Thana. I hate my bloody family, always did, that is why I went on stage to get away from the buggers, and they have haunted me ever since.

I have just heard that Poopsie pinched an enormous sum from Kabul when we were there. He did seem to have a lot of wealth lately – three watches, new suits and gold rings, so it may be true. Anyway he is not coming with us on our next trip to Malaysia, so . . . no bloody Poop . . . I shall feel young!

Don't bring any luggage, travel light, and no bloody presents – except my pork pie! See you on the beach!

In the early sixties Jennifer had been one of the first to discover Goa. The company had been there when it was still Portuguese, and it was Geoffrey's favourite date in south India. Baga Beach was empty, apart from a dozen or so hippies, there was no hotel, the airport was a dusty track, and the airport lounge an open-sided shed with wicker chairs and table fans. It was a paradise, and the golden sands stretched for miles beneath the palm trees. Fishing boats were scattered along the beaches, and small huts housed the tiny fishing community.

The road stopped yards from the beach in those days, the water came from a well, and light was generated by a tired machine that gave out around ten at night. Jennifer went once and fell in love with the peace and beauty. She persuaded Shashi to rent a large deserted house on the sands that had been lived in by visiting pot smokers for the last few years. It had a large heart painted on the tiled roof, and we called it the Love House.

The family was to spend every winter together there until Jennifer died. It was a blissful place – no cook or servants, the water was placed in buckets in the open shower room, and the lavatory was an elevated shack at the bottom of the backyard with a hole in the floor and pigs underneath. Primitive was not an adequate description and Jennifer's RULES were stuck up over the Calor gas cooker, to be disobeyed at your peril:

RULES OF THE LOVE HOUSE

1. Do not address J. K. until she has had her coffee and bread. If the breadman (or girl) is late, this could be any time – no matter.
2. Never leave any fruit or food about – the rats will come. If there is a spill, tea, beer, Coke, wipe it up at once or the ants will come. If you eat in bed you will probably get both rats and ants, serves you right.
3. Please retrieve your own towel from wherever you flung it. One towel per person – it's not hard work. Washing will be done to any garment placed in the bag, no ironing – please be reasonable.
4. No peeing in the bathrooms – and this means *all* of you.
5. Guard your torch with your life, you're likely to need it. If you lend it to some idiot visitor who came without and stayed too long, it's *yours* you lent – you can't then expect to beg someone else's.
6. *The loo.* Don't throw solid objects in it, the insides of toilet rolls, etc. – they get lodged and then so does everything else. Use plenty of water and the brush (and a disinfectant every few days – not too much, or the pigs might suffer!). It's easy to clean when you're *there*! One hour later the stuff is solid and has to be chiselled off.

It was a happy holiday with hours of relaxing on the unspoilt sands of Baga Beach. Geoffrey paraded around in his bright pink G-string, Drewe took all his clothes off and sunbathed in the nude along with various hippies, and our baby boy played in the shade of the fishing boats pulled up on the hot sand. I lost my post-pregnant plumpness and sported a silver chain and very little else on my tanned body.

It was a good time, with the three generations demonstrating their love for one another – and we tried, we really tried, to mend the cracks. But it was not to be. Away from the pressures of work and daily troubles, we could manage for a short time, but once back in England the harsh face of reality could not be denied.

I was now a kosher person of the theatre. I had done Regent's Park and the National Theatre. I had toured in the provinces; I had played the best dates; I had had good reviews and bad reviews; and I was still working. I had been in ten television shows and three series, I was doing well by any standard and, best of all, I was doing well in the theatre. England was kinder now, and although I still missed the wildness of India, my people were here. 'Tatties are the same the world over,' Geoffrey used to say. 'Except, of course, for film wallahs! Actors are actors, and there's an end to it.'

Soon after I was married, the Kendals, as they now called themselves, began to visit England every year. They had nowhere to live and, as ever, little ready cash, so they either camped on the sofa and floor of our tiny one-bedroom flat, or went to stay with Mother's family at Elmhurst, or with Geoffrey's brother Roger in the Lake District.

I loved having them around for the first few weeks, and the chatter and shouting and early-morning tea was a calming influence on my relationship. But, as the weeks turned to months and the thrill of English beer, Wall's pork sausages, and Stilton cheese wore off, Geoffrey would get itchy feet and long to return to his home. He hated the cold and cramped lifestyle in England,

and could never have returned to 'settle down'; it was out of the question, even now that he was getting older. Mother wanted very much to wind up the constant travel, to finally get a bed of her own and a place to rest her head that did not belong to someone else. But her gentle pleas fell on deaf ears, and it was never long before they were packing up and moving on. This continued way into their seventies, and only his final stroke, a year after Mother died, stopped him from returning yet again to India.

So Geoffrey was in his element when, a year after our trip to Goa, they visited us as usual, and then set off for a cruise on the *QE2* – not as paying passengers but as working crew! They performed several times and Geoffrey gave talks on his adventures. For this they were given a cabin and pocket money. He was in heaven, and although he spoke of missing us, I could tell he was really happy:

At sea on board the RMS QUEEN ELIZABETH 2, 1975

Dear Foo

I miss you so much, and I miss Charley so much, and I miss Vanski your dog so much . . . in spite of a tremendous welcome aboard from the crew. Would you mind terribly if we came back quite soon?

We are doing 11 shows between here and Bombay. I wish you great joy in the West End with The Norman Conquests.

We played our first show in a gale, quite wonderful. Food is good and we drink sherry and port as I cannot afford the beer – 22 pence for half a pint is something I cannot forgive them for. I shall buy some beer in New York. I still have my watch on London time, so I know when your show starts!

Isn't it fun really to be in Bombay next week, then

Bali, Singapore, Hong Kong. Think lucky and you'll be
lucky!

YoYo is wonderful, never looked so fit, powerful in
the show. And I feel much more youthful than I am. When
she is staying with you the domesticity and loving her
family have the effect of reducing her to an idiot. I
have to keep her on the road or she would drive herself
potty. What a barmy woman. Why should she be so good at
farting about in a house after the life I've given her?

We have the Duke and Duchess of Bedford on board and
Norma Shearer and Salvador Dali, amongst other VIPs.
The ship is full of Yanks. One used his finger bowl as an
ashtray and another complained that he did not want to
eat with the crew, when they did him the honour of
inviting him to sit at the captain's table!!

We will be in New York in the morning. I will buy YoYo a
watch at Woolworths!

Love, G.

The Norman Conquests was a hit: the three plays by Alan
Ayckbourn were some of his best work to date, they were
directed beautifully by Eric Thompson, and the cast was excellent.
The trilogy transferred from Greenwich Theatre to the Globe
in Shaftesbury Avenue. It sold out for the first nine months and
went on for a further three cast changes.

Work was going well, and so I was intrigued and delighted
to get a phone call from Robert Bolt, asking to see me. He
introduced himself over the phone in his gruff tobacco voice.
'This is Bob Bolt. Would you have lunch with me next week?'

It was a sunny day in June. Drewe and I had moved to a house
on the river in Shepperton, with a magical garden where the
weeping willows bowed into the Thames. I looked across the

lawn down to the river, where our two dogs were lying in the shade. Charley was gurgling in his cot beside me. To all appearances, my life was good. I was in a hit in London's West End; I was married to a beautiful young actor; I had a healthy baby boy; and I lived in a wonderful place. Yet beneath the surface, all was not well. Despite the good times in Goa and our best efforts, the marriage was still difficult, and I, as usual, was throwing myself into my work.

The possibility of working with Robert Bolt was thrilling. I assumed he had seen me in a play and wanted to discuss a part in something he had written or was going to direct as a film. I had seen *Lawrence of Arabia* in Singapore when I was a teenager and had been immensely impressed by the dialogue. All my life I had been trained to listen to the words of a piece – not the most respected element of most films. Bolt's screenplay was brilliant and rightly won him an Oscar.

'I hope you don't mind me phoning you at home,' Robert continued. 'I got your number from the theatre. I hope you don't mind?' I found out later that he had not got my number from the theatre, but I didn't mind at all. 'Why should I mind?' I said. 'I'd be delighted to meet you.'

We arranged to have lunch in the White Horse in Soho that coming Friday. Robert was at the height of his career, an esteemed playwright and screenwriter. I had watched him giving interviews, and seen pictures of him with his wife Sarah Miles (from whom he had just separated), so I knew that I would recognize him.

I trooped off to lunch with him in Soho, wondering what kind of part I was up for. I had asked Ros, but she knew nothing about it and said it must be early days in casting. Robert was there before me, looking very elegant in comfy slacks and a well-cut, well-worn jacket. He greeted me politely and we sat down to order. I remember noticing how much more attractive he was than his photographs suggested. His eyes, though slightly hooded, had a gaze so steady it made me feel uneasy.

'You're smaller than I thought,' he said, lighting another in his endless chain of cigarettes. We ordered lunch and the usual small-talk began. He was one of the most interesting men I had ever met; witty, charming and very down to earth. I was lulled into feeling unusually intimate and relaxed with him, and was soon behaving as if I had known him all my life. He was joking about some disaster on his last film, and I mentioned my husband having a similar problem on a dreadful thing he was making at that time. Robert suddenly went very quiet. Then he said, 'I didn't realize you were married.' 'Oh, yes,' I replied jovially. 'Very married, and with a tiny baby boy.'

I had not taken in his change of mood, and his 'I'm so sorry, Felicity, I had no idea' made me think he had gone quite mad. What did it matter? Was the part that of a nun, and even if it was, how could my married status be relevant? The lunch continued in a strained fashion; I was bewildered both by his behaviour and by my own reactions to this man I had only just met.

By the time we got to coffee, I was confused. He had not said a single word about a play or a job, and as he paid the bill he turned those eyes on me and said again, 'I'm sorry for asking you to lunch when you're not free, but I have enjoyed it. Please forgive me.'

Out on Crawford Street he hailed me a taxi, and, kissing me on the cheek, thanked me again for coming. 'Good luck,' he said. 'I hope we'll meet again sometime?' 'I'd like that,' I said, and got into the cab.

The taxi to Victoria, the train to Shepperton, the walk across the island, all passed in a haze, as I tried not to allow myself to believe the obvious truth. This was a pick-up. A nice and polite pick-up, but a pick-up nevertheless – no job opportunity in any shape or form – and as a married lady, I was not the ticket. I walked over the weir and back to my wooden house feeling rather foolish.

A letter arrived thanking me for lunch. He was off to America and he hoped I would enjoy the rest of the run in the West End. Good luck, etc. It was not until three years later that he told me that he been protecting not his high moral standards, but his need for simple relationships. He had just been through the mill of separation and a messy affair was not what he was looking for.

I forgot, or made myself forget, about him for the next two years. But at the same time I had an uncanny feeling that this person was going to be important to me. I was certain I would see him again.

I put it out of my mind and immersed myself in work. *The Norman Conquests* continued to sell out. It was a joy to be part of such a happy production.

One night, halfway through our season, Richard Briers popped his head around the door of my dressing room after the show.

'I think you're really splendid as Annie,' he said. 'Just splendid.'

'I'm going to be doing a little comedy series for the Beeb,' he added nonchalantly. 'It might not be hugely successful – it's an oddball kind of subject, but I think the writing is excellent and it would be fun to do. I wondered if you might like to read a few episodes for the part of my wife? Would you have a peek at it, if I sent you a script?'

Would I have a peek? I was stunned – and delighted. I had missed out on several television comedy series in the past few months, and Richard Briers was already an established star. Besides, to be offered something from a job I was doing was flattery of the nicest kind. I thanked him effusively and asked him to 'please, please send me a script' – although I knew I would accept the part even if I hated the script. I needed the work and I liked Richard: I felt at ease with him from the moment I met him, and his comedy technique had already made him one of the best and funniest actors of his generation.

By the following week I had read the script – and loved it. It was the story of a couple of dafties, Tom and Barbara Good, who decide to live off the land in Surbiton, turning their back garden into a smallholding, giving up work and going back to nature. The show was called *The Good Life* and each episode revolved around the catastrophic attempts of the feckless Tom and Barbara to grow their own potatoes and keep their livestock under control – to the chagrin of their nice but rather snobbish neighbours, for whom the escaping pigs, clucking chickens and bleating smelly goats are somewhat alarming. I was to play Barbara to Richard Briers's Tom. I was to be kitted out in large wellies and jeans, and sport a touch of soot to the nose and devotion to my crazy man.

The dialogue was impressive – very funny and very economic – and although the couple's long-suffering next-door neighbours had not yet been fully written, the basic idea was great. John Howard Davies, the director, came to see me in the play that week and then cast Penelope Keith as one neighbour – Margo, the smart snob with a heart of gold. It only needed Paul Eddington to join us as her patient husband and our team was complete.

From the very first day we slotted into a way of working together that was fun, fast and furious. We were all primarily theatre actors, all a bit lovey if we got the chance, but equally all extremely professional, ambitious and hard-working, and our dedication to the show was total. Dickie was the star, but never acted as though he was: it became a team effort and I think it showed. It was the whole show, not individual applause, that interested us – a rare situation in this business of enlarged egos.

We truly loved the show and worked together in complete harmony, even deciding collectively – and, I think, correctly – to quit while we were at the top.

To everyone's surprise, *The Good Life* took off. Penny won most of the awards going, and we teased her mercilessly. We all had the same quirky sense of humour and took it in turns to poke fun at one another, keeping our egos firmly on the level. The writers, Bob Larbey and John Esmonde, started writing for the actors and the characters combined, and John Howard Davies guided us with perfect taste to become one of the most popular shows on television, even achieving cult status.

I think one reason the show worked so well was the very fact that we were all theatre actors with about fifty years of rep under our collective belts. We wanted to be actors first and stars second, and this made a difference to the way we worked together. Our like-minded working methods, the chemistry between us, the brilliant scripts and the perfect timing of the back-to-nature story ensured the success of the series.

We filmed outside London, doing the exteriors at two houses, one posh and one not so posh. This not so posh one had its garden dug up for the filming on the understanding that the BBC would replace the havoc by landscaping the garden to a very high standard once filming was complete. Pigs, goats, chickens, straw, mud, manure, carrots and fully grown vegetable plants were installed. We filmed happily for two weeks, then said a fond farewell to our hosts, who waved the crew off with some relief and settled back to enjoy what would soon become a showcase garden.

None of us realized then how successful the series would be, and when the reaction to it was positive we all accepted the next series with great celebrations. Only one problem had to be overcome: someone had to go to the Goods' location house and inform the lady owner that her beautifully landscaped garden was to be dug up again and invaded once more by pigs, goats and chickens . . . This continued for the next five years, with the garden periodically being blasted with animals and mud, redesigned, then gutted again. By the last series the next-door neighbours had had enough and moved, but our hostess was a local star and had taken to plying us with coffee and cake on our first day back, then happily watching the destruction of her charming home and garden.

The pigs never did what they were told, the chickens always squawked at the wrong moment, and the goat was a devil to milk, but we approached these minor problems with humour. Our main difficulty was getting through the script without having hysterics. When the scene involved an animal, it was all we could do to get through a shot without corpsing. The trouble the animals caused was not confined to the set. A scene in which I had to milk the goat drew a very indignant letter from a viewer, informing us that she could tell the goat was male and that the BBC ought to take more care over such details. I fired off a rather beady reply, informing the lady that I would do many things for my art, but milking a billy goat was not one of them.

On the whole, however, we were the public's darlings and had to grow accustomed to being accosted in the supermarket with cries of 'Don't you grow your own then?' We enjoyed our popularity and even more the fact that there were never any quarrels between us – a rare thing on a successful show.

We were all a little in love with one another, spending weekends together whenever we could. Paul and Dickie together were two of the funniest men I have ever met. We were eccentrics playing eccentrics, but the casting was anything but to type (not that that prevented people from sending me endless scripts featuring sweet women in wellies). Dickie hated working with animals, did not like pigs or mud, loved his home comforts and would be the last person on earth to try living on a smallholding. He would leap out of the pig-pen as soon as a shot was complete, screaming abuse at the animal for treading on his toes. The idea of my being devoted and a good little loving wife, meanwhile, was a bit of a company joke.

Penny, the last word in elegance and extremely flirty and feminine in real life, was not at all like the bossy Margo. The only whisker of similarity between her and her screen character was that she was the competent one who made us pull ourselves together when we were being silly. And no one could have been less henpecked than our beloved Paul – masculine, attractive and with a twinkle for the ladies. He was always the one to joke first and make us laugh, and he became my special friend. We worked together later on another series, *The Camomile Lawn*, and on three West End plays. He teased me remorselessly and lovingly, and his death was a great personal loss. I went to see him the day before he died, and he simply turned his head, looked at me, smiled, and said, 'Oh, Foo.' He was a wonderful man.

But as *The Good Life* took off, my marriage finally fell apart. I had to face the grim reality that it was useless to continue. With sadness, we parted and started on the inevitable struggle with blame, divorce and custody. It was a time of extreme pain, neither of us behaving very well, and not an area of my life that I wish to share, explain or discuss.

Through the worst part of all this, Geoffrey was a tower of calm. He surprised me with his fairness, his sadness that I could not make my marriage work and his reluctance to apportion blame. Mother too was equally supportive, looking after her grandson and, when things got very bad, taking him off for a holiday to India. My parents, who had been so aggressive at my departure, were a close and comforting presence during this crisis in my life, strong and refusing to take sides now that I needed them. They both held the firm belief that marriage was for life, that things should be worked out, but they both refused to provoke either of us with advice they knew we would not or could no longer accept.

Jennifer, meanwhile, dropped everything to help me. I piled my baby son, my belongings and my dog into my car, and set out to look for somewhere to live. I rented a single room in Chelsea, and within a few days Jennifer flew out; and, in much the same spirit as she had cobbled together a wardrobe for me to bring to Europe, she set about looking for some property to buy that I could stay in until I had sorted out the chaos of my life.

I was doing a play eight times a week, working six nights and two matinées, and filming during the day for *The Good Life*. I had a baby and a dog and a broken marriage. For the first time since I had arrived in England, my career seemed secure and I was making a living and working with wonderful people. I had made it from hopeless outsider to accepted actor, and I knew, at last, that this country was going to be my home. A time that could have been the happiest was full of turmoil and pain.

But there, at least, was my sister, rushing about like a demented thing, with my baby under one arm, files of apartments and houses under the other, and the dog pulling her down the street. Within a week she had found and bought the lease on a little flat. She handed me the keys, some money and a budget to furnish it with; and with kisses and hugs to take my breath away, she returned to Bombay and her own small children.

This dismal time eventually passed. And it was no worse for me than for anyone else in a similar position. Our son is a blessing of such joy that no regrets are possible. And life, our lives, moved on.

And I was lucky. I had Jennifer to help me through it. In my darkest hour she was there, and she made things better. I could not do the same for her.

CHAPTER TWENTY-FOUR

MAKING GOOD

The Good Life went into a second series, then a third and a fourth. There were special Christmas shows – in all we recorded thirty episodes. Penny kept on winning just about every award for comedy known to man, Paul became the star he deserved to be, and for Richard it was yet another hit in his string of successes, making him one of the nation's most loved artists. I was voted 'Best Bottom' and the woman most men wanted to get under a duvet with.

This image did not fit at all with the picture I had had of myself during the early days of my marriage, when I keenly fashioned myself on Mother and her devotion to her one and only man. But as the years went on and I became a single, independent woman, my insecurity about my looks began to fade, and my feeling of being second best to Jennifer dissolved as my career became more secure.

I found, to my surprise, that I was not regarded as plain after all, and that a touch of wit worked wonders. My shyness was replaced by a genuine liking of the male of the species, which seemed to engender a similar response. I discovered that I was able to flirt my way into almost any pair of arms I wanted, and I experienced my personal version of the raving sixties, somewhat belatedly, in the seventies. For the next ten years I was never without a love affair, never alone, never single. The *Good Life* image of the nice girl next-door was indeed just an image.

I became the butt of many a witty remark from Paul and Richard. I was the one they teased – they were too much in awe of Penny. I was Little Foodle Doodle (Penny's nickname for me) and I was always last at learning my lines – unless they were complicated lists of things, in which case Dickie would write notes all over the set to crib from and I would hide them during the recording.

Even after several series, we were like school kids larking about, at ease and loving every minute of our success. We would tell each other our innermost secrets during tea breaks and drink enormous quantities of Paul's superb wines at the weekends. We took it in turns to cook a weekend lunch or supper, and ended up drunk and happy. We were totally loyal to one another as a team and respected each other's work. Most importantly, there was no jealousy between us. I did not realize then quite how outstanding the four of us were in our commitment to the whole rather than to our individual success.

It was sometime after our second series that we received our most unusual compliment – a request to record a show live before the Queen.

'There must be a mistake . . . this is some kind of joke,' I said when I heard the news. But no, a special script was commissioned, a date was set, and, with tremendous excitement in the ranks, we started to prepare for the first, and probably the last, ever Royal Command Performance of a recording of a sit-com at the BBC Television Centre to be played in the presence of Her Majesty the Queen and Prince Philip.

We were told that the Palace had specifically requested *The Good Life*, then a rumour started that it was the BBC's idea because it was the only clean show being filmed that month. Either way, we hardly cared. The BBC was in a frenzy of preparation. Carpenters hammered, cleaners polished; painters teetered on ladders; and men in white coats, who have never been seen before or since, fussed around in the corridors through which the royal audience would pass and Brasso-ed everything in sight. New carpets were laid on the royal route, and light bulbs were replaced in corridors that had been dark for years – the BBC had *never* looked like this before.

In the studio the very basic small seats were taken out and replaced with grand armchairs; in the front row white leather sofas appeared. Yards and yards of red, white and blue bunting were draped patriotically over the iron railings in front of the sofas; red carpet was laid over the stone floor and cables, making a walkway, and cordons were put up all over the place. Watching the preparations, I was suddenly put in mind of the sofas and splendour at the palace of Udaipur all those years before.

We rehearsed for the usual five days, with many jokes about drying up and saying 'Oh, bollocks' and being sent to the Tower. Penny, Paul, Richard and I were always like naughty kids working together, but that week we were on a high and could scarcely contain our excitement. It being the seventies, it was not yet the fashionable thing to be anti-royalist, and we were unashamedly flattered and proud.

We felt very secure as a working team and this was going to be a great show, we decided. The only slight drawback would be if things went wrong, as they invariably do during a recording. The usual pattern of dealing with this would be to say something along the lines of: 'Oh, God, it's hell working with animals. What do I say next?' Then the thing was to fall about and try to get the audience on your side by making a show of being an idiot, while the floor managers set up the cameras to re-take the mangled part of the scene. This strategy clearly would not do. It was not going to be a good idea to look Her Majesty in the eye and say, 'It's hopeless acting with pigs, Ma'am!'

John, our director, decided to take these four bad children in hand. 'The answer is simple,' he said. 'YOU WON'T GO WRONG. You will rehearse a few more hours and there will be NO re-takes!'

We watched from the backstage make-up room as our royal guests arrived. Charley was to present a bunch of flowers to Her Majesty, and I was far more nervous of this moment, for his sake, than I was of doing the show. He was very shy and bowed so low and so long that the Queen had to go and take them from him, which she did with a huge smile, caught in the photograph that I have to this day.

On the monitors we beheld the grand entrance into the now gleaming BBC of this party in full evening dress. The Queen disembarked from her Daimler in a cloud of bright pink chiffon, shaking hands in her long white gloves, while her diamonds sparkled in the flashbulb lights. Prince Philip walked behind her, chatting to the crowd and the directors of the BBC, while cameras followed the glittering group into the lobby. The procession filed in with all the pomp and ceremony of a great gala occasion, while we four frightfuls watched open-mouthed, Richard and I at our muddiest and scruffiest in jeans and wellies. I felt a strong link with Geoffrey and his love of pomp and ceremony. This would make him pleased, I thought. Granted, what we were offering was not quite Shakespeare, but at least there was a sense of tradition.

The audience was seated and without much ado we started recording. The first few minutes were very odd. We normally had a warm-up man – in our case the floor manager, Brian –

who would go out before we started, tell a few funny jokes, chat to the audience, flirt with them, explain the process and generally 'get them going'. Then he would call us out on to the floor, introduce us, and off we'd go. But today was different. Brian was spruced up in black tie instead of his usual cords, and there was to be no 'warm-up'.

However, the team was so strong by this time and worked together so comfortably that, after a few minutes of nerves, we settled down into our stride. Occasionally I would catch sight of Her Majesty's diamonds glinting in the studio lights and have to pinch myself to believe that it was really happening. It was after all a pretty strange situation. This was not a classic play in a West End theatre, it was a sit-com being recorded in a tarted-up little studio made to look as if it was posh. Very eccentric, no doubt about it.

But the show went like clockwork. The audience, though not our normal cheering crowd, were friendly and responsive, and there were no dodgy moments. And nobody said, 'Bollocks'!

After forty-five minutes it was all in the bag, so to speak, and we were lined up and formally introduced. Curtsying in my muddy dungarees was a little sad, but there was no denying the thrill of the moment.

I seemed to have come full circle from garlanding my Maharajah in his Victorian theatre, to watching my own son press flowers on the Queen of England in her BBC studios. We were part of a line that stretched from Shakespeare and his tatty players performing at court, through Geoffrey and his touring band playing to the remnants of the British Raj in a time-warp of fading pomp, through the changing face of the monarchy in England, and beyond. Still the show goes on; the tatties turn up, entertain and take a bow.

★

But while my career continued to move forward, my personal life was more of a rollercoaster. My divorce proceedings had been splashed across the *News of the World*, and my life, apart from my son, felt sad and shabby. I had forgotten all about my strange encounter with Robert Bolt several years previously. Then one night a small bunch of primroses was left for me at the stage door of the theatre I was working in, and, with it, a note: 'Would you have dinner with me on Friday, please? Love, Robert.'

There followed what can only be described as an old-fashioned, whirlwind romance. I moved again into a tiny two-up, two-down cottage in Putney, and he came with it. He was as happy on the wooden floor eating fish and chips as he was at his watermill house with its lake, gardens and rolling lawns, but he also guided me into a more sophisticated world than I had known before.

1975, Bombay

My dear Foo

    There is a rumour here that you are a sort of permanent harlot, rushing around with dirty old men years younger than even me, but dirty old men none the less . . . I have to keep my eyes down in shame as I walk through the gardens of the club!

    Today I have to go and deal with Income Tax, so I will shortly proceed to the hall of pan and spit – the income tax office. Then to the hospital to be stuck with a pin. Hate inoculations, frightened I am. Good luck in your new bachelor life.

God bless, G.

P.S. A MORTGAGE! Oh Foo, must you borrow? I would

never dare, but then I never had that sort of courage, so
you may be all right.

 Regarding the older man . . . if there is any doubt,
don't!

Geoffrey was very cross indeed at my involvement with Robert
Bolt. His worst habits surfaced and he was very rude, because
he sensed, I think, that I was not sure, and he could get away
with it. I was too happy to listen to him, however.

Robert had the gift of the gab, and, like Geoffrey and Laura, we
would talk and talk and talk. He was, I felt, my superior on every
level, yet he never made me feel young or stupid if I misunderstood
or was baffled by his philosophical or political ideas. I thought I
was completely in love with him. Then, one day, he was standing
in the kitchen, his arm leaning on the door and he said, very simply,
'I think I'd like to marry you. Shall we do that?'

It spoiled everything. I had just recovered from the dreadful
parting with Charley's father and the sadness of that was still with
me. I could not commit to any more belonging.

I made plans to be out of town on jobs or busy, and during the
next few months withdrew into a shell. Robert was strong-willed,
and I had to be tough not to give in. I took a job away from
London, away from Robert. He went to America, and we wrote
– but I was careless and did not reply well.

He came back and bought a house in Somerset. 'Come and
see it with me, Foo,' he said. 'It's an old friary and very beautiful.'
We drove down at the usual racing speed – he drove well but
always very fast. 'You can live here with me, if you like. It
would be nice.' We walked through the overgrown orchard and
wandered the main house buildings. I took photographs of him;
he had lost a great deal of weight. I made polite replies, and we
drove back to London.

He went to Hawaii not long after that and wrote the most wonderful, funny, loving letters. I started writing back – by now I was missing him. And now that he had withdrawn his demands, I was free to love him again. I wrote that I would come out and visit him and got ecstatic, silly love letters back. The tickets were arranged, and I was due to fly out to him. Then I was offered a job.

I accepted the job and did not go to Hawaii. Robert had a heart attack, came back to England and had bypass surgery. No stroke yet, but he was very ill. I went to see him with a bottle of red wine. I was young for my age, and not very wise. I was too afraid of serious loving, and not able to visit hospitals without the past years of Charley's father's illness haunting me with guilt. Our lives separated and I was to regret it for a long time to come.

My dear Foo

· You may like living alone. That is what I should have done really. Mind you, YoYo and I were lucky, we were both doing the same thing, and both not caring a bugger really. If it had not been like that, I would never have stuck it out, I can tell you. You see our job is something more than the usual, insomuch as it acts as a sort of sublimation of sex, so that the torment isn't there like it is for most people.

YoYo has decided to read my Works, and I think her opinion of me is even lower than of yore. She is ashamed of my fifth form ignorance, fancy caring whether one gets grammar right, like a bloody homework exercise.

There is nothing more to say. Should I be worried about what happens in my dotage? Am I a bloody nuisance staying on earth for a hundred years. Shall I go and live in Goa, having given away all my glad rags?

You say you need a holiday. For what? From what? I've never taken a holiday in my life, tho' I've had plenty given.

Grey sea and sky . . . hot and damp . . . unhappiness abounds.

Love, G.

CHAPTER TWENTY-FIVE

ILLUSION

For all my bravura about being the little tough one, I still felt a driving need to please Geoffrey through my work. He looked down from a great height at most of the television shows I did, and even a lead in the West End of London was not, in his eyes, comparable to the glory of being in *The Dream* at Regent's Park, or playing Juliet at the Oxford Playhouse. And as for becoming a film star, that would have been really slumming it.

But as the years went on and I did more and more work in the theatre, he gave up on the idea of my returning to tour with him, and became my biggest champion, going to absurd lengths to get me an appropriate first-night present – never valuable, always special. The telegrams and cards, with a witty quote, would arrive at the half. He read and kept all my notices, pasting them carefully into a scrap-book.

Mother would come when she could to a preview and, with a few gentle notes, nudge me in the right direction. They both insisted that it was not the point to be the best, but to do the best one could in any given performance, and never ever to allow oneself to give less than a hundred per cent, even at an empty matinée.

Jennifer, on the other hand, was not so easy to please. She

could spot the vital flaw, and she would never fail to tell me what it was. She wanted me to be the biggest and brightest star, blinding everyone with my talent. Nothing else would do, and I dreaded her seeing my work. She noticed at once where I was failing to convince and pointed it out with candour and not a little lack of sympathy. In one sentence she could destroy my confidence. She would say that I was wonderful, and clever, and yet at the same time insist that I had to do better. But I rarely did better enough for her, not in my acting.

As a sister, though, I was perfect. I had got that one down to a tee. It was easy for me. I loved everything about her, and I knew she felt the same.

When she was diagnosed with cancer, I had just got married for the second time and was on my way to meet my new husband for a two-week holiday. I cut short the honeymoon and flew to India to be with her. The choice seemed natural, and I knew she would have done the same for me.

Now she was ill, she needed me and I was beside her. She had a loving family, her husband, her three children and her parents, but I knew she still needed me – and so I was there for her during her two-year illness. I dislike the term 'fight': it implies winning or losing, and, when faced with a terminal illness, the burden of being told to fight can be as intolerable as realizing on your deathbed that you 'lost'. She was sick with cancer, she was ill, she got worse, she died. It's as simple as that. Except, of course, that it isn't.

It was a horrid, sordid business, painful and depressing, with nothing about it to be recommended. My beautiful sister, Fufu, the pretty, golden girl, the nice, kind, loving, gentle creature, turned over a period of two years into a crippled shell of the woman she once was. Even her humour left her, and certainly her will to live. She was never any good at pain; illness didn't suit her plan. She had three growing, adoring children, and she loved mothering and grooming them for adulthood. The greatest sadness of all for me was their loss of her.

Years before, in her sometimes sentimental way, she confided to me that she could not bear the thought of life without her parents. 'I don't think I'd want to live, if Mummy or Daddy died,' she said. Well, she didn't have to. And they had to bear the most painful of losses: the death of their child.

Geoffrey refused to believe she was seriously ill, and later on turned in on himself with a silent anger. Mother seemed not to ever fully recover. Her rosaries were packed away, along with her bedside Bible, and they never saw the light of day again. She stopped going to mass, a blind was pulled down on some part of her being, and she turned her heart away from India.

During Jennifer's last weeks the whole family gathered about her bedside. Shows were cancelled, tours stopped, filming halted. We clustered about the dying embers of her life, camping out around her. There was a lot of laughter, a lot of eating on and around her bed. Her hospital room we filled with jokes and funny picture cards, and desperately and helplessly waited with her, while she slowly and painfully let go. Geoffrey's visits were short; he was unable to hide his anguish, but Mother was beside her, faffing a lot and looking suddenly old and slightly mad. The three children were pillars of strength and love, constant and cheerful, and heartbreaking to watch.

Then she was gone, early one morning, with her daughter beside her.

It seemed a gigantic mistake. Someone had pushed the wrong button, this was not as it was meant to be. Any one of us should have gone, but not Jennifer. She was the nice one, she was the good one. This was not fair. 'Fairness has nothing to do with it,

Foo!' she would scold me, when I dared to say that to her. And now she was gone, and only memories of her remained, memories that would shamefully fade over the years.

During the last few days we talked and talked – sometimes nonsense plans about going to Bond Street and shopping, sometimes about books and plays. Her legs needed waxing and, with only a week to go, I shaved her legs and filed her toenails, rubbing scented cream into her stick-like shins.

We were chatting about something trivial one day when, out of the blue, she cried out, 'Who will look after my children?'

'I will, of course,' I promised.

'I know you will, Foo, but it's not the same as me, it's simply not the same,' she wept.

I wasn't wise enough to know how to comfort her, nor wise enough to calm myself.

'It will be all right!' I said stubbornly.

But she knew it would not be all right, not really.

I wish she had not died.

Your thin hands are now so twisted and crippled, I can't cut the nails any more. Your middle finger now bends into your palm, biting the flesh as it grows. It seems a lifetime away when you could sip whisky and swallow ice-cream. When I could still put your teeth in and cut your nails for you. The degree of acceptable existence is growing slowly and steadily worse, imperceptibly less tolerable.

In a few months, though, you will be eighty-nine. And we will have a party. I will give you a whisky, even if it chokes you, and fill the room with balloons and flowers. This will not be a date to remember Jennifer's death. It will be your day again, and I will spend it with you . . . if I can bear it.

Mother's not being here is still a sadness, but a natural thing, a timely thing, an inevitable passing on. But the raw pain of Jennifer's dying grows every year. Fifteen years of missing her has not healed the ache I feel in my stomach, and every year your birthday comes round and flaunts the lack of her. So much loved but always insecure. Even when she had given a superb performance, she wrote, on your birthday, a forlorn letter:

Dear Daddy

  It's your birthday today. I don't know where you are but we will drink your health and Happy Birthday.

  I am a bit depressed about my film 36 Chowringhee Lane. It WAS to go to the New York film festival – now it's not – and the San Francisco one – but we aren't sure. And I hate me in it. I'm irritating and actressy and unmoving. Anyway, it's a bit late now.

  Ismail is taking the film to London, he says, but I'm not sure I want to go and be there when all those clever people see it.

When the film came to London, she was fêted, got rave reviews and won the Evening Standard *Award for Best Actress. For the first time in her life her talent was being properly recognized; then she got cancer and she died.*

The simple entry in your journal is so sad:

On my 75th birthday early in the morning Jennifer died at the age of just 50.

  The appalling loss I cannot talk or write about . . . It seemed as if the whole Land of Promise had frozen up.

  My last communication from her was a feebly pencilled note . . . 'The readiness is all . . .' from the speech in Hamlet, which I read at her funeral. 'There is special providence in the fall of a sparrow . . .'

And I remembered her as a child during the war, standing by her window, crying as I left for India with Laura . . . my little sparrow.

What started out as a confused and sometimes aggressive need to understand you has developed into tender acceptance.

I often felt second-best to Jennifer, believing that your ambitions for me were a response to her leaving you and your company. But I had not listened carefully, and I had not read your journals or understood your strident letters of encouragement and advice.

I don't pretend to be able to pluck out your mystery, but I think I know you better than I did before. And I like you better. My image of you is strong, not sentimental, and I do not excuse your less attractive traits, nor your self-centred will. But I'd like to thank you for giving me the life you did, for showing me another way of being and offering me a choice.

I am starting a new play soon and for a month or so my visits will be fewer. I feel infinitely tired, and so much need your bullying wisdom to cheer me on.

The now all too familiar ache of frustration as I push the coins into the parking meter on the street below your window, thinking guiltily, 'One hour should be enough.'

Collecting my papers, I ring the bell. The door is buzzed open. After a quick 'hello' at the reception, I'm on my way, up the four flights of stairs. Past the tiny lady with the tiny dog, past the sad one in the chair. Up and up again. It's lunchtime and saintly nurses are delivering trays of 'school' food: stews and cottage pie, rice pudding and custard. Comfort food, all easy to chew. The doors to the rooms are always open, and the televisions' relentless activity flickers over the old bent heads.

At the top floor, pushing through the fire door on to the far landing, I pass the lovely lady with the cat asleep on her bed. The lady sits in a chair staring at the door. I wave a greeting and go on past the bathroom of amazing contraptions: handles to hold on to, chairs in the shower cubicles, lavatory seats to fix on – the trappings of the infirm, making the spacious room resemble an eccentric gym filled with pulleys and alarm cords. And at last I am at your open door.

The pictures on your walls: your favourite watercolour, a sketch from your first job, an oil painting I gave you years ago – all futile, pathetic attempts to make this room your home. The pinboard is looking a bit sad. The photograph of you on your seventy-fifth birthday is curled at the edges, and the snap of you holding your great-grandson in your arms with such tenderness reminds me of how vibrant you were and how you nearly always wore a smile in the years before . . . Birthday cards from a couple of years ago are still pinned up, and framed photos of Jennifer's children and mine are balanced on the shelf.

It's a cosy room, a kind room, but I am filled with a quiet panic when I think it will be the room you die in. After all the marble palaces, the gilded monuments, the hotels and dak bungalows, that it should come to this – to die in an old people's nursing home, however wonderful, is so very sad.

But for the moment you are still with me: still staring, still silent, but still here. And once again I start my banal prattle: 'I'm here, darling, how are you? It's Foo, Daddy . . .'

THE LAST PASSAGE

The crescent moon is shining down on the brown stone Gateway of India. It's larger than I remember and more solid and imposing. The moonshine glimmers on the water and the anchored ferry boats bob and jostle each other on their ropes. Pye-dogs strut the deserted pavements, barking out their territory. And lines of small battered black and yellow taxis are lined up in the dark streets, waiting for the morning. Under the protection of the sea wall, shrouded figures sleep, while young boys of the night ply their trade, holding hands and smoking as they stroll along the darkened causeway.

A single tiny star shines above the moon. It's one o'clock in the morning; eight p.m. in England. I have placed what's left of you, your absurdly small coffin, underneath the window of my bedroom, from which I look out at the night.

Tomorrow we will take your ashes — what a dreadful description of a person — out through the Gateway, down the steps and to a ferry boat. Once we are out beyond the second buoy, you will be scattered by your grandsons on to the waters you once sailed with such excitement and joy. It seems a fitting end and the right beginning of a time without you.

When you died, my need to return with you changed from a duty to a longing. I realized this as soon as the plane started the descent to Santa Cruz Airport, as soon as the first hot blast of pre-monsoon air struck my lungs like a sauna blast, bringing with it the first smell of spices and sewers and perfumes, the first sound of people shouting in the language I never speak. Like you, this is where I feel at home. The poverty, the corruption, the begging children, the political madness that prevails half the time – none of them can alter the spirit of the place. The apparent lack of concern for human life conceals a far greater understanding, more valuable and impossible to describe.

On the surface is a benign chaos. The cars don't start; it takes five men to do the job of one; the lights in my five-star hotel flicker because of a faulty plug; there's a definite bedbug incident in the night; and the hot water is lukewarm. But these are trifles. The things that bring real comfort are in place. The service is gracious and genuine, the smiles are meant, not bought, not surly and not pretend. The tea is Darjeeling leaf, served from a teapot with an old-world tea cosy and a silver tea strainer. The soap is sandalwood, the bedsheets smoothest Indian cotton. The pictures in the room are old Mogul prints and Daniells.

But more important are the people. Conversations are started at every given opportunity, children are cuddled and stroked by men and women, friends and servants alike. There is no shyness and everyone is welcome. There is a grasp of reality here, an acceptance of the fragility of this one life and the certainty of death, some unspoken understanding that there is more beyond our need for high achievement, that there is a past and a future as important as the moment, and that we are not to take ourselves so very seriously.

Carrying my father's ashes on the first lap of his journey back was tricky and awkward. Kind, well-meaning people averted their eyes from my beaten old brown leather holdall that was the obvious container for his remains. The lowered voices and sympathy did nothing to relieve the initial awfulness of carrying what's left of your father and presumably some of his coffin under your arm.

How bizarre, I thought, looking numbly at my old, journey-battered brown leather bag, the perfect carry-on piece, which had come with me from India, to America, to Australia, and back again. Always on tour, and always full to bursting. Now this old friend contained a stamped and sealed wooden box, which I had wrapped in an old tabard, used for years and mended and repainted by Mother again and again.

The bag perched on the tiny seat in front of me that the new first-class passengers have in the cabin. It's against the law to send ashes cargo, they must be accompanied, so here Geoffrey was, up in first for the second time in his life. The last time I upgraded him he swore never to grace the front again. 'Appalling waste of food and money! What a load of nonsense, all that drink and all those dreadful business types swanking about! I'd rather go back and enjoy myself with real people.' The fact that Mother loved the comfort did not impress, and there was never another journey made first class.

But in the frantic rush of after death, busy with funeral arrangements and air bookings, I panicked that I would not manage having to put my fragile box up in the overhead locker, among the coats and plastic duty-free bags, at landings and take-offs, and rashly upgraded to first. So Geoffrey made the last of his thousands of trips up in the front with the wastrels and the sordid extravagance.

At the security X-ray the embarrassment had reached its height. No provision was made – he went through with the cameras and the handbags and the carry-on luggage. As the nice chap swung my bag merrily out on to the collection rack, the box clunked down, just as he realized what was in it – he blushed deep red. The special services person gasped in dismay while I sheepishly retrieved my parent and handed him over to my big son to deal with for the remainder of the journey, too tired by now to cope with other people's unease.

Arriving in Bombay was quite different. We were wafted through customs, the bag was acknowledged with no sentimentality, no shyness. Eye contact was fully established, with understanding and respect. In the arrival lounge Jennifer's eldest son, Kunal, was there to meet us. With Eastern style he swept his grandfather's box protectively under his arm, kissing us all better, and, for the first time since Geoffrey had died, I felt at peace.

'Gaga's dead,' Karan said simply, using his childhood nickname for you and looking about seven years old, not his grown-up thirty-six. Standing in my hallway, he looked forlorn and rumpled, not sure how to be the messenger of this news.

'Oh, no,' I heard myself say. 'Oh, no.' Still in my dressing gown, I raced upstairs to dress. Looking at my bedside strewn with Geoffrey's letters and the last chapter of the book, I felt the numbness that I knew only too well follows information of a death. Slipping on jeans and a T-shirt, I joined Karan, who was already on the phone to India, losing my car keys twice in confusion. I took the spare set and we drove off.

'They have been calling you for an hour, but your machine was on.'

'I know. I was re-reading the last chapter and some of his letters, then I was going to see him this morning. It's strange, did he wait for me to finish the book? It's so weird. And with no warning. He wasn't ill or anything.' I couldn't stop; I babbled on and on.

Sister Margaret met us at the door. A smile of infinite sweetness and up we went, for almost the last time. As I rounded the corner to his room, I had to stop myself shouting out, 'Darling, I'm here!'

I have been blessed with a family of outspoken youngsters, due, no doubt, to their outspoken grandfather. They gathered round, your granddaughter flying in from Bombay overnight to be with us — you — for the cremation. They came with laughter, tears, hugs and unholy stories, and concern for you, and for me, now the oldest of your tribe. After me, there will be no one who remembers you as a young man with thick dark hair, a pipe, dashing clothes, the strength of ten men in your small thin body and a head full of your own teeth and mad ideas.

The night after the morning you died, I rocked myself to sleep in hot tears of loss. But in the morning I joked about where to put your ashes and what you wanted as a service. Booking seats to scatter you in India, it all seemed too sudden and silly, after all this time. And scattering sounded like what you do with birdseed; too careless for what's left of a man.

I am torn between repulsion and glorying in your final release. You're free, darling; no more pain or struggle. And yet, glad as I am for you, I miss your being part of the living. You were warm when we arrived at your bedside and, for the first time in five years, you looked rested, lying straight and still, your hair so beautifully combed and plaited into your long white pony-tail . . . God bless those saintly nurses. I felt that if I shook you, you'd turn and look at me again.

The peace in the room hung in the air. We sat beside you. I waffled on through half-tears something stupid about how I was on my way to sit with you this morning – true, but a pointless thing to say. The two boys were calm and sweet. The cook brought us some coffee and biscuits, which I insisted that we drink in front of you. We phoned India to inform relatives . . . and I wanted to sit all day just stroking your feet underneath the counterpane and touching your hair.

But after an hour you were cold as ice, and the ache of death became a reality. We left you to 'make arrangements' – a useful, if confusing, process that negates one kind of shock but introduces another. After endless procedures of the type needed to obtain a parking permit, I was free to visit you one last time. Up the stairs and along the corridor to your room – but no point in trying to say anything at all. This time really was the last. Colder than ever you were, and stiffer too. I sat in my chair by your bed, feeling numb nothingness, waiting for the relief I had expected. But all I felt was loss.

I had found a way to talk to you, about you, for you, that required no interaction, but it did require your being here. Now that that is gone, I have to stop, but I can't quite pick up my cue. What shall I do now? When do I make my exit?

It's spooky continuing to write, but somehow it's not over yet. Maybe in India, maybe that is the final chapter. I finished the book. I did not want this to be the end, but you were always one for a bit of drama, going out with a bang, as you would say.

'Has anyone got a screwdriver?'

Your ashes box, a lovely piece of wood with brass handles and a brass plate, engraved Richard Geoffrey Bragg Kendal (by courtesy of someone, since I never asked for such a thing), was screwed down so tightly that scattering was going to be an impossible task, unless we could find a screwdriver on board or, failing that, a hammer! Finally the stage manager from Prithvi Theatre produced a beauty.

The children gathered round, as Kunal, your first-born grandson, set to unscrewing the box. The bagpipers from the Kumar Regiment in the Hills of India, all dressed up in full uniform, set up a wonderful wailing. The sea was choppy, and the warm wind was blowing hard as we made our way to the prow. Someone said, 'We can't throw him in at this angle – the wind will blow him in our faces.' After some consultation with the main sailor, the engine was stopped and the boat turned round. I read 'Fear No More the Heat of the Sun', rather badly, I'm afraid. Brian had made an excellent job of it at the short service in London, but my voice shook, and you would have asked me to speak up.

The box floated out, and, as the boat circled away, the roses and jasmine floated on the waters. In the distance the Gateway glowed pink in the setting sun, dwarfed nowadays by high-rise buildings, but still an imposing reminder of old India and past glory.

Your ashes were in the warm brown waters of the Arabian Sea, poured out lovingly by two of your grandsons. I wish I could say from a cloth of gold instead of a plastic bag, but that had something to do with customs and drug-smuggling. Silver dust blew on to the side of the boat, and I couldn't help wondering what bit of you or the coffin it was. The trumpeter played the last post, and we threw garlands and handfuls of rose petals after you, your tiny cherub great-grandchildren throwing fistfuls of flowers as well.

There were wreaths and garlands, sweet white jasmine and red roses piled high in baskets. The crew and friends joined in, and when the bugle stopped we toasted you with champagne. Then we headed home in the near darkness, and went for a Chinese meal. I wish you had been there; you would have liked it. But, in a way, you were.

A week ago I finished this book, and the next morning you died. The Thames was grey and high along the Embankment, and it was too cool for spring.

But now you are back in the land you made your home. No more claustrophobia, no more imprisonment. You're free at last. I can't regret your life for you, but I wish you had not had such a struggle . . . but it's over now. You're home . . . you're here . . . you're free.

INDEX